TOWER HAMLETS

RICH
and Royal

CATHERINE MANN

Library Learning Information

To renew this item call:

0115 929 3388

or visit

www.ideastore.co.uk

TOWER HAMLETS

Created and managed by Tower Hamlets Council

WITHDRAWN

MILLS &
BOON

All rights reserved including the right of reproduction in whole or in part in any form. This edition is published by arrangement with Harlequin Books S.A.

This is a work of fiction. Names, characters, places, locations and incidents are purely fictional and bear no relationship to any real life individuals, living or dead, or to any actual places, business establishments, locations, events or incidents. Any resemblance is entirely coincidental.

This book is sold subject to the condition that it shall not, by way of trade or otherwise, be lent, resold, hired out or otherwise circulated without the prior consent of the publisher in any form of binding or cover other than that in which it is published and without a similar condition including this condition being imposed on the subsequent purchaser.

® and ™ are trademarks owned and used by the trademark owner and/or its licensee. Trademarks marked with ® are registered with the United Kingdom Patent Office and/or the Office for Harmonisation in the Internal Market and in other countries.

Published in Great Britain 2015
by Mills & Boon, an imprint of Harlequin (UK) Limited,
Eton House, 18-24 Paradise Road, Richmond, Surrey, TW9 1SR

RICH, RUGGED AND ROYAL © 2015 Harlequin Books S. A.

The Maverick Prince, His Thirty-Day Fiancée and His Heir, Her Honour were first published in Great Britain by Harlequin (UK) Limited.

The Maverick Prince © 2010 Catherine Mann
His Thirty-Day Fiancée © 2011 Catherine Mann
His Heir, Her Honour © 2011 Catherine Mann

ISBN: 978-0-263-25233-0

05-1015

Harlequin (UK) Limited's policy is to use papers that are natural, renewable and recyclable products and made from wood grown in sustainable forests. The logging and manufacturing processes conform to the legal environmental regulations of the country of origin.

Printed and bound in Spain
by CPI, Barcelona

USA TODAY bestseller **Catherine Mann** is living out her own fairytale ending on a sunny Florida beach with her Prince Charming husband and their four children. With more than thirty-five books in print in over twenty countries, she has also celebrated wins for both a RITA® Award and a Booksellers' Best Award. Catherine enjoys chatting with readers online—thanks to the wonders of the wireless internet that allows her to cyber-network with her laptop by the water! To learn more about her work, visit her website, www.catherinemann.com, or reach her by snail mail at PO box 6065, Navarre, FL 32566, USA.

TOWER HAMLETS LIBRARIES	
91000004730438	
Bertrams	15/09/2015
ROM	£5.99
THCUB	TH15000893

THE MAVERICK PRINCE

BY
CATHERINE MANN

To my favorite little princesses and princes—Megan, Frances, James and Zach. Thank you for inviting Aunt Cathy to your prince and princess tea parties. The snack cakes and sprite were absolutely magical!

Prologue

GlobalIntruder.com
Exclusive: For Immediate Release

Royalty Revealed!

Do you have a prince living next door? Quite possibly!

Courtesy of a positive identification made by one of the GlobalIntruder.com's very own photojournalists, we've successfully landed the scoop of the year. The deposed Medina monarchy has not, as was rumored, set up shop in a highly secured fortress in Argentina. The three Medina heirs—with their billions—have been living under assumed names and rubbing elbows with everyday Americans for decades.

We hear the sexy baby of the family, Antonio, is already taken in Texas by his waitress girlfriend

Shannon Crawford. She'd better watch her back now that word is out about her secret shipping magnate!

Meanwhile, never fear, ladies. There are still two single and studly Medina men left. Our sources reveal that Duarte dwells in his plush resort in Martha's Vineyard. Carlos—a surgeon, no less—resides in Tacoma. Wonder if he makes house calls?

No word yet on their father, King Enrique Medina, former ruler of San Rinaldo, an island off the coast of Spain. But our best reporters are hot on the trail.

For the latest update on how to nab a prince, check back in with the GlobalIntruder.com. And remember, you heard it here first!

One

"King takes the queen." Antonio Medina declared his victory and raked in the chips, having bluffed with a simple high-card hand in Texas Hold'Em.

Ignoring an incoming call on his iPhone, he stacked his winnings. He didn't often have time for poker since his fishing charter company went global, but joining backroom games at his pal Vernon's Galveston Bay Grille had become a more frequent occurrence of late. Since Shannon. His gaze snapped to the long skinny windows on either side of the door leading out to the main dining area where she worked.

No sign of Shannon's slim body, winding her way through the brass, crystal and white linen of the five-star restaurant. Disappointment chewed at him in spite of his win.

A cell phone chime cut the air, then a second right

afterward. Not his either time, although the noise still forced his focus back to the private table while two of Vernon Wolfe's cronies pressed the ignore button, cutting the ringing short. Vernon's poker pals were all about forty years senior to Antonio. But the old shrimp-boat captain turned restaurateur had saved Antonio's bacon back when he'd been a teen. So if Vernon beckoned, Antonio did his damnedest to show. The fact that Shannon also worked here provided extra oomph to the request.

Vernon creaked back in the leather chair, also disregarding his cell phone currently crooning "Son of a Sailor" from his belt. "Ballsy move holding with just a king, Tony," he said, his voice perpetually raspy from years of shouting on deck. His face still sported a year-round tan, eyes raccoon ringed from sunglasses. "I thought Glenn had a royal flush with his queen and jack showing."

"I was taught to bluff by the best." Antonio—or Tony Castillo as he was known these days—grinned.

A smile was more disarming than a scowl. He always smiled so nobody knew what he was thinking. Not that even his best grin had gained him forgiveness from Shannon after their fight last weekend.

Resisting the urge to frown, Tony stacked his chips on the scarred wooden table Vernon had pried from his boat before docking himself permanently at the restaurant. "Your pal Glenn needs to bluff better."

Glenn—a coffee addict—chugged his java faster when bluffing. For some reason no one else seemed to notice as the high-priced attorney banged back his third brew laced with Irish whiskey. He then simply shrugged, loosened his silk tie and hooked it on the back of the chair, settling in for the next round.

Vernon swept up the played cards, flipping the king of hearts between his fingers until the cell stopped singing vintage Jimmy Buffett. "Keep winning and they're not going to let me deal you in anymore."

Tony went through the motions of laughing along, but he knew he wasn't going anywhere. This was his world now. He'd built a life of his own and wanted nothing to do with the Medina name. He was Tony Castillo now. His father had honored that. Until recently.

For the past six months, his deposed king of a dad had sent message after message demanding his presence at the secluded island compound off the coast of Florida. Tony had left that gilded prison the second he'd turned eighteen and never looked back. If Enrique was as sick as he claimed, then their problems would have to be sorted out in heaven...or more likely in somewhere hotter even than Texas.

While October meant autumn chills for folks like his two brothers, he preferred the lengthened summers in Galveston Bay. The air conditioner still cranked in the redbrick waterside restaurant in the historic district.

Muffled live music from a flamenco guitarist drifted through the wall along with the drone of dining clientele. Business was booming for Vernon. Tony made sure of that. Vernon had given Antonio a job at eighteen when no one else would trust a kid with sketchy ID. Fourteen years and many millions of dollars later, Tony figured it was only fair some of the proceeds from the shipping business he'd built should buy the aging shrimp-boat captain a retirement plan.

Vernon nudged the deck toward Glenn to cut, then dealt the next hand. Glenn shoved his buzzing BlackBerry beside his spiked coffee and thumbed his cards up for a peek.

Tony reached for his...and stopped...tipping his ear toward the sound from outside the door. A light laugh cut through the clanging dishes and fluttering strum of the

Spanish guitar. *Her* laugh. Finally. The simple sound made him ache after a week without her.

His gaze shot straight to the door again, bracketed by two windows showcasing the dining area. Shannon stepped in view of the left lengthy pane, pausing to punch in an order at the servers' station. She squinted behind her cat-eye glasses, the retros giving her a naughty schoolmarm look that never failed to send his libido surging.

Light from the globed sconces glinted on her pale blond hair. She wore her long locks in a messy updo, as much a part of her work uniform as the knee-length black skirt and form-fitting tuxedo vest. She looked sexy as hell—and exhausted.

Damn it all, he would help her without hesitation. Just last weekend he'd suggested as much when she'd pulled on her clothes after they'd made love at his Bay Shore mansion. She'd shut him down faster than the next heartbeat. In fact, she hadn't spoken to him or returned his calls since.

Stubborn, sexy woman. It wasn't like he'd offered to set her up as his mistress, for crying out loud. He was only trying to help her and her three-year-old son. She always vowed she would do anything for Kolby.

Mentioning that part hadn't gone well for him, either.

Her lips had pursed tight, but her eyes behind those sexy black glasses had told him she wanted to throw his offer back in his face. His ears still rang from the slamming door when she'd walked out. Most women he knew would have jumped at the prospect of money or expensive gifts. Not Shannon. If anything, she seemed put off by his wealth. It had taken him two months to persuade her just to have coffee with him. Then two more months to work his way into bed with her. And after nearly four weeks of mind-bending sex, he was still no closer to understanding her.

Okay, so he'd built a fortune from Galveston Bay being

one of the largest importers of seafood. Luck had played a part by landing him here in the first place. He'd simply been looking for a coastal community that reminded him of home.

His real home, off the coast of Spain. Not the island fortress his father had built off the U.S. The one he'd escaped the day he'd turned eighteen and swapped his last name from Medina to Castillo. The new surname had been plucked from one of the many branches twigging off his regal family tree. Tony *Castillo* had vowed never to return, a vow he'd kept.

And he didn't even want to think about how spooked Shannon would be if she knew the well-kept secret of his royal heritage. Not that the secret was his to share.

Vernon tapped the scarred wooden table in front of him. "Your phone's buzzing again. We can hold off on this hand while you take the call."

Tony thumbed the ignore button on his iPhone without looking. He only disregarded the outside world for two people, Shannon and Vernon. "It's about the Salinas Shrimp deal. They need to sweat for another hour before we settle on the bottom line."

Glenn rolled his coffee mug between his palms. "So when we don't hear back from you, we'll all know you hit the ignore button."

"Never," Tony responded absently, tucking the device back inside his suit coat. More and more he looked forward to Shannon's steady calm at the end of a hectic day.

Vernon's phone chimed again—Good God, what was up with all the interruptions?—this time rumbling with Marvin Gaye's "Let's Get It On."

The grizzled captain slapped down his cards. "That's my wife. Gotta take this one." Bluetooth glowing in his ear, he shot to his feet and tucked into a corner for semiprivacy. "Yeah, sugar?"

Since Vernon had just tied the knot for the first time seven months ago, the guy acted like a twenty-year-old newlywed. Tony walled off flickering thoughts of his own parents' marriage, not too hard since there weren't that many to remember. His mother had died when he was five.

Vernon inhaled sharply. Tony looked up. His old mentor's face paled under a tan so deep it almost seemed tattooed. What the hell?

"Tony." Vernon's voice went beyond raspy, like the guy had swallowed ground glass. "I think you'd better check those missed messages."

"Is something wrong?" he asked, already reaching for his iPhone.

"You'll have to tell us that," Vernon answered without once taking his raccoonlike eyes off Tony. "Actually, you can skip the messages and just head straight for the internet."

"Where?" He tapped through the menu.

"Anywhere." Vernon sank back into his chair like an anchor thudding to the bottom of the ocean floor. "It's headlining everywhere. You won't miss it."

His iPhone connected to the internet and displayed the top stories—

Royalty Revealed!
Medina Monarchy Exposed!

Blinking fast, he stared in shock at the last thing he expected, but the outcome his father had always feared most. One heading at a time, his family's cover was peeled away until he settled on the last in the list.

Meet the Medina Mistress!

The insane speed of viral news… His gaze shot straight to the windows separating him from the waiters' station, where seconds ago he'd seen Shannon.

Sure enough, she still stood with her back to him. He wouldn't have much time. He had to talk to her before she finished tapping in her order or tabulating a bill.

Tony shot to his feet, his chair scraping loudly in the silence as Vernon's friends all checked their messages. Reaching for the brass handle, he kept his eyes locked on the woman who turned him inside out with one touch of her hand on his bare flesh, the simple brush of her hair across his chest until he forgot about staying on guard. Foreboding crept up his spine. His instincts had served him well over the years—steering him through multimillion-dollar business decisions, even warning him of a frayed shrimp net inching closer to snag his feet.

And before all that? The extra sense had powered his stride as he'd raced through the woods, running from rebels overthrowing San Rinaldo's government. Rebels who hadn't thought twice about shooting at kids, even a five-year-old.

Or murdering their mother.

The Medina cover was about more than privacy. It was about safety. While his family had relocated to a U.S. island after the coup, they could never let down their guard. And damn it all, he'd selfishly put Shannon in the crosshairs simply because he had to have her in his bed.

Tony clasped her shoulders and turned her around. Only to stop short.

Her beautiful blue eyes wide with horror said it all. And if he'd been in doubt? The cell phone clutched in Shannon's hand told him the rest.

She already knew.

* * *

She didn't want to know.

The internet rumor her son's babysitter had read over the phone had to be a media mistake. As did the five follow-up articles she'd found in her own ten-second search with her cell's internet service.

The blogosphere could bloom toxic fiction in minutes, right? People could say whatever they wanted, make a fortune off click-throughs and then retract the erroneous story the next day. Tony's touch on her shoulders was so familiar and stirring he simply couldn't be a stranger. Even now her body warmed at the feel of his hands until she swayed.

But then hadn't she made the very same mistake with her dead husband, buying into his facade because she *wanted* it to be true?

Damn it, Tony wasn't Nolan. All of this would be explained away and she could go back to her toe-curling affair with Tony. Except they were already in the middle of a fight over trying to give her money—an offer that made her skin crawl. And if he was actually a prince?

She swallowed hysterical laughter. Well, he'd told her that he had money to burn and it could very well be he'd meant that on a scale far grander than she could have ever imagined.

"Breathe," her ex-lover commanded.

"Okay, okay, okay," she chanted on each gasp of air, tapping her glasses more firmly in place in hopes the dots in front of her eyes would fade. "I'm okay."

Now that her vision cleared she had a better view of her place at the center of the restaurant's attention. And when had Tony started edging her toward the door? Impending doom welled inside her as she realized the local media would soon descend.

"Good, steady now, in and out." His voice didn't sound any different.

But it also didn't sound Texan. Or southern. Or even northern for that matter, as if he'd worked to stamp out any sense of regionality from himself. She tried to focus on the timbre that so thoroughly strummed her senses when they made love.

"Tony, please say we're going to laugh over this misunderstanding later."

He didn't answer. His square jaw was set and serious as he looked over her shoulder, scanning. She found no signs of her carefree lover, even though her fingers carried the memory of how his dark hair curled around her fingers. His wealth and power had been undeniable from the start in his clothes and lifestyle, but most of all in his proud carriage. Now she took new note of his aristocratic jaw and cheekbones. Such a damn handsome and charming man. She'd allowed herself to be wowed. Seduced by his smile.

She'd barely come to grips with dating a rich guy, given all the bad baggage that brought up of her dead husband. A crooked sleaze. She'd been dazzled by Nolan's glitzy world, learning too late it was financed by a Ponzi scheme.

The guilt of those destroyed lives squeezed the breath from her lungs all over again. If not for her son, she might very well have curled inside herself and given up after Nolan took his own life. But she would hold strong for Kolby.

"Answer me," she demanded, hoping.

"This isn't the place to talk."

Not reassuring and, oh God, why did Tony still have the power to hurt her? Anger punched through the pain. "How long does it take to say *damned rumor?*"

He slid an arm around her shoulders, tucking her to his side. "Let's find somewhere more private."

"Tell me now." She pulled back from the lure of his familiar scent, minty patchouli and sandalwood, the smell of exotic pleasures.

Tony—Antonio—Prince Medina—whoever the hell he was—ducked his head closer to hers. "Shannon, do you really want to talk here where anyone can listen? The world's going to intrude on our town soon enough."

Tears burned behind her eyes, the room going blurry even with her glasses on. "Okay, we'll find a quiet place to discuss this."

He backed her toward the kitchen. Her legs and his synched up in step, her hips following his instinctively, as if they'd danced together often...and more. Eyes and whispers followed them the entire way. Did everyone already know? Cell phones sang from pockets and vibrated on tabletops as if Galveston quivered on the verge of an earthquake.

No one approached them outright, but fragments drifted from their huddled discussions.

"Could Tony Castillo be—"

"—Medina—"

"—With that waitress—"

The buzz increased like a swarm of locusts closing in on the Texas landscape. On her life.

Tony growled lowly, "There's nowhere here we can speak privately. I need to get you out of Vernon's."

His muscled arm locked her tighter, guiding her through a swishing door, past a string of chefs all immobile and gawking. He shouldered out a side door and she had no choice but to follow.

Outside, the late-day sun kissed his bronzed face, bringing his deeply tanned features into sharper focus. She'd always known there was something strikingly foreign about him. But she'd believed his story of dead parents, bookkeepers who'd emigrated from South America. Her own parents had died in a car accident before she'd graduated from college. She'd thought they'd at least shared similar childhoods.

Now? She was sure of nothing except how her body still betrayed her with the urge to lean into his hard-muscled strength, to escape into the pleasure she knew he could bring.

"I need to let management know I'm leaving. I can't lose this job." Tips were best in the evening and she needed every penny. She couldn't afford the time it would take to get her teaching credentials current again—if she could even find a music-teaching position with cutbacks in the arts.

And there weren't too many people out there in search of private oboe lessons.

"I know the owner, remember?" He unlocked his car, the remote chirp-chirping.

"Of course. What was I thinking? You have connections." She stifled a fresh bout of hysterical laughter.

Would she even be able to work again if the Medina rumor was true? It had been tough enough finding a job when others associated her with her dead husband. Sure, she'd been cleared of any wrongdoing, but many still believed she must have known about Nolan's illegal schemes.

There hadn't even been a trial for her to state her side. Once her husband had made bail, he'd been dead within twenty-four hours.

Tony cursed low and harsh, sailor-style swearing he usually curbed around her and Kolby. She looked around, saw nothing... Then she heard the thundering footsteps a second before the small cluster of people rounded the corner with cameras and microphones.

Swearing again, Tony yanked open the passenger door to his Escalade. He lifted her inside easily, as if she weighed nothing more than the tray of fried gator appetizers she'd carried earlier.

Seconds later he slid behind the wheel and slammed the door a hair's breadth ahead of the reporters. Fists pounded on the tinted windows. Locks auto-clicked. Shannon sagged in the leather seat with relief.

The hefty SUV rocked from the force of the mob. Her heart rate ramped again. If this was the life of the rich and famous, she wanted no part.

Shifting into Reverse then forward, Tony drove, slow but steady. People peeled away. At least one reporter fell on his butt but everyone appeared unharmed.

So much for playing chicken with Tony. She would be wise to remember that.

He guided the Escalade through the historic district a hint over the speed limit, fast enough to put space between them and the media hounds. Panting in the aftermath, she still braced a hand on the dash, her other gripping the leather seat. Yet Tony hadn't even broken a sweat.

His hands stayed steady on the wheel, his expensive watch glinting from the French cuffs of his shirt. Restored brick buildings zipped by her window. A young couple dressed for an evening out stepped off the curb, then back sharply. While the whole idea of being hunted by the paparazzi scared her to her roots, right here in the SUV with Tony, she felt safe.

Safe enough for the anger and betrayal to come bubbling to the surface. She'd been mad at him since their fight last weekend over his continued insistence on giving her money.

But those feelings were nothing compared to the rage that coursed through her now. "We're alone. Talk to me."

"It's complicated." He glanced in the rearview mirror. Normal traffic tooled along the narrow street. "What do you want to know?"

She forced herself to say the words that would drive a permanent wedge between her and the one man she'd dared let into her life again.

"Are you a part of that lost royal family, the one everybody thought was hiding in Argentina?"

The Cadillac's finely tuned engine hummed in the silence. Lights clicked on automatically with the setting sun, the dash glowing.

His knuckles went white on the steering wheel, his jaw flexing before he nodded tightly. "The rumors on the internet are correct."

And she'd thought her heart couldn't break again.

Her pride had been stung over Tony's offer to give her money, but she would have gotten over it. She would have stuck to her guns about paying her own way, of course. But *this?* It was still too huge to wrap her brain around. She'd slept with a prince, let him into her home, her body, and considered letting him into her heart. His deception burned deep.

How could she have missed the truth so completely, buying into his stories about working on a shrimp boat as a teen? She'd assumed his tattoo and the closed over pierced earlobe were parts of an everyman past that seduced her as fully as his caresses.

"Your name isn't even Tony Castillo." Oh God. She pressed the back of her hand against her mouth, suddenly nauseated because she didn't even know the name of the guy she'd been sleeping with.

"Technically, it could be."

Shannon slammed her fists against the leather seat instead of reaching for him as she ached to do. "I'm not interested in technically. Actually, I'm not interested in people who lie to me. Can I even trust that you're really thirty-two years old?"

"It isn't just my decision to share specific details. I have other family members to consider. But if it's any consolation, I really am thirty-two. Are you really twenty-nine?"

"I'm not in a joking mood." Shivering, she thumbed her bare ring finger where once a three-carat diamond had rested. After Nolan's funeral, she'd taken it off and sold it along with everything else to pay off the mountain of debt. "I should have known you were too good to be true."

"Why do you say that?"

"Who makes millions by thirty-two?"

He cocked an arrogant eyebrow. "Did you just call me a moocher?"

"Well, excuse me if that was rude, but I'm not exactly at my best tonight."

His arms bulged beneath his Italian suit—she'd had to look up the exclusive Garaceni label after she'd seen the coat hanging on his bedpost.

Tony looked even more amazing out of the clothes, his tanned and muscled body eclipsing any high-end wardrobe. And the smiles he brought to her life, his uninhibited laughter were just what she needed most.

How quiet her world had been without him this week. "Sorry to have hurt your feelings, pal. Or should I say, Your Majesty? Since according to some of those stories I'm 'His Majesty's mistress.'"

"Actually, it would be 'Your Highness.'" His signature smile tipped his mouth, but with a bitter edge. "Majesty is for the king."

How could he be so flippant? "Actually, you can take your title and stuff it where the sun—"

"I get the picture." He guided the Escalade over the Galveston Island Causeway, waves moving darkly below. "You'll need time to calm down so we can discuss how to handle this."

"You don't understand. There's no calming down. You lied to me on a fundamental level. Once we made l—" she stumbled over the next word, images of him moving over her, inside her, stealing her words and breath until her stomach churned as fast as the waters below "—after we went to bed together, you should have told me. Unless the sex didn't mean anything special to you. I guess if you had to tell every woman you slept with, there would be no secret."

"Stop!" He sliced the air with his hand. His gleaming Patek Philippe watch contrasted with scarred knuckles, from his sailing days he'd once told her. "That's not true and not the point here. You were safer not knowing."

"Oh, it's for my own good." She wrapped her arms around herself, a shield from the hurt.

"How much do you know about my family's history?"

She bit back the urge to snap at him. Curiosity reined in her temper. "Not much. Just that there was a king of some small country near Spain, I think, before he was overthrown in a coup. His family has been hiding out to avoid the paparazzi hoopla."

"Hoopla? This might suck, but that's the least of my worries. There are people out there who tried to kill my family and succeeded in murdering my mother. There are people who stand to gain a lot in the way of money and power if the Medinas are wiped off the planet."

Her heart ached for all he had lost. Even now, she wanted to press her mouth to his and forget this whole insane mess.

To grasp that shimmering connection she'd discovered with him the first time they'd made love in a frenzied tangle at his Galveston Bay mansion.

"Well, believe it, Shannon. There's a big bad world outside your corner of Texas. Right now, some of the worst will start focusing on me, my family and anyone who's close to us. Whether you like it or not, I'll do whatever it takes to keep you and Kolby protected."

Her son's safety? Perspiration froze on her forehead, chilling her deeper. Why hadn't she thought of that? Of course she'd barely wrapped her brain around Tony... Antonio. "Drive faster. Get me home now."

"I completely agree. I've already sent bodyguards ahead of us."

Bodyguards?

"When?" She'd barely been able to think, much less act. What kind of mother was she not to have considered the impact on Kolby? And what kind of man kept bodyguards on speed dial?

"I texted my people while we were leaving through the kitchen."

Of course he had people. The man was not merely the billionaire shipping magnate she'd assumed, he was also the bearer of a surname generations old and a background of privilege she couldn't begin to fathom.

"I was so distracted I didn't even notice," Shannon whispered, sinking into her seat. She wasn't even safe in her own neighborhood anymore.

She couldn't wish this away any longer. "You really are this Medina guy. You're really from some deposed royal family."

His chin tipped with unmistakable regality. "My name is Antonio Medina. I was born in San Rinaldo, third son of King Enrique and Queen Beatriz."

Her heart drumming in her ears, panic squeezed harder at her rib cage. How could she have foreseen this when she met him five months ago at the restaurant, bringing his supper back to the owner's poker game? Tony had ordered a shrimp po'boy sandwich and a glass of sweet tea.

Poor Boy? How ironic was that?

"This is too weird." And scary.

The whole surreal mess left her too numb to hurt anymore. That would return later, for sure. Her hands shook as she tapped her glasses straight.

She had to stay focused now. "Stuff like this happens in movies or a hundred years ago."

"Or in my life. Now in yours, too."

"Nuh-uh. You and I?" She waggled her hand back and forth between them. "We're history."

He paused at a stop sign, turning to face her fully for the first time since he'd gripped her shoulders at the restaurant. His coal black eyes heated over her, a bold man of uninhibited emotions. "That fast, you're ready to call an end to what we've shared?"

Her heart picked up speed from just the caress of his eyes, the memory of his hands stroking her. She tried to answer but her mouth had gone dry. He skimmed those scarred knuckles down her arm until his hand rested on hers. Such a simple gesture, nothing overtly erotic, but her whole body hummed with awareness and want.

Right here in the middle of the street, in the middle of an upside down situation, her body betrayed her as surely as he had.

Wrong. Wrong. Wrong. She had to be tough. "I already ended things between us last weekend."

"That was a fight, not a breakup." His big hand splayed over hers, eclipsing her with heat.

"Semantics. Not that it matters." She pulled herself

away from him until her spine met the door, not nearly far enough. "I can't be with you anymore."

"That's too damn bad, because we're going to be spending a lot of time together after we pick up your son. There's no way you can stay in your apartment tonight."

"There's no way I can stay with *you*."

"You can't hide from what's been unleashed. Today should tell you that more than anything. It'll find you and your son. I'm sorry for not seeing this coming, but it's here and we have to deal with it."

Fear for her son warred with her anger at Tony. "You had no right," she hissed between clenched teeth, "no right at all to play with our lives this way."

"I agree." He surprised her with that. However, the reprieve was short. "But I'm the only one who can stand between you both and whatever fallout comes from this revelation."

Two

A bodyguard stood outside the front door of her first-floor apartment. A bodyguard, for heaven's sake, a burly guy in a dark suit who could have passed for a Secret Service employee. She stifled the urge to scream in frustration.

Shannon flung herself out of the Escalade before it came to a complete stop, desperate to see her child, to get inside her tiny apartment in hopes that life would somehow return to normal. Tony couldn't be serious about her packing up to go away with him. He was just using this to try to get back together again.

Although what did a *prince* want with her?

At least there weren't any reporters in the parking lot. The neighbors all seemed to be inside for the evening or out enjoying their own party plans. She'd chosen the large complex for the anonymity it offered. Multiple three-story buildings filled the corner block, making it difficult to tell one apartment from another in the stretches of yellow units with tiny white balconies. At the center of it all, there was a pool and tiny playground, the only luxuries she'd allowed herself. She might not be able to give Kolby a huge yard, but he would have an outdoor place to play.

Now she had to start the search for a haven all over again.

"Here," she said as she thrust her purse toward him, her keys in her hand, "please carry this so I can unlock the door."

He extended his arm, her hobo bag dangling from his big fist. "Uh, sure."

"This is not the time to freak out over holding a woman's purse." She fumbled for the correct key.

"Shannon, I'm here for you. For you and your hand-bag."

She glanced back sharply. "Don't mock me."

"I thought you enjoyed my sense of humor."

Hadn't she thought just the same thing earlier? How could she say good-bye to Tony—he would never be Antonio to her—forever? Her feet slowed on the walkway between the simple hedges, nowhere near as elaborate as the gardens of her old home with Nolan, but well maintained. The place was clean.

And safe.

Having Tony at her back provided an extra layer of protection, she had to admit. After he'd made his shocking demand that she pack, he'd pulled out his phone and began checking in with his lawyer. From what she could tell hearing one side of the conversation, the news was spreading fast, with no indication of how the Global Intruder's people had cracked his cover. Tony didn't lose his temper or even curse.

But her normally lighthearted lover definitely wasn't smiling.

She ignored the soft note of regret spreading through her for all she would leave behind—this place. *Tony.* He strode alongside her silently, the outside lights casting his shadow over hers intimately, moving, tangling the two together as they walked.

Stopping at her unit three doors down from the corner, Tony exchanged low words with the guard while she slid the key into the lock with shaking hands. She pushed her way inside and ran smack into the babysitter already trying to open up for her. The college senior was majoring in elementary education and lived in the same complex. There might only be seven years between her and the girl in a concert T-shirt, but Shannon couldn't help but feel her own university days spent studying to be a teacher happened eons ago.

Shannon forced herself to stay calm. "Courtney, thanks for calling me. Where's Kolby?"

The sitter studied her with undisguised curiosity— who could blame her?—and pointed down the narrow hall toward the living room. "He's asleep on the couch. I thought it might be better to keep him with me in case any reporters started showing up outside or something." She hitched her bulging backpack onto one shoulder. "I don't think they would stake out his window, but ya never know. Right?"

"Thank you, Courtney. You did exactly the right thing." She angled down the hall to peek in on Kolby.

Her three-year-old son slept curled on the imported leather sofa, one of the few pieces that hadn't been sold to pay off debts. Kolby had poked a hole in the armrest with a fountain pen just before the estate sale. Shannon had strapped duct tape over the tear, grateful for one less piece of furniture to buy to start her new life.

Every penny she earned needed to be tucked away for

emergencies. Kolby counted on her, her sweet baby boy in his favorite Thomas the Tank Engine pj's, matching blanket held up to his nose. His blond hair was tousled and spiking, still damp from his bath. She could almost smell the baby-powder sweetness from across the room.

Sagging against the archway with relief, she turned back to Courtney. "I need to pay you."

Shannon took back her hobo bag from Tony and tunneled through frantically, dropping her wallet. Change clanked on the tile floor.

What would a three-year-old think if he saw his mother's face in some news report? Or Tony's, for that matter? The two had only met briefly a few times, but Kolby knew he was Mama's friend. She scooped the coins into a pile, picking at quarters and dimes.

Tony cupped her shoulder. "I've got it. Go ahead and be with your son."

She glanced up sharply, her nerves too raw to take the reminder of how he'd offered her financial help mere moments after sex last weekend. "I can pay my own way."

Holding up his hands, he backed away.

"Fine, Shannon. I'll sit with Kolby." He cautioned her with a look not to mention their plans to pack and leave.

Duh. Not that she planned to follow all *his* dictates, but the fewer who knew their next move the better for avoiding the press and anyone else who might profit from tracking their moves. Even the best of friends could be bought off.

Speaking of payoffs… "Thank you for calling me so quickly." She peeled off an extra twenty and tried not to wince as she said goodbye to ice cream for the month. She usually traded babysitting with another flat-broke single mom in the building when needed for work and dates.

Courtney was only her backup, which she couldn't—and didn't—use often. "I appreciate your help."

Shaking her head, Courtney took the money and passed back the extra twenty. "You don't need to give me all that, Mrs. Crawford. I was only doing my job. And I'm not gonna talk to the reporters. I'm not the kind of person who would sell your story or something."

"Really," Shannon urged as she folded the cash back into her hand, "I want you to have it."

Tony filled the archway. "The guard outside will walk you home, just to make sure no one bothers you."

"Thanks, Mr. Castillo. Um, I mean…" Courtney stuffed the folded bills into her back pocket, the college coed eyeing him up and down with a new awareness. "Mr. Medina… Sir? I don't what to call you."

"Castillo is fine."

"Right, uh, bye." Her face flushed, she spun on her glitter flip-flops and took off.

Shannon pushed the door closed, sliding the bolt and chain. Locking her inside with Tony in a totally quiet apartment. She slumped back and stared down the hallway, the ten feet shrinking even more with the bulk of his shoulders spanning the arch. Light from the cheap brown lamp glinted off the curl in his black hair.

No wonder Courtney had been flustered. He wasn't just a prince, but a fine-looking, one-hundred-percent *man*. The kind with strong hands that could finesse their way over a woman's body with a sweet tenderness that threatened to buckle her knees from just remembering. Had it only been a week since they'd made love in his mammoth jetted tub? God knows she ached as if she'd been without him for months.

Even acknowledging it was wrong with her mind, her body still wanted him.

* * *

Tony wanted her.

In his arms.

In his bed.

And most of all, he wanted her back in his SUV, heading away from here. He needed to use any methods of persuasion possible and convince her to come to his house. Even if the press located his home address, they wouldn't get past the gates and security. So how to convince Shannon? He stared down the short tiled hallway at her.

Awareness flared in her eyes. The same slam of attraction he felt now and the first time he'd seen her five months ago when he'd stopped by after a call to play cards. Vernon had mentioned hiring a new waitress but Tony hadn't thought much of it—until he met her.

When Tony asked about her, the old guy said he didn't know much about Shannon other than her crook of a husband had committed suicide rather than face a jury. Shannon and her boy had been left behind, flat broke. She'd worked at a small diner for a year and a half before that and Vernon had hired her on a hunch. Vernon and his softie heart.

Tony stared at her now every bit as intently as he had that first time she'd brought him his order. Something about her blue-gray eyes reminded him of the ocean sky just before a storm. Tumultuous. Interesting.

A challenge. He'd been without a challenge for too long. Building a business from nothing had kept him charged up for years. What next?

Then he'd seen her.

He'd spent his life smiling his way through problems and deals, and for the first time he'd found someone who saw past his bull. Was it the puzzle that tugged him? If so, he wasn't any closer to solving the mystery of Shannon.

Every day she confused him more, which made him want her more.

Pushing away from the door, she strode toward him, efficiently, no hip swish, just even, efficient steps. Then she walked out of her shoes, swiping one foot behind her to kick them to rest against the wall. No shoes in the house. She'd told him that the two times he'd been allowed over her threshold for no more than fifteen minutes. Any liaisons between them had been at his bayside mansion or a suite near the restaurant. He didn't really expect anything to happen here with her son around, even asleep.

And given the look on her face, she was more likely to pitch him out. Better to circumvent the boot.

"I'll stay with your son while you pack." He removed his shoes and stepped deeper into her place, not fancy, the sparse generic sort of a furnished space in browns and tan—except for the expensive burgundy leather sofa with a duct-taped *X* on the armrest.

Her lips thinned. "About packing, we need to discuss that further."

"What's to talk about?" He accepted their relationship was still on hold, but the current problems with his identity needed to be addressed. "Your porch will be full by morning."

"I'll check into a hotel."

With the twenty dollars and fifty-two cents she had left in her wallet? He prayed she wasn't foolish enough to use a credit card. Might as well phone in her location to the news stations.

"We can talk about where you'll stay *after* you pack."

"You sound like a broken record, Tony."

"*You*'re calling *me* stubborn?"

Their standoff continued, neither of them touching, but he was all too aware of her scrubbed fresh scent.

Shannon, the whole place, carried an air of some kind of floral cleaner. The aroma somehow calmed and stirred at the same time, calling to mind holding her after a mind-bending night of sex. She never stayed over until morning, but for an hour or so after, she would doze against his chest. He would breathe in the scent of her and him and *them* blended together.

His nose flared.

Her pupils widened.

She stumbled back, her chest rising faster. "I do need to change my clothes. Are you sure you'll be all right with Kolby?"

It was no secret the couple of times he'd met the boy, Kolby hadn't warmed up to him. Nothing seemed to work, not ice cream or magic coin tricks. Tony figured maybe the boy was still missing his father.

That jerk had left Shannon bankrupt and vulnerable. "I can handle it. Take all the time you need."

"Thank you. I'm only going to change clothes though. No packing yet. We'll have to talk more first, Tony—um, Antonio."

"I prefer to be called *Tony*." He liked the sound of it on her tongue.

"Okay…Tony." She spun on her heel and headed toward her bedroom.

Her steps still efficient, albeit faster, were just speedy enough to bring a slight swing to her slim hips in the pencil-straight skirt. Thoughts of peeling it down and off her beautiful body would have to wait until she had the whole Antonio/Tony issue sorted out.

If only she could accept that he'd called himself Tony Castillo almost longer than he'd remembered being Antonio Medina.

He even had the paperwork to back up the Castillo

name. Creating another persona hadn't been that difficult, especially once he'd saved enough to start his first business. From then on, all transactions were shuttled through the company. Umbrella corporations. Living in plain sight. His plan had worked fine until someone, somehow had pierced the new identities he and his brothers had built. In fact, he needed to call his brothers, who he spoke to at most a couple of times a year. But they might have insights.

They needed a plan.

He reached inside his jacket for his iPhone and ducked into the dining area where he could see the child but wouldn't wake him. He thumbed the seven key on his speed dial...and Carlos's voice mail picked up. Tony disconnected without leaving a message and pressed the eight key.

"Speak to me, my brother." Duarte Medina's voice came through the phone. They didn't talk often, but these weren't normal circumstances.

"I assume you know." He toyed with one of Shannon's hair bands on the table.

"Impossible to miss."

"Where's Carlos? He's not picking up." Tony fell back into their clipped shorthand. They'd only had each other growing up and now circumstances insisted they stay apart. Did his brothers have that same feeling, like they'd lost a limb?

"His secretary said he got paged for an emergency surgery. He'll be at least another couple of hours. Apparently Carlos found out as he was scrubbing in, but you know our brother." Duarte, the middle son, tended to play messenger with their father. The three brothers spoke and met when they could, but there were so many crap memories from their childhood, those reunions became further apart.

Tony scooped up the brown band, a lone long strand

of her blond hair catching the light. "When a patient calls…"

"Right."

It could well be hours before they heard from Carlos, given the sort of painstaking reconstructive surgeries he performed on children. "Any idea how this exploded?"

His brother hissed a long angry curse. "The Global Intruder got a side-view picture of me while I was visiting our sister."

Their half sister Eloisa, their father's daughter from an affair shortly after they had escaped to the States. Enrique had still been torn up with grief from losing his wife… not to mention the guilt. But apparently not so torn up and remorseful he couldn't hop into bed with someone else. The woman had gone on to marry another man who'd raised her daughter as his own.

Tony had only met his half sister once as a teen, a few years before he'd left the island compound. She'd only been seven at the time. Now she'd married into a high-profile family jam-packed with political influence and a fat portfolio. Could she be at fault for bringing the media down on their heads for some free PR for her new in-laws? Duarte seemed to think she wanted anonymity as much as the rest of them. But could he have misjudged her?

"Why were you visiting Eloisa?" Tony tucked the band into his pocket.

"Family business. It doesn't matter now. Her in-laws were there. Eloisa's sister-in-law—a senator's wife—slipped on the dock. I kept her from falling into the water. Some damn female reporter in a tree with a telephoto lens caught the mishap. Which shouldn't have mattered, since Senator Landis and his wife were the focus of the picture. I still don't know how the photographer pegged me from a side view, but there it is. And I'm sorry for bringing this crap down on you."

Duarte hadn't done anything wrong. They couldn't live in a bubble. In the back of Tony's mind, he'd always known it was just a matter of time until the cover story blew up in their faces. He'd managed to live away from the island anonymously for fourteen years, his two older brothers even longer.

But there was always the hope that maybe he could stay a step ahead. Be his own man. Succeed on his own merits. "We've all been caught in a picture on occasion. We're not vampires. It's just insane that she was able to make the connection. Perfect storm of bad luck."

"What are your plans for dealing with this perfect storm?"

"Lock down tight while I regroup. Let me know when you hear from Carlos."

Ending the call, Tony strode back into the living room, checked on Kolby—still snoozing hard—and dropped to the end of the sofa to read messages, his in-box already full again. By the time Tony scrolled through emails that told him nothing new, he logged on to the internet for a deeper peek. And winced. Rumors were rampant.

That his father had died of malaria years ago—false.

Supposition that Carlos had plastic surgery—again, false.

Speculation that Duarte had joined a Tibetan monastery—definitely false.

And then there were the stories about him and Shannon, which actually happened to be true. The whole "Monarch's Mistress" was really growing roots out there in cyberspace. Guilt kicked him in the gut that Shannon would suffer this kind of garbage because of him. The media feeding frenzy would only grow, and before long they would stir up all the crap about her thief of a dead husband. He tucked away his phone in disgust.

"That bad?" Shannon asked from the archway.

She'd changed into jeans and a simple blue tank top. Her silky blond hair glided loosely down her shoulders, straight except for a slight crimped ring where she'd bound it up on her head for work. She didn't look much older than the babysitter, except in her weary—wary—eyes.

Leaning back, he extended his legs, leather creaking as he stayed on the sofa so as not to spook her. "The internet is exploding. My lawyers and my brothers' lawyers are all looking into it. Hopefully we'll have the leak plugged soon and start some damage control. But we can't stuff the genie back into the bottle."

"I'm not going away with you." She perched a fist on one shapely hip.

"This isn't going to die down." He kept his voice even and low, reasonable. The stakes were too important for all of them. "The reporters will swarm you by morning, if not sooner. Your babysitter will almost inevitably cave in to one of those gossip rag offers. Your friends will sell photos of the two of us together. There's a chance people could use Kolby to get to me."

"Then we're through, you and I." She reached for her sleeping son on the sofa, smoothing his hair before sliding a hand under his shoulders as if to scoop him up.

Tony touched her arm lightly, stopping her. "Hold on before you settle him into his room." As far as Tony was concerned, they would be back in his Escalade in less than ten minutes. "Do you honestly think anyone's going to believe the breakup is for real? The timing will seem too convenient."

She sagged onto the arm of the sofa, right over the silver X. "We ended things last weekend."

Like hell. "Tell that to the papers and see if they believe you. The truth doesn't matter to these people. They probably printed photos of an alien baby last week. Pleading a breakup isn't going to buy you any kind of freedom from their interest."

"I know I need to move away from Galveston." She glanced around her sparsely decorated apartment, two pictures of Kolby the only personal items. "I've accepted that."

There wouldn't be much packing to do.

"They'll find you."

She studied him through narrowed eyes. "How do I know you're not just using this as an excuse to get back together?"

Was he? An hour ago, he would have done anything to get into her bed again. While the attraction hadn't diminished, since his cover was blown, he had other concerns that overshadowed everything else. He needed to determine the best way to inoculate her from the toxic fallout that came from associating with Medinas. One thing for certain, he couldn't risk her striking out on her own.

"You made it clear where we stand last weekend. I get that. You want nothing to do with me or my money." He didn't move closer, wasn't going to crowd her. The draw between them filled the space separating them just fine on its own. "We had sex together. Damn good sex. But that's over now. Neither one of us ever asked for or expected more."

Her gaze locked with his, the room silent but for their breathing and the light snore of the sleeping child. Kolby. Another reminder of why they needed to stay in control.

In fact, holding back made the edge sharper. He skimmed his knuckles along her collarbone, barely touching. A week ago, that pale skin had worn the rasp of his beard. She didn't move closer, but she didn't back away, either.

Shannon blinked first, her long lashes sweeping closed while she swallowed hard. "What am I supposed to do?"

More than anything he wanted to gather her up and tell her everything would be okay. He wouldn't allow anything less. But he also wouldn't make shallow promises.

Twenty-seven years ago, when they'd been leaving San Rinaldo on a moonless night, his father had assured them everything would be fine. They would be reunited soon.

His father had been so very wrong.

Tony focused on what he could assure. "A lot has happened in a few hours. We need to take a step back for damage assessment tonight at my home, where there are security gates, alarms, guards watching and surveillance cameras."

"And after tonight?"

"We'll let the press think we are a couple, still deep in that affair." He indulged himself in one lengthy, heated eye-stroke of her slim, supple body. "Then we'll stage a more public breakup later, on our terms, when we've prepared a backup plan."

She exhaled a shaky breath. "That makes sense."

"Meanwhile, my number one priority is shielding you and Kolby." He sifted through options, eliminating one idea after another until he was left with only a single alternative.

Her hand fell to rest on her sleeping son's head. "How do you intend to do that?"

"By taking you to the safest place I know." A place he'd vowed never to return. "Tomorrow, we're going to visit my father."

Three

"Visit your father?" Shannon asked in total shock. Had Tony lost his mind? "The King of San Rinaldo? You've got to be kidding."

"I'm completely serious." He stared back at her from the far end of the leather sofa, her sleeping son between them.

Resisting Tony had been tough enough this past week just knowing he was in the same town. How much more difficult would it be with him in the same house for one night much less days on end? God, she wanted to run. She bit the inside of her lip to keep from blurting out something she would regret later. Sorting through her options could take more time than they appeared to have.

Kolby wriggled restlessly, hugging his comfort blanket tighter. Needing a moment to collect her thoughts and her resolve, she scooped up her son.

"Tony, we'll have to put this discussion on hold." She

cradled her child closer and angled down the hall, ever aware of a certain looming prince at her back. "Keep the lights off, please."

Shadows playing tag on the ceiling, she lowered Kolby into the red caboose bed they'd picked out together when she moved into the apartment. She'd been trying so hard to make up for all her son had lost. As if there was some way to compensate for the loss of his father, the loss of security. Shannon pressed a kiss to his forehead, inhaling his precious baby-shampoo smell.

When she turned back, she found Tony waiting in the doorway, determination stamped on his square jaw. Well, she could be mighty resolute too, especially when it came to her son. Shannon closed the curtains before she left the room and stepped into the narrow hall.

She shut the door quietly behind her. "You have to know your suggestion is outrageous."

"The whole situation is outrageous, which calls for extraordinary measures."

"Hiding out with a king? That's definitely what I would call extraordinary." She pulled off her glasses and pinched the bridge of her nose.

Before Nolan's death she'd worn contacts, but couldn't afford the extra expense now. How much longer until she would grow accustomed to glasses again?

She stared at Tony, his face clear up close, everything in the distance blurred. "Do you honestly think I would want to expose myself, not to mention Kolby, to more scrutiny by going to your father's? Why not just hide out at your place as we originally discussed?"

God, had she just agreed to stay with him indefinitely?

"My house is secure, up to a point. People will figure out where I live and they'll deduce that you're with me.

There's only one place I can think of where no one can get to us."

Frustration buzzed in her brain. "Seems like their telephoto lenses reach everywhere."

"The press still hasn't located my father's home after years of trying."

But she thought… "Doesn't he live in Argentina?"

He studied her silently, the wheels almost visibly turning in his broad forehead. Finally, he shook his head quickly.

"No. We only stopped off there to reorganize after escaping San Rinaldo." He adjusted his watch, the only nervous habit she'd ever observed in him. "My father did set up a compound there and paid a small, trusted group of individuals to make it look inhabited. Most of them also escaped San Rinaldo with us. People assumed we were there with them."

What extreme lengths and expense their father had gone to. But then wasn't she willing to do anything to protect Kolby? She felt a surprise connection to the old king she'd never met. "Why are you telling me this much if it's such a closely guarded secret?"

He cupped her shoulder, his touch heavy and familiar, *stirring*. "Because it's that important I persuade you."

Resisting the urge to lean into him was tougher with each stroke of his thumb against the sensitive curve of her neck. "Where *does* he live then?"

"I can't tell you that much," he said, still touching and God, it made her mad that she didn't pull away.

"Yet you expect me to just pack up my child and follow you there." She gripped his wrist and moved away his seductive touch.

"I detect a note of skepticism in your voice." He shoved his hands in his pockets.

"A note? Try a whole freaking symphony, Tony." The sense of betrayal swelled inside her again, larger and larger until it pushed bitter words out. "Why should I trust you? Especially now?"

"Because you don't have anyone else or they would have already been helping you."

The reality deflated her. She only had a set of in-laws who didn't want anything to do with her or Kolby since they blamed her for their son's downfall. She was truly alone.

"How long would we be there?"

"Just until my attorneys can arrange for a restraining order against certain media personnel. I realize that restraining orders don't always work, but having one will give us a stronger legal case if we need it. It's one thing to stalk, but it's another to stalk and violate a restraining order. And I'll want to make sure you have top-of-the-line security installed at your new home. That should take about a week, two at the most."

Shannon fidgeted with her glasses. "How would we get there?"

"By plane." He thumbed the face of his watch clean again.

That meant it must be far away. "Forget it. You are not going to isolate me that way, cut me off from the world. It's the equivalent of kidnapping me and my son."

"Not if you agree to go along." He edged closer, the stretch of his hard muscled shoulders blocking out the light filtering from the living area. "People in the military get on planes all the time without knowing their destination."

She tipped her chin upward, their faces inches apart. Close enough to feel his heat. Close enough to kiss.

Too close for her own good. "Last time I checked, I wasn't wearing a uniform." Her voice cracked ever so slightly. "I didn't sign on for this."

"I know, Shanny…." He stroked a lock of her hair intimately. "I *am* sorry for all this is putting you through, and I will do my best to make the next week as easy for you as possible."

The sincerity of his apology soothed the ragged edges of her nerves. It had been a long week without him. She'd been surprised by how much she had missed his spontaneous dates and late-night calls. His bold kisses and intimate caresses. She couldn't lie to herself about how much he affected her on both an emotional and physical level. Otherwise this mess with his revealed past wouldn't hurt her so deeply.

Her hand clenched around her glasses. He gently slid them from her hand and hooked them on the front of her shirt. The familiarity of the gesture kicked her heart rate up a notch.

Swaying toward him, she flattened her hands to his chest, not sure if she wanted to push him away or pull him nearer. Thick longing filled the sliver of space between them. An answering awareness widened his pupils, pushing and thinning the dark brown of his eyes.

He lowered his head closer, closer still until his mouth hovered over hers. Heated breaths washed over her, stirring even hotter memories and warm languid longing. She'd thought the pain of Nolan's deceit had left her numb for life…until she saw Tony.

"Mama?"

The sound of her son calling out from his room jolted her back to reality. And not only her. Tony's face went from seductive to intent in a heartbeat. He pulled the door open just as Kolby ran through and into his mother's arms.

"Mama, Mama, Mama…" He buried his face in her neck. "Monster in my window!"

* * *

Tony shot through the door and toward the window in the child's room, focused, driven and mentally kicking himself for letting himself be distracted.

He barked over his shoulder, "Stay in the hall while I take a look."

It could be nothing, but he'd been taught at a young age the importance of never letting down his guard. Adrenaline firing, he jerked the window open and scanned the tiny patch of yard.

Nothing. Just a Big Wheel lying on its side and a swing dangling lazily from a lone tree.

Maybe it was only a nightmare. This whole blast from the past had him seeing bogeymen from his own childhood, too. Tony pushed the window down again and pulled the curtains together.

Shannon stood in the door, her son tucked against her. "I could have sworn I closed the curtains."

Kolby peeked up. "I opened 'em when I heard-ed the noise."

And maybe this kid's nightmare was every bit as real as his own had been. On the off chance the boy was right, he had to check. "I'm going outside. The guard will stay here with you."

She cupped the back of her child's head. "I already warned the guard. I wasn't leaving you to take care of the 'monster' by yourself."

Dread kinked cold and tight in his gut. What if something had happened to her when she had stepped outside to speak to the guard? He held in the angry words, not wanting to upset her son.

But he became more determined by the second to persuade her and the child to leave Galveston with him.

"Let's hope it was nothing but a tree branch. Right, kiddo?"

Tony started toward the door just as his iPhone rang. He glanced at the ID and saw the guard's number. He thumbed the speaker phone button. "Yes?"

"Got him," the guard said. "A teenager from the next complex over was trying to snap some pictures on his cell phone. I've already called the police."

A sigh shuddered through Shannon, and she hugged her son closer, and God, how Tony wanted to comfort her.

However, the business of taking care of her safety came first. "Keep me posted if there are any red flags when they interview the trespasser. Good work. Thanks."

He tucked his phone back into his jacket, his heart almost hammering out of his chest at the close call. This could have been worse. He knew too well from past experience how bad it could have been.

And apparently so did Shannon. Her wide blue eyes blinked erratically as she looked from corner to corner, searching shadows.

To hell with giving her distance. He wrapped an arm around her shoulders until she leaned on him ever so slightly. The soft press of her against him felt damn right in a day gone wrong.

Then she squeezed her eyes closed and straightened. "Okay, you win."

"Win what?"

"We'll go to your home tonight."

A hollow victory, since fear rather than desire motivated her, but he wasn't going to argue. "And tomorrow?"

"We'll discuss that in morning. Right now, just take us to your house."

* * *

Tony's Galveston house could only be called a mansion.

The imposing size of the three-story structure washed over Shannon every time they drove through the scrolled iron gates. How Kolby could sleep through all of this boggled her mind, but when they'd convinced him the "monster" was gone—thanks to the guard—Kolby had been all yawns again. Once strapped into the car seat in the back of Tony's Escalade, her son had been out like a light in five minutes.

If only her own worries could be as easily shaken off. She had to think logically, but fears for Kolby nagged her. Nolan had stolen so much more than money. He'd robbed her of the ability to feel safe, just before he took the coward's way out.

Two acres of manicured lawn stretched ahead of her in the moonlight. The estate was intimidating during the day, and all the more ominously gothic at night with shadowy edges encroaching. It was one thing to visit the place for a date.

It was another to take shelter here, to pack suitcases and accept his help.

She'd lived in a large house with Nolan, four thousand square feet, but she could have fit two of those homes inside Tony's place. In the courtyard, a concrete horse fountain was illuminated, glowing in front of the burgundy stucco house with brown trim so dark it was almost black. His home showcased the Spanish architecture prevalent in Texas. Knowing his true heritage now, she could see why he would have been drawn to this area.

Silently he guided the SUV into the garage, finally safe and secure from the outside world. For how long?

He unstrapped Kolby from the seat and she didn't argue. Her son was still sleeping anyway. The way Tony's big hands managed the small buckles and shuffled the sleeping child onto his shoulder with such competence touched her heart as firmly as any hothouse full of roses.

Trailing him with a backpack of toy trains and trucks, she dimly registered the house that had grown familiar after their dates to restaurants, movies and the most amazing concerts. Her soul, so starved for music, gobbled up every note.

Her first dinner at his home had been a five-course catered meal with a violinist. She could almost hear the echoing strains bouncing lightly off the high-beamed ceiling, down to the marble floor, swirling along the inlay pattern to twine around her.

Binding her closer to him. They hadn't had sex that night, but she'd known then it was inevitable.

That first time, Tony had been thoughtful enough to send out to a different restaurant than his favored Vernon's, guessing accurately that when a person worked eight hours a day in one eating establishment, the food there lost its allure.

He'd opted for Italian cuisine. The meal and music and elegance had been so far removed from paper plate dinners of nuggets and fries. While she adored her son and treasured every second with him, she couldn't help but be wooed by grown-up time to herself.

Limited time as she'd never spent the night here. Until now.

She followed Tony up the circular staircase, hand on the crafted iron banister. The sight of her son sleeping so limp and relaxed against Tony brought a lump to her throat again.

The tenderness she felt seeing him hold her child reminded her how special this new man in her life was. She'd chosen him so carefully after Nolan had died, seeing

Tony's innate strength and honor. Was she really ready to throw that away?

He stopped at the first bedroom, a suite decorated in hunter green with vintage maps framed on the walls. Striding through the sitting area to the next door, he flipped back the brocade spread and set her son in the middle of the high bed.

Quietly, she put a chair on either side as a makeshift bed rail, then tucked the covers over his shoulders. She kissed his little forehead and inhaled his baby-fresh scent. Her child.

The enormity of how their lives had changed tonight swelled inside her, pushing stinging tears to the surface. Tony's hand fell to rest on her shoulder and she leaned back….

Holy crap.

She jolted away. How easily she fell into old habits around him. "I didn't mean…"

"I know." His hand fell away and tucked into his pocket. "I'll carry up your bags in a minute. I gave the house staff the night off."

She followed him, just to keep their conversation soft, not because she wasn't ready to say good-night. "I thought you trusted them."

"I do. To a point. It's also easier for security to protect the house with fewer people inside." He gestured into the sitting area. "I heard what you said about feeling cut off from the world going to my father's and I understand."

His empathy slipped past her defenses when they were already on shaky ground being here in his house again. Remembering all the times they'd made love under this very roof, she could almost smell the bath salts from last weekend. And with him being so understanding on top of everything else…

He'd lied. She needed to remember that.

"I realize I have to do what's right for Kolby." She sagged onto the striped sofa, her legs folding from an emotional and exhausting night. "It scares the hell out of me how close a random teenager already got to my child, and we're only a couple of hours into this mess. It makes me ill to think about what someone with resources could do."

"My brothers and I have attorneys. They'll look into pressing charges against the teen." He sat beside her with a casual familiarity of lovers.

Remember the fight. Not the bath salts. She inched toward the armrest. "Let me know what the attorneys' fees are, please."

"They're on retainer. Those lawyers also help us communicate with each other. My attorney will know we're going to see my father if you're worried about making sure someone is aware of your plans."

Someone under his employ, all of this bought with Tony's money that she'd rejected a few short days ago. And she couldn't think of any other way. "You trust this man, your lawyer?"

"I have to." The surety in his voice left little room for doubt. "There are some transactions that can't be avoided no matter how much we want to sever ties with the past."

A darker note in his voice niggled at her. "Are you talking about yourself now?"

He shrugged, broad shoulders rippling the fabric of his fine suit.

Nuh-uh. She wasn't giving up that easily. She'd trusted so much of her life to this man, only to find he'd misled her.

Now she needed something tangible, something honest from him to hold on to. Something to let her know if that honor and strength she'd perceived in him was real. "You said you didn't want to break off our relationship. If that's true, this would be a really good time to open up a little."

Angling toward her, Tony's knee pressed against hers, his eyes heating to molten dark. "Are you saying we're good again?"

"I'm saying…" She cleared her throat that had suddenly gone cottony dry. "Maybe I could see my way clear to forgiving you if I knew more about you."

He straightened, his eyes sharp. "What do you want to know?"

"Why Galveston?"

"Do you surf?"

What the hell? She watched the walls come up in his eyes. She could almost feel him distancing himself from her. "Tony, I'm not sure how sharing a *Surf's Up* moment is going to make things all better here."

"But have you ever been surfing?" He gestured, his hands riding imaginary waves. "The Atlantic doesn't offer as wild a ride as the Pacific, but it gets the job done, especially in Spain. Something to do with the atmospheric pressure coming down from the U.K. I still remember the swells tubing." He curled his fingers around into the cresting circle of a wave.

"You're a *surfer?*" She tried to merge the image of the sleek business shark with the vision of him carefree on a board. And instead an image emerged of his abandon when making love. Her breasts tingled and tightened, awash in the sensation of sea spray and Tony all over her skin.

"I've always been fascinated with waves."

"Even when you were in San Rinaldo." The picture of him began to make more sense. "It's an island country, right?"

She'd always thought the nautical art on his walls was tied into his shipping empire. Now she realized the affinity for such pieces came from living on an island. So much about him made sense.

His surfing hand soared to rest on the gold flecked globe beside the sofa. Was it her imagination or was the gloss dimmer over the coast of Spain? As if he'd rubbed his finger along that area more often, taking away the sheen over time.

He spun the globe. "I thought you didn't know much about the Medinas."

"I researched you on Google on my phone while we were driving over." Concrete info had been sparse compared to all the crazy gossip floating about, but there were some basics. Three sons. A monarch father. A mother who'd been killed as they were escaping. Her heart squeezed thinking of him losing a parent so young, not much older than Kolby.

She pulled a faltering smile. "There weren't any surfer pictures among the few images that popped up."

Only a couple of grainy formal family portraits of three young boys with their parents, everyone happy. Some earlier photos of King Enrique looking infinitely regal.

"We scrubbed most pictures after we escaped and regrouped." His lighthearted smile contrasted with the darker hue deepening his eyes. "The internet wasn't active in those days."

The extent of his rebuilding shook her to her shoes. She'd thought she had it rough leaving Louisiana after her husband's arrest and death. How tragic to have your past wiped away. The enormity of what had happened to his family, of how he'd lived since then, threatened to overwhelm her.

How could she not ache over all he'd been through? "I saw that your mother died when I read up on your past. I'm so sorry."

He waved away her sympathy. "When we got to…where my father lives now, things were isolated. But at least we still had the ocean. Out on the waves, I could forget about everything else."

Plowing a hand through his hair, he stared just past her, obviously locked in some deep memories. She sensed she was close, so close to the something she needed to reassure her that placing herself and her son in his care would be wise, even if there weren't gossip seekers sifting through her trash.

She rested her hand on his arm. "What are you thinking?"

"I thought you might like to learn next spring. Unless you're already a pro."

"Not hardly." Spring was a long way off, a huge commitment she wasn't anywhere near ready to make to anyone. The thought of climbing on a wave made her stomach knot almost as much as being together that long. "Thanks for the offer, but I'll pass."

"Scared?" He skimmed his knuckles over her collarbone, and just that fast the sea-spray feel tingled through her again.

"Hell, yes. Scared of getting hurt."

His hand stilled just above her thumping heart. Want crackled in the air. Hers? Or his? She wasn't sure. Probably equal measures from both of them. That had never been in question. And too easily he could draw her in again. Learning more about him wasn't wise after all, not tonight.

She pulled away, her arms jerky, her whole body out of whack. She needed Tony's lightness now. Forget about serious peeks into each other's vulnerable pasts. "No surfing for me. Ever try taking care of a toddler with a broken leg?"

"When did you break your leg?" His eyes narrowed. "Did he hurt you? Your husband?"

How had Tony made that leap so quickly?

"Nolan was a crook and a jerk, but he never raised a hand to me." She shivered, not liking the new direction their conversation had taken at all. This was supposed to teach her more about him. Not the other way around. "Do we have to drag more baggage into this?"

"If it's true."

"I told you. He didn't abuse me." Not physically. "Having a criminal for a husband is no picnic. Knowing I missed the signs... Wondering if I let myself be blind to it because I enjoyed the lifestyle... I don't even know where to start in answering those questions for myself."

She slumped, suddenly exhausted, any residual adrenaline fizzling out. Her head fell back.

"Knowing you as I do, I find it difficult to believe you would ever choose the easy path." Tony thumbed just below her eyes where undoubtedly dark circles were all but tattooed on her face. "It's been a long day. You should get some rest. If you want, I'll tuck you in," he said with a playful wink.

She found the old Tony much easier to deal with than the new. "You're teasing, of course."

"Maybe..." And just that fast the light in his eyes flamed hotter, intense. "Shanny, I would hold you all night if you would let me. I would make sure no one dared threaten you or your son again."

And she wanted to let him do just that. But she'd allowed herself to depend on a man before... "If you hold me, we both know I won't get any rest, and while I'll have pleasure tonight, I'll be sorry tomorrow. Don't you think we have enough wrong between us right now without adding another regret to the mix?"

"Okay…." Tony gave her shoulder a final squeeze and stood. "I'll back off."

Shannon pushed to her feet alongside him, her hands fisted at her sides to keep from reaching for him. "I'm still mad over being kept in the dark, but I appreciate all the damage control."

"I owe you that much and more." He kissed her lightly on the lips without touching her anywhere else, lingering long enough to remind her of the reasons they clicked. Her breath hitched and it was all she could do not to haul him in closer for a firmer, deeper connection.

Pulling back, he started toward the door.

"Tony?" Was that husky voice really hers?

He glanced over his shoulder. So easily she could take the physical comfort waiting only a few feet away in his arms. But she had to keep her head clear. She had to hold strong to carve out an independent life for her and her son and that meant drawing clear boundaries.

"Just because I might be able to forgive you doesn't mean you're welcome in my bed again."

Four

She wasn't in her own bed.

Shannon wrestled with the tenacious grip of her shadowy nightmare, tough as hell to do when she couldn't figure out where she was. The ticking grandfather clock, the feel of the silky blanket around her, none of it was familiar. And then a hint of sandalwood scent teased her nose a second before…

"Hey." Tony's voice rumbled through the dark. "It's okay. I'm here."

Her heart jumped. She bolted upright, the cashmere afghan twisting around her legs and waist. Blinking fast, she struggled to orient herself to the surroundings so different from her apartment, but the world blurred in front of her from the dark and her own crummy eyesight. Shannon pressed her hands to the cushiony softness of a sofa and everything came rushing back. She was at Tony's, in the sitting room outside where Kolby slept.

"It's okay," Tony continued to chant, squeezing her shoulder in his broad hand as he crouched beside the couch.

Swinging her feet to the ground, she gathered the haunting remnants of her nightmare. Shadows smoked through her mind, blending into a darker mass of memories from the night Nolan died, except Tony's face superimposed itself over that of her dead husband.

Nausea burned her throat. She swallowed back the bite of bile and the horror of her dream. "Sorry, if I woke you." Oh, God, her son. "Is Kolby all right?"

"Sleeping soundly."

"Thank goodness. I wouldn't want to frighten him." She took in Tony's mussed hair and hastily hauled on jeans. The top button was open and his chest was bare. Gulp. "I'm sorry for disturbing you."

"I wasn't asleep." He passed her glasses to her.

As she slid them on, his tattoo came into focus, a nautical compass on his arm. Looking closer she realized his hair was wet. She didn't want to think about him in the shower, a tiled spa cubicle they'd shared more than once. "It's been a tough night all around."

"Want to talk about what woke you up?"

"Not really." Not ever. To anyone. "I think my fear for Kolby ran wild in my sleep. Dreams are supposed to help work out problems, but sometimes, it seems they only make everything scarier."

"Ah, damn, Shanny, I'm sorry for this whole mess." He sat on the sofa and slid an arm around her shoulders.

She stiffened, then decided to hell with it all and leaned back against the hard wall of chest. With the nightmare so fresh in her mind, she couldn't scavenge the will to pull away. His arms banded around her in an instant and her head tucked under his chin. Somehow it was easier to accept this comfort when she didn't have to look in his eyes. She'd been alone with her bad dreams for so long. Was it wrong to take just a second's comfort from his arms roped so thick with muscles nothing could break through to her? She would be strong again in a minute.

The grandfather clock ticked away minutes as she stared at his hands linked over her stomach—at the lighter band of skin where his watch usually rested. "Thanks for coming in to check on us, especially so late."

"It can be disconcerting waking in an unfamiliar place alone." His voice vibrated against her back, only her thin nightshirt between them and his bare chest.

Another whiff of his freshly showered scent teased her nose with memories of steam-slicked bodies.

"I've been here at least a dozen times, but never in this room. It's a big house." They'd met five months ago, started dating two months later…had starting sleeping together four weeks ago. "Strange to think we've shared the shower, but I still haven't seen all of your home."

"We tended to get distracted once our feet hit the steps," he said drily.

True enough. They'd stayed downstairs on early dinner dates here, but once they'd ventured upstairs…they'd always headed straight for his suite.

"That first time together—" Shannon remembered was after an opera when her senses had been on overload and her hormones on hyperdrive from holding back "—I was scared to death."

The admission tumbled out before she could think, but somehow it seemed easier to share such vulnerabilities in the dark.

His muscles flexed against her, the bristle of hair on his arms teasing goose bumps along her skin. "The last thing I ever want to do is frighten you."

"It wasn't your fault. That night was a big leap of faith for me." The need to make him understand pushed past walls she'd built around herself. "Being with you then, it was my first time since Nolan."

He went completely still, not even breathing for four ticks of the clock before she felt his neck move with a swallow against her temple. "No one?"

"No one." Not only had Tony been her sole lover since Nolan, he'd been her second lover ever.

Her track record for picking men with secrets sucked.

His gusty sigh ruffled her hair. "I wish you would have told me."

"What would that have changed?"

"I would have been more…careful."

The frenzy of their first time stormed her mind with a barrage of images…their clothes fluttering to carpet the stairs on their way up. By the top of the steps they were naked, moonlight bathing his olive skin and casting shadows along the cut of muscles. Kissing against the wall soon had her legs wrapped around his waist and he was inside her. That one thrust had unfurled the tension into shimmering sensations and before the orgasm finished tingling all the way to the roots of her hair, he'd carried her to his room, her legs still around him. Again, she'd found release in bed with him, then a languid, leisurely completion while showering together.

Just remembering, an ache started low, throbbing between her legs. "You were great that night, and you know it." She swatted his hand lightly. "Now wipe the arrogant grin off your face."

"You can't see me." His voice sounded somber enough.

"Am I right, though?"

"Look at me and see."

She turned around and dared to peer up at him for the first time since he'd settled on the couch behind her. Her intense memories of that evening found an echo in his serious eyes far more moving than any smile.

Right now, it was hard to remember they weren't a couple anymore. "Telling you then would have made the event too serious."

Too important.

His offer to "help" her financially still loomed unresolved between them, stinging her even more than last weekend after the enormous secret he'd kept from her. Why couldn't they be two ordinary people who met at the park outside her apartment complex? What would it have been like to get to know Tony on neutral, normal ground? Would she have been able to see past the pain of her marriage?

She would never know.

"Shannon." His voice came out hoarse and hungry. "Are you okay to go back to sleep now? Because I need to leave."

His words splashed a chill over her heated thoughts. "Of course, you must have a lot to take care of with your family."

"You misunderstand. I *need* to leave, because you're killing me here with how much I've hurt you. And as if that wasn't enough to bring me to my knees, every time you move your head, the feel of your hair against my chest just about sends me over the edge." His eyes burned with a coal-hot determination. "I'll be damned before I do anything to break your trust again."

Before she could unscramble her thoughts, he slid his arms from her and ducked out the door as silently as he'd arrived. Colder than ever without the heat of Tony all around her, she hugged the blanket closer.

No worries about any more nightmares, because she was more than certain she wouldn't be able to go back to sleep.

By morning, Tony hadn't bothered turning down the covers on his bed. After leaving Shannon's room, he'd spent most of the night conferring with his lawyer and a security firm. Working himself into the ground to distract himself from how much he hurt from wanting her.

With a little luck and maneuvering, he could extend his week with her into two weeks. But bottom line, he *would* ensure her safety.

At five, he'd caught a catnap on the library sofa, jolting awake when Vernon called him from the front gate. He'd buzzed the retired sea captain through and rounded up breakfast.

His old friend deserved some answers.

Choosing a less formal dining area outside, he sat at the oval table on the veranda shaded by a lemon tree, Vernon beside him with a plate full of churros. Tony thumbed the edge of the hand-painted stoneware plate—a set he'd picked up from a local craftsman to support the dying art of the region.

Today of all days, he didn't want to think overlong on why he still ate his same childhood breakfast—deep fried strips of potato dough. His mother had always poured a thick rich espresso for herself and mugs of hot chocolate for her three sons, an informal ritual in their centuries-old castle that he now knew was anything but ordinary.

Vernon eyed him over the rim of his coffee cup. "So it's all true, what they're saying in the papers and on the internet?"

Absurd headlines scrolled through his memory, alongside reports that had been right on the money. "My brother's not a Tibetan monk, but the general gist of that first report from the Global Intruder is correct."

"You're a prince." He scrubbed a hand over his dropped jaw. "Well, hot damn. Always knew there was something special about you, boy."

He preferred to think anything "special" about him came from hard work rather than a genetic lottery win. "I hope you understand it wasn't my place to share the details with you."

"You have brothers and a father." He stirred a hefty dollop of milk into his coffee, clinking the spoon against the edges of the stoneware mug. "I get that you need to consider their privacy, as well."

"Thanks, I appreciate that."

He wished Shannon could see as much. He'd hoped bringing her here would remind her of all that had been good between them. Instead those memories had only come back to bite him on the ass when she'd told him that he was her first since her husband died. The revelation still sucker punched the air from his gut.

Where did they go from there? Hell if he knew, but at least he had more time to find out. Soon enough he would have her in his private jet that waited fueled and ready a mile away.

The older man set down his mug. "I respect that you gotta be your own man."

"Thank you again." He'd expected Vernon to be angry over the secrecy, had even been concerned over losing his friendship.

Vernon's respect meant a lot to him, as well as his advice. From day one when Tony had turned in his sparse job application, Vernon had treated him like a son, showing him the ropes. They had a lot of history. And just like fourteen years ago, he offered unconditional acceptance now.

His mentor leaned forward on one elbow. "What does your family have to say about all of this?"

"I've only spoken with my middle brother." He pinched off a piece of a churro drizzled with warm honey. Popping it into his mouth, he chewed and tried not think of how much of his past stayed imprinted on him.

"According to the papers, that would be Duarte. Right?" When Tony nodded, Vernon continued, "Any idea how the story broke after so many years?"

And wasn't that the million-dollar question? He, his brothers and their lawyers were no closer to the answer on that one today than they'd been last night. "Duarte doesn't have any answers yet, other than some photojournalist caught him in a snapshot and managed to track down details. Which is damn strange. None of us look the same since we left San Rinaldo as kids."

"And there are no other pictures of you in the interim?"

"Only a few stray shots after I became Tony. Carlos's face has shown up in a couple of professional magazines." But the image was so posed and sterile, Tony wasn't sure he would recognize his own sibling on the street. For the best.

His father always insisted photos would provide dangerous links, as if he'd been preparing them from the beginning to split up. Or preparing them for his death.

Not the normal way for a kid to live, but they weren't a regular family. He'd grown accustomed to it eventually... until it almost seemed normal. Until he was faced with a regular person's life, like Shannon's treasured photos of her son.

He broke off another inch of a churro. His hand slowed halfway to his mouth as he got that feeling of "being watched." He checked right fast—

Kolby stood in the open doorway, blanket trailing from his fist.

Uh, okay. So now what? He'd only met the child a few times before last night and none had gone particularly well. Tony had chalked it up to Kolby being shy around strangers or clingy. Judging by the thrust of his little jaw and frown now, there was no mistaking it. The boy didn't like him.

That needed to change. "Hey, kiddo. Where's your mom?"

Kolby didn't budge. "Still sleepin'."

Breaking the ice, Vernon tugged out a chair. "Wanna have a seat and join us?"

Never taking his eyes off Tony, Kolby padded across the tile patio and scrambled up to sit on his knees. Silently, he simply blinked and stared with wide blue-gray eyes just like Shannon's, his blond hair spiking every which way.

Vernon wiped his mouth, tossed his linen napkin on the plate and stood. "Thanks for the chow. I need to check on business. No need to see me out."

As his old friend deserted ship, unease crawled around inside Tony's gut. His experience with children was nonexistent, even when he'd been a kid himself. He and his brothers had been tutored on the island. They'd been each other's only playmates.

The island fortress had been staffed with security guards, not the mall cop sort, but more like a small deployed military unit. Cleaning staff, tutors, the chef and groundskeepers were all from San Rinaldo, older supporters of his father who'd lost their families in the coup. They shared a firm bond of loyalty, and a deep-seated need for a safe haven.

Working on the shrimp boat had felt like a vacation, with the wide open spaces and no boundaries. Most of all he enjoyed the people who didn't wear the imprint of painful loss in their eyes.

But still, there weren't any three-year-olds on the shrimp boat.

What did kids need? "Are you hungry?"

"Some of that." Kolby pointed to Tony's plate of churros. "With peanut bubber."

Grateful for action instead of awkward silence, he shoved to his feet. "Peanut butter it is then. Follow me."

Once he figured out where to look. He'd quit cooking for himself about ten years ago and the few years he had, he wasn't whipping up kiddie cuisine.

About seven minutes later he unearthed a jar from the cavernous pantry and smeared a messy trail down a churro before chunking the spoon in the sink.

Kolby pointed to the lid on the granite countertop. "We don't waste."

"Right." Tony twisted the lid on tight. Thinking of Shannon pinching pennies on peanut butter, for crying out loud, he wanted to buy them a lifetime supply.

As he started to pass the plate to Kolby, a stray thought broadsided him. Hell. Was the kid allergic to peanuts? He hadn't even thought to ask. Kolby reached. Tony swallowed another curse.

"Let's wait for your mom."

"Wait for me why?" Her softly melodic voice drifted over his shoulder from across the kitchen.

He glanced back and his heart kicked against his ribs. They'd slept together over the past month but never actually *slept*. And never through the night.

Damn, she made jeans look good, the washed pale fabric clinging to her long legs. Her hair flowed over her shoulders and down her back, still damp from a shower. He remembered well the silky glide of it through his fingers... and so not something he should be thinking about with her son watching.

Tony held up the plate of churros. "Can he eat peanut butter?"

"He's never tried it that way before, but I'm sure he'll like it." She slipped the dish from his grip. "Although, I'm not so certain that breakable stoneware is the best choice for a three-year-old."

"Hey, kiddo, is the plate all right with you?"

"'S okay." Kolby inched toward his mother and wrapped an arm around her leg. "Like trains better. And milk."

"The milk I can handle." He yanked open the door on the stainless steel refrigerator and reached for the jug. "I'll make sure you have the best train plates next time."

"Wait!" Shannon stopped him, digging into an oversized bag on her shoulder and pulling out a cup with a vented lid. "Here's his sippy cup. It's not Waterford, but it works better."

Smoothly, she filled it halfway and scooped up the plate. Kolby held on to his mother all the way back to the patio.

For the first time he wondered why he hadn't spent more time with the boy. Shannon hadn't offered and he hadn't pushed. She sat and pulled Kolby in her lap, plate in front just out of his reach. The whole family breakfast scenario wrapped around him, threatening his focus. He skimmed a finger along his shirt collar— Hell. He stopped short, realizing he wasn't wearing a tie.

She pinched off a bite and passed it to her son. "I had a lot of time to think last night."

So she hadn't slept any better than he had. "What did you think about after I left?"

Her eyes shot up to his, pink flushing her face. "Going to see your father, of course."

"Of course." He nodded, smiling.

"Of course," Kolby echoed.

As the boy licked the peanut butter off the churro, she traced the intricate pattern painted along the edge of the plate, frowning. "I would like to tell Vernon and your lawyer about our plans for the week and then I'll come with you."

He'd won. She would be safe, and he would have more time to sway her. Except it really chapped his hide that she trusted him so little she felt the need to log her travel itinerary. "Not meaning to shoot myself in the foot here, but why Vernon instead of my lawyer? Vernon is my friend. I financed his business."

"You own the restaurant?" Her slim fingers gravitated back to the china. "*You* are responsible for my paychecks? I thought the Grille belonged to Vernon."

"You didn't know?" Probably a good thing or he might well have never talked her into that first date. "Vernon was a friend when I needed one. I'm glad I could return the favor. He's more than delivered on the investment."

"He gave you a job when your past must have seemed spotty," she said intuitively.

"How did you figure that out?"

"He did the same for me when I needed a chance." A bittersweet smile flickered across her face much like how the sunlight filtered through the lemon tree to play in her hair. "That's the reason I trust him."

"You've worked hard for every penny you make there."

"I know, but I appreciate that he was fair. No handouts, and yet he never took advantage of how much I needed that job. He's a good man. Now back to our travel plans." She rested her chin on her son's head. "Just to be sure, I'll also be informing my in-laws—Kolby's grandparents."

His brows slammed upward. She rarely mentioned them, only that they'd cut her out of their lives after their son died. The fact that she would keep such cold fish informed about their grandson spoke of an innate sense of fair play he wasn't sure he would have given in her position.

"Apparently you trust just about everyone more than me."

She dabbed at the corners of her mouth, drawing his attention to the plump curve of her bottom lip. "Apparently so."

Not a ringing endorsement of her faith in him, but he would take the victory and focus forward. Because before sundown, he would return to his father's island home off the coast of Florida.

She was actually in a private plane over...

Somewhere.

Since the window shades were closed, she had no idea whether they were close to land or water. So where were they? Once airborne, she'd felt the plane turn, but quickly lost any sense of whether they were going north or south, east or west. Although north was unlikely given he'd told her to pack for warm weather.

How far had they traveled? Tough to tell since she'd napped and she had no idea how fast this aircraft could travel. She'd been swept away into a world beyond anything she'd experienced, from the discreet impeccable service to the sleeping quarters already made up for her and Kolby on arrival. Questions about her food preferences had resulted in a five-star meal.

Shannon pressed a hand to her jittery stomach. God,

she hoped she'd made the right decision. At least her son seemed oblivious to all the turmoil around them.

The cabin steward guided Kolby toward the galley kitchen with the promise of a snack and a video. As they walked toward the back, he dragged his tiny fingers along the white leather seats. At least his hands were clean.

But she would have to make a point of keeping sharp objects out of Kolby's reach. She shuddered at the image of a silver taped X on the luxury upholstery.

Her eyes shifted to the man filling the deep seat across from her couch. Wearing gray pants and a white shirt with the sleeves rolled up, he focused intently on the laptop screen in front of him, seemingly oblivious to anyone around him.

She hated the claustrophobic feeling of needing his help, not to mention all the money hiding out entailed. Dependence made her vulnerable, something she'd sworn would never happen again. Yet here she was, entrusting her whole life to a man, a man who'd lied to her.

However, with her child's well-being at stake, she couldn't afford to say no.

More information would help settle the apprehension plucking at her nerves like heart strings. Any information, since apparently everything she knew about him outside of the bedroom was false. She hadn't even known he owned the restaurant where she worked.

Ugh.

Of course it seemed silly to worry about being branded as the type who sleeps with the boss. Having an affair with a drop-dead sexy prince trumped any other gossip. "How long has it been since you saw your father?"

Tony looked up from his laptop slowly. "I left the island when I was eighteen."

"Island?" Her hand grazed the covered window as she

envisioned water below. "I thought you left San Rinaldo as a young boy."

"We did." He closed the computer and pivoted the chair toward her, stretching his legs until his feet stopped intimately close to hers. "I was five at the time. We relocated to another island about a month after we escaped."

She scrunched her toes in her gym shoes. Her scuffed canvas was worlds away from his polished loafers and a private plane. And regardless of how hot he looked, she wouldn't be seduced by the trappings of his wealth.

Forcing her mind back on his words rather than his body, she drew her legs away from him. Was the island on the east coast or west coast? Provided Enrique Medina's compound was even near the U.S. "Your father chose an island so you and your brothers would feel at home in your new place?"

He looked at her over the white tulips centered on the cherry coffee table. "My father chose an island because it was easier to secure."

Gulp. "Oh. Right."

That took the temperature down more than a few degrees. She picked at the piping on the sofa.

Music drifted from the back of the plane, the sound of a new cartoon starting. She glanced down the walkway. Kolby was buckled into a seat, munching on some kind of crackers while watching the movie, mesmerized. Most likely by the whopping big flat screen.

Back to her questions. "How much of you is real and what's a part of the new identity?"

"My age and birthday are real." He tucked the laptop into an oversized briefcase monogrammed with the Castillo Shipping Corporation logo. "Even my name is technically correct, as I told you before. Castillo comes from my mother's family tree. I took it as my own when I turned eighteen."

Resting her elbow on the back of the sofa, she propped her head in her palm, trying her darnedest to act as casual as he appeared. "What does your father think of all you've accomplished since leaving?"

"I wouldn't know." He reclined, folding his hands over his stomach, drawing her eyes and memories to his rock-hard abs.

Her toes curled again until they cracked inside her canvas sneakers. "What does he think of us coming now?"

"You'll have to ask him." His jaw flexed.

"Did you even tell him about the extra guests?" She resisted the urge to smooth the strain away from the bunched tendons in his neck. How odd to think of comforting him when she still had so many reservations about the trip herself.

"I told his lawyer to inform him. His staff will make preparations. Kolby will have whatever he needs."

Who was this coolly factual man a hand stretch away? She almost wondered if she'd imagined carefree Tony... except he'd told her that he liked to surf. She clung to that everyday image and dug deeper.

"Sounds like you and your father aren't close. Or is that just the way royalty communicates?" If so, how sad was that?

He didn't answer, the drone of the engines mingling with the cartoon and the rush of recycled air through the vents. While she wanted her son to grow up independent with a life of his own, she also planned to forge a bond closer than cold communications exchanged between lawyers and assistants.

"Tony?"

His eyes shifted to the shuttered window beside her

head. "I didn't want to live on a secluded island any longer. So I left. He disagreed. We haven't resolved the issue."

Such simple words for so deep a breach where attorneys handled *all* communiqués between them. The lack of communication went beyond distant to estrangement. This wasn't a family just fractured by location. Something far deeper was wrong.

Tucking back into his line of sight, she pressed ahead. This man had already left such a deep imprint on her life, she knew she wouldn't forget him. "What have your lawyers told your father about Kolby and me? What did they tell your dad about our relationship?"

"Relationship?" He pinned her with his dark eyes, the intensity of his look—of him—reaching past the tulips as tangibly as if he'd taken that broad hand and caressed her. He was such a big man with the gentlest of touches.

And he was thorough. God, how he was thorough.

Her heart pounded in her ear like a tympani solo, hollow and so loud it drowned out the engines.

"Tony?" she asked. She *wanted*.

"I let him know that we're a couple. And that you're a widow with a son."

It was one thing to carry on a secret affair with him. Another to openly acknowledge to people—to family—that they were a couple.

She pressed hard against her collarbone, her pulse pushing a syncopated beat against her fingertips. "Why not tell your father the truth? That we broke up but the press won't believe it."

"Who says it's not the truth? We slept together just a week ago. Seems like less than that to me, because I swear I can still catch a whiff of your scent on my skin." He leaned closer and thumbed her wrist.

Her fingers curled as the heat of his touch spread farther. "But about last weekend—"

"Shanny." He tapped her lips once, then traced her rounded sigh. "We may have argued, but when I'm in the room with you, my hand still gravitates to your back by instinct."

Her heart drummed faster until she couldn't have responded even if she tried. But she wasn't trying, too caught up in the sound of him, the desire in his every word.

"The pull between us is that strong, Shannon, whether I'm deep inside you or just listening to you across a room." A half smile kicked a dimple into one cheek. "Why do you think I call you late at night?"

She glanced quickly at the video area checking to make sure her son and the steward where still engrossed in Disney, then she whispered, "Because you'd finished work?"

"You know better. Just the sound of you on the other end of the line sends me rock—"

"Stop, please." She pressed her fingers to his mouth. "You're only hurting us both."

Nipping her fingers lightly first, he linked his hand with hers. "We have problems, without a doubt, and you have reason to be mad. But the drive to be together hasn't eased one bit. Can you deny it? Because if you can, then that is it. I'll keep my distance."

Opening her mouth, she formed the words that would slice that last tie to the relationship they'd forged over the past few months. She fully intended to tell him they were through…. But nothing came out. Not one word.

Slowly, he pulled back. "We're almost there."

Almost where? Back together? Her mind scrambled to keep up with him, damn tough when he kept jumbling her brain. She was a flipping magna cum laude graduate. She resented feeling like a bimbo at the mercy of her libido. But how her libido sang arias around this man...

He shoved to his feet and walked away. Just like that, he cut their conversation short as if they both hadn't been sinking deep into a sensual awareness that had brought them both such intense pleasure in the past. She tracked the lines of his broad shoulders, down to his trim waist and taut butt showcased so perfectly in tailored pants.

Her fingers dug deep into the sofa with restraint. He stopped by Kolby and slid up the window covering.

"Take a look, kiddo, we're almost there." Tony pointed at the clear glass toward the pristine sky.

Ah. *There.* As in they'd arrived there, at his father's island. She'd been so caught up in the sensual draw of undiluted Tony that she'd temporarily forgotten about flying away to a mystery location.

Scrambling down the sofa, she straightened her glasses and stared out the window, hungry for a peek at their future—temporary—home. And yes, curious as hell about the place where Tony had grown up. Sure enough, an island stretched in the distance, nestled in miles and miles of sparkling ocean. Palm trees spiked from the lush landscape. A dozen or so small outbuildings dotted a semicircle around a larger structure.

The white mansion faced the ocean in a *U* shape, constructed around a large courtyard with a pool. She barely registered Kolby's "oohs" and "aahs" since she was pretty much overwhelmed by the sight herself.

Details were spotty but she would get an up-close view soon enough of the place Tony had called home for most of his youth. Even from a distance she couldn't miss the grand scale of the sprawling estate, the unmistakable sort that housed royalty.

The plane banked, lining up with a thin islet alongside the larger island. A single strip of concrete marked the private runway. As they neared, a ferryboat came into focus. To ride from the airport to the main island? They sure were serious about security.

The intercom system crackled a second before the steward announced, "We're about to begin our descent to our destination. Please return to your seats and secure your lap belts. Thank you, and we hope you had a pleasant flight."

Tony pulled away from the window and smiled at her again. Except now, the grin didn't reach his eyes. Her stomach fluttered, but this time with apprehension rather than arousal.

Would the island hold the answers she needed to put Tony in her past? Or would it only break her heart all over again?

Five

Daylight was fading fast and a silence fourteen years old between him and his father was about to be broken.

Feet braced on the ferry deck, Tony stared out over the rail at the island where he'd spent the bulk of his childhood and teenage years. He hated not being in command of the boat almost as much as he hated returning to this place. Only concern for Shannon and her son could have drawn him back where the memories grew and spread as tenaciously as algae webbing around coral.

Just ahead, a black skimmer glided across the water, dipping its bill into the surface. With each lap of the waves against the hull, Tony closed off insidious emotions before they could take root inside him and focused on the shore.

An osprey circled over its nest. Palm trees lined the beach with only a small white stucco building and a two-lane road. Until you looked closer and saw the guard tower.

When he'd come to this island off the coast of St. Augustine at five, there were times he'd believed they were home...that his father had moved them to another part of San Rinaldo. In the darkest nights, he'd woken in a cold sweat, certain the soldiers in camouflage were going to cut through the bars on his windows and take him. Other nights he imagined they'd already taken him and the bars locked him in prison.

On the worst of nights, he'd thought his mother was still alive, only to see her die all over again.

Shannon's hand slid over his elbow, her touch tentative, her eyes wary. "How long did I sleep on the plane?"

"A while." He smiled to reassure her, but the feeling didn't come from his gut. Damn, but he wished the past week had never happened. He would pull her soft body against him and forget about everything else.

Wind streaked her hair across her face. "Oh, right. If you tell me, I might get a sense of how far away we are from Galveston. I might guess where we are. Being cut off from the world is still freaking me out just a little."

"I understand, and I'll to do my best to set things right as soon as possible." He wanted nothing more than to get off this island and return to the life he'd built, the life he chose. The only thing that made coming back here palatable was having Shannon by his side. And that rocked the deck under his feet, realizing she held so much influence over his life.

"Although, I have to admit," she conceded as she tucked her son closer, "this place is so much more than I expected."

Her gaze seemed to track the herons picking their way along the shore, sea oats bowing at every gust. Her grayish-blue eyes glinted with the first hints of excitement. She must not have noticed the security cameras tucked in trees and the guard on the dock, a gun strapped within easy reach.

Tony gripped the rail tighter. "There's no way to prepare a person."

Kolby squealed, pitching forward in his mother's arms.

"Whoa…" Tony snagged the kid by the back of his striped overalls. "Steady there."

A hand pressed to her chest, Shannon struggled for breath. "Thank God you moved so fast. I can't believe I looked away. There's just so much to see, so many distractions."

The little guy scowled at Tony. "Down."

"Buddy," Tony stated as he shook his head, "sometime you're going to have to like me."

"Name's not buddy," Kolby insisted, bottom lip out.

"You're right. I'm just trying to make friends here." Because he intended to use this time to persuade Shannon breaking up had been a crappy idea. He wondered how much the child understood. Since he didn't know how else to approach him, he opted for straight up honesty. "I like your mom, so it's important that you like me."

Shannon's gasp teased his ear like a fresh trickle of wind off the water. As much as he wanted to turn toward her, he kept his attention on the boy.

Kolby clenched Tony's shirt. "Does you like *me?*"

"Uh, sure." The question caught him off guard. He hadn't thought about it other than knowing it was important to win the son over for Shannon's sake. "What do you like?"

"Not you." He popped his bottom lip back in. "Down, pwease."

Shannon caught her son as he leaned toward her. Confusion puckering her brow, her eyes held Tony's for a second before she pointed over the side. "Is that what you wanted to see, sweetie?"

A dolphin zipped alongside the ferry. The fin sliced through the water, then submerged again.

Clapping his tiny hands, Kolby chanted, "Yes, yes, yes."

Again, Shannon saw beauty. He saw something entirely different. The dolphins provided port security. His father had gotten the idea from his own military service, cutting-edge stuff back then. The island was a minikingdom and money wasn't an object. Except this kingdom had substantially fewer subjects.

Tony wondered again if the secluded surroundings growing up could have played into his lousy track record with relationships as an adult. There hadn't been any teenage dating rituals for practice. And after he left, he'd been careful with relationships, never letting anything get too complicated. Work and a full social life kept him happy.

But the child in front of him made things problematic in a way he hadn't foreseen.

For years he'd been pissed off at his father for the way they'd had to live. And here he was doing the same to Kolby. The kid was entertained for the moment, but that would end fast for sure.

Protectiveness for both the mother and son seared his veins. He wouldn't let anything from the Medina past mark their future. Even if that meant he had to reclaim the very identity he'd worked his entire adulthood to shed.

The ferry slid against the dock. They'd arrived at the island.

And Prince Antonio Medina was back.

What was it like for Tony to come back after so long away? And it wasn't some happy homecoming, given the estrangement and distance in this family that communicated through lawyers.

Shannon wanted to reach across the limousine to him, but Tony had emotionally checked out the moment the ferry docked. Of course he'd been Mr. Manners while leaving the ferry and stepping into the Mercedes limo.

Watch your step... Need help? However, the smiles grew darker by the minute.

Maybe it was her own gloomy thoughts tainting her perceptions. At least Kolby seemed unaffected by their moods, keeping his nose pressed to the window the whole winding way to the pristine mansion.

Who wouldn't stare at the trees and the wildlife and finally, the palatial residence? White stucco with a clay tiled roof, arches and opulence ten times over, the place was the size of some hotels or convention centers. Except no hotel she'd stayed in sported guards armed with machine guns.

What should have made her feel safer only served to remind her money and power didn't come without burdens. To think, Tony had grown up with little or no exposure to the real world. It was a miracle he'd turned out normal.

If you could call a billionaire prince with a penchant for surfing "normal."

The limousine slowed, easing past a towering marble fountain with a "welcome" pineapple on top—and wasn't that ironic in light of all those guards? Once the vehicle stopped, more uniformed security appeared from out of nowhere to open the limo. Some kind of servant—a butler perhaps—stood at the top of the stairs. While Tony had insisted he wanted nothing to do with his birthplace, he seemed completely at ease in this surreal world. For the first time, the truth really sunk in.

The stunningly handsome—stoically silent—man walking beside her had royal blood singing through his veins.

"Tony?" She touched his elbow.

"After you," he said, simply gesturing ahead to the double doors sweeping open.

Scooping Kolby onto her hip, she took comfort in his sturdy little body and forged ahead. Inside. *Whoa.*

The cavernous circular hall sported gold gilded archways leading to open rooms. Two staircases stretched up either side, meeting in the middle. And, uh, stop the world, was that a Picasso on the wall?

Her canvas sneakers squeaked against marble floors as more arches ushered her deeper into the mansion. And while she vowed money didn't matter, she still wished she'd packed different shoes. Shannon straightened the straps on Kolby's favorite striped overalls, the ones he swore choo-choo drivers wore. She'd been so frazzled when she'd tossed clothes into a couple of overnight bags, picking things that would make him happy.

Just ahead, French doors opened on to a veranda that overlooked the ocean. Tony turned at the last minute, guiding her toward what appeared to be a library. Books filled three walls, interspersed with windows and a sliding brass ladder. Mosaic tiles swirled outward on the floor, the ceiling filled with frescos of globes and conquistadors. The smell of fresh citrus hung in the air, and not just because of the open windows. A tall potted orange tree nestled in one corner beneath a wide skylight.

An older man slept in a wingback by the dormant fireplace. Two large brown dogs—some kind of Ridgeback breed, perhaps?—lounged to his left and right.

Tony's father. A no-kidding king.

Either age or illness had taken a toll, dimming the family resemblance. But in spite of his nap, he wasn't going gently into that good night. No slippers and robe for this meeting. He wore a simple black suit with an ascot rather than a tie, his silver hair slicked back. Frailty and his pasty pallor made her want to comfort him.

Then his eyes snapped open. The sharp gleam in his coal dark eyes stopped her short.

Holy Sean Connery, the guy might be old but he hadn't lost his edge.

"Welcome home, *hijo prodigo*." *Prodigal son*.

Enrique Medina spoke in English but his accent was still unmistakably Spanish. And perhaps a bit thick with emotion? Or was that just wishful thinking on her part for Tony's sake?

"Hello, Papa." Tony palmed her back between her shoulder blades. "This is Shannon and her son Kolby."

The aging monarch nodded in her direction. "Welcome, to you and to your son."

"Thank you for your hospitality and your help, sir." She didn't dare wade into the whole *Your Highness* versus *Your Majesty* waters. Simplicity seemed safest.

Toying with a pocket watch in his hand, Enrique continued, "If not for my family, you would not need my assistance."

Tony's fingers twitched against her back. "Hopefully we won't have to impose upon you for long. Shannon and her son only need a place to lay low until this blows over."

"It won't blow over," Enrique said simply.

Ouch. She winced.

Tony didn't. "Poor choice of words. Until things calm down."

"Of course." He nodded regally before shifting his attention her way. "I am glad to have you here, my dear. You brought Tony home, so you have already won favor with me." He smiled and for the first time, she saw the family resemblance clearly.

Kolby wriggled, peeking up from her neck. "Whatsa matter with you?"

"Shhh…Kolby." She pressed a quick silencing kiss to his forehead. "That's a rude question."

"It's an honest question. I do not mind the boy." The king shifted his attention to her son. "I have been ill. My legs are not strong enough to walk."

"I'm sorry." Kolby eyed the wheelchair folded up and tucked discreetly alongside the fireplace. "You musta been bery sick."

"Thank you. I have good doctors."

"You got germs?"

A smile tugged at the stern face. "No, child. You and your mother cannot catch my germs."

"That's good." He stuffed his tiny fists into his pockets. "Don't like washin' my hands."

Enrique laughed low before his hand fell to rest on one dog's head. "Do you like animals?"

"Yep." Kolby squirmed downward until Shannon had no choice but to release him before he pitched out of her arms. "Want a dog."

Such a simple, painfully normal wish and she couldn't afford to supply it. From the pet deposit required at her apartment complex to the vet bills… It was out of her budget. Guilt tweaked again over all she couldn't give her child.

Yet hadn't Tony been denied so much even with such wealth? He'd lost his home, his mother and gained a gilded prison. Whispers of sympathy for a motherless boy growing up isolated from the world softened her heart when she most needed to hold strong.

Enrique motioned Kolby closer. "You may pet my dog.

Come closer and I will introduce you to Benito and Diablo. They are very well trained and will not hurt you."

Kolby didn't even hesitate. Any reservations her son felt about Tony certainly didn't extend to King Enrique—or his dogs. Diablo sniffed the tiny, extended hand.

A cleared throat startled Shannon from her thoughts. She glanced over her shoulder and found a young woman waiting in the archway. In her late twenties, wearing a Chanel suit, she obviously wasn't the housekeeper.

But she was stunning with her black hair sleeked back in a simple clasp. She wore strappy heels instead of sneakers. God, it felt silly to be envious of someone she didn't know, and honestly, she only coveted the pretty red shoes.

"Alys," the older man commanded, "enter. Come meet my son and his guests. This is my assistant, Alys Reyes de la Cortez. She will show you to your quarters."

Shannon resisted the urge to jump to conclusions. It wasn't any of her business who Enrique Medina chose for his staff and she shouldn't judge a person by their appearance. The woman was probably a rocket scientist, and Shannon wouldn't trade one single sticky hug from her son for all the high-end clothes on the planet.

Not that she was jealous of the gorgeous female with immaculate clothes, who fit perfectly into Tony's world. After all, he hadn't spared more than a passing glance at the woman.

Still, she wished she'd packed a pair of pumps.

An hour later, Shannon closed her empty suitcases and rocked back on her bare heels in the doorway of her new quarters.

A suite?

More like a luxury condominium within the mansion. She sunk her toes into the Persian rug until her chipped pink polish disappeared in the apricot and gray pattern. She and Kolby had separate bedrooms off a sitting area with an eating space stocked more fully than most kitchens. The balcony was as large as some yards.

Had the fresh-cut flowers been placed in here just for her? She dipped her face into the crystal vase of lisianthus with blooms that resembled blue roses and softened the gray tones in the decor.

After Alys had walked them up the lengthy stairs to their suite, Kolby had run from room to room for fifteen minutes before winding down and falling asleep in an exhausted heap under the covers. He hadn't even noticed the toy box at the end of his sleigh bed yet, he'd been so curious about their new digs. Tony had given them space while she unpacked, leaving for his quarters with a simple goodbye and another of those smiles that didn't reach his eyes.

The quiet echoed around her, leaving her hyperaware of other sounds...a ticking grandfather clock in the hall... the crashing ocean outside... Trailing her fingers along the camelback sofa, she looked through the double doors, moonlight casting shadows along her balcony. Her feet drew her closer until the shadows took shape into the broad shoulders of a man leaning on the railing.

Tony? He felt like a safe haven in an upside down day. But how had he gotten there without her noticing his arrival?

Their balconies must connect, which meant someone had planned for them to have access to each other's rooms. Had he been waiting for her? Anticipation hummed through her at the notion of having him all to herself.

Shannon unlocked and pushed open the doors to the patio filled with topiaries, ferns and flowering cacti. A swift ocean breeze rolled over her, lifting her hair and fluttering her shirt along her skin in whispery caresses. God, she was tired and emotional and so not in the right frame of mind to be anywhere near Tony. She should go to bed instead of staring at his sinfully sexy body just calling to her to rest her cheek on his back and wrap her arms around his waist. Her fingers fanned against her legs as she remembered the feel of him, so much more intense with his sandalwood scent riding the wind.

Need pooled warm and languid and low, diluting her already fading resistance.

His shoulders bunched under his starched white shirt a second before he glanced over his shoulder, his eyes haunted. Then they cleared. "Is Kolby asleep?"

"Yes, and thank you for all the preparations. The toys, the food...the flowers."

"All a part of the Medina welcome package."

"Perhaps." But she'd noticed a few too many of their favorites for the choices to have been coincidental. She moved forward hesitantly, the tiles cool against the bottoms of her feet. "This is all...something else."

"Leaving San Rinaldo, we had to downsize." He gave her another of those dry smiles.

More sympathy slid over her frustration at his secrets. "Thank you for bringing us here. I know it wasn't easy for you."

"I'm the reason you have to hide out in the first place until we line up protection for you. Seems only fair I should do everything in my power to make this right."

Her husband had never tried to fix any of his mistakes, hadn't even apologized after his arrest in the face of irrefutable evidence. She couldn't help but appreciate the way Tony took responsibility. And he cared enough to smooth the way for her.

"What about you?" She joined him at the swirled iron

railing. "You wouldn't have come here if it weren't for me. What do you hope to accomplish for yourself?"

"Don't worry about me." He leaned back on his elbows, white shirt stretching open at the collar to reveal the strong column of his neck. "I always look out for myself."

"Then what are you gaining?"

"More time with you, at least until the restraining order is in place." The heat of his eyes broadcast his intent just before he reached for her. "I've always been clear about how much I want to be with you, even on that first date when you wouldn't kiss me good-night."

"Is that why you chased me? Because I said no?"

"But you didn't keep saying no and still, here I am turned on as hell by the sound of your voice." He plucked her glasses off, set them aside and cradled her face in his palms. "The feel of your skin."

While he owned an empire with corporate offices that took up a bayside block, his skin still carried the calluses of the dockworker and sailor he'd been during his early adulthood. He was a man who certainly knew how to work with his hands. The rasp as he lightly caressed her cheekbones reminded her of the sweet abrasion when he explored farther.

He combed through along her scalp, strands slithering across his fingers. "The feel of your hair."

A moan slipped past her lips along with his name, "Tony…"

"Antonio," he reminded her. "I want to hear you say my name, know who's here with you."

And in this moment, in his eyes, he was that foreign prince, less accessible than her Tony, but no less exciting and infinitely as irresistible, so she whispered, "Antonio."

His touch was gentle, his mouth firm against hers. She parted her lips under his and invited in the familiar sweep, taste and pure sensation. Clutching his elbows, she swayed, her breasts tingling, pulling tight. Before she could think or stop herself, she brushed slightly from side to side, increasing the sweet pleasure of his hard chest teasing her. His hard thigh between her legs.

She stepped backward.

And tugged him with her.

Toward the open French doors leading into her bedroom, her body overriding her brain as it always seemed to do around Tony. She squeezed her legs together tighter against the firm pressure of his muscled thigh, so close, too close. She wanted, *needed* to feel him move inside her first.

Sinking her fingernails deeper, she ached to ask him to stay with her, to help her forget the worries waiting at home. "Antonio—"

"I know." He eased his mouth from hers, his chin scraping along her jaw as he nuzzled her hair and inhaled. "We need to stop."

Stop? She almost shrieked in frustration. "But I thought... I mean, you're here and usually when we let things go this far, we finish."

"You're ready to resume our affair?"

Affair. Not just one night, one satisfaction, but a relationship with implications and complications. Her brain raced to catch up after being put on idle while her body took over. God, what had she almost done? A few kisses along with a well-placed thigh, and she was ready to throw herself back in his bed.

Planting her hands on his chest, she stepped away. "I can't deny that I miss you and I want you, but I have no desire to be labeled a Medina mistress."

His eyebrows shot up toward his hairline. "Are you saying you want to get married?"

Six

"**M**arried?" Shannon choked on the word, her eyes so wide with shock Tony was almost insulted. "No! No, definitely not."

Her instant and emphatic denial left zero room for doubt. She wasn't expecting a proposal. Good thing, since that hadn't crossed his mind. Until now.

Was he willing to go that far to protect her?

She turned away fast, her hands raised as she raced back into the sitting area. "Tony—Antonio—I can't talk to you, look at you, risk kissing you again. I need to go to bed. To sleep. Alone."

"Then what do you want from me?"

"To end this craziness. To stop thinking about you all the time."

All the time?

He homed in on her words, an obvious slip on her part because while she'd been receptive and enthusiastic in bed, she'd given him precious little encouragement once they had their clothes back on again. Their fight over his simple offer of money still stung. Why did she have to reject his attempt to help?

She paced, restlessly lining up her shoes beside the sofa, scooping Kolby's tiny train from a table, lingering to rearrange the blue flowers. "You've said you feel the same. Who the hell wants to be consumed by this kind of ache all the time? It's damned inconvenient, especially when it can't lead anywhere. It's not like you were looking for marriage."

"That wasn't my intention when we started seeing each other." Yet somehow the thought had popped into his head out there on the patio. Sure, it had shocked the crap out of him at first. Still left him reeling. Although not so much that he was willing to reject the idea outright. "But since you've brought it up—"

Her hands shot up in front of her, between them. "Uh-uh, no sirree. You were the one to mention the *M* word."

"Fine, then. The marriage issue is out there, on the table for discussion. Let's talk it through."

She stopped cold. "This isn't some kind of business merger. We're talking about our lives here, and not just ours. I don't have the luxury of making another mistake. I already screwed up once before, big time. My son's well-being depends on my decisions."

"And I'm a bad choice because?"

"Do not play with my feelings. Damn it, Tony." She jabbed him in the chest with one finger. "You know I'm attracted to you. If you keep this up, I'll probably cave and we'll have sex. We probably would have on the plane if the steward and my son hadn't been around. But I would have been sorry the minute the orgasm chilled and is that really how you want it to be between us? To have me waking up regretting it every time?"

With images of the two of them joining the mile-high club fast-tracking from his brain to his groin, he seriously considered saying to hell with regrets. Let this insanity between them play out, wherever it took them.

Her bed was only a few steps away, offering a clear and tempting place to sink inside her. He would sweep away her clothes and the covers— His gaze hooked on the afghan draped along the end corner of the mattress.

Damn. Who had put that there? Could his father be deliberately jabbing him with reminders of their life as a family in hopes of drawing him back into the fold? Of course Enrique would, manipulative old cuss that he was.

That familiar silver blanket sucker punched him back to reality. He would recognize the one-of-a-kind afghan anywhere. His mother had knitted it for him just before she'd been killed, and he'd kept it with him like a shield during the whole hellish escape from San Rinaldo. Good God, he shouldn't have had to ask her why he was a bad choice. He knew the reason well.

Tony stumbled back, away from the memories and away from this woman who saw too much with her perceptive gray-blue eyes.

"You're right, Shannon. We're both too exhausted to make any more decisions today. Sleep well." His voice as raw as his memory-riddled gut, he left.

Dazed, Shannon stood in the middle of the sitting room wondering what the hell had just happened.

One second she'd been ready to climb back into Tony's arms and bed, the next they'd been talking about marriage.

And didn't that still stun her numb with thoughts of how horribly things had ended with Nolan?

But only seconds after bringing up the marriage issue, Tony had emotionally checked out on her again. At least he'd prevented them from making a mistake. It was a mistake, right?

Eyeing her big—empty—four-poster bed, she suddenly wasn't one bit sleepy. Tony overwhelmed her as much as the wealth. She walked into her bedroom, studying the Picasso over her headboard, this one from the artist's rose period, a harlequin clown in oranges and pinks. She'd counted three works already by this artist alone, including some leggy elephant painting in Kolby's room.

She'd hidden the crayons and markers.

Laughing at the absurdity of it all, she fingered a folded cashmere afghan draped over the corner of the mattress. So whispery soft and strangely worn in the middle of this immaculately opulent decor. The pewter-colored yarn complemented the apricot and gray tones well enough, but she wondered where it had come from. She tugged it from the bed and shook it out.

The blanket rippled in front of her, a little larger than a lap quilt, not quite long enough for a single bed. Turning in a circle she wrapped the filmy cover around her and padded back out to the balcony. She hugged the cashmere wrap tighter and curled up in a padded lounger, letting the ocean wind soothe her face still warm from Tony's touch.

Was it her imagination or could she smell hints of him even on the blanket? Or was he that firmly in her senses as well as her thoughts? What was it about Tony that reached to her in ways Nolan never had? She'd responded to her husband's touch, found completion, content with her life right up to the point of betrayal.

But Tony… Shannon hugged the blanket tighter. She

hadn't been hinting at marriage, damn it. Just the thought of giving over her life so completely again scared her to her toes.

So where did that leave her? Seriously considering becoming exactly what the media labeled her—a monarch's mistress.

Tony heard...the silence.

Finally, Shannon had settled for the night. Thank God. Much longer and his willpower would have given out. He would have gone back into her room and picked up where they'd left off before he'd caught sight of the damn blanket.

This place screwed with his head, so much so he'd actually brought up marriage, for crying out loud. It was like there were rogue waves from his past curling up everywhere and knocking him off balance. The sooner he could take care of business with his father the sooner he could return to Galveston with Shannon, back to familiar ground where he stood a better chance at reconciling with her.

Staying out of her bed for now was definitely the wiser choice. He walked down the corridor, away from her and that blanket full of memories. He needed his focus sharp for the upcoming meeting with his father. This time, he would face the old man alone.

Charging down the hall, he barely registered the familiar antique wooden benches tucked here, a strategic table and guard posted there. Odd how quickly he slid right back into the surroundings even after so long away. And even stranger that his father hadn't changed a thing.

The day had been one helluva ride, and it wasn't over yet. Enrique had been with his nurse for the past hour, but should be ready to receive him now.

Tony rounded the corner and nodded to the sentinel outside the open door to Enrique's personal quarters. The space was made for a man, no feminine touches to soften the room full of browns and tans, leather and wood. Enrique saved his Salvador Dali collection for himself, a trio of the surrealist's "soft watches" melting over landscapes.

The old guy had become more obsessed with history after his had been stolen from him.

Enrique waited in his wheelchair, wearing a heavy blue robe and years of worries.

"Sit," his father ordered, pointing to his old favored chair.

When Tony didn't jump at his command, Enrique sighed heavily and muttered under his breath in Spanish. "Have a seat," he continued in his native tongue. "We need to talk, *mi hijo.*"

They did, and Tony had to admit he was curious— concerned—about his father's health. Knowing might not have brought him home sooner, but now that he was here, he couldn't ignore the gaunt angles and sallow pallor. "How sick are you really?" Tony continued in Spanish, having spoken both languages equally once they'd left San Rinaldo. "No sugar coating it. I deserve the truth."

"And you would have heard it earlier if you had returned when I first requested."

His father had never *requested* anything in his life. The stubborn old cuss had been willing to die alone rather than actually admit how ill he was.

Of course Antonio had been just as stubborn about ignoring the demands to show his face on the island. "I am here now."

"You and your brothers have stirred up trouble." A great big *I told you so* was packed into that statement.

"Do you have insights as to how this leaked? How did

that reporter identify Duarte?" His middle brother wasn't exactly a social guy.

"Nobody knows, but my people are still looking into it. I thought you would be the one to expose us," his father said wryly. "You always were the impetuous one. Yet you've behaved decisively and wisely. You have protected those close to you. Well done."

"I am past needing your approval, but I thank you for your help."

"Fair enough, and I'm well aware that you would not have accepted that help if Shannon Crawford was not involved. I would be glad to see one of my sons settled and married before I die."

His gut pitched much like a boat tossed by a wave. "Your illness is that bad?" An uneasy silence settled, his father's rattling breaths growing louder and louder. "Should I call a nurse?"

Or his assistant? He wasn't sure what Alys Reyes de la Cortez was doing here, but she was definitely different from the older staff of San Rinaldo natives Enrique normally hired.

"I may be old and sick, but I don't need to be tucked into bed like a child." His chin tipped.

"I'm not here to fight with you."

"Of course not. You're here for my help."

And he had the feeling his father wasn't going to let him forget it. They'd never gotten along well and apparently that hadn't changed. He started to rise. "If that's all then, I will turn in."

"Wait." His father polished his eighteen-karat gold pocket watch with his thumb. "My assistance comes at a price."

Shocked at the calculating tone, Tony sank back into his chair. "You can't be serious."

"I am. Completely."

He should have suspected and prepared himself. "What do you want?"

"I want you to stay for the month while you wait for the new safety measures to be implemented."

"Here? That's all?" He made it sound offhand but already he could feel the claustrophobia wrap around his throat and tighten. The Dali art mocked him with just how slippery time could be, a life that ended in a flash or a moment that extended forever.

"Is it so strange I want to see what kind of man you have matured into?"

Given Enrique had expected Tony to break their cover, he must not have had high expectations for his youngest son. And that pissed him off. "If I don't agree? You'll do what? Feed Shannon and her son to the lions?"

"Her son can stay. I would never sacrifice a child's safety. The mother will have to go."

He couldn't be serious. Tony studied his father for some sign Enrique was bluffing...but the old guy didn't have a "tell." And his father hadn't hesitated to trust his own wife's safety to others. What would stop him from sending Shannon off with a guard and a good-luck wish?

"She would never leave without her child." Like his mother. Tony restrained a wince.

"That is not my problem. Are you truly that unwilling to spend a month here?"

"What if the restraining order comes through sooner?"

"I would ask you to stay as a thanks for my assistance. I have risked a lot for you in granting her access to the island."

True enough, or so it would feel to Enrique with his near agoraphobic need to stay isolated from the world.

"And there are no other conditions?"

A salt and pepper eyebrow arched. "Do you want a contract?"

"Do you? If Shannon decides to leave by the weekend, I could simply go, too. What's the worst you can do? Cut me out of the will?" He hadn't taken a penny of his father's money.

"You always were the most amusing of my sons. I have missed that."

"I'm not laughing."

His father's smile faded and he tucked the watch into a pocket, chain jingling to a rest. "Your word is sufficient. You may not want any part of me and my little world here, but you are a Medina. You are my son. Your honor is not in question."

"Fair enough. If you're willing to accept my word, then a month it is." Now that the decision was made, he wondered why his father had chosen that length of time. "What's your prognosis?"

"My liver is failing," Enrique said simply without any hint of self-pity. "Because of the living conditions when I was on the run, I caught hepatitis. It has taken a toll over the years."

Thinking back, Tony tried to remember if his father had been sick when they'd reunited in South America before relocating to the island...but he only recalled his father being coolly determined. "I didn't know. I'm sorry."

"You were a child. You did not need to be informed of everything."

He hadn't been told much of *anything* in those days, but even if he had, he wasn't sure he would have heard. His grief for his mother had been deep and dark. That, he remembered well. "How much longer do you have?"

"I am not going to kick off in the next thirty days."

"That isn't what I meant."

"I know." His father smiled, creases digging deep. "I have a sense of humor, too."

What had his father been like before this place? Before the coup? Tony would never know because time was melting away like images in the Dali paintings on the wall.

While he had some memories of his mother from that time, he had almost none of his father until Enrique had met up with them in South America. The strongest memory he had of Enrique in San Rinaldo? When his father gathered his family to discuss the evacuation plan. Enrique had pressed his pocket watch into Tony's hands and promised to reclaim it. But even at five, Tony had known his father was saying goodbye for what could have been the last time. Now, Enrique wanted him back to say goodbye for the last time again.

How damned ironic. He'd brought Shannon to this place because she needed him. And now he could only think of how much he needed to be with her.

Seven

Where was Tony?

The next day after lunch, Shannon stood alone on her balcony overlooking the ocean. Seagulls swooped on the horizon while long legged blue herons stalked prey on the rocks. Kolby was napping. A pot of steeped herbal tea waited on a tiny table along with dried fruits and nuts.

How strange to have such complete panoramic peace during such a tumultuous time. The balcony offered an unending view of the sea, unlike the other side with barrier islands. The temperature felt much the same as in Galveston, humid and in the seventies.

She should make the most of the quiet to regain her footing. Instead, she kept looking at the door leading into Tony's suite and wondering why she hadn't seen him yet.

Her morning had been hectic and more than a little overwhelming learning her way around the mansion with Alys. As much as she needed to resist Tony, she'd missed having his big comforting presence at her side while she explored the never-ending rooms packed nonchalantly with priceless art and antiques.

And they'd only toured half of the home and grounds.

Afterward, Alys had introduced two women on hand for sitter and nanny duties. Shannon had been taken aback by the notion of turning her son over to total strangers, although she had to confess, the guard assigned to shadow Kolby reassured her. She'd been shown letters of recommendation and résumés for each individual. Still, Shannon had spent the rest of the morning getting to know each person in case she needed to call on their help.

Interestingly, none of the king's employees gave away the island's location despite subtle questions about traveling back to their homes. Everyone on Enrique's payroll seemed to understand the importance of discretion, as well as seeing to her every need. Including delivering a closet full of clothes that just happened to fit. Not that she'd caved to temptation yet and tried any of it on. A gust rolling off the ocean teased the well-washed cotton of her sundress around her legs as she stood on the balcony.

The click of double doors opening one suite down snapped her from her reverie. She didn't even need to look over her shoulder to verify who'd stepped outside. She knew the sound of his footsteps, recognized the scent of him on the breeze.

"Hello, Tony."

His Italian loafers stopped alongside her feet in simple pink and brown striped flip-flops. *Hers*. Not ones from the new stash.

Leaning into her line of sight, he rested his elbows on the iron rail. "Sorry not to have checked in on you sooner. My father and I spent the morning troubleshooting on a conference call with my brothers and our attorneys."

Of course. That made sense. "Any news?"

"More of the same. Hopefully we can start damage control with some valid info leaked to the press to turn the tide. There's just so much out there." He shook his head sharply then forced a smile. "Enough of that. I missed you at lunch."

"Kolby and I ate in our suite." The scent of Tony's sandalwood aftershave had her curling her toes. "His table manners aren't up to royal standards."

"You don't have to hide in your rooms. There's no court or ceremony here." Still, he wore khakis and a monogrammed blue button-down rolled up at the sleeves rather than the jeans and shorts most everyday folks would wear on a beach vacation.

And he looked mighty fine in every starched inch of fabric.

"Formality or not, there are priceless antiques and art all easily within a child's reach." She trailed her fingers along the iron balustrade. "This place is a lot to absorb. We need time. Although I hope life returns to normal sooner rather than later."

Could she simply pick up where she'd left off? Things hadn't been so great then, given her nearly bankrupt account and her fight with Tony over more than money, over her very independence. Yet hadn't she been considering resuming the affair just last night?

Sometimes it was tough to tell if her hormones or her heart had control these days.

He extended his hand. "You're right. Let's slow things down. Would you like to go for a walk?"

"But Kolby might wake up and ask for m—"

"One of the nannies can watch over him and call us the second his eyes open. Come on. I'll update you on the wackiest of the internet buzz." A half grin tipped one side of his tanned face. "Apparently one source thinks the Medinas have a space station and I've taken you to the mother ship."

Laughter bubbled, surprising her, and she just let it roll free with the wind tearing in from the shore. God, how she needed it after the stressful past couple of days—a stressful week for that matter, since she had broken off her relationship with Tony. "Lead the way, my alien lover."

His smile widened, reaching his eyes for the first time since their ferry had pulled up to the island. The power outshone the world around her until she barely noticed the opulent surroundings on their way through the mansion to the beach.

The October sun high in the sky was blinding and warm, hotter than when she'd been on the balcony, inching up toward eighty degrees perhaps. Her mind started churning with possible locations. Could they be in Mexico or South America? Or were they still in the States? California or—

"We're off the coast of Florida."

Glancing up sharply, she swallowed hard, not realizing until that moment how deeply the secrecy had weighed on her. "Thank you."

He waved aside her gratitude. "You would have figured it out on your own in a couple of days."

Maybe, but given the secrecy of Enrique's employees, she wasn't as certain. "So, what about more of those wacky internet rumors?"

"Do you really want to discuss that?"

"I guess not." She slid off her flip-flops and curled her toes in the warm sand. "Thank you for all the clothes for me and for Kolby, the toys, too. We'll enjoy them while we're here. But you know we can't keep them."

"Don't be a buzz kill." He tapped her nose just below the

bridge of her glasses. "My father's staff ordered everything. I had nothing to do with it. If it'll make you happy, we'll donate the lot to Goodwill after you leave."

"How did he get everything here so fast?" She strode into the tide, her shoes dangling from her fingers.

"Does it matter?" He slid off his shoes and socks and joined her, just into the water's reach.

With the more casual and familiar Tony returning, some of the tension left her shoulders. "I guess not. The toys are awesome, of course, but Kolby enjoys the dogs most. They seem incredibly well trained."

"They are. My father will have his trainers working with the dogs to bond with your son so they will protect him as well if need be while you are here."

She shivered in spite of the bold beams of sunshine overhead. "Can't a dog just be a pet?"

"Things aren't that simple for us." He looked away, down the coast at an osprey spreading its wings and diving downward.

How many times had he watched the birds as a child and wanted to fly away, too? She understood well the need to escape a golden cage. "I'm sorry."

"Don't be." He rejected her sympathy outright.

Pride iced his clipped words, and she searched for a safer subject.

Her eyes settled on the rippling crests of foam frosting the gray-blue shore. "Is this where you used to surf?"

"Actually, the cove is pretty calm." He pointed ahead to an outcropping packed with palm trees. "The best spot is about a mile and a half down. Or at least it was. Who knows after so many years?"

"You really had free rein to run around the island." She stepped onto a sandbar that fingered out into the water. As a mother, she had a tough time picturing her child exploring this junglelike beach at will.

"Once I was a teenager, pretty much. After I was through with schooling for the day, of course." A green turtle popped his head from the water, legs poking from the shell as he swam out and slapped up the beach. "Although sometimes we even had class out here."

"A field trip to the beach? What fun teachers you had."

"Tutors."

"Of course." The stark difference in their upbringings wrapped around her like seaweed lapping at her ankles. She tried to shake free of the clammy negativity. "Surfing was your P.E.?"

"Technically, we had what you would call phys ed, but it was more of a health class with martial arts training."

During her couple of years teaching high school band and chorus before she'd met Nolan, some of her students went to karate lessons. But they'd gone to a gym full of other students, rather than attending in seclusion with only two brothers for company. "It's so surreal to think you never went to prom, or had an after-school job or played on a basketball team."

"We had games here…but you're right in that there was no stadium of classmates and parents. No cheerleaders." He winked and smiled, but she sensed he was using levity as a diversion.

How often had he done that in the past and she'd missed out hearing his real thoughts or feelings because she wanted things to be uncomplicated?

Shannon squeezed his bulging forearm. "You would have been a good football player with your size."

"Soccer." His bicep twitched under her touch. "I'm from Europe, remember?"

"Of course." Unlikely she would ever forget his roots now that she knew. And she wanted to learn more about this strong-jawed man who thought to order a miniature motorized Jeep for her son—and then give credit to his father.

She tucked her hand into the crook of his arm as she swished through the ebbs and flow of the tidewaters. "So you still think of yourself as being from Europe? Even though you were only five when you came to the U.S.?"

His eyebrows pinched together. "I never really thought of this as the U.S. even though I know how close we are."

"I can understand that. Everything here is such a mix of cultures." While the staff spoke English to her, she'd heard Spanish spoken by some. Books and magazines and even instructions on labels were a mix of English, Spanish and some French. "You mentioned thinking this was still San Rinaldo when you got here."

"Only at first. My father told us otherwise."

What difficult conversations those must have been between father and sons. So much to learn and adjust to so young. "We've both lost a lot, you and I. I wonder if I sensed that on some level, if that's what drew us to each other."

He slid an arm around her shoulders and pulled her closer while they kicked through the surf. "Don't kid yourself. I was attracted to how hot you looked walking away in that slim black skirt. And then when you glanced over your shoulder with those prim glasses and do-me eyes." He whistled long and low. "I was toast from the get-go."

Trying not to smile, her skin heating all the same, she elbowed him lightly. "Cro-Magnon."

"Hey, I'm a red-blooded male and you're sexy." He traced the cat-eye edge of her glasses. "You're also entirely too serious at the moment. Life will kick us in the ass all on its own soon enough. We're going to just enjoy the moment, remember? No more buzz kills."

"You're right." Who knew how much longer she would have with Tony before this mess blew up in her face? "Let's go back to talking about surfing and high school dances. You so would have been the bad boy."

"And I'll bet you were a good girl. Did you wear those studious glasses even then?"

"Since I was in the eighth grade." She'd hated how her nose would sweat in the heat when she'd marched during football games. "I was a dedicated musician with no time for boys."

"And now?"

"I want to enjoy this beautiful ocean and a day with absolutely nothing to do." She bolted ahead, kicking through the tide, not sure how to balance her impulsive need for Tony with her practical side that demanded she stay on guard.

Footsteps splashed behind her a second before Tony scooped her up. And she let him.

The warm heat of his shoulder under her cheek, the steady pump of his heart against her side had her curling her arms around his neck. "You're getting us all wet."

His eyes fell to her shirt. His heart thumped faster. "Are you having fun?"

"Yes, I am." She toyed with the springy curls at the nape of his neck. "You always make sure of that, whether it's an opera or a walk by the beach."

"You deserve to have more fun in your life." He held her against his chest with a familiarity she couldn't deny. "I would make things easier for you. You know that."

"And you know where I stand on that subject." She cupped his face, his stubble so dark and thick that he wore a perpetual five o'clock shadow. "This—your protection, the trip, the clothes and toys—it's already much more than I'm comfortable taking."

She needed to be clear on that before she even considered letting him closer again.

He eased her to her feet with a lingering glide of her body down his. "We should go back."

The desire in his eyes glinted unmistakably in the afternoon sun. Yet, he pulled away.

Her lips hungered and her breasts ached—and *he* was walking away again, in spite of all he'd said about how much he wanted her. This man confused the hell out of her.

Five days later, Shannon lounged on the downstairs lanai and watched her son drive along the beach in his miniature Jeep, dogs romping alongside. This was the first time she'd been left to her own devices in days. She'd never been romanced so thoroughly in her life. True to his word, over the past week Tony had been at his most charming.

Could her time here already be almost over?

Sipping freshly squeezed lemonade—although the drink tasted far too amazing for such a simple name—she savored the tart taste. Of course everything seemed sharper, crisper as tension seeped from her bones. The concerns of the world felt forever away while the sun warmed her skin and the waves provided a soothing sound track to her days.

And she had Tony to thank for it all. She'd never known there were so many entertainment options on an island. Of course Enrique Medina had spared no expense in building his compound.

A movie screening room with all the latest films piped in for private viewing.

Three different dining rooms for everything from family style to white-tie.

Rec room, gym, indoor and outdoor swimming pools.

She could still hear Kolby's squeal of delight over the stable of horses and ponies.

Throughout it all, Tony had been at her side with tantalizing brushes of his strong body against hers. All the while his rich chocolate brown eyes reminded Shannon that the next move was up to her. Not that they stood a chance at finding privacy today. The grounds buzzed with activity, and today, no sign of Tony.

Behind her, the doors snicked open. Tony? Her heart stuttered a quick syncopation as she glanced back.

Alys walked toward her, high heels clicking on the tiled veranda as she angled past two guards comparing notes on their twin BlackBerry phones. Shannon forced herself to keep the smile in place. It would be rude to frown in disappointment, especially after how helpful the woman had been.

Too bad the disappointment wasn't as easy to hide from herself. No doubt about it, Tony was working his way back into her life.

The king's assistant stopped at the fully stocked outdoor bar and poured a glass of lemonade from the crystal pitcher.

Shannon thumbed the condensation on the cold glass. "Is there something you need?"

"Antonio wanted me to find you, and I have." She tapped her silver BlackBerry attached to the waistband of her linen skirt. Ever crisp with her power suit and French manicure. As usual the elegant woman didn't have a wrinkle in sight, much less wince over working in heels all day. "He'll be out shortly. He's finishing up a meeting with his father."

"I should get Kolby." She swung her feet to the side.

How silly to be glad she'd caved and used some of the new clothes. She had worn everything she brought with her twice and while the laundry service easily kept up with her limited wardrobe, she'd begun to feel a little ungrateful not to wear at least a few of the things that someone had gone to a lot of trouble to provide. Shannon smoothed the de la Renta scoop-necked dress, the fabric so decadently soft it caressed her skin with every move.

"No need to stop the boy's fun just yet. Antonio is on his way." Alys perched on the edge of the lounger, glass on her knee.

Shannon rubbed the hem of her dress between two fingers much like Kolby with his blanket when he needed soothing. "I hear you're the one who ordered all the new clothes. Thank you."

Alys saw to everything else in this smoothly run place. "No need for thanks. It's my job."

"You have excellent taste." She tugged the hem back over her knees.

"I saw your photo online and chose things that would flatter your frame and coloring. It's fun to shop on someone else's dime."

More than a dime had gone into this wardrobe. Her closet sported new additions each morning. Everything from casual jeans and designer blouses to silky dresses and heels to wear for dinner. An assortment of bathing suits to choose from….

And the lingerie. A decadent shiver slid down her spine at the feel of the fine silks and satins against her skin. Although it made her uncomfortable to think of this woman choosing everything.

Alys turned her glass around and around on her knee. "The expense you worry about is nothing to them. They can afford the finest. It would bother them to see you struggling. Now you fit in and that gives the king less to worry about."

God forbid her tennis shoes should make the king uncomfortable. But saying as much would make her sound ungrateful, so she toyed with her glasses, pulling them off and cleaning them with her napkin even though they were already crystal clear. The dynamics of this place went beyond any household she'd ever seen. Alys seemed more comfortable here than Tony.

Shannon slid her glasses back on. "If you don't mind my asking, how long have you been working for the king?"

"Only three months."

How long did she intend to stay? The island was luxurious, but in more of a vacation kind of way. It was so cut off from the world, time seemed to stand still. What kind of life could the woman build in this place?

Abruptly, Alys leaped to her feet. "Here is Antonio now."

He charged confidently through the door, eyes locked on Shannon. "Thank you for finding her, Alys."

The assistant backed away. "Of course." Alys stepped out of hearing range, giving them some privacy.

Forking a hand through his hair—messing up the precise combing from his conference with his father—Tony wore a suit without a tie. The jacket perhaps a nod toward meeting with his father? His smile was carefree, but his shoulders bore the extra tension she'd come to realize accompanied time he had spent with the king.

"How did your meeting go?"

"Don't want to talk about that." Tony plucked a lily from the vase on the bar, snapped the stem off and tucked the bloom behind her ear. "Would much rather enjoy the view. The flower is almost as gorgeous as you are."

The lush perfume filled each breath. "All the fresh flowers are positively decadent."

"I wish I could take credit, but there's a hothouse with a supply that's virtually unlimited."

Yet another amenity she wouldn't have guessed, although it certainly explained all the fresh-cut flowers. "Still," she repeated as she touched the lily tucked in her hair, "I appreciate the gesture."

"I would make love to you on a bed of flowers if you let me." He thumbed her earlobe lightly before skimming his knuckles along her collarbone.

How easy it would be to give over to the delicious seduction of his words and his world. Except she'd allowed herself to fall into that trap before.

And of course there was that little technicality that *he* had been the one holding back all week. "What about thorns?"

He laughed, his hand falling away from her skin and palming her back. "Come on, my practical love. We're going out."

Love? She swallowed to dampen her suddenly cottony mouth. "To lunch?"

"To the airstrip."

Her stomach lurched. This slice of time away was over already? "We're leaving?"

"Not that lucky, I'm afraid. Your apartment is still staked out with the press and curious royalty groupie types. You may want to consider a gated community on top of the added security measures. I know the cost freaks you out, but give my lawyer another couple of days to work on those restraining orders and we can take it from there. As for where we're going today, we're greeting guests and I'd like you to come along."

They weren't leaving. Relief sang through her so intensely it gave her pause.

Tony cocked his head to the side. "Would you like to come with me?"

"Uh, yes, I think so." She struggled to gather her scrambled thoughts and composure. "I just need to settle Kolby."

Alys cleared her throat a few feet away. "I've already notified Miss Delgado, the younger nanny. She's ordering a picnic lunch and bringing sand toys. Then of course she will watch over him during his naptime if needed. I assume that's acceptable to you?"

Her son would enjoy that more than a car ride and waiting around for the flight. She was growing quite spoiled having afternoons completely free while Kolby napped safely under a nanny's watchful care. "Of course. That sounds perfect."

Shannon smiled her thanks and reached out to touch the woman's arm. Except Alys wasn't looking at her. The king's assistant had her eyes firmly planted elsewhere.

On Tony.

Shock nailed her feet to the tiles. Then a fierce jealousy vibrated through her, a feeling that was most definitely ugly and not her style. She'd thought herself above such a primitive emotion, not to mention Tony hadn't given the woman any encouragement.

Still, Shannon fought the urge to link her arm with his in a great big "mine" statement. In that unguarded moment, Alys revealed clearly what she hoped to gain from living here.

Alys wanted a Medina man.

Eight

Tony guided the Porsche Cayenne four-wheel drive along the island road toward the airstrip, glad Shannon was with him to ease the edge on the upcoming meeting. Although having her with him brought a special torment all its own.

The past week working his way back into her good graces had been a painful pleasure, sharpening the razor edge on his need to have her in his bed again. Spending time with her had only shown him more reasons to want her. She mesmerized him with the simplest things.

When she sat on the pool edge and kicked her feet through the water, he thought of those long legs wrapped around him.

Seeing her sip a glass of lemonade made him ache to taste the tart fruit on her lips.

The way she cleaned her glasses with a gust of breath

fogging the frames made him think of her panting in his ear as he brought her to completion.

Romancing his way back into her good graces was easier said than done. And the goal of it all made each day on this island easier to bear.

And after they returned to Galveston? He would face that then. Right now, he had more of his father's past to deal with.

"Tony?" Bracing her hand against the dash as the rutted road challenged even the quality shock absorbers, she looked so right sitting in the seat next to him. "You still haven't told me who we're picking up. Your brothers, perhaps?"

Steering the SUV under the arch of palm trees lining both sides of the road, he searched for the right words to prepare Shannon for something he'd never shared with a soul. "You're on the right track." His hands gripped the steering wheel tighter. "My sister. Half sister, actually. Eloisa."

"A sister? I didn't know...."

"Neither does the press." His half sister had stayed under the radar, growing up with her mother and stepfather in Pensacola, Florida. Only recently had Eloisa reestablished contact with their father. "She's coming here to regroup, troubleshoot. Prepare. Now that the Medina secret is out, her story will also be revealed soon enough."

"May I ask what that story might be?"

"Of course." He focused on the two-lane road, a convenient excuse to make sure she didn't see any anger pushing past his boundaries. "My father had a relationship with her mother after arriving in the U.S., which resulted in Eloisa. She's in her mid-twenties now."

Shannon's eyes went wide behind her glasses.

"Yeah, I know." Turning, he drove from the jungle road

onto a waterside route leading to the ferry station. "That's a tight timeline between when we left San Rinaldo and the hookup." Tight timeline in regard to his mother's death.

"That must have been confusing for you. Kolby barely remembers his father and it's been tough for him to accept you. And we haven't had to deal with adding another child to the mix."

A child? With Shannon? An image of a dark-haired baby—his baby—in her arms blindsided him, derailing his thoughts away from his father in a flash. His foot slid off the accelerator. Shaking free of the image was easier said than done as it grew roots in his mind—Kolby stepping into the picture until a family portrait took shape.

God, just last week he'd been thinking how he knew nothing about kids. She was the one hinting at marriage, not him. Although she said the opposite until he didn't know what was up.

Things with Shannon weren't as simple as he'd planned at the outset. "My father's affair was his own business."

"Okay, then." She pulled her glasses off and fogged them with her breath. She dried them with the hem of her dress. "Do you and your sister get along?"

He hauled his eyes from Shannon's glasses before he swerved off onto the beach. Or pulled onto the nearest side road and to hell with making it to the airstrip on time.

"I've only met her once before." When Tony was a teenager. His father had gone all out on that lone visit with his seven-year-old daughter. Tony didn't resent Eloisa. It wasn't her fault, after all. In fact, he grew even more pissed off at his father. Enrique had responsibilities to his daughter. If he wanted to stay out of her life, then fine. Do so. But half measures were bull.

Yet wasn't that what he'd been offering Shannon? Half measures?

Self-realization sucked. "She's come here on her own since then. She and Duarte have even met up a few times, which in a roundabout way brought on the media mess."

"How so?" She slid her glasses back in place.

"Our sister married into a high-profile family. Eloisa's husband is the son of an ambassador and brother to a senator. He's a Landis."

She sat up straighter at the mention of America's political royalty. Talk about irony.

Tony slowed for a fuel truck to pass. "The Landis name naturally comes with media attention." He accelerated into the parking lot alongside the ferry station, the boat already close to shore. An airplane was parked on the distant airstrip. "Her husband—Jonah—likes to keep a low profile, but that's just not possible."

"What happened?"

"Duarte was delivering one of our father's messages, which put him on a collision course with a press camera. We're still trying to figure out how the Global Intruder made the connection. Although, it's a moot point now. Every stray photo of all of us has been unearthed, every detail of our pasts."

"Of my past?" Her face drained of color.

"I'm afraid so."

All the more reason for her to stay on the island. Her husband's illegal dealings, even his suicide, had hit the headlines again this morning, thanks to muckrakers looking for more scandal connected to the Medina story. He would only be able to shield Shannon from that for so long. She had a right to know.

"I've grown complacent this week." She pressed a hand to her stomach. "My poor in-laws."

The SUV idled in the parking spot, the ferry already

preparing to dock. He didn't have much time left alone with her.

Tony skimmed back her silky blond hair. "I'm sorry all this has come up again. And I hate it that I can't do more to fix things for you."

Turning toward his touch, she rested her face in his hand. "You've helped this week."

He wanted to kiss her, burned to recline the seats and explore the hint of cleavage in her scoop-necked dress. And damned if that wasn't exactly what he planned to do.

Slanting his mouth over her, he caught her gasp and took full advantage of her parted lips with a determined sweep of his tongue. Need for her pumped through his veins, fast-tracked blood from his head to his groin until he could only feel, smell, taste undiluted *Shannon*. Her gasp quickly turned to a sigh as she melted against him, the curves of her breasts pressed to his chest, her fingernails digging deeply into his forearms as she urged him closer.

He was more than happy to accommodate.

It had been so long, too long since they'd had sex before their argument over his damned money. Nearly fourteen days that seemed like fourteen years since he'd had his hands on her this way, fully and unrestrained, tunneling under her clothes, reacquainting himself with the perfection of her soft skin and perfect curves. She fit against him with a rightness he knew extended even further with their clothes off. A hitch in her throat, the flush rising on the exposed curve of her breasts keyed him in to her rising need, as if he couldn't already tell by the way she nearly crawled across the seat to get closer.

Shannon wanted sex with him every bit as much as he wanted her. But that required privacy, not a parking lot in clear view of the approaching ferry.

Holding back now was the right move, even if it was killing him.

"Come on. Time to meet my sister." He slid out of her arms and the SUV and around to her door before she could shuffle her purse from her lap to her shoulder.

He opened the door and she smiled her thanks without speaking, yet another thing he appreciated about her. She sensed when he didn't want to talk anymore. He'd shared things with women over the years, but until her, he'd never found one with whom he could share silence.

The lapping waves, the squawk of gulls, the endless stretch of water centered him, steadying his steps and reminding him how to keep his balance in a rocky world.

Resting his head on Shannon's back, he waited while the ferry finished docking. His sister and her husband stood at the railing. Eloisa's husband hooked an arm around her shoulders, the couple talking intently.

Eloisa might not be a carbon copy of their father, but she carried an air of something unmistakably Medina about her. His father had once said she looked like their grandmother. Tony wouldn't know, since he couldn't remember his grandparents who'd all died before he was born.

The loudspeaker blared with the boat captain announcing their arrival. Disembarking, the couple stayed close together, his brother-in-law broadcasting a protective air. Jonah was the unconventional Landis, according to the papers. If so, they should get along just fine.

The couple stepped from the boat to the dock, and up close Eloisa didn't appear nearly as calm as from a distance. Lines of strain showed in her eyes.

"Welcome," Tony said. "Eloisa, Jonah, this is Shannon Crawford, and I'm—"

"Antonio, I know." His sister spoke softly, reserved. "I recognize you both from the papers."

He'd met Eloisa once as a child when she'd visited the island. She'd come back recently, but he'd been long gone by then.

They were strangers and relatives. Awkward, to say the least.

Jonah Landis stepped up. "Glad you could accommodate our request for a visit so quickly."

"Damage control is important."

Eloisa simply took his hand, searching his face. "How's our father?"

"Not well." Had Shannon just stepped closer to him? Tony kept his eyes forward, knowing in his gut he would see sympathy in her eyes. "He says his doctors are doing all they can."

Blinking back tears, Eloisa stood straighter with a willowy strength. "I barely know him, but I can't envision a world without him in it. Sounds crazy, I'm sure."

He understood too well. Making peace was hard as hell, yet somehow she seemed to have managed.

Jonah clapped him on the back. "Well, my new bro, I need to grab Eloisa's bags and meet you at the car."

A Landis who carried his own luggage? Tony liked the unpretentious guy already.

And wasn't that one of the things he liked most about Shannon? Her down-to-earth ways in spite of her wealthy lifestyle with her husband. She seemed completely unimpressed with the Medina money, much less his defunct title.

For the first time he considered she might be right. She may be better off without the strain of his messed-up family.

Which made him a selfish bastard for pursuing her. But

he couldn't seem to pull back now when his world had been rocked on its foundation. The sailor in him recognized the only port in the storm, and right now, only a de la Renta dress separated him from what he wanted—needed—more than anything.

However, he needed to choose his time and place carefully with the private island growing more crowded by the minute.

The next afternoon, Shannon sat beside Tony in the Porsche four-wheel drive on the way to the beach. He'd left her a note to put on her bathing suit and meet him during Kolby's naptime. She'd been taken aback at the leap of excitement in her stomach over spending time alone with him.

The beach road took them all the way to the edge of the shoreline. He shifted the car in Park, his legs flexing in black board shorts as he left the car silently. He'd been quiet for the whole drive, and she didn't feel the need to fill the moment with aimless babbling. Being together and quiet had an appeal all its own.

Tugging on the edge of the white cover-up, she eyed the secluded stretch of beach. Could this be the end of the "romancing" and the shift back to intimacy? Her stomach fluttered faster.

She stepped from the car before he could open her door. Wind ruffled his hair and whipped his shorts, low slung on his hips. She knew his body well but still the muscled hardness hitched her breath in her throat. Bronzed and toned—smart, rich and royal to boot. Life had handed him an amazing hand, and yet he still chose to work insane hours. In fact, she'd spent more time with him this past week than during the months they'd dated in Galveston.

And everything she learned confused her more than solving questions.

She jammed her hands in the pockets of her cover-up. "Are you going to tell me why we're here?"

"Over there." He pointed to a cluster of palm trees with surfboards propped and waiting.

"You're kidding, right? Tony, I don't surf, and the water must be cold."

"You'll warm up. The waves aren't high enough today for surfing. But there're still some things even a beginner can do." He peeled off his T-shirt and she realized she was staring, damn it. "You won't break anything. Trust me."

He extended a hand.

Trust? Easier said than done. She eyed the boards and looked back at him. They were on the island, she reminded herself, removed from real life. And bottom line, while she wasn't sure she trusted him with her heart, she totally trusted him with her body. He wouldn't let anything happen to her.

Decision made, she whipped her cover-up over her head, revealing her crocheted swimsuit. His eyes flamed over her before he took her cover-up and tossed it in the SUV along with his T-shirt. He closed his hands around hers in a warm steady grip and started toward the boards.

She eyed the pair propped against trees—obviously set up in advance for their outing. One shiny and new, bright white with tropical flowers around the edges. The other was simpler, just yellow, faded from time and use. She looked at the water again, starting to have second—

"Hey." He squeezed her hand. "We're just going to paddle out. Nothing too adventurous today, but I think you're going to find even slow and steady has some unexpected thrills."

And didn't that send her heart double timing?

Thank goodness he moved quickly. Mere minutes later she was on her stomach, on the board, paddling away from shore to…nowhere. Nothing but aqua blue waters blending into a paler sky. Mild waves rolled beneath her but somehow never lifted her high enough to be scary, more of a gentle rocking. The chilly water turned to a neutral sluice over her body, soothing her into becoming one with the ocean.

One stroke at a time she let go of goals and racing to the finish line. Her life had been on fast-paced frenetic since Nolan died. Now, for the first time in longer than she could remember, she was able to unwind, almost hypnotized by the dip, dip, dip of her hands and Tony's into the water.

Tension she hadn't even realized kinked her muscles began to ease. Somehow, Tony must have known. She turned her head to thank him and found him staring back at her.

She threaded her fingers through the water, sun baking her back. "It's so quiet out here."

"I thought you would appreciate the time away."

"You were right." She slowed her paddling and just floated. "You've given over a lot of your time to make sure Kolby and I stayed entertained. Don't you need to get back to work?"

"I work from the island using my computer and telecoms." His hair, even darker when wet, was slicked back from his face, his damp skin glinting in the sun. "More and more of business is being conducted that way."

"Do you ever sleep?"

"Not so much lately, but that has nothing to do with work." He held her with his eyes locked on her face, no suggestive body sweep, just intense, undiluted Tony.

And she couldn't help but wonder why he went to so much trouble when they weren't sleeping together anymore.

If his conscience bothered him, he could have assigned guards to watch over her and she wouldn't have argued for Kolby's sake. Yet here he was. With her.

"What do you see in me?" She rested her cheek on her folded hands. "I'm not fishing for compliments, honest to God, it's just we seem so wrong for each other on so many levels. Is it just the challenge, like building your business?"

"Shanny, you take *challenge* to a whole 'nother level."

She flicked water in his face. "I'm being serious here. No joking around, please."

"Seriously?" He stared out at the horizon for a second as if gathering his thoughts. "Since you brought up the business analogy, let's run with that. At work you would be someone I want on my team. Your tenacity, your refusal to give up—even your frustrating rejection of my help—impress the hell out of me. You're an amazing woman, so much so that sometimes I can't even look away."

He made her feel strong and special with a few words. After feeling guilty for so long, of wondering if she could hold it all together for Kolby, she welcomed the reassurance coursing through her veins as surely as the current underneath her.

Tony slid from his board and ducked under. She watched through the clear surface as he freed the ankle leash attaching him to his board.

Resurfacing beside her, he stroked the line of her back. "Sit up for a minute."

"What?" She'd barely heard him, too focused on the feel of his hand low on her waist.

"Sit up on the board and swing your legs over the side." He held the edge. "I won't let you fall."

"But your board's drifting." She watched the faded yellow inch away.

"I'll get it later. Come on." He palmed her back, helping her balance as finally, she wriggled her way upright.

She bobbled. Stifled a squeal. Then realized what was the worst that could happen? She would be in the water. Big deal. And suddenly the surfboard steadied a little, still rocking but not out of control. The waters lapped around her legs, cool, exciting.

"I did it." She laughed, sending her voice out into that endlessness.

"Perfect. Now hold still," he said and somehow slid effortlessly behind her.

Her balance went haywire again for a second, the horizon tilting until she was sure they would both topple over.

"Relax," he said against her ear. "Out here, it's not about fighting, it's the one place you can totally let go."

The one place *he* could let go? And suddenly she realized this was about more than getting her to relax. He was sharing something about himself with her. Even a man as driven and successful as himself needed a break from the demands of everyday life. Perhaps because of moments like these he kept it all together rather than letting the tension tighten until it snapped.

She fit herself against him, his legs behind hers as they drifted. Her muscles slowly melted until she leaned into him. The waves curled underneath, his chest wet and bristly against her skin. A new tension coiled inside her, deep in her belly. Her swimsuit suddenly felt too tight against her breasts that swelled and yearned for the brush of the air and Tony's mouth.

His palms rested on her thighs. His thumbs circled a light massage, close, so close. Water ebbed and flowed over her heated core, waves sweeping tantalizing caresses on her aching flesh. Her head sagged onto his shoulder.

With each undulation of the board, he rocked against her, stirring, growing harder until he pressed fully erect along her spine. Every roll of the board rubbing their bodies against each other had to be as torturous for him as it was for her. His hands moved higher on her legs, nearer to what she needed. Silently. Just as in tune with each other as when they'd been paddling out.

She worried at first that someone might see, but with their backs to the shore and water…she could lose herself in the moment. Already his breaths grew heavier against her ear, nearly as fast as her own.

They could both let go and find completion right here without ever moving. Simply feeling his arousal against her stirred Shannon to a bittersweet edge. And good God, that scared the hell out of her.

The wind chilled, and she recognized the sting of fear all too well. She'd thought she could ride the wave, so to speak, and just have an affair with Tony.

But this utter abandon, the loss of control, the way they were together, it was anything but simple, something she wasn't sure she was ready to risk.

Scavenging every bit of her quickly dwindling willpower, she grabbed his wrists, moved his hands away…

And dived off the side of the board.

Nine

Tony propped his surfboard against a tree and turned to take Shannon's. The wariness in her eyes frustrated the hell out of him. He could have sworn she was just as into the moment out there as he was—an amazing moment that had been seconds away from getting even better.

And then she'd vaulted off the board and into the water.

Staying well clear of him, she'd said she was ready to return to shore. She hadn't spoken another word since. Had he blown a whole week's worth of working past her boundaries only to wreck it in one afternoon? Problem was, he still didn't know what had set her off.

She stroked a smudge of sand from his faded yellow board. "Is it all right to leave them here so far from where we started?"

They'd drifted at least a mile from the SUV. "I'll buy new ones. I'm a filthy rich prince, remember?"

Yeah, sexual frustration was making him a little cranky, and he suspected no amount of walking would take the edge off. Worse yet, she didn't even rise to the bait of his crabby words full of reminders of why they'd broken up in the first place.

Fine. Who the hell knew what she needed?

He started west and she glided alongside him. The wind picked up, rustling the trees and sweeping a layer of sand around his ankles.

Shannon gasped.

"What?" Tony looked fast. "Did you step on something? Are you getting chilly?"

Shaking her head, she pointed toward the trees, branches and leaves sweeping apart to reveal the small stone chapel. "Why didn't I notice that when we drove here?"

"We approached the beach from a different angle."

"It's gorgeous." Her eyes were wide and curious.

"No need to look so surprised. I told you that we lived here 24/7. My father outfitted the island with everything we would need, from a small medical clinic to that church." He took in the white stone church, mission bell over the front doors. It wasn't large, but big enough to accommodate everyone here. His older brother had told him once it was the only thing on the island built to resemble a part of their old life.

"Were you an altar server?"

Her voice pulled him back to the present.

"With a short-lived tenure." He glanced down at her, so damn glad she was talking to him again. "I couldn't sit still and the priest frowned on an altar server bringing a bag of books and Legos to keep himself entertained during the service."

"Legos?" She started walking again. "Really?"

"Every Sunday as I sat out in the congregation. I would

have brought more, but the nanny confiscated my squirt gun."

"Don't be giving Kolby any ideas." She elbowed him lightly, then as if realizing what she'd done, picked up her pace.

Hell no, he wasn't losing ground that fast. "The nanny didn't find my knife though."

Her mouth dropped open. "You brought a knife to church?"

"I carved my initials under the pew. Wanna go see if they're still there?"

She eyed the church, then shook her head. "What's all this about today? The surfing and then stories about Legos?"

Why? He hadn't stopped to consider the reasons, just acting on instinct to keep up with the crazy, out-of-control relationship with Shannon. But he didn't do things without a reason.

His gut had pointed him in this direction because… "So that you remember there's a man in here." He thumped his chest. "As well as a filthy rich prince."

But no matter what he said or how far he got from this place, the Medina heritage coursed through his veins. Regardless of how many times he changed his name or started over, he was still Antonio Medina. And Shannon had made it clear time and time again, she didn't want that kind of life. Finally, he heard her.

Several hours later, Shannon shoved her head deeper into the industrial sized refrigerator in search of a midnight snack. A glass of warm milk just wasn't going to cut it.

Eyeing the plate of *trufas con cognac* and small cups of *crema catalana,* she debated whether to go for the brandy truffles or cold custard with caramel on top…. She picked one of each and dropped into a seat at the steel table.

Silence bounced and echoed in the cavernous kitchen. She was sleepy and cranky and edgy. And it was all Tony's fault for tormenting her with charming stories and sexy encounters on the water—then shutting her out. She nipped an edge of the liqueur-flavored chocolate. Amazing. Sighing, she sagged back in the chair.

Since returning from their surfing outing, he'd kept his distance. She'd thought they were getting closer on a deeper level when he'd shared about his sister and even the Lego, then, wham. He'd turned into the perfect—distant—host at the stilted family dinner.

Not that she'd been able to eat a bite.

Now, she was hungry, in spite of the fact she'd finished off the truffle. She spooned a scoop of custard into her mouth, although she suspected no amount of gourmet pastries would satisfy the craving gnawing her inside.

When she'd started dating Tony, she'd taken a careful, calculated risk because her hormones had been hollering for him and she'd been a long, long time without sex. Okay, so her hormones hadn't been shouting for just any man. Only Tony. A problem that didn't seem to have abated in the least.

"Ah, hell." Tony's low curse startled her upright in her seat.

Filling the archway, he studied her cautiously. He wore jeans and an open button-down that appeared hastily tossed on. He fastened two buttons in the middle, slowly shielding the cut of his six-pack abs.

Cool custard melted in her mouth, her senses singing. But her heart was aching and confused. She toyed with the neck of her robe nervously. The blue peignoir set covered her from neck to toes, but the loose-fitting chiffon and lace brushed sensual decadence against her skin. The froufrou little kitten heels to match had seemed over-the-top in her room, but now felt sexy and fun.

Her hands shook. She pressed them against the steel topped table. "Don't mind me. I'm just indulging in a midnight feeding frenzy. I highly recommend the custard cups in the back right corner of the refrigerator."

He hesitated in the archway as if making up his mind, then walked deeper into the kitchen, passing her without touching. "I was thinking in terms of something more substantial, like a sandwich."

"Are princes allowed to make their own snacks?"

"Who's going to tell me no?" He kicked the fridge closed, his hands full of deli meat, cheese and lettuce, a jar of spread tucked under his elbow.

"Good point." She swirled another spoonful. "I hope the cook doesn't mind I've been foraging around. I actually used the stove, too, when I cooked a late night snack for Kolby. He woke up hungry."

Tony glanced over from his sandwich prep. "Is he okay?"

"Just a little homesick." Her eyes took in the sight of the Tony she remembered, a man who wore jeans low-slung on his hips. And rumpled hair...she enjoyed the disobedient swirls in his hair most.

"I'm sorry for that." His shoulders tensed under the loose chambray.

"Don't get me wrong, I appreciate how everyone has gone out of their way for him. The gourmet kid cuisine makes meals an adventure. I wish I had thought to tell him rolled tortillas are snakes and caterpillars." Pasta was called worms or a nest. "I'm even becoming addicted to Nutella crepes. But sometimes, a kid just needs the familiar feel of home."

"I understand." His sandwich piled high on a plate, he took a seat—across from her rather than beside as he would have in the past.

"Of course you do." She clenched her hands together to keep from reaching out to him. "Well, I'll have to make sure the cook knows I tried to put everything back where I found it."

"He's more likely to be upset that you called him a cook rather than a chef."

"Ah, a chef. Right. All those nuances between your world and mine." How surreal to be having a conversation with a prince over a totally plebian hoagie.

Tony swiped at his mouth with a linen napkin and draped it over his knee again. "You ran in a pretty high-finance world with your husband."

Her husband's dirty money.

She shoved away the custard bowl. Thoughts of the media regurgitating that mess for public consumption made her nauseated. She wasn't close to her in-laws, but they would suffer hearing their precious son's reputation smeared again.

And God help them all if her own secrets were somehow discovered.

Best to lie low and keep to herself. Although she was finding it increasingly difficult to imagine how she would restart her life. Even if she was able to renew her teaching credentials, who was going to want to hire the infamous Medina Mistress who'd once been married to a crook? When this mess was over, she would have to dig deep to figure out how to recreate a life for herself and Kolby.

Could Tony be having second thoughts about their relationship? His strict code of honor would dictate he take care of her until the media storm passed, but she didn't want to be his duty.

They'd dated. They'd had sex. But she only just realized how much of their relationship had been superficial as they both dodged discussing deeper, darker parts of their past.

Still, she wasn't ready to plunge into the murkiest of waters that made up her life with Nolan. She wasn't even sure right now if Tony would want to hear.

But regardless of how things turned out between them, she needed him to understand the real her. "I didn't grow up with all those trappings of Nolan's world. My dad was a high school science teacher and a coach. My mom was the elementary school secretary. We had enough money, but we were by no means wealthy." She hesitated, realizing… "You probably already know all of that."

"Why would you think so?" he asked, although he hadn't denied what she said.

"If you've had to be so worried about security and your identity, it makes sense you or your lawyer or some security team you've hired would vet people in your life."

"That would be the wise thing to do."

"And you're a smart man."

"I haven't always acted wisely around you."

"You've been a perfect gentleman this week and you know it," she said, as close as she could come to hinting that she ached for his touch, his mouth on her body, the familiar rise of pleasure and release he could bring.

Tony shrugged and tore into his sandwich again, a grandfather clock tolling once in the background.

"Kolby thinks we're on vacation."

"Good." He finished chewing, tendons in his strong neck flexing. "That's how he should remember this time in his life."

"It's unreal how you and your father have shielded him from the tension in your relationship."

"Obviously not well enough to fool you." His boldly handsome face gave nothing away.

"I know some about your history, and it's tough to miss how little the two of you talk. Your father's an interesting man." She'd enjoyed after-dinner discussions with Enrique and Eloisa about current events and the latest book they'd read.

The old king may have isolated himself from the world, but he'd certainly stayed abreast with the latest news. The discussions had been enlightening on a number of levels, such as how the old king wasn't as clipped and curt with his daughter as he was with Tony.

Tony stared at the last half of his snack, tucking a straggly piece of lettuce back inside. "What did you make for Kolby?"

His question surprised her, but if it kept him talking…

"French toast. It's one of his favorite comfort foods. He likes for me to cut the toast into slices so he can dip it into the syrup. Independence means a lot, even to a three-year-old." It meant a lot to adults. She reached for her bowl to scrape the final taste of custard and licked the spoon clean. The caramel taste exploded into her starving senses like music in her mouth.

Pupils widening with awareness until they nearly pushed away his brown irises, Tony stared back at her across the table, intense, aroused. Her body recognized the signs in him well even if he didn't move so much as an inch closer.

She set the spoon down, the tiny clink echoing in the empty kitchen. "Tony, why are you still awake?"

"I'm a night owl. Some might call me an insomniac."

"An insomniac? I didn't know that." She laughed darkly. "Although how could I since we've never spent an entire night together? Have you had the problem long?"

"I've always been this way." He turned the plate around on the table. "My mother tried everything from warm milk to a 'magic' blanket before just letting me stay up. She used to cook for me too, late at night."

"Your mother, the queen, cooked?" She inched to the edge of her chair, leaning on her elbows, hoping to hold his attention and keep him talking.

"She may have been royalty even before she married my father, but there are plenty in Europe with blue blood and little money." Shadows chased each other across his eyes. "My mother grew up learning the basics of managing her own house. She insisted we boys have run of the kitchen. There were so many everyday places that were off-limits to us for safety reasons, she wanted us to have the normalcy of popping in and out of the kitchen for snacks."

Like any other child. A child who happened to live in a sixteenth-century castle. She liked his mother, a woman she would never meet but felt so very close to at the moment. "What did she cook for you?"

"A Cyclops."

"Excuse me?"

"It's a fried egg with a buttered piece of bread on top." He swirled his hand over his plate as if he could spin an image into reality. "The bread has a hole pinched out of the middle so the egg yolk peeks out like a—"

"Like a Cyclops. I see. My mom called it a Popeye." And with the memory of a simple egg dish, she felt the connection to Tony spin and gain strength again.

He glanced up, a half smile kicking into his one cheek. "Cyclops appealed to the bloodthirsty little boy in me. Just like Kolby and the caterpillar and snake pasta."

To hell with distance and waiting for him to reach out, she covered his hand with hers. "Your mother sounds wonderful."

He nodded briefly. "I believe she was."

"Believe?"

"I have very few memories of her before she...died." He turned his hand over and stroked hers with his thumb. "The beach. A blanket. Food."

"Scents do tend to anchor our memories more firmly."

More shadows drifted through his eyes, darker this time, like storm clouds. *Died* seemed such a benign word to describe the assassination of a young mother, killed because she'd married a king. A vein pulsed visibly in Tony's temple, faster by the second. He'd dealt with such devastating circumstances in life honorably, while her husband had turned to stealing and finally, to taking the ultimate coward's way out.

She held herself very still, unthreatening. Her heart ached for him on a whole new and intense level. "What do you remember about when she died? About leaving San Rinaldo?"

"Not much really." He stayed focused on their connected hands, tracing the veins on her wrist with exaggerated concentration. "I was only five."

So he'd told her before. But she wasn't buying his nonchalance. "Traumatic events seem to stick more firmly in our memory. I recall a car accident when I couldn't have been more than two." She wouldn't back down now, not when she was so close to understanding the man behind the smiles and bold gestures. "I still remember the bright red of the Volkswagen bug."

"You probably saw pictures of the car later," he said dismissively, then looked up sharply, aggressively full of bravado. The storm clouds churned faster with each throb of the vein on his temple. He stroked up her arm with unmistakable sensual intent. "How much longer are you going to wait before you ask me to kiss you again? Because right now, I'm so on fire for you, I want to test out the sturdiness of that table."

"Tony, can you even hear yourself?" she asked, frustrated and even a bit insulted by the way he was jerking her around. "One minute you're Prince Romance and Restraint, the next you're ignoring me over dinner. Then you're spilling your guts. Now, you proposition me—and not too suavely, I might add. Quite frankly, you're giving me emotional whiplash."

His arms twitched, thick roped muscles bulging against his sleeves with restrained power. "Make no mistake, I have wanted you every second of every day. It's all I can do not to haul you against me right now and to hell with the dozens of people that might walk in. But today on the water and tonight here, I'm just not sure this crazy life of mine is good enough for you."

Her body burned in response to his words even as her mind blared a warning. Tony had felt the increasing connection too, and it scared him. So he'd tried to run her off with the crude offer of sex on the table.

Well too damn bad for him, she wasn't backing down. She'd wanted this, *him,* for too long to turn away.

Ten

He'd wanted Shannon back in his bed, but somewhere between making a sandwich and talking about eggs, she'd peeled away walls, exposing thoughts and memories that were better forgotten. They distracted. Hurt. Served no damn purpose.

Anger grated his raw insides. "So? What'll it be? Sex here or in your room?"

She didn't flinch and she didn't leave. Her soft hand stayed on top of his as she looked at him with sad eyes behind her glasses. "Is that what this week has been about?"

He let his gaze linger on the vee of her frothy nightgown set. Lace along the neckline traced into the curve of her breasts the way his hands ached to explore. "I've been clear from the start about what I want."

"Are you so sure about that?"

"What the hell is that supposed to mean?" he snapped.

Sliding from her chair, she circled the table toward him, her heels clicking against the tile. She stopped beside him, the hem of her nightgown set swirling against his leg. "Don't confuse me with your mother."

"Good God, there's not a chance of that." He toppled her into his lap and lowered his head, determined to prove it to her.

"Wait." She stopped him with a hand flattened to his chest just above the two closed buttons. Her palm cooled his overheated skin, calming and stirring, but then she'd always been a mix of contradictions. "You suffered a horrible trauma as a child. No one should lose a parent, especially in such an awful way. I wish you could have been spared that."

"I wish my *mother* had been spared." His hands clenched in her robe, his fists against her back.

"And I can't help but wonder if you helping me—a mother with a young child—is a way to put her ghost to rest. Putting your own ghosts to rest in the process."

Given the crap that had shaken down in his past, he'd done a fine job turning his life around. Frustration poured acid on his burning gut. "You've spent a lot of time thinking about this."

"What you told me this afternoon and tonight brought things into focus."

"Well, thanks for the psychoanalysis." His words came out harsh, but right now he needed her to walk away. "I would offer to pay you for the services, but I wouldn't want to start another fight."

"Sounds to me like you're spoiling for one now." Her eyes softened with more of that concern that grated along his insides. "I'm sorry if I overstepped and hit a nerve."

A nerve? She'd performed a root canal on his emotions. His brain echoed with the retort of gunfire stuttering, aimed at him, his brothers. His mother. He searched for what to say to shut down this conversation, but he wasn't sure of anything other than his need for a serious, body-draining jog on the beach. Problem was? The beach circled right back around to this place.

Easing from his lap, she stood and he tamped down the swift kick of disappointment. Except she didn't leave. She extended her hand and linked her fingers with his.

Just a simple connection, but since he was raw to the core, her touch fired deep.

"Shannon," he said between teeth clenched tight with restraint, "I'm about a second from snapping here. So unless you want me buried heart deep inside you in the next two minutes, you need to go back to your room."

Her hold stayed firm, cool and steady.

"Shannon, damn it all, you don't know what you're doing. You don't want any part of the mood I'm in." Her probing may have brought on the mood, but he wouldn't let it contaminate her.

Angling down with slow precision, she pressed her lips to his. Not moving. Only their mouths and hands linked.

He wanted—needed—to move her away gently. But his fingers curled around the softness of her arm.

"Shanny," he whispered against her mouth, "tell me to leave."

"Not a chance. I only have one question."

"Go ahead." He braced himself for another emotional root canal.

She brought his hand to her chest, pressing his palm against her breast. "Do you have a condom?"

Relief splashed over him like a tidal wave. "Hell, yes, I have one, two in fact, in my wallet. Because even when we're not talking, I know the way we are together could combust at any second. And I will always, always make sure you're protected and safe."

Standing, he scooped her into his arms. Purring her approval, she hooked her hands behind his neck and tipped her face for a full kiss. The soft cushion of her breasts against his chest sent his libido into overdrive. He throbbed against the sweet curve of her hip. At the sweep of tongue, the taste of caramel and *her,* he fought the urge to follow through on the impulse to have her here, now, on the table.

He sketched his mouth along her jaw, down to her collarbone, the scent of her lavender body wash reminding him of shared showers at his place. "We need to go upstairs."

"The pantry is closer." She nipped his bottom lip. "And empty. We can lock the door. I need you now."

"Are you su—?"

"Don't even say it." She dipped her hands into the neckline of his loose shirt, her fingernails sinking insistently deep. "I want you. No waiting."

Her words closed down arguments and rational thought. He made a sure-footed beeline across the tiled floor toward the pantry. Shannon nuzzled his neck, kissed along his jaw, all the while murmuring disjointed words of need that stoked him higher—made his feet move faster. As he walked, her silky blond hair and whispery robe trailed, her sexy little heels dangling from her toes.

Dipping at the door, he flipped the handle and shouldered inside the pantry, a food storage area the size of a small bedroom. The scent of hanging dried herbs coated the air, the smell earthy. He slid her glasses from her face and set them aside on a shelf next to rows of bottled water.

As the door eased closed, the space darkened and his

other senses increased. She reached for the light switch and he clasped her wrist, stopping her.

"I don't need light to see you. Your beautiful body is fired into my memory." His fingers crawled up her leg, bunching the frothy gown along her soft thigh, farther still to just under the curve of her buttocks. "Just the feel of you is about more than my willpower can take."

"I don't want your willpower. I'm fed up with your restraint. Give me the uninhibited old Tony back." Her husky voice filled the room with unmistakable desire.

Pressing her hips closer, he tasted down her neck, charting his way to her breasts. An easy swipe cleared the fabric from her shoulders and he found a taut nipple. Damn straight he didn't need light. He knew her body, knew just how to lave and tease the taut peak until she tore at his shirt with frantic hands.

His buttons popped and cool air blanketed his back, warm Shannon writhing against his front. Hooking a finger along the rim of her bikini panties, he stroked her silky smooth stomach. Tugging lightly, he started the scrap of fabric downward until she shimmied them the rest of the way off.

Stepping closer, the silky gown bunched between them, she flattened her hand to the fly of his jeans. He went harder against the pleasure of her touch. Shannon. Just Shannon.

She unzipped his pants and freed his arousal. Clasping him in her fist, she stroked once, and again, her thumb working over his head with each glide. His eyes slammed shut.

Her other hand slipped into his back pocket and pulled out his wallet. A light crackle sounded as she tore into the packet. Her deft fingers rolled the sheath down the length of him with torturous precision.

"Now," she demanded softly against his neck. "Here. On the stepstool or against the door, I don't care as long as you're inside me."

Gnawing need chewed through the last of his restraint. She wanted this. He craved her. No more waiting. Tony backed her against the solid panel of the door, her fingernails digging into his shoulders, his back, lower as she tucked her hand inside his jeans and boxers.

Arching, urging, she hooked her leg around his, opening for him. Her shoe clattered to the floor but she didn't seem to notice or care. He nudged at her core, so damp and ready for him. He throbbed—and thrust.

Velvet heat clamped around him, drew him deeper, sent sparks shooting behind his eyelids. In the darkened room, the pure essence of Shannon went beyond anything he'd experienced. And the importance of that expanded inside him, threatening to drive him to his knees.

So he focused on her, searching with his hands and mouth, moving inside and stroking outside to make sure she was every bit as encompassed by the mind-numbing ecstasy. She rocked faster against him. Her sighs came quicker, her moans of pleasure higher and louder until he captured the sound, kissing her and thrusting with his tongue and body. He explored the soft inside of her mouth, savoring the soft clamp of her gripping him with spasms he knew signaled her approaching orgasm.

Teeth gritted, he held back his own finish. Her face pressed to his neck. Her chants of *yes, yes, yes* synced with his pulse and pounding. Still, he held back, determined to take her there once more. She bowed away from the door, into him, again and again until her teeth sunk into his shoulder on a stifled cry of pleasure.

The scent of her, of slick sex and *them* mixed with the already earthy air.

Finally—*finally*—he could let go. The wave of pleasure pulsing through him built higher, roaring louder in his ears. He'd been too long without her. The wave crested. Release crashed over him. Rippling through him. Shifting the ground under his feet until his forehead thumped against the door.

Hauling her against his chest, heart still galloping, as they both came back down to earth in the pantry.

The pantry, for God's sake?

His chances of staying away from Shannon again were slim. That path didn't work for either of them. But if they were going to be together, he would make sure their next encounter was total fantasy material.

Sun glinting along the crystal clear pool, Shannon tugged Kolby's T-shirt over his head and slid his feet into tiny Italian leather sandals. She'd spent the morning splashing with her son and Tony's sister, and she wasn't close to working off pent-up energy. Even the soothing ripple of the heated waters down the fountain rock wall hadn't stilled the jangling inside her.

After making love in the pantry, she and Tony had locked themselves in her room where he'd made intense and thorough love to her. Her skin remembered the rasp of his beard against her breasts, her stomach, the insides of her thighs. How could she still crave even more from him? She should be in search of a good nap rather than wondering when she could get Tony alone again.

Of course she would have to find him first.

He'd left via her balcony just as the morning sun peeked over the horizon. Now that big orange glow was directly overhead and no word from him. She deflated her son's water wings. The hissing air and the maternal ritual reminded her of Tony's revelations just before they'd ended up in the closet.

Could he be avoiding her to dodge talking further? He'd made no secret of using sex to skirt the painful topic. She couldn't even blame him when she'd been guilty of the same during their affair. What did this do to their deadline to return home?

Kolby yanked the hem of her cover-up. "Want another movie."

"We'll see, sweetie." Kolby was entranced by the large home theater, but then what child wouldn't be?

Tony's half sister shaded her eyes in the lounger next to them, an open paperback in her other hand. "I can take him in if you want to stay outside. Truly, I don't mind." She toyed with her silver shell necklace, straightening the conch charm.

"But you're reading. And aren't you leaving this afternoon? I don't want to keep you from your packing."

"Do you honestly think any guest of Enrique Medina is bothered by packing their own suitcases? Get real." She snorted lightly. "I have plenty of time. Besides, I've been wanting to check out the new Disney movie for my library's collection."

She'd learned Eloisa was a librarian, which explained the satchel of books she'd brought along. Her husband was an architect who specialized in restoring historic landmarks. They were an unpretentious couple caught up in a maelstrom. "What if the screening room doesn't have the movie you w—" She stopped short. "Of course they have whatever you're looking for on file."

"A bit intimidating, isn't it?" Eloisa pulled on her wraparound cover-up, tugging her silver necklace out so the conch charm was visible. "I didn't grow up with all of this and I suspect you didn't, either."

Shannon rubbed her arms, shivering in spite of the eighty-degree day. "How do you keep from letting it overwhelm you?"

"I wish I could offer you reassurance or answers, but honestly I'm still figuring out how to deal with all of this myself. I had only begun to get to know my birth father a few months ago." She looked back at the mission-style mansion, her eyebrows pinching together. "Now the whole royal angle has gone public. They haven't figured out about me. Yet. That's why we're here this week, to talk with Enrique and his attorneys, to set up some preemptive strikes."

"I'm sorry."

Thank God Eloisa had the support of her husband. And Tony had been there for her. Who was there for him? Even his brothers hadn't shown up beyond sterile conference calls.

"You have nothing to apologize for, Shannon. I'm only saying it's okay to feel overwhelmed. Cut yourself some slack and do what you can to stay level. Let me watch a movie with your son while you swim or enjoy a bubble bath or take a nap. It's okay."

Indecision warred inside her. These past couple of weeks she'd had more help with Kolby than since he was born. Guilt tweaked her maternal instincts.

"Please, Mama?" Kolby sidled closer to Eloisa. "I like Leesa."

Ah, and just like that, her maternal guilt worried in another direction, making her fret that she hadn't given her son enough play dates or socialization. Funny how a mother worried no matter what.

Shannon nodded to Tony's sister. "If you're absolutely sure."

"He's a cutie, and I'm guessing he will be asleep before

the halfway point. Enjoy the pool a while longer. It'll be good practice for me to spend time with him." She smiled whimsically as she ruffled his damp hair. "Jonah and I are hoping to have a few of our own someday."

"Thank you. I accept gratefully." Shannon remembered well what it felt like to be young and in love and hopeful for the future. She couldn't bring herself to regret Nolan since he'd given her Kolby. "I hope we'll have the chance to speak again before you leave this afternoon?"

"Don't worry." Eloisa winked. "I imagine we'll see each other again."

With a smile, Shannon hugged her little boy close, inhaling his baby fresh scent with a hint of chlorine.

He squirmed, his cheeks puffed with a wide smile. "Wanna go."

She pressed a quick kiss to his forehead. "Be good for Mrs. Landis."

Eloisa took his hand. "We'll be fine."

Kolby waved over his shoulder without a backward glance.

Too restless for a bath or nap, she eyed the pool and whipped off her cover-up. Laps sounded like the wisest option. Diving in, she stared through the chlorinated depths until her eyes burned, forcing her to squeeze them shut. She lost herself in the rhythm of slicing her arms through the heated water, no responsibilities, no outside world. Just the *thump, thump, thump* of her heart mingling with the roar of the water passing over her ears.

Five laps later, she flipped underwater and resurfaced face up for a backstroke. She opened her eyes and, oh my, the view had changed. Tony stood by the waterfall in black board shorts.

Whoa. Her stomach lurched into a swan dive. Tony's bronzed chest sprinkled with hair brought memories of their night together, senses on overload from the darkened herb-scented pantry, later in the brightly lighted luxury of her bedroom. Who would have thought dried oregano and rosemary could be aphrodisiacs?

His eyes hooked on her crocheted two piece with thorough and unmistakable admiration. He knew every inch of her body and made his appreciation clear whether she wore high-end garb or her simple black waitress uniform, wilted from a full shift. God, how he was working his way into her heart as well as her life.

She swam toward the edge with wide lazy strokes. "Is Kolby okay?"

"Enjoying the movie and popcorn." He knelt by the edge, his elbow on one knee drawing her eye to the nautical compass tattooed on his bicep. "Although with the way his head is drooping, chances are he'll be asleep anytime now."

"Thank you for checking on him." She resisted the urge to ask Tony what *he*'d been doing since he left her early this morning.

"Not a problem." His fingers played through the water in front of her without touching but so close the swirls caressed her breasts. "I said I intended to romance you and I got sidetracked. I apologize for that. The woman I'm with should be treated like a princess."

His *princess?* Shock loosened her hold on the edge of the pool. Tony caught her arm quickly and eased her from the water to sit next to him. His gaze swept her from soaking wet hair to dripping toes. Appreciation smoked, darkening his eyes to molten heat she recognized well.

He tipped her chin with a knuckle scarred from handling sailing lines. "Are you ready to be royally romanced?"

Eleven

A five-minute walk later, Tony flattened his palm to Shannon's back and guided her down the stone path leading from the mansion to the greenhouse. Her skin, warmed from the sun, heated through her thin cover-up. Soon, he hoped to see and feel every inch of her without barriers.

He'd spent the morning arranging a romantic backdrop for their next encounter. Finding privacy was easier said than done on this island, but he was persistent and creative. Anticipation ramped inside him.

He was going to make things right with her. She deserved to be treated like a princess, and he had the resources to follow through. His mind leaped ahead to all the ways he could romance her back on the mainland now that he understood her better—once he fulfilled the remaining weeks he'd promised his father.

A kink started in his neck.

Squeezing his hand lightly, she followed him along the

rocky path, the mansion smaller on the horizon. Few trees stood between them and the glass building ahead. Early on, Enrique had cleared away foliage for security purposes.

"Where are we going?"

"You'll see soon."

Farther from shore, a sprawling oak had been saved. The mammoth trunk declared it well over a hundred years old. As a kid, he'd begged to keep this one for climbing. His father had gruffly agreed. The memory kicked over him, itchy and ill timed.

He brushed aside a branch, releasing a flock of butterflies soaring toward the conservatory, complete with two wings branching off the main structure. "This is the greenhouse I told you about. It also has a café style room."

Enrique had done his damnedest to give his sons a "normal" childhood, as much as he could while never letting them off the island. Tony had undergone some serious culture shock after he'd left. At least working on a shrimper had given him time to absorb the mainland in small bites. Back then, he'd even opted to rent a sailboat for a home rather than an apartment.

As they walked past a glass gazebo, Shannon tipped her face to his. Sunlight streaked through the trees, bathing her face. "Is that why the movie room has more of a theater feel?"

Nodding, he continued, "There's a deli at the ferry station and an ice cream parlor at the creamery. I thought we could take Kolby there."

He hoped she heard his intent to try with her son as well, to give this relationship a real chance at working.

"Kolby likes strawberry flavored best," she said simply.

"I'll remember that," he assured her. And he meant it.

"We also have a small dental clinic. And of course there's the chapel."

"They've thought of everything." Her mouth oohed over a birdbath with doves drinking along the edge.

"My father always said a monarch's job was to see to the needs of his people. This island became his minikingdom. Because of the isolation, he needed to make accommodations, try to create a sense of normalcy." Clouds whispered overhead and Tony guided her faster through the garden. "He's started a new round of renovations. A number of his staff members have died of old age. That presents a new set of challenges as he replaces them with employees who aren't on the run, people who have options."

"Like Alys."

"Exactly," he said, just as the skies opened up with an afternoon shower. "Now, may I take you to lunch? I know this great little out-of-the-way place with kick-ass fresh flowers."

"Lead on." Shannon tugged up the hood on her cover-up and raced alongside him.

As the rain pelted faster, he charged up the stone steps leading to the conservatory entrance. Tony threw open the double doors, startling a sparrow into flight around the high glass ceiling in the otherwise deserted building. A quick glance around assured him that yes, everything was exactly as he'd ordered.

"Ohmigod, Tony!" Shannon gasped, taking in the floral feast for her eyes as well as her nose. "This is breathtaking."

Flipping the hood from her head, she plunged deeper into the spacious greenhouse where a riot of scents and colors waited. Classical music piped lowly from hidden speakers. Ferns dangled overhead. Unlike crowded nurseries she'd visited in the past, this space sprawled more like an indoor floral park.

An Italian marble fountain trickled below a skylight, water spilling softly from a carved snake's mouth as it curled around some reclining Roman god. Wrought iron screens sported hydrangeas and morning glories twining throughout, benches in front for reading or meditation. Potted palms and cacti added height to the interior landscape. Tiered racks of florist's buckets with cut flowers stretched along a far wall. She spun under the skylight, immersing herself in the thick perfume, sunbeams and Debussy's *Nocturnes*.

While she could understand Tony's point about not wanting to be isolated here indefinitely, she appreciated the allure of the magical retreat Enrique had created. Even the rain *tap, tap, tapping* overhead offered nature's lyrical accent to the soft music.

Slowing her spin, she found Tony staring at her with undeniable arousal. Tony, and only Tony because the space appeared otherwise deserted. Her skin prickled with awareness at the muscular display of him in nothing but board shorts and deck shoes.

"Are we alone?" she asked.

"Completely," he answered, gesturing toward a little round table set for two, with wine and finger foods. "Help yourself. There are stuffed mussels, fried squid, vegetable skewers, cold olives and cheese."

She strode past him, without touching but so close a magnetic field seemed to activate, urging her to seal her body to his.

"It's been so wonderful here indulging in grown-up food after so many meals of chicken nuggets and pizza." She broke off a corner of ripe white cheese and popped it in her mouth.

"Then you're going to love the beverage selection." Tony scooped up a bottle from the middle of the table. "Red wine from Basque country or sherry from southern Spain?"

"Red, please. But can we wait a moment on the food? I want to see everything here first."

"I was hoping you would say that." He passed her a crystal glass, half full.

She sipped, staring at him over the rim. "Perfect."

"And there's still more." His fingers linked with hers, he led her past an iron screen to a secluded corner.

Vines grew tangled and dense over the windows, the sun through the glass roof muted by rivulets of rain. A chaise longue was tucked in a corner. Flower petals speckled the furniture and floor. Everything was so perfect, so beautiful, it brought tears to her eyes. God, it still scared her how much she wanted to trust her feelings, trust the signals coming from Tony.

To hide her eyes until she could regain control, she rushed to the crystal vase of mixed flowers on the end table and buried her face in the bouquet. "What a unique blend of fragrances."

"It's a specially ordered arrangement. Each flower was selected for you because of its meaning."

Touched by the detailed thought he'd put into the encounter, she pivoted to face him. "You told me once you wanted to wrap me in flowers."

"That's the idea here." His arms banded around her waist. "And I was careful to make sure there will be no thorns. Only pleasure."

If only life could be that simple. With their time here running out, she couldn't resist.

"You're sure we won't be interrupted?" She set her wine glass on the end table and linked her fingers behind his neck. "No surveillance cameras or telephoto lenses?"

"Completely certain. There are security cameras outside, but none inside. I've given the staff the afternoon off and our guards are not Peeping Toms. We are totally and completely alone." He anchored her against him, the rigid length of his arousal pressing into her stomach with a hefty promise.

"You prepared for this." And she wanted this, wanted him. But... "I'm not sure I like being so predictable."

"You are anything but predictable. I've never met a more confusing person in my life." He tugged a damp lock of her hair. "Any more questions?"

She inhaled deeply, letting the scents fill her with courage. "Who can take off faster the other person's clothes?"

"Now there's a challenge I can't resist." He bunched her cover-up in his hands and peeled the soft cotton over her head.

Shaking her hair free, she leaned into him just as he slanted his mouth over hers. His fingers made fast work of the ties to her bathing suit top. The crocheted triangles fell away, baring her to the steamy greenhouse air.

She nipped his ear where a single dot-shaped scar stayed from a healed-over piercing. A teenage rebellion, he'd told her once. She could envision him on a Spanish galleon, a swarthy and buffed pirate king.

For a moment, for *this* moment, she let herself indulge in foolish fantasies, no fears. She would allow the experience to sweep her away as smoothly as she brushed off his board shorts. She pushed aside the sterner responsible voice inside her that insisted she remember past mistakes and tread cautiously.

"It's been too damn long." He thumbed off her swimsuit bottom.

"Uh, hello?" She kicked the last fabric barrier away and

prayed other barriers could be as easily discarded. "It's been less than eight hours since you left my room."

"Too long."

She played her fingers along the cut of his sculpted chest, down the flat plane of his washboard stomach. Pressing her lips to his shoulder, she kissed her way toward his arm until she grazed the different texture of his tattooed flesh—inked with a black nautical compass. "I've always wanted to ask why you chose this particular tattoo."

His muscles bunched and twitched. "It symbolizes being able to find my way home."

"There's still so much I don't know about you." Concerns trickled through her like the rain trying to find its way inside.

"Hey, we're here to escape. All that can wait." He slipped her glasses from her face and placed them on the end table.

Parting through the floral arrangement to the middle, he slipped out an orchid and pinched off the flower. He trailed the bloom along her nose, her cheekbones and jaw in a silky scented swirl. "For magnificence."

Her knees went wobbly and she sat on the edge of the chaise, tapestry fabric rough on the backs on her thighs, rose-petal smooth. He tucked the orchid behind her ear, easing her back until she reclined.

Returning to the vase, he tugged free a long stalk with indigo buds and explored the length of her arm, then one finger at a time. Then over her stomach to her other hand and back up again in a shivery path that left her breathless.

"Blue salvia," he said, "because I think of you night and day."

His words stirred her as much as the glide of the flower

over her shoulder. Then he placed it on the tiny pillow under her head.

A pearly calla lily chosen next, he traced her collarbone before lightly dipping between her breasts.

"Shannon," he declared hoarsely, "I chose this lily because you are a majestic beauty."

Detouring, he sketched the underside of her breast and looped round again and again, each circle smaller until he teased the dusky tip. Her body pulled tight and tingly. Her back arched into the sweet sensation and he transferred his attention to her other breast, repeating the delicious pattern.

Reaching for him, she clutched his shoulders, aching to urge him closer. "Tony…"

Gently, he clasped her wrists and tucked them at her sides. "No touching or I'll stop."

"Really?"

"Probably not, because I can't resist you." He left the lily in her open palm. "But how about you play along anyway? I guarantee you'll like the results."

Dark eyes glinting with an inner light, Tony eased free… "A coral rose for passion."

His words raspy, his face intense, he skimmed the bud across her stomach, lower. Lower still. Her head fell back, her eyes closed as she wondered just how far he would dare go.

The silky teasing continued from her hip inward, daring more and even more. A husky moan escaped between her clenched lips.

Still, he continued until the rose caressed…oh my. Her knee draped to the side giving him, giving the flower, fuller access as he teased her. Gooseflesh sprinkled her skin. Her body focused on the feelings and perfumes stoking desire higher.

A warm breath steamed over her stomach with only a second's warning before his mouth replaced the flower. Her fingers twitched into a fist, crushing the lily and releasing a fresh burst of perfume. A flick of his tongue, alternated with gentle suckles, caressed and coaxed her toward completion.

Her head thrashed as she chased her release. He took her to the brink, then retreated, drawing out the pleasure until the pressure inside her swelled and throbbed...

And bloomed.

A cry of pleasure burst free and she didn't bother holding it back. She rode the sensation, gasping in floral-tinged breaths.

His bold hands stroked upward as he slid over her, blanketing her with his hard, honed body. She hooked a languid leg over his hip. Her arm draped his shoulders as she drew him toward her, encouraging him to press inside.

The smell of crushed flowers clung to his skin as she kissed her way along his chest, back up his neck. He filled her, stretched her, moved inside her. She was surprised to feel desire rising again to a fevered pitch. Writhing, she lost herself in the barrage of sensations. The bristle of his chest hair against her breasts. The silky softness of flower petals against her back.

And the scents—she gasped in the perfect blend of musk and sex and earthy greenhouse. She raked his back, broad and strong and yet so surprisingly gentle, too.

He was working his way not only into her body but into her heart. When had she ever stood a chance at resisting him? As much as she tried to tell herself it was only physical, only an affair, she knew this man had come to mean so much more to her. He reached her in ways no one ever had before.

She grappled at the hard planes of his back, completion so close all over again.

"Let go and I'll catch you," he vowed against her ear and she believed him.

For the first time in so long, she totally trusted.

The magnitude exploded inside her, blasting through barriers. Pleasure filled every niche. Muscles knotted in Tony's back as he tensed over her and growled his own hoarse completion against her ear.

Staring up at the rain-splattered skylight, tears burning her eyes again, she held Tony close. She felt utterly bare and unable to hide any longer. She'd trusted him with her body.

Now the time had come to trust him with her secrets.

Twelve

Tony watched Shannon on his iPhone as she talked to Kolby. She'd assured him that she wanted to stay longer in their greenhouse getaway, once she checked on her son.

Raindrops pattered slowly on the skylight, the afternoon shower coming to an end. Sunshine refracted off the moisture, casting prisms throughout the indoor garden.

He had Shannon back in his bed and in his life and he intended to do anything it took to keep her there. The chemistry between them, the connection—it was one of a kind. The way she'd calmly handled his bizarre family set-up, keeping her down-to-earth ways in the face of so much wealth… Finally, he'd found a woman he could trust, a woman he could spend his life with. Coming back to the island had been a good thing after all, since it had made him realize how unaffected she was by the trappings. In a compass, she would be the magnet, a grounding center.

And he owed her so much better than he'd delivered thus

far. He'd wrecked Shannon's life. It was up to him to fix it. Here, alone with her in the bright light of day, he couldn't avoid the truth.

They would get married.

The decision settled inside him with a clean fit, so much so he wondered why he hadn't decided so resolutely before now. His feelings for her ran deep. He knew she cared for him, too. And marrying each other would solve her problems.

They were making progress. He could tell she'd been swayed by the flowers, the ambience.

A plan formed in his mind. Later tonight he would take her to the chapel, lit with candles, and he would propose, while the lovemaking they'd shared here was still fresh in her memory.

Now he just had to figure out the best way to persuade her to say yes.

Thumbing the off button, she disconnected her call. "The nanny says Kolby has only just woken up and she's feeding him a snack." She passed his phone to him and curled against his side on the chaise. "Thanks for not teasing me about being overprotective. I can't help but worry when I'm not with him."

"I would too, if he was mine," he said. Then her surprised expression prompted him to continue, "Why do you look shocked?"

"No offense meant." She smoothed a hand along his chest. "It's just obvious you and he haven't connected."

Something he would need to rectify in order to be a part of Shannon's life. "I will never let you or him down the way his father did."

She winced and he could feel her drawing back into herself. He wanted all barriers gone between them as fully as they'd tossed aside their clothes.

"Hey, Shannon, stay with me here." He cupped her bare hip. "I asked you before if your husband hit you and you said no. Did you lie about that?"

Sitting up abruptly, she gathered her swimsuit off the floor.

"Let's get dressed and then we can talk." She yanked on the suit bottom briskly.

Waiting, he slid on his board shorts. She tied the bikini strings behind her neck with exaggerated effort, all the while staring at the floor. A curtain of tousled blond locks covered her face. Just when he'd begun to give up on getting an answer, she straightened, shaking her hair back over her shoulders.

"I was telling the truth when I said Nolan never laid a hand on me. But there are things I need to explain in order for you to understand why it's so difficult for me to accept help." Determination creased her face. "Nolan was always a driven man. His perfectionism made him successful in business. And I'd been brought up to believe marriage is forever. How could I leave a man because he didn't like the way I hung clothes in the closet?"

He forced his hands to stay loose on his knees, keeping his body language as unthreatening as possible when he already sensed he would want to beat the hell out of Nolan Crawford by the end of this conversation—if he wasn't already dead.

Plucking a flower petal from her hair, she rubbed the coral-colored patch between two fingers. "Do you know how many people laughed at me because I was upset that he didn't want me to work? He said he wanted us to have more time together. Somehow any plans I made with others were disrupted. After a while I lost contact with my friends."

The picture of isolation came together in his head with startling clarity. He understood the claustrophobic feeling of being cut off from the rest of the world. Although he couldn't help but think his father's need to protect his children differed from an obsessive—abusive—husband dominating his wife. Rage simmered, ready to boil.

She scooped her cover-up from the floor and clutched it to her stomach. "Then I got pregnant. Splitting up became more complicated."

Hating like hell the helpless feeling, he passed her glasses back to her. It was damn little, but all he could see her accepting from him right now.

With a wobbly smile, she slid them on her face and seemed to take strength from them. "When Kolby was about thirteen months old, he spiked a scary high fever while I was alone with him. Nolan had always gone with us to pediatric check-ups. At the ER, I was a mess trying to give the insurance information. I had no idea what to tell them, because Nolan had insisted I not 'worry' about such things as medical finances. That day triggered something in me. I needed to take care of my son."

He took her too-cold hand and rubbed it between his.

"Looking back now I see the signs were there. Nolan's computer and cell phone were password protected. He considered it an invasion of privacy if I asked who he was speaking to. I thought he was cheating. I never considered…"

He squeezed her hand in silent encouragement.

"So I decided to learn more about the finances, because if I needed to leave him, I had to make sure my son's future was protected and not spirited away to some Cayman account." She fidgeted, her fingers landing on the blue salvia—*I think of you often* took on a darker meaning. "I was lucky enough to figure out his computer password."

"*You* discovered the Ponzi scheme?" Good God,

what kind of strength would it take to turn in her own husband?

"It was the hardest thing I've ever done, but I handed over the evidence to the police. He'd stolen so much from so many people, I couldn't stay silent. His parents posted bail, and I wasn't given warning." She spun the stem between her thumb and forefinger. "When he walked back into the house, he had a gun."

Shock nailed him harder than a sail boom to the gut.

"My God, Shannon. I knew he'd committed suicide but I had no idea you were there. I'm so damn sorry."

"That's not all, though. For once the media didn't uncover everything." She drew herself up straight. "Nolan said he was going to kill me, then Kolby and then himself."

Her words iced the perspiration on his brow. This was so much worse than he'd foreseen. He cupped an arm around her shoulders and pulled her close. She trembled and kept twirling the flower, but she didn't stop speaking.

"His parents pulled up in the driveway." A shuddering sigh racked her body, her profile pained. "He realized he wouldn't have time to carry out his original plan. Thank God he locked himself in his office before he pulled the trigger and killed himself."

"Shannon." Horror threatened to steal his breath, but for her, he would hold steady. "I don't even know what to say to fix the hell you were put through."

"I didn't tell his parents what he'd planned. They'd lost their son and he'd been labeled a criminal." She held up the blue salvia. "I couldn't see causing them more grief when they thought of him."

Her eyes were filled with tears and regret. Tony kissed her forehead, then pulled her against his chest. "You were generous to the memory of a man who didn't deserve it."

"I didn't do it for him. No matter what, he's the father

of my child." She pressed her cheek harder against him and hugged him tightly. "Kolby will have to live with the knowledge that his dad was a crook, but I'll be damned before I'll let my son know his own father tried to kill him."

"You've fought hard for your son." He stroked her back. "You're a good mother and a strong woman."

She reminded him of a distant memory, of his own mother wrapping him in a silver blanket as they left San Rinaldo and telling him the shield would keep him safe. She'd been right. If only he could have protected her, as well.

Easing away, Shannon scrubbed her damp cheeks. "Thank God for Vernon. I'd sold off everything to pay Nolan's debts, even my piano and my oboe. The first waitressing job I landed in Louisiana didn't cover expenses. We were running out of options when Vernon hired me. Everyone else treated me like a pariah. Even Nolan's parents didn't want anything to do with either of us. So many people insisted I must have known what he was doing. That I must have tucked away money for myself. The gossip and the rumors were hell."

Realization, understanding spewed inside him like the abrupt shower of the sprinklers misting over the potted plants. He'd finally found a woman he could trust enough to propose marriage.

Only to find a husband was likely the last thing she ever wanted again.

Three hours later, Shannon sat on the floor in her suite with Kolby, rolling wooden trains along a ridged track. An ocean breeze spiraled through the open balcony door. She craved the peace of that boundless horizon. Never again would she allow herself to be hedged in as she'd been in her marriage.

After she'd finished dredging up her past, she'd needed to see her son. Tony had been understanding, although she could sense he wanted to talk longer. Once she'd returned to her suite, she'd showered and changed—and had been with her son ever since.

The past twenty-four hours had been emotionally charged on so many levels. Tony had been supportive and understanding, while giving her space. He'd also been a tender—thorough—lover.

Could she risk giving their relationship another try once they returned to the mainland? Was it possible for her to be a part of a normal couple?

A tug on her shirt yanked her attention back to the moment. Kolby looked up at her with wide blue eyes. "I'm hungry."

"Of course, sweetie. We'll go down to the kitchen and see what we can find." Hopefully the cook—the *chef*—wouldn't object since he must be right in the middle of supper prep. "We just need to clean up the toys first."

As she reached for the train set's storage bin, she heard a throat clear behind her and jerked around to find her on-again lover standing in the balcony doorway.

Her stomach fluttered with awareness, and she pressed her sweaty palms to her jeans. "How long have you been there?"

"Not long." Tony had showered and changed as well, wearing khakis and a button-down. "I can make his snack."

Whoa, Tony was seeking time with her son? That signaled a definite shift in their relationship. Although she'd seen him make his own breakfast in the past, she couldn't miss the significance of this moment and his efforts to try.

Turning him away would mean taking a step back. "Are you sure?"

Because God knows, she still had a boatload of fears.

"Positive," he said, his voice as steady as the man.

"Okay then." She pressed a hand over her stomach full of butterflies. "I'll just clean up here—"

"We've got it, don't we, pal?"

Kolby eyed him warily but he didn't turn away, probably because Tony kept his distance. He wasn't pushing. Maybe they'd both learned a lot these past couple of weeks.

"Okay, then." She stood, looking around the room, unsure what to do next. "I'll just, uh…"

Tony touched her hand lightly. "You mentioned selling your piano and I couldn't miss the regret in your voice. There's a Steinway Grand in the east wing. Alys or one of the guards can show you where if you would like to play."

Would she? Her fingers twitched. She'd closed off so much of her old life, including the good parts. Her music had been a beautiful bright spot in those solitary years of her life with Nolan. How kind of Tony to see beyond the surface of the harrowing final moments that had tainted her whole marriage. In the same way he'd chosen flowers based on facets of her personality, he'd detected the creativity she'd all but forgotten, honoring it in a small, simple offer.

Nodding her head was tougher than she thought. Her body went a little jerky before she could manage a response. "I would like that. Thank you for thinking of it and for spending time with Kolby."

He was a man who saw beyond her material needs…a man to treasure.

Her throat clogging with emotion, she backed from the room, watching the tableau of Tony with her son. Antonio Medina, a prince and billionaire, knelt on the floor with Kolby, cleaning up a wooden train set.

Tony chunked the caboose in the bin. "Has your mom ever cooked you a Cyclops?"

"What's a cycle-ops?" His face was intent with interest.

"The sooner we clean up the trains, the sooner I can show you."

She pressed a hand to her swelling heart. Tony was handling Kolby with ease. Her son would be fine.

After getting directions from Alys, Shannon found the east wing and finally the music room. What a simple way to describe such an awe-inspiring space. More of a circular ballroom, wooden floors stretched across, with a coffered ceiling that added texture as well as sound control. Crystal chandeliers and sconces glittered in the late afternoon sun.

And the instruments… Her feet drew her deeper into the room, closer to the gold gilded harp and a Steinway grand piano. She stroked the ivory keys reverently, then zipped through a scale. Pure magic.

She perched on the bench, her hands poised. Unease skittered up her spine like a double-timed scale, a sense of being watched. Pivoting around, she searched the expansive room….

Seated in a tapestry wingback, Enrique Medina stared back at her from beside a stained glass window. Even with his ill health, the deposed monarch radiated power and charisma. His dogs asleep on either side, he wore a simple dark suit with an ascot, perfectly creased although loose fitting. He'd lost even more weight since her arrival.

Enrique thumbed a gold pocket watch absently. "Do not mind me."

Had Tony sent her to this room on purpose, knowing his father would be here? She didn't think so, given the stilted relationship between the two men. "I don't want to disturb you."

"Not at all. We have not had a chance to speak alone, you and I," he said with a hint of an accent.

The musicality was pleasing to the ear. Every now and then, a lilt in certain words reminded her of how Tony spoke, small habits that she hadn't discerned as being raised with a foreign language. But she could hear the similarity more clearly when listening to his father.

While she'd seen the king daily during her two weeks on the island, those encounters had been mostly during meals. He'd spent the majority of his time with his daughter. But since Eloisa and her husband had left this afternoon, Enrique must be at loose ends. Shannon envied them that connection, and missed her own parents all the more. How much different her life might have been if they hadn't died. Her mother had shared a love of music.

She stroked the keyboard longingly. "Who plays the piano?"

"My sons took lessons as a part of the curriculum outlined by their tutors."

"Of course, I should have realized," she said. "Tony can play?"

Laughter rattled around inside his chest. "That would be a stretch. My youngest son can read music, but he did not enjoy sitting still. Antonio rushed through lessons so he could go outside."

"I can picture that."

"You know him well then." His sharp brown eyes took in everything. "Now my middle boy, Duarte, is more disciplined, quite the martial arts expert. But with music?" Enrique waved dismissively. "He performs like a robot."

Her curiosity tweaked for more details on Tony's family. Over the past couple of weeks, their relationship had deepened, and she needed more insights to still the fears churning her gut. "And your oldest son, Carlos? How did he fare with the piano lessons?"

A dark shadow crossed Enrique's face before he schooled his regal features again. "He had a gift. He's a surgeon now, using that touch in other ways."

"I can see how the two careers could tap into the same skill," she said, brushing her fingers over the gleaming keys.

Perhaps she could try again to find a career that tapped into her love of music. What a gift it would be to bring joy deeper into her life again.

Enrique tucked one hand into his pocket. "Do you have feelings for my son?"

His blunt question blindsided her, but she should have realized this cunning man never chatted just for conversation's sake. "That is a personal question."

"And I may not have time to wait around for you to feel comfortable answering."

"You're playing the death card? That's a bit cold, don't you think, sir?"

He laughed, hard and full-out like Tony did—or like he used to. "You have a spine. Good. You are a fine match for my stubborn youngest."

Her irritation over his probing questions eased. What parent didn't want to see their children settled and happy? "I appreciate your opening your home to me and my son and giving us a chance to get to know you."

"Diplomatically said, my dear. You are wise to proceed thoughtfully. Regrets are a terrible thing," he said somberly. "I should have sent my family out of San Rinaldo sooner. I waited too long and Beatriz paid the price."

The darker turn of the conversation stilled her. She'd wanted more insights into Tony's life, yet this was going so much deeper than she had anticipated.

Enrique continued, "It was such chaos that day when the coup began. We had planned for my family to take one escape route and I would use another." His jaw flexed sharply in his gaunt face. "I made it out, and the rebels found my family. Carlos was injured trying to save his mother."

The picture of violence and terror he painted sounded like something from a movie, so unreal, yet they'd lived it. "Tony and your other sons witnessed the attack on their mother?"

"Antonio had nightmares for a year, and then he became obsessed with the beach and surfing. From that day on, he lived to leave the island."

She'd known the bare bones details of their escape. But the horror they'd lived through, the massive losses rolled over her with a new vividness. Tony's need to help her had more to do with caring than control. He didn't want to isolate her or smother her by managing everything the way her husband had. Tony tried to help her because he'd failed to save someone else he cared about.

Somehow, knowing this made it easier for her to open her heart. To take a chance beyond their weeks here.

Without question, he would have to understand her need for independence, but she also had to appreciate how he'd been hurt, how those hurts had shaped him. And as Antonio Medina and Tony Castillo merged in her mind, she couldn't ignore the truth any longer.

She loved him.

Approaching footsteps startled her, drawing her focus from the past and toward the arched entry. Tony stepped into view just when her defenses were at their lowest. No doubt her heart was in her eyes. She started toward him, only to realize *his* eyes held no tender feelings.

The harsh angles of his face blared a forewarning before he announced, "There's been a security breach."

Thirteen

Shock jolted through Shannon, followed closely by fear. "A security breach? Where's Kolby?"

She shot to her feet and ran across the music room to Tony. The ailing king reached for his cane, his dogs waking instantly, beating her there by a footstep. Enrique steadied himself with a hand against the wall, but he was up and moving. "What happened?"

"Kolby is fine. No one has been hurt, but we have taken another hit in the media."

Enrique asked, "Have they located the island?"

"No," Tony said as Alys slid into view behind him. "It happened at the airport when Eloisa and Jonah's flight landed in South Carolina. The press was waiting, along with crowds of everyday people wanting a picture to sell for an easy buck."

Shannon's stomach lurched at another assault in the

news. "Could the frenzy have to do with the Landis family connections?"

"No," Tony said curtly. "The questions were all about their vacation with Eloisa's father the king."

Alys angled past Tony with a wheelchair. "Your Majesty, I'll take you to your office so you can speak to security directly."

The king dropped into the wheelchair heavily. "Thank you, Alys." His dogs loped into place alongside him. "I am ready."

Nerves jangled, Shannon started to follow, but Tony extended a hand to stop her.

"We need to talk."

His chilly voice stilled her feet faster than any arm across the entranceway. Had he been holding back because of concerns for his father's health? "What's wrong? What haven't you told me?"

She stepped closer for comfort. He crossed his arms over his chest.

"The leak came from this house. There was a call placed from here this afternoon—at just the right time—to an unlisted cell number."

"Here? But your father's security has been top notch." No wonder he was so concerned.

Tony unclipped his iPhone from his waistband. "We have security footage of the call being made."

Thumbing the controls, he filled the screen with a still image of a woman on the phone, a woman in a white swimsuit cover-up, hood pulled over her head.

A cover-up just like hers? "I don't understand. You think this is *me?* Why would I tip off the media?"

His mouth stayed tight-lipped and closed, and his eyes... Oh God, she recognized well that condemning look from the days following Nolan's arrest and then his death.

Steady. Steady. She reminded herself Tony wasn't Nolan or the other people who'd betrayed her, and he had good reasons to be wary. She drew in a shuddering breath.

"I understand that Enrique brought you up to be unusually cautious about the people in your life. And he had cause after what happened to your mother." Thoughts of Tony as a small child watching his mother's murder brushed sympathy over her own hurt. "But you have to see there's nothing about me that would hint at this kind of behavior."

"I know you would do anything to secure your son's future. Whoever sold this information received a hefty payoff." He stared back at her with cold eyes and unswerving surety.

In a sense he was right. She would do anything for Kolby. But again, Tony had made a mistake. He'd offered her money before, assuming that would equate security to her. She had deeper values she wanted to relay to her son, like the importance of earning a living honorably. Tony had needed to prove that himself in leaving the island. Why was it so difficult to understand she felt the same way?

Her sympathy for him could only stretch so far.

"You actually believe I betrayed you? That I placed everyone here at risk for a few dollars?" Anger frothed higher and higher inside her. "I never wanted any of this. My son and I can get by just fine without you and your movie theater." She swatted his arm. "Answer me, damn you."

"I don't know what to think." He pinched the bridge of his nose. "Tell me it was an accident. You called a friend just to shoot the breeze because you were homesick and that friend sold you out."

Except as she'd already told him and he must remember, she didn't have friends, not anymore. Apparently she didn't even have Tony. "I'm not going to defend myself to you. Either you trust me or you don't."

He gripped her shoulders, his touch careful, his eyes more tumultuous. "I want a future with you. God, Shannon, I was going to ask you to marry me later tonight. I planned to take you back to the chapel, go inside this time and propose."

Her heart squeezed tight at the image he painted. If this security nightmare hadn't occurred, she would have been swept off her feet. She would have been celebrating her engagement with him tonight, because by God, she would have said yes. Now, that wasn't possible.

"You honestly thought we could get married when you have so little faith in me?" The betrayal burned deep. And hadn't she sworn she'd never again put herself in a position to feel that sting from someone she cared about? "You should have included some azaleas in the bouquet you chose for us. I hear they mean fragile passion."

She shrugged free of his too tempting touch. The hole inside her widened, ached.

"Damn it all, Shannon, we're talking." He started toward her.

"Stop." She held up a hand. "Don't come near me. Not now. Not ever."

"Where are you going?" He kept his distance this time. "I need to know you're safe."

"Has the new security system been installed at my apartment?"

His mouth tight, he nodded. "But we're still working on the restraining orders. Given the renewed frenzy because of Eloisa's identity—"

"The new locks and alarms will do for now."

"Damn it, Shannon—"

"I have to find Alys so she can make the arrangements."

She held her chin high. Pride and her child were all she had left now that her heart was shattered to pieces. "Kolby and I are returning to Texas."

"Where are Shannon and her son?"

His father's question hammered Tony's already pounding head. In his father's study, he poured himself three fingers of cognac, bypassing the Basque wine and the memories it evoked. Shannon wrapped around him, the scent of lilies in her hair. "You know full well where she is. Nothing slips past you here."

They'd spent the past two hours assessing the repercussions of the leak. The media feeding frenzy had been rekindled with fresh fuel about Eloisa's connection to the family. Inevitable, yet still frustrating. It gnawed at his gut to think Shannon had something to do with this, although he reassured himself it must have been an accident.

And if she'd simply slipped up and made a mistake, he could forgive her. She hadn't lived the Medina way since the cradle. Remembering all the intricacies involved in maintaining such a high level of security was difficult. If she would just admit what happened, they could move on.

His father rolled back from the computer desk, his large dogs tracking his every move from in front of the fireplace. "Apparently I do not know everything happening under my roof, because somebody placed a call putting Eloisa's flight at risk. I trusted someone I shouldn't have."

"You trusted me and my judgment." He scratched his tightening rib cage.

His father snorted with impatience. "Do not be an impulsive jackass. Think with your brain and not your heart."

"Like you've always done?" Tony snapped, his patience for his father's cryptic games growing short. "No thank you."

Once he finished his one-month obligation, he wouldn't set foot on this godforsaken island again. If memories of his life here before were unhappy, now they were gut-wrenching. His father should come to the mainland anyway for medical treatment. Even Enrique's deep coffers couldn't outfit the island with unlimited hospital options.

Enrique poured himself a drink and downed it swiftly. "I let my heart guide me when I left San Rinaldo. I was so terrified something would happen to my wife and sons that I did not think through our escape plan properly."

Invincible Enrique was admitting a mistake? Tony let that settle inside him for a second before speaking.

"You set yourself up as a diversion. Sounds pretty self-less to me." He'd never doubted his father's bravery or cool head.

"I did not think it through." He refilled his glass and stared into the amber liquid, signs of regret etched deep in his forehead. Illness had never made the king appear weak, but at this moment, the ghosts of an old past showed a vulnerability Tony had never seen before. "If I had, I would have taken into account the way Carlos would react if things went to hell. I arrogantly considered my plan foolproof. Again, I thought with my emotions and those assassins knew exactly how to target my weakness."

Tony set aside his glass without touching a drop. Empathy for his father seared him more fully than alcohol. Understanding how it felt to have his feelings ripped up through his throat because of a woman gave him insights to his father he'd never expected. "You did your best at the time."

Could he say the same when it came to Shannon?

"I tried to make that right with this island. I did everything in my power to create a safe haven for my sons."

"But we all three left the protection of this place."

"That doesn't matter to me. My only goal was keeping you safe until adulthood. By the time you departed, you took with you the skills to protect yourself, to make your way in the world. That never would have been possible if you'd grown up with obligations to a kingdom. For that, I'm proud."

Enrique's simply spoken words enveloped him. Even though his father wasn't telling him anything he didn't already know, something different took root in him. An understanding. Just as his mother had made the silver security blanket as a "shield," to make him feel protected, his father had been doing the same. His methods may not have been perfect, but their situation had been far from normal. They'd all been scrambling to patch together their lives.

Some of his understanding must have shown on his face, because his father smiled approvingly.

"Now, son, think about Shannon logically rather than acting like a love-sick boy."

Love-sick boy? Now that stung more than a little. And the reason? Because it was true. He did love her, and that had clouded his thinking.

He loved her. And he'd let his gut drive his conclusions rather than logic. He forced his slugging heart to slow and collected what he knew about Shannon. "She's a naturally cautious woman who wouldn't do anything to place her son at risk. If she had a call to make, she would check with you or I to make sure the call was safe. She wouldn't have relied on anyone else's word when it comes to Kolby."

"What conclusion does that lead you to?"

"We never saw the caller's face. I made an assumption

based on a female in a bathing suit cover-up. The caller must have been someone with detailed knowledge of our security systems in order to keep her face shielded. A woman of similar build. A person with something to gain and little loyalty to the Medinas…" His brain settled on… "Alys?"

"I would bet money on it." The thunderous anger Enrique now revealed didn't bode well for the assistant who'd used her family connections to take advantage of an ailing king with an aging staff. "She was even the one to order Shannon's clothes. It would be easy to make sure she had the right garb…."

Shannon had done nothing wrong.

"God, I wonder if Alys could have even been responsible for tipping off the Global Intruder about that photo of Duarte when it first ran, before he was identified." The magnitude of how badly he'd screwed up threatened to kick his knees out from under him. He braced a hand on his father's shoulder, touching his dad for the first time in fourteen years. "Where the hell is Alys?"

Enrique swallowed hard. He clapped his hand over Tony's for a charged second before clearing his throat.

"Leave Alys to me." His royal roots showed through again as he assumed command. "Don't you have a more pressing engagement?"

Tony checked his watch. He had five minutes until the ferry pulled away for the airstrip. No doubt his father would secure the proof of Alys's deception soon, but Shannon needed—hell, she deserved—to know that he'd trusted in her innocence without evidence.

He had a narrow, five-minute window to prove just how much he loved and trusted her.

* * *

The ferry horn wailed, signaling they were disconnecting from the dock. The crew was stationed at their posts, lost in the ritual of work.

Kolby on her hip, Shannon looked at the exotic island for the last time. This was hard, so much harder than she'd expected. How would she ever survive going back to Galveston where even more memories of Tony waited? She couldn't. She would have to start over somewhere new and totally different.

Except there was no place she could run now that would be free of Medina reminders. The grocery store aisles would sport gossip rags. Channel surfing could prove hazardous. And she didn't even want to think of how often she would be confronted with Tony's face peering back at her from an internet headline, reminding her of how little faith he'd had in her. As much as she wanted to say to hell with it all and accept whatever he offered, she wouldn't settle for half measures ever again.

Tears blurred the exotic shoreline, sea oats dotting the last bit of sand as they pulled away. She squeezed her eyes closed, tears cool on her heated cheeks.

"Mommy?" Kolby patted her face.

She scavenged a wobbly smile and focused on his precious face. "I'm okay, sweetie. Everything's going to be fine. Let's look for a dolphin."

"Nu-uh," he said. "Why's Tony running? Can he come wif us, pretty pwease?"

What? She followed the path of her son's pointing finger....

Tony sprinted down the dock, his mouth moving but his words swallowed up by the roar of the engines and churning water behind the ferry. Her heart pumped in time with his long-legged strides. She almost didn't dare hope, but then Tony had always delivered the unexpected.

Lowering Kolby to the deck with one arm, she leaned over the rail, straining to hear what he said. Still, the wind whipped his words as the ferry inched away. Disappointment pinched as she realized she would have to wait for the ferry to travel back again to speak to him. So silly to be impatient, but her heart had broken a lifetime's worth in one day.

Just as she'd resigned herself to waiting, Tony didn't stop running. Oh my God, he couldn't actually be planning to—

Jump.

Her heart lodged in her throat for an expanded second as he was airborne. Then he landed on deck with the surefooted ease of an experienced boater. Tony strode toward her with even, determined steps, the crew parting to make way.

He extended his hand, his fist closed around a clump of sea oats, still dripping from where he'd yanked them up. "You'll have to use your imagination here because I didn't have much time." He passed her one stalk. "Imagine this is a purple hyacinth, the 'forgive me' flower. I hope you will accept it, along with my apology."

"Go ahead. I'm listening." Although she didn't take his pretend hyacinth. He had a bit more talking to do after what he'd put her through.

Kolby patted his leg for attention. Winking down at the boy, Tony passed him one of the sea oats, which her son promptly waved like a flag. With Kolby settled, Tony shifted his attention back to Shannon.

"I've been an idiot," he said. Sea spray dampened his hair, increasing the rebellious curls. "I should have known you wouldn't do anything to put Kolby or my family at risk.

And if you'd done so inadvertently, you would have been upfront about it." He told her all the things she'd hoped to hear earlier.

While she appreciated the romanticism of his gesture, a part of her still ached that he'd needed proof. Trust was such a fragile thing, but crucial in any relationship.

"What brought about this sudden insight to my character? Did you find some new surveillance tape that proves my innocence?"

"I spoke to my father. He challenged me, made me think with my head instead of my scared-as-hell heart. And thank God he did, because once I looked deeper I realized Alys must have made the call. I can't help but wonder if she's the one who made the initial leak to the press. We don't have proof yet, but we'll find it."

Alys? Shannon mulled over that possibility, remembering the way the assistant had stared at Tony with such hunger. She'd sensed the woman wanted to be a Medina. Perhaps Alys had also wanted all the public princess perks to go with it rather than a life spent in hiding.

Tony extended his hand with the sea oats again, tickling them across Kolby's chin lightly before locking eyes with Shannon. "But none of that matters if you don't trust me."

Touching the cottony white tops of the sea oats, she weighed her words carefully. This moment could define the rest of her life. "I realize the way you've grown up has left marks on you…what happened with your mother… living in seclusion here. But I can't always worry when that's going to make you push me away again just because you're afraid I'll betray you."

Her fingers closed around his. "I've had so many people turn away from me. I can't—I won't—spend my life proving myself to you."

"And I don't expect you to." He clasped both hands around hers, his skin callused and tough, a little rough around the edges like her impetuous lover. "You're absolutely right. I was wrong. What I feel for you, it's scary stuff. But the thought of losing you is a helluva lot scarier than any alternative."

"What exactly are you saying?" She needed him to spell it out, every word, every promise.

"My life is complicated and comes with a lot more cons than pros. There's nothing to stop Alys from spilling everything she knows, and if so, it's really going to hit the fan. A life with me won't be easy. To the world, I am a Medina. And I hope you will consent to be a Medina, too."

He knelt in front of her with those sea oats—officially now her favorite plant.

"Shannon, will you be my bride? Let me be your husband and a father to Kolby." He paused to ruffle the boy's hair, eliciting a giant smile from her son. "As well as any other children we may have together. I can't promise I won't be a jackass again. I can almost guarantee that I will. But I vow to stick with it, stick with us, because you mean too much to me for me to ever mess this up again."

Sinking to her knees, she fell into his arms, her son enclosed in the circle. "Yes, I'll marry you and build a family and future with you. Tony Castillo, Antonio Medina, and any other name you go by, I love you, too. You've stolen my heart for life."

"Thank God." He gathered her closer, his arms trembling just a hint.

She lost track of how long they knelt that way until Kolby squirmed between them, and she heard the crew applauding and cheering. Together, she and Tony stood as the ferry captain shouted orders to turn the boat around.

Standing at the deck with Tony, she stared at the approaching island, a place she knew they would visit over the years. She clasped his arm, her cheek against his compass tattoo. Tony rested his chin on her head.

His breath caressed her hair. "The legend about the compass is true. I've found my way home."

Surprised, she glanced up at him. "Back to the island?"

Shaking his head, he tucked a knuckle under her chin and brushed a kiss across her mouth. "Ah, Shanny, *you* are my home."

* * * * *

HIS THIRTY-DAY
FIANCÉE

BY
CATHERINE MANN

To Mollie Saunders,
a real-life princess and a magical storyteller!

One

Catching a royal was tough. But catching an elusive Medina was damn near impossible.

Teeth chattering, photojournalist Kate Harper inched along the third-story ledge leading to Prince Duarte Medina's living quarters. The planked exterior of his Martha's Vineyard resort offered precious little to grab hold of as she felt her way across in the dark, but she'd never been one to admit defeat.

Come hell or high water, she would snag her top-dollar picture. Her sister's future teetered even more precariously than Kate's balance on the twelve-inch beam.

Wind whipped in off the harbor, slapping her mossy green Dolce & Gabbana knockoff around her legs. Her cold toes curled along the wooden ridge since she'd ditched her heels on the balcony next door before climbing out. Thank God it wasn't snowing tonight.

Wrangling her way into an event at the posh Medina resort hadn't been easy. But she'd nabbed a ticket to a Fortune 500 mogul's rehearsal dinner for his son by promising a dimwit dilettante to run a tabloid piece on her ex in exchange for the woman's invitation. Once in, however, Kate was on her own to dodge security, locate Prince Duarte and snap the shot. As best she could tell, this was her only hope to enter his suite. Too bad her coat and gloves had been checked at the door.

The minicameras embedded in her earrings were about to tear her darn earlobes in half. She'd transformed a couple old button cameras into what looked like gold-and-emerald jewelry.

The lighthouse swooped a dim beam through the cottony-thick fog, Klaxon wailing every twenty seconds and temporarily drowning out the sound of wedding-party guests mingling on the first floor. She scooched closer to the prince's balcony.

Kate stretched her leg farther, farther still until… Pay dirt. Her pounding heart threatened to pop a seam on her thrift-shop satin gown. She grabbed the railing fast and swung her leg over.

A hand clamped around her wrist. A strong hand. A *masculine* hand.

She yelped as another hand grabbed her ankle and hauled, grip strong on her arm and calf. His fingers seared her freezing skin just over her anklet made by her sister. A good-luck charm to match the earrings. She sure hoped it helped.

A swift yank sent her tumbling over onto the balcony. Her dress twisted around her thighs and hopefully not higher. She scrambled for firm footing, her arms flailing as her gown slid back into place. She landed hard against a wall.

No, wait. Walls didn't have crisp chest hair and defined muscles, and smell of musky perspiration. Under normal circumstances, she'd have been more than a little turned on. If she wasn't so focused on her sister's future and her lips weren't turning blue from the cold.

Kate peeked…and found a broad male torso an inch from her nose. A black shirt or robe hung open, exposing darkly tanned skin and brown hair. Her fingers clenched in the silky fabric. Some kind of karate workout clothes?

Good God, did Medina actually hire ninjas for protection like monarchs in movies?

Kate looked up the strong column of the ninja's neck, the tensed line of his square jaw in need of a shave. Then, holy crap, she met the same coal-black eyes she'd been planning to photograph.

"You're not a ninja," she blurted.

"And you are not much of an acrobat." Prince Duarte Medina didn't smile, much less say cheese.

"Not since I flunked out of kinder-gym." This was the strangest conversation ever, but at least he hadn't pitched her over the railing. Yet.

He also didn't let go of her arms. The restrained strength of his calloused fingers sparked an unwelcomed shiver of awareness along her chilled skin.

Duarte glanced down at her bare feet. "Were you booted for a balance beam infraction?"

"Actually, I broke another kid's nose." She'd tripped the nasty little boy after he'd called her sister a moron.

Kate fingered her earring. She had to snap her pictures and punch out. This was an opportunity rarer than a red diamond.

The Medina monarchy had pretty much fallen off the map twenty-seven years ago after King Enrique Medina was deposed in a coup that left his wife dead. For decades rumors swirled that the old widower had walled up with his three sons in an Argentinean fortress. After a while, people stopped wondering about the Medinas at all. Until she'd felt the journalistic twitch to research an individual in the background of a photo she'd taken. That twitch had led to her news story which popped the top off a genie bottle. She'd exposed the secret lives of three now-grown princes who were hiding in plain sight in the United States.

But that hadn't been enough. The paycheck on that story hadn't come close to hauling her out of the financial difficulties life had thrust upon her.

Her window of opportunity to grab an up-close picture was shrinking. Already paparazzi from every corner of the globe were scrambling for a photo op now that news of her initial find leaked like water through a crumbling sandcastle.

Yet somehow, she'd beaten them all because Duarte Medina was really here. In the flesh. In front of her. And so much hotter in person. She swayed and couldn't even blame it on vertigo.

He scooped her into his arms, apparently sporting real strength to go with those ninja workout clothes.

"You are turning to a block of ice." His voice rumbled with the barest hint of an exotic accent, the bedroom sort of inflection perfect for voice-overs in commercials that would convince a woman to buy anything if he came with it. "You need to come in from the cold before you pass out."

So he could call security to lock her up? Her angle with the earring cameras wasn't great, but she hoped she'd snagged some workable shots while she jostled around in his arms.

"Uh, thanks for the save." Should she call him Prince Duarte or Your Majesty?

Coming into this, she'd envisioned getting her photos on the sly and hadn't thought to brush up on protocol when confronted with a prince in karate pajamas. A very hot, swarthy prince carrying her inside to his suite.

Now that she studied his face inches from hers, his ancestry was unmistakable. The Medina monarchy had originated on the small island of San Rinaldo off the coast of Spain. And in the charged moment she could see his bold Mediterranean heritage as clearly as his arrogance. With fog rolling along the rocky shore at his back through the open balcony doors, she could envision him reigning over his native land. In fact it was difficult to remember at all that he'd lived for so many years in the United States.

He set her on her feet again, her toes sinking for miles into the plush rug. The whole room spoke of understated wealth and power from the pristine white sofas, to the mahogany antique armoire, to a mammoth four-poster bed with posts as thick as tree trunks.

A bed? She tried to swallow. Her throat went dry.

Duarte smiled tightly, heavy lidded eyes assessing. "Ramon has really outdone himself this time."

"Ramon?" Her editor's name was Harold. "I'm not sure what you mean." But she would play along if it meant staying put a few minutes more. To get her pictures, of course.

"The father of the groom has a reputation for supplying the best, uh—" his pulse beat slowly along his bronzed neck "—companionship to woo his business associates, but you surpass them all in originality."

"Companionship?" Shock stunned her silent. He couldn't be implying what she thought.

"I assume he paid you well, given the whole elaborate entrance." His upper lip curled with a hint of disdain.

Paid companionship. Ah, hell. He thought she was a high-priced call girl. Or at least she hoped he thought high-priced. Well, she wasn't going that far for her sister, but maybe she could scavenge another angle for the story by sticking around just a question or two longer.

Kate placed a tentative hand on his shoulder. No way was she touching his bared chest. "How many times has he so generously gifted you?"

His smoky dark eyes streamed over the tops of her breasts darn near spilling out of the wretched thrift-store dress. "I have never availed myself of—how shall we say? Paid services."

A good journalist would ask. "Not even once?" Maybe she could inch just her pinky past his open neck-line.

"Never." His hard tone left no room for doubt.

She held back her sigh of relief and let herself savor the heat of his skin under her touch.

Her fingers curled. "Oh, uh…just oh."

"I am a gentleman, after all. And as such, I can't simply send you back onto the balcony. Stay while I make arrangements to slip you out." His palm lay low on her waist. "Would you like a drink?"

Her stomach squeezed into an even tighter ball of anticipation. Why was she this hyped-up over an assignment? This was her job, one she was well-trained to do. Thoughts of her days as a photojournalist for news magazines bombarded her. Days when her assignments ranged from a Jerusalem pilgrimage to the aftermath of an earthquake in Indonesia.

Now, she worked for GlobalIntruder.com.

She stifled a hysterical laugh. God, what had she

sunk to? And what choice did she have with a shrinking newspaper industry?

Sure, she was nervous, damn it. This photo was about more than staying in the media game. It was about finding enough cash fast to make sure her special-needs sister wasn't booted out of her assisted-living facility next month. Jennifer had a grown-up's body with a child's mind. She needed protection and Kate was all she had left keeping her from becoming an adult ward of the state.

Too bad Kate was only a couple of rent payments away from bankruptcy court.

The prince's hand slid up her spine, clasping the back of her neck. Her traitorous body tingled.

She needed a moment to regroup—away from this guy's surprising allure—if she hoped to get the information she needed. "Is there a powder room nearby where I can freshen up while you pour the drinks? When I leave your suite, I shouldn't *look* like I climbed around outside the balcony."

"I'll show you the way."

Not what she had in mind. But she'd kept her cool during a mortar attack before. She could handle this. "Just point, please. I've got good internal navigational skills."

"I imagine you're good at a great many things." His breath heated over her neck as he dipped his head closer to speak. "I may have never had use for offers such as yours before, but I have to confess, there is something captivating about you."

Oh, boy.

His warm breath grazed her exposed shoulder, his lips so close to touching her skin without closing that final whisper for connection. Her breasts beaded against the already snug bodice of her gown. She pushed her heels deeper into the carpet to keep her balance. Her anklet rubbed against her other leg. Her good-luck charm from Jennifer. Remember her sister.

"About that bathroom?" Frantically, she looked around the bedroom suite with too many tall, paneled doors, all closed.

"Right over here." His words heated over her neck, raising goose bumps along her arms.

"Uh, but…" Was that breathy gasp hers? "I prefer to go solo."

"We wouldn't want you to get lost on your way." He stopped just at her earlobe as if to share a secret.

Had he touched her? His breath against her skin left her light-headed. He cupped the other side of her head. Hunger gnawed deep within her as she ached to lean into his cradling touch.

Then he backed away, his hand teasing a tempting trail and his black workout clothes rustling a lethal whisper. "Just through that door, Ms. Kate Harper."

Duarte gestured right, both of her earrings dangling from between his fingers.

Duarte had been waiting for this moment since the second he'd learned which tabloid scumbag had blown apart his family's carefully crafted privacy. He held Kate Harper's earrings in his hands along with her hopes of a new scoop. He'd been alerted she might be on the premises and determined her hidden cameras' locations before they'd left the balcony.

He'd spent his whole life dodging the press. He knew their tricks. His father had drummed into his sons at a young age how their safety depended on anonymity. They'd been protected, educated and, above all, trained.

Sweat trickled between his shoulder blades from his workout—a regimen that had been interrupted by security concerns.

One look at the intruder on the screen and he'd decided to see how far she would go.

In that form-fitting dress, she personified seduction. Like a pinup girl from days past, she had a timeless air and feminine allure that called to the primal male inside him. Good Lord, what a striking picture she would make draped on the white sofa just behind her. Or better yet, in his bed.

But he was an expert at self-control. And just calling to mind her two-bit profession made it easier to rein in his more instinctive thoughts.

Kate Harper perched a hand on her hip. "I can't believe you knew who I really was the whole time."

"From the second you left the party." He'd been sent pictures of her when he'd investigated the photojournalist who cracked a cover story that had survived intense scrutiny for decades.

Background photos of her portrayed something very different: an earthy woman in khaki pants and generic white T-shirts, no makeup, her sleek brown hair in an unpretentious ponytail as opposed to the windswept twist she wore now. A hint of cinnamon apple fragrance drifted his way.

Her bright red lips pursed tight with irritation. "Then why pretend I'm a call girl?"

"That's too high-class for the garbage you peddle." He pocketed her earrings, blocking thoughts of her pretty pout.

His family's life had been torn apart just when his father needed peace more than ever. Too much stress could kill Enrique Medina faster than any extremist assassin from San Rinaldo.

"So the gloves are off." She folded her arms over her chest, rubbing her hands along her skin. From fear or the cold ocean wind blasting through the open French doors? "What do you intend to do? Call your security or the police?"

"I have to admit, I wouldn't mind seeing more than gloves come off your deceitful body." Duarte closed the balcony doors with a click and a snick of a lock.

"Uh, listen, Prince Duarte, or Your Majesty, or whatever I'm supposed to call you." Her words tumbled faster and faster. "Let's both calm down."

He glanced over his shoulder, cocking an eyebrow.

"Okay, *I* will be calm. You be whatever you want." She swiped back a straggling hair with a shaky hand. "My point is I'm here. You don't want invasive media coverage. So why not pose for just one picture? It can be staged any way you choose. You can be in total control."

"Control? Is this some kind of game to you, like a child's video system where we pass the controller back and forth?" He stalked closer, his feet as bare as hers on the carpet. "Because for me, this isn't anywhere near a game. This is about my family's privacy, our safety."

Royals—even ones without a country—were never safe from threats. His mother had been killed in the rebellion overthrowing San Rinaldo, his older brother severely injured trying to save her. As a result, his father—King Enrique Medina—became obsessed with security. He'd constructed an impenetrable fortress on an island off the coast of St. Augustine, Florida, where he'd brought up his three young sons. Only when they'd become adults had Duarte and his brothers been able to break free. By scattering to the far corners of the U.S., they'd kept low profiles and were able to lead normal adult lives—with him on Martha's Vineyard, Antonio in Galveston Bay and Carlos in Tacoma.

Kate touched his wrist lightly. "I'm sorry about what has happened to your family, how you lost your mother."

Her touch seared at a raw spot hidden deep inside, prompting him to lash out in defense. Duarte sketched his knuckles over her bare ears. "How sorry are you?"

He had to give her credit. She didn't back down. She met his gaze dead-on with eyes bluer than the San Rinaldo waters he just barely remembered.

Kate pulled her hand away. "What about a picture of you in your ninja clothes lounging against the balcony railing?"

"How about a photo of you naked in my arms?"

She gasped. "Of all the arrogant, self-aggrandizing, pompous—"

"I'm a prince." He held up a finger. "But of course everyone knows that now, thanks to your top-notch journalistic instincts."

"You're angry. I get that." She inched behind the sofa as if putting a barrier between them, yet her spine stayed rigid, her eyes sparking icicles. "But just because you're royalty doesn't give you a free pass along with all these plush trappings."

He'd left his father's Florida fortress with nothing more than a suitcase full of clothes. Not that he intended to dole out that nugget for her next exposé. "Can't blame a prince for trying."

She didn't laugh. "Why did you let me in here? Am I simply around for your amusement so you can watch me flinch when you flush my camera?"

Kate Harper was a woman who regained her balance fast. He admired that. "You really want this picture."

Her fingers sunk so deep in the sofa that her short red nails disappeared. "More than you can possibly know."

How far would she go to get it?

For an immoral moment he considered testing those boundaries. His identity had been exposed already anyway, a reality that drained his father's waning strength. Anger singed the edges of his control, fueling memories of how soft Kate's skin had felt under his touch when he'd pulled her onto the balcony, how perfectly her curves had shaped themselves to his chest.

Turning away, he forced his more civilized nature to quench the heat. "You should leave now. Use the door directly behind you. The guard in the corridor will escort you out."

"You're not going to give me my camera back, are you?"

He pivoted toward her again. "No." He slid his hand in his pocket and toyed with her earrings. "Although, you're more than welcome to try to retrieve your jewelry."

"I prefer battles I have a chance of winning." Her lips tipped in a half smile. "Can I at least have a cigar to hock on eBay?"

Again she'd surprised him. He wasn't often entertained anymore. "You're funny. I like that."

"Give me my camera and I'll become a stand-up comedian—" she snapped her fingers "—that fast."

Who was this woman in an ill-fitting gown with an anklet made of silver yarn and white plastic beads? Most would have been nervous as hell or sucking up.

Although, perhaps she was smarter than the rest, in spite of her dubious profession.

This woman had cost him more than could be regained. He would forge ahead, but already his father feared for his sons' safety, a concern the ailing old man didn't need. An alarming possibility snaked through his mind, one he should have considered before. Damn the way she took the oxygen and reason from a room. What if her minicamera sent the photos instantly by remote to a portal? Photos already on their way to flood the media?

Photos of the two of them?

Duarte sifted the earrings between his fingers. A plan formed in his mind to safeguard against all possibilities, a way to satisfy his urges on every level—lust and revenge without any annoying loose ends. Some might think over such a large decision, but his father had taught him to trust his instincts.

"Ms. Harper," he said, closing in on her, following her behind the sofa. "I have another proposition instead."

"Uh, a *proposition?*" She stepped backed, bumping an end table, rattling the glass lamp filled with coins. "I thought we already cleared the air on that subject. Even I have limits."

"Too bad for both of us. That could have been..." He stopped mid-sentence and steadied the lamp—a gift from his brother Antonio—filled with Spanish doubloons from a shipwreck off San Rinaldo. No need to torment her for the hell of it, not when he had a more complex plan in mind. "It's not that kind of proposition. Believe me, I don't have to trade money—or media exclusives—for sex."

She eyed him warily, surreptitiously hitching up the

sinking neckline of her gown. "Then what kind of trade are we talking about here?"

He watched her every move. The way she picked at her painted thumbnail with her forefinger. How she rubbed her heel over the silly little anklet she wore. He savored up every bit of reeling her in, the plan growing more fulfilling by the second.

This was the best way. The only way. "I have a bit of a, uh, shall we say 'family situation.' My father is in ill health—as the world now knows thanks to your invasive investigative skills."

She winced visibly for the first time. "I'm very sorry about that. Truly." Then her nervousness fell away and her azure-blues gleamed with intelligence. "About the trade?"

"My father wants to see me settled down, married and ready to produce the next Medina heir. He even has a woman chosen—"

Her eyes went wide. "You have a fiancée?"

"My, how you reporters gobble up tidbits like fish snapping at crumbs on the water. But no. I do not have a fiancée." Irritation nipped, annoying him all the more since it signaled a bit of control sliding to her side. "If you want another bread crumb, don't anger me."

"My apologies again." She fingered her empty earlobe. "What about our trade?"

Back to the intriguing problem in front of him.

He would indulge those impulses with her later. When she was ready. And gauging by her air of desperation, it wouldn't take much persuasion. Just a little time he could buy while settling a score and easing his father's concerns about future heirs.

"As I said, my father is quite ill." Near death from the damage caused by hepatitis contracted during his days on the run. The doctors feared liver failure at any time. He shut off distracting images of his pale father. "Obviously I don't want to upset him while his health is so delicate."

"Of course not. Family is important." Her eyes filled with sympathy.

Ah. He'd found her weakness. The rest would be easy.

"Exactly. So, I have something you want, and you can give me something in return." He lifted her chilly hand and kissed her short red nails. Judging by the way her pupils dilated, this revenge would be a pleasure for them both. "You cost our family much with your photos, destroying our carefully crafted anonymity. Now, let's discuss how you're going to repay that debt."

Two

"Repay the debt," Kate repeated, certain he couldn't be implying what she'd thought. And she would look like a fool if she let him know what she'd assumed. She inched her chilly hand from his encompassing grip. "I'm going to work for you?"

"Nice try." He stepped closer, his ninja workout pants whispering a dark, sexy hello.

Holding her silence, she crossed her arms to hide her shivery response and keep him from moving closer. This man's magnetism was mighty inconvenient. Her toes curled into the Aubusson rug.

He tipped his head regally, drawing her attention to the strong column of his neck, his pulse steady and strong. "I want you to be my fiancée."

Shock unfurled her toes. "Are you smoking crack?"

"Never have. Never intend to." He clasped her wrists

and unfolded her arms slowly, deliberately until they stood closer still. His eyes bored into hers. "I'm stone-cold sober and completely serious. In case you haven't noticed, I do not joke."

Her breasts strained against the bodice of her dress with each breath growing deeper, more erratic. She didn't know what he was up to. Right now, he held all the cards, including all her photos.

Any hope of salvaging an article from this required playing with fire. "Seems to me like you have a fine sense of humor to suggest something as ridiculous as this. What do you really hope to accomplish?"

"If my father thinks I'm already locked into a relationship—" he skimmed his knuckles up her arm "—with you, he will quit pressing me to hook up with one of the daughters of his old pals from San Rinaldo."

"Why choose me?" She plucked his hand away with a nonchalance she certainly didn't feel inside. "Surely there must be plenty of women who would be quite happy to pretend to be your fiancée."

He leaned on the back of the sofa, muscular legs mouth-wateringly showcased in his ninja pants. "There are women who want to be my fiancée, but not pretend."

"What a shame you're suffering from such ego problems." She playfully kicked his bare foot with hers.

Oops. Wrong move. Her skin flamed from the simple touch. An answering heat sparked in his eyes.

It was just their feet, for pity's sake. Still, she'd never felt such an intense and instantaneous draw to a man in her life, and she resented her body's betrayal.

Heels staying on the ground, Duarte toed her anklet, flicking at the beads. "I fully realize my bank balance offers a hefty enticer. With you, however, we both know where we stand."

Her yarn and plastic contrasted sharply with his suite sporting exclusive artwork. The seascape paintings weren't from some roadside stand bought simply to accent a Martha's Vineyard decor. She recognized the distinctive brushstrokes of Spanish master painter Joaquín Sorolla y Bastida from her college art classes.

She forced herself not to twitch away from Duarte's power play, not too tough actually since the simple strokes felt so good against her adrenaline-pumped nerves. "Won't your father wonder why he's never heard you mention me before now?"

"We're not a Sunday-dinners sort of family. You can use that as a quote for articles if you wish, once we're finished."

Articles. Plural. But would they be timely enough to generate the money to settle her sister's bill for next month? "How long from now until that finish date?"

"My father has asked for thirty days of my time to handle estate business around the country while he's ill. You can accompany and compile notes for your exclusive. I'll be hitting a number of hot spots around the U.S., including a stop in Washington, D.C., for a black-tie dinner with some politicians who could put your name on the map. And of course you'll get to meet my family along the way. I ask only that I get to approve any material you plan to submit."

Thirty days?

She did a quick mental calculation of her finances and Jennifer's bills. With some pinching she could squeak through until then. Except what kind of scoop would she have when every news industry out there could have jumped in ahead of her? "The story could be cold by then. I need some assurance of a payoff—at work—that will help advance my career."

Bleck, but that made her sound money-grubbing. How come men struck hard bargains and they were corporate wizards, but the same standards didn't apply to women? She had a career to look after and responsibilities to her sister.

Duarte's eyes brimmed with cynicism. "So we're going to barter here? Quite bold on your part."

"Arrest me, then. I'll text a story from my jail cell. I'll describe the inside of your personal suite along with details about your aftershave and that birthmark right above your belly button. People can draw their own conclusions and believe me, the click-throughs will be plentiful."

"You're willing to insinuate we had an affair? You're prepared to compromise your journalistic integrity?"

For her sister? She didn't have any choice. "I work for the *Global Intruder.* Obviously journalistic integrity isn't a high priority."

A glint of respect flecked his eyes. "You drive a hard bargain. Good for you." He straightened, topping her by at least half a foot. "Let's get down to business, then. There's going to be a family wedding at the end of the month at my father's estate. If you hold up your end of the bargain for the next thirty days, you get exclusive photos of the private ceremony. The payoff from those photos should be more than adequate to meet your needs."

A Medina wedding? Wow. Just. Wow.

Before she could push a resounding yes past her lips, he continued, "And in a show of good faith, you can submit a short personal interview about our engagement."

"All I have to do is *pretend* to be your fiancée?" It sounded too good to be true. Could this Hail Mary pass for Jennifer work out just right?

"Of course it's pretend. I most certainly do not want you to be my real fiancée."

"You're serious here. You're actually going to take me with you to your father's estate?" And give her photos of a family wedding.

"Ah, I can see the dollar signs in your lovely eyes."

"Sure I want a story and I have bills to pay like anybody else—well, anybody other than Medinas—but I work for that payday." Hey wait, he thought her eyes were lovely? "What reporter in their right mind would say no to this? But what's the catch? Because I can't imagine anyone would willingly invite a reporter into the intimate circle of their lives. Especially someone with as many secrets as you."

"Let's call it a preemptive strike. Better to know the snake's identity rather than wonder. And I also gain four weeks of your charming presence."

Suddenly an ugly suspicion bloomed in her mind. "I'm not going to sleep with you to land this exclusive."

Her eyes darted back to the bed, an image blossoming in her brain of the two of them tangled together in the sheets, their discarded clothes mating on the floor in a silky blend of green and black.

A humorless chuckle rumbled in his chest. "You really are obsessed with having sex with me. First, you believe I've mistaken you for a prostitute. Then, you think I want to trade my story for time in your bed. Truly, I'm not that hard up."

She blinked away the dizzying fantasy he'd painted of the two of them together. "This just seems so... bizarre."

"My life is far from normal." The luxury that wrapped so effortlessly around him confirmed that.

"I should simply accept what you're offering at face value?"

"It's a month of your life to make appearances with a prince while I settle Dad's estate. Our family is rather well connected. You'll have some very influential new contacts for future stories."

Now, didn't he know how to tempt a girl? On too many levels. "If we're not sleeping together, what do you get out of this?"

He held up one finger, tapping it on her shoulder. "I give my father peace." He added a second touch, thumbing her collarbone. "I retain control of my own personal life. And three—" he curled his whole hand around her in a hold that was both arousing and a little dangerous "—I manage all cameras, all the time. You don't have access to any shots unless I okay them. The press hears nothing without my approval. And before you get too excited, when we go to my father's, you will not know where he lives."

She laughed in hopes of dispersing the tingles tightening her breasts. "Do you intend to put a bag over my head before you stuff me in a limo?"

"Nothing so plebian, my dear." His thumb continued to work its magic. "Suffice it to say, you will get on an airplane and then land on a private island, somewhere warmer than here in Massachusetts. Beyond that..." He shrugged, sliding past her, a hint of cedar drifting along with him.

Pivoting, she watched him stride across the room, his steps silent, his hips trim and decidedly hot. "You're taking me to an untraceable island so you can kill me and dump my body in the ocean for exposing your family—which, for the record, is just my job. Nothing personal."

Shaking his head, he stopped in front of a painting of a wooden sailboat beached on its side. "Pull a bag over your head? Feed you to the sharks? You are a bloodthirsty one." Pulling back the gold-framed artwork, he revealed a wall safe. Duarte punched in numbers and the door hissed open. "Nobody is going to kill anyone. We're going to let the world know we're engaged right away. Then if you disappear, all fingers will point to me."

"If they can find you on that 'warm island.'"

"Thanks to you, I'm sure my father's secluded hideaway will be found sooner or later." He pulled out one flat velvet box after another, each with an exclusive jeweler's name imprinted on the top. "One last point. If you break any of my rules about distribution of information, I will turn over the security footage of you breaking into my estate and press charges for unlawful entry. It won't matter that you've been my fiancée. The world will believe the tape was taken after our breakup and that you were a scorned woman bent on revenge."

The unrelenting line of his back, strong column of his neck exposed by closely shorn hair spoke of cool determination. She wasn't dealing with a rookie. "You would really send me to jail?"

"Only if you betray me. If you didn't want to play in the big leagues, then you shouldn't have climbed onto my balcony. You can always just walk away free and clear now." He plucked the smallest jewelry box from the back and creaked it open to reveal an emerald-cut ruby flanked with diamond baguettes. "Negotiations are over. Take it or leave it. That's my deal."

She eyed the platinum-set engagement ring, jewels

clearly perfect yet curiously understated. No gaudy Hollywood flash, but rather old-money class that appealed to her more than some princess-cut satellite dish in a six-pronged setting. For Jennifer's sake, she would make this work. She had to. She would regret it for the rest of her life if she didn't take this risk, a chance to provide for her sister forever.

Decision made, Kate extended her hand. "Why on earth would I betray you when we've obviously come to a mutually beneficial agreement?"

Duarte hardened his focus as he did in the workout room and plucked the ring out of the cushiony bed. Best not to think about any other kind of bed.

Cradling her left hand in his, he slid the ring in place, a ruby-and-diamond antique from the Medina family collection. He could buy her something more contemporary and ornate later, but now that he had Kate's agreement, he wasn't going to give her time to wriggle out. He had a month to exact revenge on her. And no, he wasn't going to dump her in the ocean or cause her any bodily harm.

Instead, he would seduce her completely, thoroughly and satisfyingly. He wanted this woman and would have pursued her regardless of how they'd crossed paths. But they hadn't met under normal circumstances. He couldn't forget what she'd done to his family. The best way to discredit any future reports from her would come from casting her in the role of a bitter ex.

A month should be plenty of time to accomplish all of his goals.

Closing his hand around hers, he sealed the ring in place. "The bride and groom have left the rehearsal dinner downstairs, so we will not be stealing their spotlight by showing up together."

"Together? Tonight?"

"Within the hour." He thumbed the ring until the ruby centered on top of her delicate finger. "I told you I wanted to spread the word soon."

"This is more than soon." She rubbed her foot against the yarn anklet, betraying nerves she didn't let show on her face.

"It's in your best interest that we establish ourselves as a couple right away." Just saying the word *couple* brought to mind images of how thoroughly he intended to couple with her. "Especially if you're still concerned about me feeding you to the fishes."

"Then, uh, okay. I guess there's no time like the present." She tugged up the bodice of her dress, drawing his eyes right back to her cleavage.

His teeth ached, he wanted her so much. He liked to think he appreciated the whole package when it came to women, mind as well as body. But good God, this woman had a chest that could send a strong man to his knees. He burned with the urge to ease down the sides of her gown and reveal each creamy swell, slowly taking his time to explore and appreciate with his hands, with his mouth.

Patience. "There's a large party downstairs with plenty of movers and shakers from social and political scenes. You'll get to share details with your boss. My word. Fifteen minutes downstairs and then I'll have the reassurance that you're committed. You'll have the reassurance that I can't kill you without pinging police radar."

"Okay, okay, I see your point." Her laughter tickled his ears. "It's just all moving so fast I want to make sure

I think of everything. I need to make one call before we go public."

"To your editor? I think not." He tugged her closer, the soft curves of her breasts grazing his chest. He could almost taste the milky softness of her skin. "I need your commitment to this plan first. Can't have you going rogue on me out there."

The fight crept back into her eyes, chasing away the nervousness he'd seen earlier. Her grit fired his insides every bit as much as her pinup-girl curves.

She locked his hand in a firm hold, her eyes meeting his dead-on. "I need to call my sister. We can put her on speakerphone if you don't trust me about what's being said, but I have to speak to her first. It's nonnegotiable. If the answer's no, then I'll accept your offer to walk away and settle for an exposé on your birthmark."

With the top of her head at nose level, he could smell the apple-fresh scent of her shampoo, see the rapid pulse in her neck bared by her upswept do. A simple slide of his hands around her back and he would be able to cup her bottom and cradle her between his legs before he kissed her. He couldn't remember when he'd wanted a woman this much. And although he tried to tell himself it had something to do with a stretch of abstinence since the Medina story broke, he knew full well he would have ached to have her anytime. Anywhere.

Why hadn't photos of her in the private investigator's report captured his attention the way she did now? He'd registered she was an attractive woman, but hadn't felt this gut-leveling kick. She chewed her bottom lip, and he realized he was staring.

His fingers tightened around her hand wearing his ring. "What about speaking to the rest of your family?"

"Just my sister," she said softly. Her eyes were wary but she didn't pull away. "What about *your* family?"

And would he tell his brothers the truth? He would have to decide on the best strategy for approaching them later. "They'll get the memo. You could call your sister immediately after we make our announcement downstairs."

She shook her head quickly, a light brown lock sliding loose to caress her cheek the way he longed to. "I don't want to risk any chance of her hearing it from someone else first." Kate tipped her chin defiantly, as if prepping for battle. "My sister is a special-needs adult. Okay? She will be confused if this leaks before I can speak to her. It's not like I would lie about something you can easily verify."

Every word she shared was so obviously against her will that his conscience engaged for the first time. But that couldn't change his course. Kate had set this in motion when she'd climbed onto the ledge, in fact back when she'd identified his face in a picture that launched an exposé on his family. Still, his inconvenient kick of conscience could be silenced by acquiescing to her request for a call.

"Fine, then." He unclipped his cell from his waistband and passed it to her. "Feel free to phone your sister before she finds out on Facebook. But I would hurry if I were you. We all know how quickly internet news can spread."

She scrunched her nose. "You cut me to the quick with your not-so-subtle reference to my news story of the century."

God, she was hot. And he wanted her.

While he would have to wait to have her, before the

night was over, he would claim a seal-the-deal kiss from his new fiancée.

Meanwhile, it wouldn't hurt to keep her on her toes. "Make your call quickly. You have until I've changed for our appearance downstairs."

With slow and unmistakably sexual deliberation, he untied the belt on his workout clothes.

Kate damn near swallowed her tongue. "Uh, do you want me to step into the hall?"

"You promised to use speakerphone, remember?" Duarte turned his back to her but he didn't leave. He simply strode toward the mahogany armoire.

The jacket slid from his shoulders.

Holy hell.

He draped the black silk over one of the open cabinet doors, muscles shifting along his back. She saw sparks like a camera flash snapping behind her retinas.

Oh. Right. She needed to breathe.

God, this man was ripped with long, lean—lethal—definition. She'd felt those muscles up close when she'd fallen against him on the balcony.

How much further would he carry this little display? Her fingers had been wowed, for sure, but her photographer eyes picked up everything she'd missed in that frantic moment earlier.

She was female. With a heartbeat. And swaying on her feet. The cell phone bit into her tight grip, reminding her of the reason she'd come here in the first place. Keeping Jennifer happy and secure was top priority.

Thumbing in her sister's number, she considered blowing off the whole speakerphone issue. But she'd probably pushed her luck far enough tonight. There was no reason not to let him hear and he would have

Jennifer's number anyway now that it was stored in his cell history.... And hey, might Jennifer have his as well after this call? Interesting. She would have to check once she could steal a moment away from him. She activated the speaker phone just as her sister picked up.

"Hello?" Jennifer's voice came through, hesitant, confused. "Who's this?"

"Jennifer? It's Katie, calling from a, uh, friend's phone." Her eyes zipped back to Duarte and his silky pants riding low on his trim hips. "I have some important news for you."

"Are you coming to see me?" She pictured Jennifer in her pj's, eating popcorn with other residents at the first-rate facility outside Boston.

"Not tonight, sweetie." She had a date with an honest-to-God prince. The absurdity of it all bubbled hysteria in her throat.

"Then when?"

That depended on a certain sexy stranger who was currently getting mouth-wateringly naked.

"I'm not sure, Jennifer, but I promise to try my best to make it as soon as possible."

Duarte pulled out a tuxedo and hung it on the door. She caught the reflection of his chest in the mirror inside the wardrobe. The expanse of chest she'd only seen a slice of from his open jacket—

"Katie?" Jennifer's voice cut through the airwaves. "What's your news?"

"Oh, uh…" She gulped in air for confidence—and to still her stuttering heart as Duarte knelt to select shoes. "I'm engaged."

"To be married?" Jennifer squealed. "When?"

Wincing, Kate opted to deliberately misunderstand

the whole timing question since there wasn't going to be a wedding. "He gave me a ring tonight."

"And you said yes." Her sister squealed again, her high-pitched excitement echoing around the room. "Who is he?"

At least she could answer the second question honestly. "He's someone I met through work. His name is Duarte."

"Duarte? That's a funny name. I've never heard it before. Do you think he would mind if I call him Artie? I like art class."

He glanced over his shoulder, an eyebrow arched, his first sign that he even noticed or cared that she was still in the room while he stripped.

Kate cradled the phone. "Artie is a nice name, but I think he prefers Duarte."

A quick smile chased across his face before he turned back to the tux. His thumbs hooked in the waistband of his whispery black workout pants. Oh, boy. Her breath went heavy in her lungs and she couldn't peel her eyes off him to save her soul. So silly. So wrong. And so compelling in his arrogant confidence.

Then she realized he was watching her watch him in the mirror. His eyes were dark and unreadable. But he wasn't laughing or mocking, because that would have shown, surely.

Silence stretched between them, his thumbs still hooked on the waistband. His biceps flexed in anticipation of motion.

She spun away, zeroing in on the conversation instead of the man. "You will probably see something in the paper, so I want you to understand. Duarte is a real-life Prince Charming."

God, it galled her to say that.

The whistle of sliding fabric carried, the squeak of the floor as he must have shuffled from foot to foot to step out of his pants.

"A Prince Charming? Like in the stories?" Jennifer gasped. "Cool. I can't wait to tell my friends."

What would all those friends think and say when they learned he was a prince in more than some fairy-tale fashion? Would people try to get to Duarte through especially vulnerable Jennifer? The increasing complications of what she'd committed to hit her. "Sweetie, please promise me that if people ask you any questions, you just tell them to ask your sister. Okay?"

Jennifer hesitated, background sounds of a television and bingo game bleeding through. "For how long?"

"I'll talk to you by tomorrow morning. I swear." And she always kept her promises to Jennifer. She always would.

"Okay, I promise, too. Not a word. Cross my heart. Love you, Katie."

"I love you, too, Jennifer. Forever and always."

The phone line went dead and Katie wondered if she'd done the right thing. Bottom line, she had to provide for her sister and right now her options were limited. The lure of those wedding photos tempted her. A family member, Duarte had said. One of his brothers? An unknown cousin? His father even?

A hanger clanked behind her and she resisted the urge to pivot back around. Right now she cursed her artistic imagination as it filled in the blanks. In her mind's eye, she could see those hard, long legs sliding into the fine fabric tailored to fit him. The zipper rasped and she decided it was safe to look.

Although that also put his chest back in her line of sight. He was facing her now, pulling his undershirt over his head, shoes on, his tuxedo pants a perfect fit as predicted. As the cotton cleared his face, his eyes were undiluted. And she could read him well now.

She saw desire.

Duarte was every bit as turned on as she was, which seemed ironic given she was wearing that god-awful dress and he was putting on a custom-cut tuxedo. Somewhere in that contrast, a compliment to her lurked if he could see past the thrift-store trappings of her unflattering dress.

"We need to talk about my sister," she blurted.

"Speak," he commanded.

Duarte carried this autocratic-prince thing a little far, but she wasn't in the mood to call him on it. She had other more pressing matters to address, making sure he fully understood about her sister.

"Earlier, I told you that my sister has special needs. I imagine you couldn't misunderstand after hearing our conversation." Hearing the childlike wordings with an adult pitch.

"I heard two sisters who are very close to each other," he said simply, striding toward the stack of jewelry boxes he'd set on a table beside the safe, his shirttails flapping. He creaked open the one on top to reveal shirt studs and cuff links, monogrammed, and no doubt platinum. "You said there's nobody else to call. What happened to the rest of your family?"

She watched his hands at work fastening his shirt and cuffs, struck again by the strange intimacy of watching a stranger dress. "Our mother died giving birth to Jennifer."

Glancing over at her, the first signs of some kind of genuine emotion flickered through his eyes. A hint of compassion turned his coal-dark eyes to more of a chocolate brown. "I am sorry to hear that."

The compassion lingered just for a second, but long enough to soften her stiff spine. "I wish I remembered more about her so I could tell Jennifer. I was seven when our mother died." Jennifer was twenty now. Kate had taken care of her since their father walked out once his youngest daughter turned eighteen. "We have a few photos and home videos of Mom."

"That is good." He nodded curtly, securing his cummerbund. "Did your mother's death have something to do with your sister's disability?"

She didn't like discussing this, and frankly considered it none of people's business, but if she would even consider being around this man for a full month, he needed to understand. Jennifer came first for her. "Our mother had an aneurysm during the delivery. The doctors delivered Jennifer as soon as possible, but she was deprived of oxygen for a long time. She's physically healthy, but suffered brain damage."

He looped his tie with an efficiency that could only come from frequent repetition. "How old is your sister?"

Now wasn't that a heartbreaking question? "She's an eight-year-old in a twenty-year-old's body."

"Where's your father?"

Sadly, not in hell yet. "He isn't in the picture."

"Not in the picture how?"

"As in, he's not a part of our lives now." Or ever again, if she had anything to say about contact with the self-centered jackass. Anger spiked through her so hot and furious she feared it might show in her eyes and reveal a major chink in her armor. "He skipped the country once

Jennifer turned eighteen. If you want to know more, hire a private investigator."

"You chose to be Jennifer's legal guardian." He slid his tuxedo coat off the hanger. "No law says you had to assume responsibility."

"Don't make it sound like she's a burden," she responded defensively. "She's my sister and I love her. Your family may not be close, but I am very close to Jennifer. If you do anything at all to hurt her, I will annihilate you in the press—"

"Hold on." He paused shrugging on his jacket. "No one said anything about hurting your sister. I will see to it that she's protected 24/7. Nobody will get near her."

How surprising that he would commit such resources to her family. She relaxed her guard partway, if not fully. She couldn't imagine ever being completely at ease around this man. "And you won't let your guards scare her?"

"They take into account the personality of whomever they're protecting. Your sister will be treated with sensitivity and professionalism."

"Thank you," she said softly, lacing her hands and resisting the urge to smooth his satiny lapels. She hadn't expected such quick and unreserved understanding from him.

"Turn around," he commanded softly, hypnotically, and without thinking she pivoted.

His hand grazed the back of her neck. Delicious awareness tingled along her skin. What was he doing? Hell, what was *she* doing?

Something chilly slithered over her heated skin, cold and metallic. Her fingers slid up to his fingers...

Jewels. Big ones. She gasped.

He cupped her shoulders and walked her toward the

full-length mirror inside the armoire door. "It's not bad for having to make do with what I had in the safe."

His eyes held hers as they had earlier when he'd been changing. Diamonds glinted around her neck in a platinum setting, enough jewels to take care of Jennifer for years.

"Stand still and I'll put on the matching earrings." They dangled from between his fingertips in much the same way her purloined camera earrings had earlier. Except these were worth a mint.

What if she lost one in a punch bowl?

"Can't I just have my own back?"

"I think not." He looped the earrings through effortlessly until a cascade of smaller diamonds shimmered from her ears almost to her shoulders. "I'll send a guard to retrieve your shoes, and then we can go."

"Go where?" she asked, her breath catching at his easy familiarity in dressing her. He sure knew his way around a woman's body.

Duarte offered his elbow. "Time to introduce my fiancée to the world."

Three

In a million years, he never would have guessed that tonight he would introduce a fiancée to Martha's Vineyard movers and shakers. Even though the engaged couple had left the rehearsal, the band, food and schmoozing would continue long into the night.

Duarte had expected to spend the bulk of his evening working out until he decided how to approach his father's request for a month of his time. He needed to simplify his life and instead he'd added a curvaceous complication.

No looking back, he reminded himself. And by introducing Kate to a ballroom full of people he ensured she couldn't fade away. Once in the Medina spotlight, always in the spotlight.

Kate stood at his side in the elevator—more private than the two flights of stairs. As the button for the ground level lit up, he slid his iPhone back into his pocket. He'd just sent a text to his head of security, ordering protection for Jennifer Harper, securing all the identification information for Kate. He would follow up on those instructions after the announcement.

The parting doors revealed the back hall, muffled sounds swelling inside. Clinking glasses and laughter mingled as guests downed crate after crate of Dom Perignon. A dance band finished a set and announced their break. His event planners oversaw these sorts of gigs, but he spot-checked details, especially for a seven-figure event.

Offering his arm to Kate, he gestured through the open elevator doors into the hall. This part of the resort was original to the hundred-year-old building, connecting to the newly constructed ballroom he'd added to accommodate larger events. He'd started his chain of resorts as a way to build a cash base of his own, independent of the Medina fortune.

While he spent most of his time in Martha's Vineyard, scooping up properties around the U.S. allowed him to move frequently, a key to staying undetected. There was no chain name for his acquisitions. Each establishment stood on its own as an exclusive getaway for hosting private events. He didn't have any interest in owning a home—his had been taken away long ago—so moving from hotel to hotel throughout the year posed no problem for him.

Kate's hand on his arm seared through his tuxedo, making him ache to feel her touch on his bare skin. His body was still on edge from the glide of her eyes on him as he changed.

Yet, listening to her on the phone with her sister, he'd been intrigued on a deeper level than just sex and revenge. Suddenly Kate's anklet of yarn and plastic beads made sense. There were layers to this woman that intrigued him, made him want her even more.

And he intended to make sure she wanted him every bit as much before he took her to bed.

Duarte stopped in front of the side door that would open into the ballroom reception area. He reached for the knob.

Her feet stumbled, ensconced in her retrieved black high heels. "You're really going to go through with this."

"The ring did not come out of a gum-ball machine."

"No kidding." She held it up, the light refracting off the ruby and diamonds. "Looks more like an heirloom, actually."

"It is, Katie."

"I'm Kate," she snapped. "Only Jennifer calls me Katie."

Jennifer, the sister who'd wanted to call him Artie. If his brothers heard, they would never let him live that one down.

"All right then, Kate, time to announce our arrival." He wondered what Kate thought of his other name, the one he'd called himself after leaving the island at eighteen. An assumed name he could no longer use thanks to her internet exposé. Now people would always think of him as Duarte Medina instead of Duarte Moreno, the name he'd assumed after leaving his father's island.

Sweeping the ballroom doors open, he scanned the tables and dance floor illuminated by crystal chandeliers, searching for the father of the groom. He spotted Ramon with his wife a few feet away.

The pharmaceutical heir smiled his welcome and

reached for the microphone. "Dear friends and family," he called for his guests' attention.

Some still milled over their dinner of beef tenderloin, stuffed with crab and scallops. Others collected around the stage waiting for the band to return from their break.

Ramon continued, "—please welcome our special guest who has generously graced us with his presence—"

Bowing and scraping was highly overrated.

"—Prince Duarte Medina."

Applause, gasps and the general crap he'd already grown weary of bounced around the half-toasted wedding guests who'd been whooping it up for a week's worth of celebration. Times like these he almost understood his father's decision to live in total seclusion.

Once the hubbub died down, Ramon pulled the mic to his mouth again. "A hearty welcome as well to his lovely date for the evening—"

Duarte stopped alongside Ramon and spoke, filling the room without artificial aid. "I hope you will all join me in celebrating a second happy event this evening. This lovely woman at my side, Kate Harper, has agreed to be my wife."

Lifting her left hand, he kissed her fingers, strategically displaying the ring. Cameras flashed, thanks to the select media that had been invited. Kate had been on target by calling her sister. This news would be all over the internet within the hour—just as he intended.

Comments jumbled on top of each other from the partyers, while Kate stayed silent, a smile pasted on her face. Smart woman. The less said, the better.

"Congratulations!"

"How did you two m—?"

"No wonder he dumped Chelsea—"

"Oh, you both must come to our—"

"Why haven't we heard anything about her before now?"

Duarte decided that last question deserved addressing. "Why would I let the press chew Kate alive before I could persuade her to marry me?"

Good-natured laughter increased, as did the curiosity in the sea of faces. He needed to divert their thoughts. And the best way?

Claim that kiss he'd been craving since the second he'd felt the give of Kate's soft body against him on the balcony.

Her ring hand still clasped in his, he folded her arm against his chest. The pulse in her wrist beat faster under his thumb, her pupils widening with a clear signal of awakening desire. She didn't like him, and he didn't like her much either after what she'd put his family through.

But neither of them could look away.

The whispers and shuffling from the guests dulled in his ears as he focused only on her. He brushed his mouth across hers, lightly, only close enough to graze the barest friction across her bottom lip. She gasped, opening just enough to send a surge of success through him. As much as he wanted to draw this out and see how long it would take her to melt fully against him, they did have an audience and this kiss served a purpose other than seduction.

Time to seal the deal.

A second after Duarte sealed his mouth to hers, Kate had to grab the front of his tuxedo jacket to keep from stumbling. Shock. It must be shock.

But her tingling body called her a great big liar.

The seductive rasp of his calloused hand cupping her face, the light tug on her bottom lip between his teeth threatened her balance far more than any surprise. Her fingers twisted tighter in the fine weave of fabric. Tingles sparked until her eyes fluttered closed, blocking out their audience, the very reason for this display in the first place. But whatever the reason, she wanted his mouth on hers.

Sure, the attraction had been evident from the start, but still she hadn't been prepared for this. There were kisses...

And then there were *kisses*.

Duarte's slow and deliberate intensity clearly qualified as one of the latter. Tension from the whole crazy night unfurled inside her, flooding her body with a roaring need that blocked out the gawkers and whispers. The cool firm pressure of his lips to hers—confident and persuasive—had her swaying against him, her clenched hands between them.

Memories of his bronzed flesh flashed through her mind. How much more of him would she see in the coming month? And if she was this tempted after a mere couple of hours together, how much worse might the attraction become with a month of these pretend fiancée kisses and touches?

His mandarin-cedar scent enfolded her as seductively as his arms. She splayed her fingers on the hard wall of his chest. The twitch of muscles under her touch offered a cold splash of reality.

What in the world was wrong with her that she could be so thoroughly entranced by a guy she'd just met? Her bank balance, her career, her sister's very future demanded she keep a level head.

Easier said than done when the stroke of his tongue along the seam of her lips sent a lightning bolt straight through her.

She pulled away sharply before she did something reckless, like ask him to continue this later. Kate scavenged a smile and gave Duarte a playful pat on the chest for the benefit of their witnesses, people dressed in designer clothes and wearing jewels that rivaled even those around her neck. This was his world, not hers. She was just a thirty-day guest and she would do well to remember that.

This party alone offered plenty of lavish reminders. Duarte took her arm and excused them both from the festivities. A legion of uniformed staff gathered the remains of the meal as she walked past. Her mouth watered at the leftover beef tenderloin, stuffed lobster tail…and wedding cake. Okay, technically it was a groom's cake for the rehearsal dinner, but still.

Her empty stomach grumbled. Embarrassed, she clapped a hand over it.

Lord, she loved wedding cake, had a serious weakness for it, which totally pissed her off since she considered herself far from a romantic. It was as if the cake called to her, laughing the whole time. *Mock me, will you?*

And speaking of negative vibes, more than one woman shot daggers with her eyes as Kate made her way back to the door with Duarte. She wanted to reassure them. She would be out of the picture soon. But somehow she didn't think that would help these females who'd set their hopes on a wealthy prince. One wafer-thin woman even dabbed at tears with a napkin.

Could that be the one somebody had said he'd dumped?

Arching up on her toes, Kate whispered against his chin, "Who's Chelsea?"

The question fell out of her mouth before she could think.

"Chelsea?" He glanced down. "Are you taking notes for the *Intruder* already?"

"Just curious." She shrugged more nonchalantly than she felt. "I am not a popular person among the young and eligible female crowd."

Duarte squeezed her hand on his elbow. "No one will dare be rude to you. They believe you're going to be a princess."

"For the next month anyway." With his kiss still singing on her lips, thirty days seemed like a very long time to resist him.

"I think we've milled around enough for now." He pushed through the side door back into the hall, deserted but for a security guard. The elevator doors stood open, at Duarte's beck and call as everyone else appeared to be around this place.

Once inside the private elevator, Kate stomped her foot. "What were you doing out there with that whole kiss?"

Duarte tapped his floor number. "They expected a kiss. We gave them a kiss."

"That wasn't a kiss." Her toes curled in her high-heeled pumps until the joints popped. "That was, well, a lot more than it needed to be to make your point."

His heated gaze swept down, his lashes longer than she'd noticed before. "How much more was it?"

The elevator cab shrunk in size, canned music suddenly romantic and mood setting. What a time to realize she'd never had sex in an elevator. Worse yet, what a time to realize she *wanted* to have sex in an elevator.

With Duarte.

She reached behind her neck to unhook the necklace. "Call me a cab so I can leave."

"How did you get here in the first place?" He caught the necklace that she all but threw at him to keep their hands from accidentally brushing. "Slow down before you tear off your earlobes."

"I came in a taxi." She slid the second cascade of diamonds from her earlobe. "I paid him to wait for an hour but that's long past, and I'm sure he's left."

"For the best, because really—" he extended his palm as she dropped the rest of the jewelry there "—do you think I trust you'll walk out of here and come back? We're past the point where you're free to punch out of our plan."

"I'll leave your damn ruby ring behind, too, and you can assign more of your guards to watch me." Would he threaten again to have her arrested? Would that really even hold up after the announcement they'd just made?

"That's not the point, and if you take off that engagement ring, you'll be losing the chance for those wedding photos."

The elevator doors swooshed open to his private quarters. He motioned for her to enter ahead of him. Going forward meant committing to the plan.

She stepped into the hall but no farther. Was this the point where he would turn into a jerk and proposition her? He had kissed her with skilled deliberation. "A part of our deal included no sex."

"I always keep my word. We will not have sex—unless you ask." He stepped closer. "Although be aware, there will be more kisses in the coming weeks. It's expected that I would shower my fiancée with affection. It's also expected that you would reciprocate."

"Fair enough," she conceded, then rushed to add, "but only when we're in public."

"That's logical. Know, too, though, that we will have to spend time alone with each other. This evening, for example, we need to get our stories straight before we face the world on a larger scale."

So much for her assumption of darker motives for his refusal to call a cab. What he said made sense. "Know that I'm staying under duress."

"Duly noted. Just keep remembering that black-tie dinner in D.C. with politicians and ambassadors."

"You're wicked bad with the temptation."

He steamed her with another smoky once-over. "You're one to lecture on that subject."

"I thought we were going to talk."

"We will. Soon." He stepped away and she exhaled. Hard. "I have a quick errand to take care of, but I'll have dinner sent up to your room while you wait. I hear tonight's special is tenderloin and stuffed lobster."

"And cake," she demanded, even knowing it wouldn't come close to satisfying the hunger gnawing as her insides tonight. "I really need a slice of that groom's cake."

Duarte watched his head of security shovel a bite of chocolate cake in his mouth in between reviewing surveillance footage and internet headlines on the multiple screens. A workaholic, Javier Cortez frequently ate on the job, rather than take off so much as a half hour for a meal. He even kept an extra suit in his office for days he didn't make it home.

Wheeling out a chair from the monitor station, Duarte

took a seat. "What were you able to pull together on security for Jennifer Harper?"

Javier swiped a napkin across his mouth before draping the white linen over his knee again. "Two members of our team are currently en route to her assisted-living facility outside Boston. They're already in phone contact with security there and will be reporting back to me within the hour."

"Excellent work, as always." He didn't dispense praise lightly, but Javier deserved it.

The head of security had also endured a crappy month every bit as bad as Duarte's. Javier's cousin, Alys, had betrayed the Medina family by confirming the *Global Intruder*'s suspicions about Duarte's identity. She had served as the inside source for other leaks as well, even offering up Enrique Medina's "love child" he'd fathered shortly after arriving in the U.S.

Javier had weathered intense scrutiny after Alys's betrayal had been discovered. He'd turned in his resignation the second his cousin had been confronted, vowing he bore no ill will against the Medinas and was shamed by his cousin's behavior.

Duarte had torn up the resignation. He trusted his instincts on this one.

How odd that he found it easier to trust Javier than his own father. That could have something to do with Enrique Medina's "love child" the whole world now knew about. Their grief-stricken widower father hadn't taken long to hook up with another woman. The affair had only lasted long enough to produce Eloisa. Duarte made a point of not blaming his half sister. He tried not to judge his father, but that part was tougher.

Making peace with the old man was more pressing than ever with Enrique's failing health.

Javier set aside his plate with a clink of the fork. "No disrespect, my friend, but are you sure you know what you're doing?"

Most wouldn't risk asking him such a personal question, but Javier's past wasn't that different from Duarte's. Javier's family had escaped San Rinaldo along with the king. Enrique had set up a compound in Argentina as a red herring. The press had believed the deposed king and his family had settled there.

However, the highly secured estate in South America had housed the close circle who'd been forced out of San Rinaldo with the Medinas—including the Reyes de la Cortez family. Javier understood fully the importance of security as well as the burning need to break free of smothering seclusion.

Duarte tapped a screen displaying an image of Kate at the antique dinner cart, plucking the long-stem red rose from the bud vase. "I know exactly what I was doing. I was introducing my fiancée to the world."

"Oh, really?" Javier leaned closer, pulling his tie from over his shoulder, where he must have draped it when he started his dinner. "Less than two hours ago she was scaling the side of the building to get a photo of you."

His eyes cruised back to the screen. Kate stroked the rose under her nose as she settled in the chair. Her brown hair tousled, her feet bare, she had the look of a woman who'd been thoroughly kissed and seduced.

Thinking of the way she'd made her entrance on the balcony earlier… He couldn't help but smile at her audacity. "Quite an entrance she makes."

"Now you've invited her into your inner sanctum?" Javier shook his head. "Why not simply hand over a journal with your life story?"

"What better way to watch your enemy than keeping

her close?" In his room. Where she waited for him now, savoring the beef tenderloin with the gusto of a woman who appreciated pleasures of the senses. "She will only see what I want her to see. The world will only know what I want it to know."

"And if she goes to the press later with the whole fake engagement?" Javier's eyes followed his to the screen, to Kate.

Duarte clicked off the image and the monitor went blank. "By then, people will label anything she says as the ramblings of a scorned woman. And if a handful of people believe her, what does that matter to me?"

"You really don't care." Javier tapped the now-dark screen, a skeptical look on his face.

"She will have served her purpose."

"You're a cold one."

"And you are not very deferential to the man who signs your extremely generous paychecks," he retorted, not at all irritated since he knew his friend was right. And a man needed people like that in his inner circle, individuals unafraid to declare when the emperor wore no clothes. "I assume you want to continue working for me?"

"You keep me on because I don't kowtow to you." Javier picked up his cake plate again. "You've never thought much of brownnosers. Perhaps that's why she intrigues you."

"I told you already—"

"Yeah, yeah, inner sanctum, blah-blah-blah." He shoveled a bite of the chocolate rum cake, smearing basket-weave frosting into the fork tines.

"Perhaps I am not as cold as you say. Revenge is sweet." So why wasn't he seeking this sort of "revenge" with Javier's cousin? Alys was attractive. They'd even dated briefly in the past.

"If you wanted revenge you could have gotten Kate Harper fired or arrested. She's snagged your interest."

Javier was too astute, part of what made him excel at his job as head of security. But then what was wrong with sleeping with Kate? In fact, an affair made perfect sense, lending credibility to their engagement.

"Kate is…entertaining. I'll grant her that." And his life was so damn boring of late.

Work did not provide a challenge. How many millions did a man need to make? He was a warrior without an army.

If he'd grown up in San Rinaldo, he would have served in her military. But with his history, he'd never had the option of signing on for service in his new home.

How ironic to be a thirty-five-year-old billionaire suffering from a career crisis? "She's also helping take heat off me with my father. The old man is in a frenzy to ensure the next generation of Medinas before he dies."

"Whatever you say, my friend." Javier tipped back a bottled water.

Ah, hell. He couldn't hide the truth from himself any more than from his friend. Duarte was off balance, tied up in knots over his father because he'd promised his mother he would watch Enrique's back. But how did a person defend someone against a failing liver?

He sometimes wondered why Beatriz had asked him when Carlos had been older, when Carlos had been the one to come through for her. She'd reminded him then he had always been the family's little soldier. He'd done his best to protect his family, a drive he saw equaled in Kate's eyes when she spoke of her sister. How ironic that their similar goals of protecting family put them so at odds.

Standing, Duarte returned the rolling chair under the console of monitors and tapped the blank screen that had held an image of Kate relishing her dinner. "Make sure you leave that one off. I'll take care of security in Kate's suite."

Four

Thank goodness no one was looking, because she'd tossed out table manners halfway through the lobster tail. Kate washed down the bite of chocolate rum cake with sparkling water. She was hungrier than she'd realized, having skipped supper due to nerves over crashing the Medina party.

Sipping from her crystal goblet, she opted for the Fuiggi water rather than the red wine. She needed to keep her mind clear around Duarte, especially after that kiss.

A promise of temporary pleasures that could lead to a host of regrets.

Footsteps sounded in the hall, a near-silent tread she was beginning to recognize as his. Would he go to his suite or stop by her room? He'd said he wanted to talk through details about their supposed dating past before they faced the world.

He stopped outside her door. Her toes curled. She licked her fork clean quickly and pushed away from the small table. Her shoes? Where had she ditched them before digging into her meal?

The door swung open.

Time had run out so she stayed seated, tucking her bare feet underneath the chair. Duarte filled the open frame to her room, blocking out the world behind him, reminding her that they were completely alone with each other and the memory of one unforgettable kiss. She straightened with as much nonchalance as she could, given her heart pumped as fast as a rapid-shot camera.

"Supper is to your liking?" He draped his tuxedo coat over the back of a carved mahogany chair.

"It's amazing and you know it." She wished she could take a slice of the cake to Jennifer.

"You were hungry." He loosened his tie.

Her heart stuttered. "How about you keep your pants on this time, cowboy."

"Whatever makes you happy, my dear."

Smiling, he slid the tie from his collar slowly, a sleigh bed with a fluffy comforter warm and inviting behind him. Then he stopped across from her at the intimate table for two, complete with silver and roses. Thank heaven he was still clothed—for the most part.

She placed her fork precisely along the top of her dessert china, the gold-rimmed pattern gleaming in the candlelight. "My compliments to your chef."

"I'll let him know." He scooped up her cut crystal glass of untasted wine and swirled the red vintage along the sides. "I have to confess, it's refreshing to hear a woman admit to appreciating a full dinner rather than models who starve themselves." He eyed her over the top of the Waterford goblet. "Eating can be a sensual experience."

Just the way he lingered over the word *sensual* with the slightest hint of an exotic accent made her mouth go moist. She swallowed hard and reminded herself to gather as much information as possible for future articles. While her primary job focused on taking the photos, an inside scoop could only help sell those shots.

This time with Duarte wasn't about her. She was here for her job, for her sister. "You don't strike me as the sort to overindulge when the dinner bell clangs. You seem very self-disciplined."

"How so?" He tipped back the glass.

She watched his throat work with a long swallow, his every move precise. "I would peg you as a health-food nut, a workout fiend."

"Do you have a problem with a sweaty round in the gym?"

"I don't love it, but I adore food more than I dislike exercise. So I log a few miles on a stationary bike when I can." Wait, how had this suddenly become about her when she was determined to learn more about him?

"You need to stay in shape for scaling ledges." He tapped the rim of his glass to her water goblet, right over the spot where her mouth had rested.

The *ting* of crystal against crystal resonated through her. "You said you saw me on security footage before I ever entered your room. What if those tapes of me crawling around outside somehow leak to the media? Won't that shoot a hole in our engagement story? And what about the part I played in exposing your half sister?"

"About the balcony incident, we'll blame it on the

paparazzi chasing you out of your room. As for Alys, we can always say you let it slip at work." He dropped into the chair across from her, lean and long, his power harnessed but humming.

"What's to stop me from claiming any of that if you decide to use the video feed against me?"

"Do you think I've revealed all the ammunition in my arsenal?" He turned the glass on the table, the thin stem so fragile in his hand.

"Are you trying to worry me?" She refused to be intimidated.

His breathing stayed even, but his eyes narrowed. "Only letting you know I play at an entirely different level than anyone you've ever come up against. I have to. The stakes are higher."

"I don't know about that." An image of Jennifer's smile when she'd passed over the braided anklet filled Kate's mind. "My stakes feel pretty high to me."

He set aside his drink and reached back into his tux jacket. His hand came back with a computer disc in a case. He slid it across the table toward her. "Copies of the photos from your camera and from my own press team for you to share with the *Intruder*."

"All of my photos?" she asked with surprise—and skepticism.

"Most of your photos." The hard angles of his face creased into a half smile. "You can pass these along to your editor. If he questions why you're still speaking to him when you have a rich fiancé, tell him that we want to control the release of information and as long as he plays nice, the flow will continue. I'll have a laptop computer sent up for you. I keep my word."

She traced an intricate *M* scrolled on a label, the

gilded letter taking on the shape of a crown. Her brain spun headlines... Medina Men. Medina Monarchs.

Medina Money, because without question pure gold rested under her fingertips. And he'd promised her so much more in four weeks. "I need to stop by my apartment tomorrow before we leave."

"Cat or dog?"

"What?" She glanced up quickly.

"Do you have a cat or a dog? What kind?" He cradled his iPhone in his broad palm. "I'll pass along the details to my assistant and your animal will be boarded."

His arrogance almost managed to overshadow his thoughtfulness. Almost, but not quite. "I didn't know that ninjas read minds. And it's a cat. I'm away from home too much to have a dog. My neighbor usually watches him for me."

"No need to bother your neighbor. My people will see to everything, like with your sister's security." He began tapping in instructions.

How easy it would be to let him take charge, especially when what he offered was actually helpful...even thoughtful. "That's nice of you. Thanks."

He waved aside her gratitude and continued texting. "Before you mention packing clothes, forget it. I'm already ordering everything you'll need. You'll have some of the new wardrobe by morning."

She glanced down at her green Gabbana knockoff. "Cinderella makeover time?"

"Believe me, you don't need a makeover. Even wearing a, uh—" He stumbled over his words for the first time, his brow furrowing....

"A secondhand-store bargain, you mean?" She found his hesitation, this first sign of human emotion, unsettling...and a little charming. "You don't have to worry about offending me. I'm not embarrassed by the fact my bank balance is smaller than yours. That's just a fact."

"Very good that you're not going to waste our time with ridiculous arguments. What's your dress size?"

"Eight for dresses, pants, shirts."

"Got it." He input the information. "Shoe size."

"Seven. Narrow."

"Bra?"

She gasped. "Excuse me?"

"What is your bra size?" He quirked an eyebrow, without raising his onyx gaze. "Some of the evening gowns will have a fitted bodice and special cut. Last-minute alterations in person can be made, but it's helpful to have a ballpark number to start with."

Resisting the urge to flatten her hands to her breasts required a Herculean effort. "Thirty-four C."

He didn't look away from his iPhone, but a slow sexy smile creased his face. The air between them crackled and her nipples ached inside her strapless pushup. This man was entirely too audacious. And enticing. Finally, he put away his phone and returned his focus to her.

"A new 'princess' wardrobe will be waiting in the morning with enough garments to see you through our first few days of travel. The rest of your clothing for the month will arrive before the end of the week." He thumbed the engagement ring on her finger, nudging the ruby back to the center again.

His simple touch stirred her as much now as his kiss had earlier, and this time they were alone rather than in a ballroom full of onlookers. His gaze fell to her mouth, brown eyes turning lava-dark with desire.

He'd told her the engagement was mutually beneficial for practical reasons, but at the moment she wondered if he had a different agenda. Could he really be so interested in getting her into his bed that he would expose himself to press coverage? That he would want her so much after one meeting was mind-blowing. Who wouldn't be complimented?

Except it also felt so far out of the realm of possibility that she felt conceited for considering it. Revenge seemed a far more logical reason for the seductive gleam he directed at her.

Either way, she needed to keep her guard up at all times. "Thank you. I will be certain the reporter who pens the stories accompanying my photos notes that you have impeccable, princely manners."

"No thanks or credit needed. I won't even notice the expense of a few dresses and 34C bras."

Her fingers curved into a fist under his touch. "I was referring to your consideration in looking after my cat before we leave."

"Again, that has nothing to do with being nice." He enfolded her curled hand in his until it disappeared. "I'm only taking care of loose ends so we can move forward."

This man was such a strong presence he could eclipse a person as fully as his palm covered her hand. "Of course I'll also have to make note in the article that you're bossy."

"I prefer to think I'm a take-charge sort of man."

"You would have made a great general."

He traced from her ring finger around to the vein leading to the pulse in her wrist. "Why do I feel like you're not complimenting me?"

"Don't you worry about how I'll present you in stories once this is over? Photography may be my main focus, but I do write articles on occasion."

The warmth of his clasp seared her skin. They were

just linking fingers, for crying out loud, something as innocent as two teens in a movie theater. But they weren't in some public locale.

They were alone, and she questioned the wisdom of letting him touch her in private. The heated look in his eyes was most definitely anything but innocent.

"You'll be the ex-fiancée. It'll all sound like sour grapes." He released her fist and stood before she could pull away. "Regardless, I don't give a flying f—"

"Right. Got it." She raised both hands. "You don't care what people think of you."

"I only cared about privacy, and now that's a moot point." He walked around the table, stopping beside her and tipping her chin with a knuckle. "So let's get back to talking about how smoking-hot you look regardless of what you wear, and how much better you must look in nothing at all."

She saw this for what it was, a gauntlet moment where she could either back down—or let him know she wasn't a pushover. No dancing around the subject or pretending to ignore his seductive moves to keep some kind of peace. She'd always met life head-on and now wouldn't be any different.

"Stop trying to throw me off balance." She stared at him without flinching or pulling away. "I've kept a steady hand taking pictures through bomb blasts in a war zone and during aftershocks in earthquake rubble. I think I can handle a come-on from you."

A flicker of approval mingled with the desire in his dark eyes at her moxie. And how silly to be excited because she'd impressed him with something other than her cup size. She wasn't interested in the man beyond what he had to offer in a photo op.

Okay, not totally true. Truth be told, just looking at

him turned her on. Hearing his light Spanish accent stoked that a notch. He was a handsome man, and a big-time winner in the genetic gene pool when it came to charisma.

But that didn't mean she intended to act on the attraction.

"I can handle you," she repeated, just as much to reassure herself as to convince him.

"Good, an easy victory isn't nearly as much fun." He reached behind her, his hand coming back with a thick white robe. He passed the folded terry cloth bearing the resort logo to her. "Enjoy your shower."

Kate was naked under the robe.

The terry cloth was thick and long and covered her completely from Duarte's eyes as he lounged in her suite. But deep in his gut, he knew. She wore nothing more.

He went utterly still in his chair by her fireplace. He'd waited for a half hour in her suite, a large room with a sitting area in the bay window, sleigh bed across the room. She stood in the doorway from her bathroom, her fluffy robe accenting the crisp blue-and-white decor. Her wet hair was gathered in a low ponytail draped over one shoulder.

It was longer than he'd expected. He also expected her to demand that he leave. But she simply tucked her feet into the complimentary slippers by the door and padded across the room toward him.

Unflinching, she stared back at him, her eyes sweeping down him as if taking in every detail of his tuxedo shirt open at the neck, dark pants sans cummerbund, feet propped on the ottoman. She stopped alongside him and sank smoothly into the blue checkered chair on the other side of the fireplace. She was fearless.

And magnificent.

She crossed her legs, baring a creamy calf. "What else do we need to cover before facing the world tomorrow?"

The fire crackled and warmed. He'd started the blaze to set a more intimate tone. Except now it tormented him by heating her pale leg to an even more tempting rosy pink. "Let's discuss how we met. You spin mythical stories from a thread of truth. How about take a stab at it by creating our dating history?"

"Hmm…" Her foot swung slowly, slipper dangling from her toes, her yarn jewelry still circling her ankle. "After I broke the story about your family, you confronted me…at my apartment… You didn't want to risk being seen at my office. You know where I live, right? Since you knew to send someone to take care of my cat."

"You're based out of Boston, but travel frequently," he confirmed correctly. "So you just keep a studio apartment."

"Your detectives have done their homework well." Her smile went tight, her plump lips thinning. "Did you already know about Jennifer?"

"No, I only know your address and work history."

Perhaps there he'd dropped the ball. He, above all people, should know how family concerns shaped a person's perspective. Pieces of the Kate puzzle readjusted in his mind, and he resolved to get back to the issue of her sister.

Although Kate's tight mouth let him know he would have to tread warily. "Tell me, Ms. Harper, how does someone who covered the wars in Iraq and Afghanistan end up working for the *Global Intruder?*"

"Downsizing in the newspaper industry." She blinked fast as if working hard not to look away nervously.

"Taking care of your sister had nothing to do with your decisions?" He understood her protectiveness when it came to her sibling. The bond was admirable, but he wouldn't let softer feelings blur his goal.

"Jennifer needs me." Kate picked at the white piping along the club chair.

"There were plenty of people willing to roll out for an assignment at the drop of the hat." Unanswered questions about her career descent now made perfect sense. "By the time you settled your sister, you'd lost out on assignments. Other reporters moved ahead of you. Have I got it right?"

Fire snapped in her eyes as hotly as the flames popping in the fireplace. "How does this pertain to fielding questions about our engagement? If the subject of Jennifer comes up, we'll tell the media it's none of their business."

"Well, damn." He thumped himself on the forehead. "Why didn't my family and I come up with that idea ourselves? To think we hid out and changed our identity for nothing."

"Are you sure we'll be able to convince anyone we even like each other, much less that we're in love?"

He tamped down the anger that would only serve to distract. This woman was too adept at crawling under his skin. "We're only talking about your basic life story. Surely you can trust me with that."

"Give me a good reason why I should trust you with anything. I don't really know you." She toyed with the tip of her damp ponytail, releasing a waft of shower-fresh *woman*. "Perhaps if you would tell me more about your past, I'll feel more comfortable opening up in return."

"Touché," he said softly as a lighthouse horn wailed in the distance. "Instead, we'll move back to creating our dating history."

She dropped her ponytail and stared upward as if plucking the story from the air. "On the day we met, I was wearing khaki pants, a Bob Marley T-shirt, and Teva sandals. You remember it perfectly because you were entranced by my purple toenail polish." Her gaze zipped and locked with his again. "You get bonus points if you remember the polish had glitter. We ended up talking for hours."

"What was *I* wearing?"

"A scowl." She grinned wickedly.

"You sound positively besotted."

She flattened a hand to her chest dramatically, drawing his eyes to the sweet curves of her breasts. "I *swooned*." Kate leaned forward, her robe gaping enough to tease him with a creamy swell but not enough to give him a clear view. "I took your picture because I found you darkly intriguing and the feeling increased when you came to confront me about exposing your identity. The attraction was instantaneous. Undeniable."

"That part will be very easy to remember." His groin tightened the longer he looked at the peekaboo flesh of her generous breasts.

"You wooed me. I resisted, of course." Clasping the neck of her robe closed, she sat back. Had she tormented him on purpose? "But ultimately I fell for you."

"Do tell what I did to convince you." Any edge with Kate would be helpful.

Her grin turned mischievous. "You won me over with your love poem."

He leaned back. "Afraid not."

"I was joking." She toe-tapped his feet, propped and crossed on the ottoman.

"Oh. Okay. I see that now. I'm not artistic." His family also said he lacked a sense of humor, which had never bothered him before, but could prove problematic in dealing with this woman. He needed to turn the tables back in his favor. "I can be romantic without resorting to sappy sonnets."

"Then let's hear how you spin the story of our first date." She waved with a flourish for him to take over. "How did it go?"

"I picked you up in my Jaguar."

Kate crinkled her nose, shaking her head. "Nuh-uh. Too flashy to wow me."

"It's vintage."

"That's better," she conceded.

"And red."

"Even better yet."

He searched his mental catalogue of information about her for the right detail... "I brought you catnip and *cat*viar, instead of flowers and candy."

"You remembered I have a cat?" The delighted surprise in her voice rewarded his effort.

"I remembered everything you told me, although you neglected to mention her name and breed."

"*He* is a gray tabby named Ansel."

"As in Ansel Adams, the photographer. Nice." He filed away another piece of information about the intriguing woman in front of him.

"No flowers and candy at all, though. I'm surprised. I would expect you to be the exotic bouquet and expensive truffle sort."

"Too obvious. I can see you're intrigued by my unusual choice, which makes my point." That little strip of braided yarn she wore told him that Kate had a sentimental side. "Moving on. We ate a catered dinner on my private jet, so as not to attract attention in a restaurant."

"Your airplane? Where were we going?"

"The Museum of Contemporary Photography in Chicago."

"I haven't been there before," she said wistfully.

He vowed then and there to take her before the month was over. "We learned a lot about each other, such as food preferences—" He paused.

"Chili dogs with onions and a thick slice of wedding cake, extra frosting," she answered, toying with the tassel on the tapestry wall hanging behind her. "What about you?"

"Paella for me, a Spanish rice dish." Although he'd never been able to find a chef who could replicate the taste he remembered from San Rinaldo. "And your favorite color?"

"Red. And yours?"

"Don't have one." His world was a clear-cut image of black and white, right and wrong. Colors were irrelevant. "Coffee or tea drinker?"

"Coffee, thick and black served with New Orleans–style beignets."

"We're in agreement on the coffee, churros for me." Now on to the important details. "Favorite place to be kissed?"

She gasped, fidgeting with the tie to her robe. "Not for public knowledge."

"Just want to make sure I get it right when the cameras start. For the record, we kissed on the first date but you wouldn't let me get to second base until—"

"I don't intend for any interview to reach that point and neither will you."

"But we did kiss on our first date." He swung his feet to the floor and leaned forward, elbows on his knees. Closer to her.

"After your display in the ballroom, the whole world knows we've, uh, kissed."

He clamped his fingers around her ankle, over the beaded yarn. "From what I've learned about you tonight, kissing you, touching you, I think you have very sensitive earlobes."

Her pupils widened, her lips parting and for a moment he thought she would sway forward, against him, into him. The memory of her curves pressed to his chest earlier imprinted his memory. How much more mind-blowing the sensation would be bare flesh to flesh.

Kate drew in a shuddering breath. "I think we've learned quite enough about each other for one evening." She crossed her arms just below her breasts. "You should go so I can get some sleep."

The finality in her tone left no room for doubt. He'd pushed her as far as he could for one night. And while he would have preferred to end the evening revealing every inch of her body beneath that robe, he took consolation in knowing he had a month to win her over.

Easing back, he shoved to his feet. Was that regret in her eyes? Good. That would heighten things for them both when he won her over.

Five

The next morning, Kate pulled on her borrowed clothes, made of fabric so fine it felt like she wore nothing at all.

The silk lined linen pants were both warm and whispery. A turtleneck, cool against her skin, still insulated her from the crisp nip in the winter air leaching into her suite. They'd gotten everything right from the size of the clothes to her favored cinnamon-apple fragrance. Had he noticed even that detail about her?

Everything fit perfectly, from the brown leather ankle boots—to her bra. Toying with the clasp between her breasts, she wondered how much he knew about the selections.

All had been brought to her by the resort staff, along with a note, beignets and black coffee. The aftertaste of her breakfast stirred something deeper inside her, a place already jittery at the notion of him envisioning her underwear. He'd listened to her preferences about food choices. He'd remembered.

He'd even come through on his promise to deliver a secured laptop for her to send her photos to Harold Hough, her editor at the *Global Intruder*. Duarte had kept his word on everything he'd promised.

She trailed her fingers over the two packed bags with her other new clothes neatly folded and organized, along with shoes and toiletries. She plucked out a brush and copper hair clamp. What a different world, having anything appear with the snap of his fingers.

Sweeping the brush through her hair, she shook it loose around her shoulders. Excitement twirled in her belly like the snowflakes sifting from the clouds. She scooped up the fur-lined trench and matching suede gloves, wondering where they would go after stopping by her place for her cameras.

How could she want to spend time with a man who, underneath the trappings, was all but blackmailing her? She churned the dichotomy around in her brain until finally resolving to look at this as a business deal. She'd agreed to that deal wholeheartedly out of desperation, and she would make the best of her choice.

Kate stepped into the hall and locked her door behind her. Duarte's note with her breakfast had instructed her to meet him in his office after she ate and dressed.

Pivoting, she nearly slammed into a man who seemed to have materialized out of nowhere.

"Excuse me." She jolted back a step, away from the guy in a dark suit with an even darker glower.

"Javier Cortez—I work for Duarte Medina," he introduced himself, his accent thicker than his boss's. "I am here to escort you to his office." Javier was even more somber than his employer.

Duarte was intense. This guy was downright severe.

Something about his name tugged at her memory—and was that a gun strapped to his belt? "What exactly do you do here for Duarte?"

"I am head of security."

That explained the gun, at least. "Thank you for the help. I don't know my way around the resort yet."

His footsteps thudded menacingly down the Persian runner. "You managed quite well last night."

She winced. He must be the keeper of the video footage from her not-so-successful entrance. Which meant he also likely knew the engagement was a farce. She thumbed the ring and gauged her words.

"Last night was a memorable evening for many reasons, Mr. Cortez."

Pausing outside a paneled wood door, Javier faced her down. Why did he look so familiar? The other two Medina brothers were named Antonio and Carlos, not Javier. Roughly the same age and bearing as Duarte, still Javier didn't look like a relative.

And she couldn't help but notice that while he was undoubtedly handsome, this guy didn't entice her in the least.

"Is this his office?"

"The back entrance. Yes." His arm stretched across it barred her from entering—and parted his jacket enough to put his gun in plain sight. "Betray my friend and you will regret it."

She started to tell him to drop the B-grade-movie melodrama, then realized he was serious. She didn't give ground. Bullies never respected a wimp anyway. "So he tells me."

"This time, *I* am telling you. Know that I will be

watching your every step. Duarte may trust you with your cameras and that secure laptop, but I'm not so easily fooled."

Irritation itched through two dings of the elevator down the hall before she cleared her brain enough to realize what had bothered her about the man's name and why he looked familiar. "You're angry about your cousin getting booted out of royal favor for tipping me off."

His jaw flexed with restraint, his eyes cold. "Alys is an adult. She chose wrong. My cousin was disloyal not only to our family and the Medinas, but she also betrayed our entire country. I'm angry with *her*. Alys must accept responsibility for her actions, and you can feel free to cite me on that in your gossip e-zine."

"Thank you for the quote. I'll be sure they spell your name correctly." She hitched her hands on her hips. "I'm just curious about clarifying one point. If you're only mad at her and realize I was just doing my job, why are you reading me the riot act about not hurting Duarte?"

"Because I do not trust you." Javier stepped closer, his intent obviously to intimidate. "I understand you made your decision for practical reasons. Yes, you were doing your job. Understand, I am doing mine, and I am far more ruthless than you could ever hope to be."

As much as she resented being towered over, she understood and respected the need to protect the people you cared about. Javier might be a bully, but he wasn't just looking out for himself.

"You know what, Javier Cortez? Everybody should have a friend like you."

"Compliments won't work with me." He stared down his sharp nose at her. "Remember, I'll be watching you."

The door swung open abruptly. The security guru jerked upright.

Duarte frowned, looking from one to the other. "Is something wrong here, Javier?"

"Not at all," he answered. "I was only introducing myself to your fiancée."

"Kate?" Duarte asked her, his gaze skeptical.

She stepped in front of Javier and a little too close to Duarte. His hair still damp, she caught a whiff of her faux fiancé's aftershave and a hint of crisp air. Had he already been for a walk outside?

And ouch, how silly to wonder how he'd spent his morning.

A cleared throat behind her reminded Kate of the bodyguard. "Your buddy Javier was just giving me the lowdown on security around here."

As much as she wanted to tell Javier to shove it, the guy had a point. She needed to watch her step.

She couldn't allow herself to be swayed by Duarte's charming images of jet-setting dates and catnip gifts. This was a man who lived with security cameras and ruthless armed guards. He was every bit as driven as she was. She needed to harden her resolve and shore up her defenses if she expected to survive this month unscathed.

Which meant keeping tempting touches to a minimum.

Outside Kate's Boston apartment, Duarte slid inside the limousine, heater gusting full blast. The door closed, locking him in the vehicle with Kate and his frustration over finding her with Javier earlier. Not that he was jealous. He didn't do that emotion. However, seeing them standing close together made him...

Hell, he didn't know what it made him feel, but he didn't like the way his collar suddenly seemed too tight. He swiped the sleet from his coat sleeves.

After they'd taken the ferry from Martha's Vineyard, they'd spent the past couple hours driving through snow turned to sleet on their way to her place. She'd insisted on retrieving her cameras herself, stating she didn't want one of his "people" pawing through her things. He understood the need for privacy and had agreed. He controlled his own travel plans, after all. A few hours' wiggle room didn't pose a problem.

A hand's reach away, Kate sorted through her camera bag she'd retrieved from her tiny efficiency. The bland space where she lived had relayed clearly how little time she spent there.

She looked up from her voluminous black bag as ice and packed snow crunched under the limo's tires. "May I ask what's next on the agenda or are we going to an undisclosed location?"

"I have a private jet fueled and waiting to fly us to D.C. as soon as the weather clears. After we land, we'll stay at one of my hotels." He selected a card from his wallet and passed it to her. "Here's the address, in case you want to let your sister—or the *Intruder*—know."

Not that anyone would get past his security.

He'd bought the nineteenth-century manor home in D.C. ten years ago. With renovations and an addition, he'd turned it into an elite hotel. He catered to the wealthy who spent too much time on the road and appreciated the feeling of an exclusive home away from home while doing business in the nation's capital.

Silently, she pulled out her cell phone from her bag and began texting, her silky hair sliding forward over one shoulder. She was a part of the press. He couldn't forget for a second that he walked a fine line with her.

He needed to be sure she remembered, as well. "Don't make the mistake of thinking Javier is cut from the same cloth as his cousin. You were able to trick Alys, but Javier is another matter."

She kept texting without answering, sleet pinging off the roof. He studied her until she glanced over at him, tight-lipped.

Anger frosted Kate's blue eyes as chilly as the bits of melted sleet still spiking her eyelashes. "For your information, I didn't have to trick your pal Alys. Yes, I approached her about the photo I accidentally snapped of you at Senator Landis's beach house. But *she* came to *me* about your half sister."

Duarte registered her words, but he could only think about her determination, her drive…and her 34C breasts. He wondered what his assistant had chosen for Kate. As much as he wanted to know, checking out the clothes before they were sent to her felt…invasive. Privacy was important.

He understood that firsthand. "You made the contact with Alys when you chased her down about that photo of me with the senator."

"Believe what you want." She changed out the lens on a camera with the twist of her wrist. "I merely traced people in the picture until one of them was willing to give up more information on the mysterious past of a guy who called himself Duarte Moreno."

Hearing how easily someone in his father's inner circle could turn angered him. But it also affirmed what he'd thought during his entire isolated childhood on the island. There was no hiding from the Medina legacy. "You'll be wise to remember how easy it is to misstep. If our secret is out, I'll have no reason to keep you around until the wedding."

A small yellow rag in hand, she cleaned a lens. "One screwup and that's it? No room for mistakes and forgiveness? Everyone deserves an occasional do over."

"Not when the stakes are so high." A single mistake, a break in security, could cost a life. His mother had died and Carlos still carried scars from that day.

"Aren't you curious as to why Alys was willing to sell out your family?"

"The 'why' doesn't matter."

"There, you are wrong." She handled her camera reverently. "The 'why' can matter very much."

"What happened to neutral reporting of the facts?" He hooked a finger along her black camera strap.

"The 'why' can help a good journalist get more information from a source."

"All right, then. Why did Alys turn on us?"

Kate raised the camera to her face, lens pointed in his direction, and when he didn't protest, she clicked.

He forced himself not to flinch, tough to do after so long hiding from having his image captured as if the camera could steal his spirit. "Kate?"

"Alys wanted to be a Medina princess." Kate lowered the camera to her lap. "But how much fun would the tiara be worth if she couldn't show it off to the world? She wanted everyone to know about the Medinas, and my camera made that possible."

"Don't even try to say she had feelings for one of us. She wouldn't have betrayed us if she cared."

"True enough." Her voice drifted off and he could all but see the investigative wheels turning in her mind. "Did *you* love *her?* Is that why you're so edgy today?"

His restlessness had everything to do with Kate and nothing to do with Alys, a woman he considered past history. "What do you think?"

"I believe it must have hurt seeing a trusted friend turn on your family, especially if she meant something more to you."

"I'm not interested in Alys, never was beyond a couple dates. Any princess dreams she may have harbored were of her own making."

In a flash of insight, he realized she was curious about his past relationships, and not as a reporter, but as a woman. Suddenly his frustration over finding her with Javier didn't irritate him nearly as much.

He slid his arm along the back of the leather seat.

"Uh…" Kate jumped nervously. "What do you think you're doing?"

Dipping his face toward her hair, he nuzzled her ear. When she purred softly, he continued, "Kissing my fiancée, or I will be," he said on his way toward her parted lips, "momentarily."

Catching her gasp, his mouth met hers. His hand between her shoulder blades drew her closer. The rigid set of her spine eased and she flowed into him, her lips softening. The tip of her tongue touched his with the first tentative sweep. Then more boldly.

Carefully, he moved her camera from her lap to the seat. He untied her belt and pushed her coat from her shoulders. The turtleneck hugged her body to perfection, the fabric so thin he could almost imagine the feel of her skin under his hands. He cupped her rib cage, just below her breasts. If his thumb just twitched even an inch, he could explore the lush softness pressed against him.

Heat surged through his veins so quickly he could have sworn it would melt the sleet outside. Shivering, she brushed against him, her breasts pebbling against his chest in unmistakable arousal.

Kate's breathy gasp caressed his face and she wriggled closer. "What are we doing?"

"I want to reassure you. You have no worries where Alys is concerned." He swept her hair from her face, silky strands gliding between his fingers, catching on calluses. "You have my complete and undivided attention."

"Whoa, hold on there a minute, Prince Charming." She eased away. "That's quite an ego you're sporting there."

"You wanted to know if I had a relationship with Alys. And you weren't asking for some article. Am I wrong?"

"I'm the one who's wrong. I should have stopped that kiss sooner. I'm not even sure why..." She pulled her coat back over her shoulders. "Last night was a different matter. That display was for the public."

"I had no idea you were into voyeurism."

"Don't be dense."

"I'm complimenting you. I enjoyed that kiss so much I want a repeat."

"To what end?"

He simply smiled.

Her pupils widened in unmistakable arousal even as she scooted away, crossing her arms firmly and defensively across her chest. "We made a month-long business deal, and then we walk away. You said sleeping together wasn't a part of the plan unless I asked. And I do not intend to ask. I don't do casual sex."

He eased her tight arms from her chest and looped the trench tie closed again. "Then we'll have to make sure there's nothing casual about it."

Six

Two days later, Kate let the live band's waltz number sweep her away on the dance floor with Duarte in his D.C. hotel. The tuxedoed musicians played a mix of slower show tunes, segueing out of a *Moulin Rouge* hit and into a classic from *Oklahoma*. Duarte's hand linked with hers, his other at her back. Crystal chandeliers dimming, he guided her through the steps with an effortless lead. For the moment, at least, she was content to pass over control and simply enjoy the dazzling evening with her handsome date.

She'd been endlessly impressed by all she'd seen of his restored hotel and this ballroom was no exception. Greco-Roman architectural details mirrored many of the Capital City's earliest buildings. Wide Doric columns soared high to murals painted on the ceilings, depicting characters from classic American literature. Huck Finn stared down at her alongside Rip Van Winkle. Moby Dick rode a wave on another wall.

The black-tie dinner packed with politicians and embassy officials had been a journalistic dream come true. The five-course meal now over, she one-two-threed past a senator partnered with an undersecretary in the State department. Her fingers had been itching all night long to snap pictures, but Duarte had been generous with allowing other photographs while they were in D.C. She had to play by his rules and be patient.

And he'd been open to her sharing tips with her boss at the *Global Intruder.* Duarte had spent the past two days meeting with embassy officials from San Rinaldo and neighboring countries. He'd delivered a press conference on behalf of his family. She'd racked up plenty of tips and images to send on the laptop.

Although, sticky politics had quickly taken a backseat to questions about the fiancée at his side. Kate had to applaud his savvy. He'd been right in deciding an engagement could prove useful as he steered the media dialogue.

The press as a whole was having a field day with the notion of a Medina prince engaged to the woman who'd first broken his cover. Their concocted courtship story packed the blogosphere.

Undoubtedly images of them waltzing together would continue the Cinderella theme in the society pages. Her off-the-shoulder designer dress tonight was a world away from the ill-fitting gown she'd worn when breaking into Duarte's Martha's Vineyard resort. The shimmer of champagne-colored satin slithered over her with each sweeping step, giving her skin a warm glow. Duarte's hand on her back, his even breaths brushing her brow, took that warm glow to a whole new and deeper level.

She glanced up into his dark eyes and saw past the somber air to the thoughtfulness he tried so hard to hide. "Thank you for the clothes and the dinner. You really have come through on what you promised."

"Of course." He swept her toward the outer edges of the dance floor, around a marble pillar, farther from the swell of music. "I gave you my word."

"People lie to the press all the time." People lied period. "I accept it."

"I never expected to meet a woman as jaded as myself." His hand on her back splayed wider, firmer. "Who broke your heart?"

She angled closer, resting her head against his jaw so she wouldn't have to look in his too-perceptive eyes. "Let's not wreck this perfect evening with talk about my past." With talk about her father. "Just because you've got a packed romantic history doesn't mean everyone else does."

Wait! Where had that come from? It seemed they bumped into his old girlfriends around every corner. Not that she cared other than making sure they kept their stories straight about the engagement.

Maybe if she told herself that often enough, she might start believing it. Somewhere over the past few days, she'd started enjoying his presence. She really didn't want him to be a jerk.

"Hmm…" He nuzzled her upswept hair, a loose bundle of fat curls dotted with tiny yellow diamonds, courtesy of a personal stylist brought in for her for the afternoon. "What do you know about my dating history?"

"You're like a royal George Clooney. Except younger." And hotter. And somehow here, with her.

"Did you expect me to be a monk just because I had

to live under the radar?" His hand on her back pressed slightly, urging her closer as the music slowed.

"Best as I can tell from the women I've met during our time in D.C.—" she paused, her brain scrambling with each teasing brush of his body against hers, nothing overt, but just enough to make her ache for a firmer pressure "—you've never had a relationship that lasted more than three months."

His ex-girlfriends had wished her luck, *lots* of luck. Their skepticism was obvious. Women he hadn't dated were equally restrained in their good wishes.

"Would you prefer I led someone on by continuing a relationship beyond the obvious end?"

"Don't you care that you broke hearts?" Money and good looks, too, not fair. And then she realized... "Those women didn't even know you're a prince. You're positively a dangerous weapon now."

Why was she pushing this? Old news wouldn't make for much of a media tip. It shouldn't matter that this man who collected luxury hotels around the country had never committed to a single house, much less a particular woman.

He exhaled dismissively. "Anyone who's interested in me because of my bank balance or defunct title isn't worth your concern. Now can we discuss something else? There's the U.S. ambassador to Spain."

"I've already met him. Thank you." She had nabbed award-winning photos by never backing down. She wouldn't change now. "Didn't it bother you, lying to women about your past?"

"Perhaps that's why I never stayed in a relationship." He tucked their clasped hands closer and flicked her dangling earring. Yellow diamonds in a filigree gold setting tickled her shoulder. "Now there are no more constraints."

Her heart hitched in her chest at his outlandish implication. Even knowing he couldn't possibly be serious, she couldn't resist asking, "Are you trying to seduce me?"

"Absolutely. And I intend to make sure you enjoy every minute of it."

With a quick squeeze of their linked hands, he stepped back. The song faded to an end. He applauded along with the rest of the guests while she stood stunned and tingling.

Only seventy-two hours since she'd climbed onto his balcony and already she was wondering just how much longer she could hold out against Duarte Medina.

Abruptly, Duarte frowned and reached into his tuxedo coat. His hand came back out with his iPhone.

"Excuse me a second." The phone buzzed in his hand again. "Javier? Speak."

As he listened, his frown shifted to an outright scowl. His body tensed and his eyes scanned the room. Kate went on alert. Something was wrong. She looked around, but saw nothing out of the ordinary.

He disconnected with a low curse and slid an arm around her waist. His touch was different this time, not at all seductive, but rather proprietary.

Protective.

"What's wrong?" she asked.

"We need to duck out. Now." He hauled her toward a side exit. "Security alert. We have party crashers."

Duarte hurried Kate the rest of the way down the hall and into the elevator. No one followed, but he wasn't taking any chances or wasting a minute. Even a second's delay could prove catastrophic.

The old-fashioned iron grate rattled shut, then the doors slid closed on the wooden compartment, sealing him inside with Kate and jazz Muzak.

Finally, he had her safely alone, away from cameras, party crashers and the scores of other people wanting a piece of her simply because she wore his ring. Growing up, he'd resented like hell the island isolation his father had imposed on them all. But right now, he wouldn't have minded some of that seclusion.

He stabbed the stop button and reached for his phone to check for text updates from Javier.

"Duarte?" Kate gripped his wrist. "Why aren't we going upstairs?"

"Soon." He needed to ensure her security before he let himself enjoy how easily she touched him now. "We are going to hang out here until Javier gets the lowdown on those party crashers." Duarte scrolled through the incoming texts.

Inching closer, she eyed the corners of the wood elevator suspiciously. The side of her breast brushed his arm. His hand gripped the phone tighter.

Even if they were only in the elevator, he had her all to himself for the first time since he'd seen the shift in her eyes. He'd known she felt the same attraction from the start and seventy-two hours straight spent together had crammed months' worth of dates and familiarity into a short period.

On the dance floor, he'd sensed any residual resistance melting from her spine. However, he couldn't think of that now. He needed to get Kate to a secure location, and then find out how the pair of party crashers had slipped through security.

Picking nervously at the yellow diamond earring, Kate nodded toward his phone. "What's the report? Can we talk in here?"

"Yes." He tucked his phone back into his coat.

"You're sure? No bugs or cameras? Remember, I know how sneaky the press can be."

"This is my hotel, with my security." Although right now his security had suffered a serious breach in the form of two struggling actors seeking to increase their visibility. If the party crashers' confessions were even true. They had every reason to lie. "I stay in my own establishments whenever possible. Javier has two people in custody. He's checking their story and also making sure there aren't more people involved. Luckily, the initial pair never made it past the coat check."

"Sounds like Javier earned his Christmas bonus tonight."

"He's a valuable member of my staff."

Sighing, she sagged onto the small bench lining the back of the elevator, red velvet cushion giving slightly beneath her. "So the crisis is over?"

"We should know soon. Javier is questioning them directly." As security concerns eased, his other senses ramped into overdrive, taking in the scent of Kate's hair, the gentle rise and fall of her chest in her off-the-shoulder gown. "Anything more?"

Possibilities for that bench marched through his mind with unrelenting temptation.

"No, nothing, well, except you confuse me. You've been such a prince—in a good way—for the past three days. Then you go all autocratic on me." Her head fell back against the mirror behind her. "Never mind. It doesn't matter. A grumpy prince is easier to resist than a charming prince."

He stepped closer. "You're having trouble resisting me?"

Her fingers dug into the crushed velvet. "You have a certain appeal."

"Glad to hear it." He liked the way she didn't gush with overblown praise. Duarte sat beside her.

"What are you doing?"

"Waiting for the okay from Javier." He slid his arm around her shoulders and nuzzled her neck.

"What about the mirror? Are you sure it's not a two-way?" she asked but didn't pull back.

"Thinking like a journalist, I see. Smart." He grazed his knuckles along her bared collarbone, eliciting a sexy moan from her.

Flattening her hands against his chest, she dug her fingers in lightly. Possessively? "I'm thinking like the paranoid fiancée of a prince. Unless your whole intent is for someone to snap pictures of us making out in an elevator. I guess that would go a long way toward persuading the public we're a happily engaged couple."

"What I want to do with you right now goes beyond simple making out, and you can be sure, I don't want anyone seeing you like that except me. I pay top dollar to my security people. Everything from my phones, to my computers, to my hotels—this is *my* domain," he declared, his mouth just over hers. "Although you're right in that it's always wise to double-check the mirrors."

He reached behind her and ran his fingers along the frame. "This one is hung on the elevator wall rather than mounted in it. And when you press against the pane…" He angled toward her until their bodies met, her back to the glass. "Hear that? Not a hollow thump. A regular mirror for me to see the beautiful curve of your back."

"Duarte…" She nipped his lower lip.

"Not that I need to see your reflection when the real deal right in front of me is so damn mesmerizing," he growled.

Sliding his hands down, he cupped her waist and shifted her around until she straddled his lap. Champagne-colored satin pooled around them, her knees on either side of him. His groin tightened. The need to have her burned through him.

And then she smiled.

Her soft cool hands cupped either side of his face and she slanted her lips more firmly across his. Just as she gave no quarter in every word and moment of her day, she demanded equal time here and now. He was more than happy to accommodate.

Liquid heat pumped through him as finally he had unfettered access to her mouth. Champagne and strawberries from their dinner lingered. He was fast becoming drunk on the taste of Kate alone. Her fingers crawled under his coat, digging into his back, urgent, insistent.

Demanding.

He thrust his hand in her hair. Tiny diamonds *tink, tink, tinked* from her updo onto the floor.

"Duarte," she mumbled against his mouth.

"We'll find them later." To hell with anything but being with her. He couldn't remember when he'd ached so much to be inside a woman. This woman. He'd known her for three intense days that felt a lot longer than his three-month relationships of the past.

Of course he'd never met anyone like Kate.

His phone buzzed in his coat pocket. She stiffened against him. His phone vibrated again, her fingers between the cell and his chest, so the sensation buzzed through her and into him. She wriggled in his lap. He throbbed in response, so hard for her that he couldn't think of anything else.

"Ignore the phone." He gathered her closer, not near enough with the bunching satin of her evening gown between them.

"The call could be important," she said, regret tingeing her voice as she cupped his face and kissed him quickly again. "It could be Javier with an update. Or something even more important," she insisted between quick nibbles. "You said your father is sick. You don't want to be sorry you ignored a message."

Her words slowly penetrated his passion-fogged brain. What had he been thinking? Of course that was the whole point. Kate had a way of scrambling rational thought.

He pulled out his phone and checked the screen. His gut clenched with dread.

"Duarte?" Kate asked, sliding to sit beside him. "Is everything okay?"

"It's my brother Antonio." He reached for the elevator button, already preparing himself for the worst—that their father had died. "Let's go to our suite. I need to call him back."

Standing in her walk-in closet that rivaled the size of her studio apartment, Kate stepped out of her princess gown and hung it up carefully among the rest of her extravagant wardrobe. Another elaborate fiction, covering up the sham of her engagement with layers of beaded and embroidered fabrics. She smoothed the front of tonight's dress, releasing a whiff of Duarte's cedar scent and memories of the elevator.

As they'd returned to the suite, Duarte had asked

for privacy for his conversation with his brother and suggested she change clothes. Her heart ached to think what he might be hearing now. She wanted to stand beside him and offer silent comfort. Without question, the proud prince wouldn't stand for any overt signs of sympathy. Apparently he saved unrestrained emotions for elevator encounters.

Her body hummed with the memory of embracing him, straddling his lap with the hard press of his arousal evident even through the folds of his dress. Warm air from the vent whispered over her skin as she stood in her matching champagne-colored underwear with nothing more than diamond earrings and a lopsided updo.

How different the evening might have been if the call hadn't come through. She wouldn't have stopped at just a kiss. Right now they could have been living out her fantasy of making love in an elevator.

Or here, in her room, with him peeling off her thigh-high silk stockings. What came next for them now? Would they be leaving right away? Or staying overnight?

She was used to pulling up stakes in a heartbeat for a story. In fact, she kept a change of clothes in her camera case for just such occasions. A camera case that wasn't monogrammed or even made of real leather, for that matter. She was in over her head playing make-believe with a real live prince.

Her cell phone rang from across the room, and she almost jumped out of her skin. Oh, God. Her sister. They hadn't spoken today and Kate had promised. She snatched up an oversized T-shirt from the top of her camera case and yanked it over her head as she sprinted across the room.

She scooped her ringing phone from the antique dresser without looking at the screen. "Hello? Jennifer?"

"'Fraid not," answered her editor from the *Global Intruder.*

Harold Hough kept the e-zine afloat through his dogged determination. She should have known she couldn't avoid him for long.

"Is there some emergency, boss? It's a little late to be calling, don't you think?"

"You're a tough lady to reach now that you're famous. Hope you haven't forgotten us little people."

Sagging on the end of the bed, she puffed out her cheeks with a hefty sigh while she weighed her words. "I explained that my fiancé is fine with me talking to you. I will relay more snippets when Duarte and I have discussed what we're comfortable with the world knowing."

Resentment scratched inside her. Thank God she hadn't told him about her plans to sneak into Duarte's Martha's Vineyard resort. As far as Harold knew, she'd been hiding a relationship with Duarte these past few months and now was attempting to control the fallout with her leaks to him. And she sure wasn't going to tell him about a surprise call from Duarte's brother.

She stared at her closed door, her heart heavy for Duarte and what he might be facing in that conversation.

Harold's voice crackled over the line. "But you were at that exclusive embassy dinner tonight. I've already heard rumblings about some party crashers. I'd hoped to get more pictures from you. Did you receive my latest email tonight? Is there something you're not telling me?" he ended suspiciously.

"Have I ever been anything but honest? I've worked my tail off for the *Intruder*." She paused to apply a little pressure in hopes Harold would back off. "So hard, in fact, maybe I need a vacation."

Tucking the phone against her shoulder, she rolled down a thigh-high stocking while waiting for Harold's response.

"Right, you're distancing yourself from the *Intruder*." His chair squeaked in the background and she could picture him leaning back to grab a pack of gum, his crutch to help him through giving up cigarettes. "You've forgotten I'm the one who made it possible for you to pay your bills."

She rolled off the other stocking, back to her pre-Cinderella self in a familiar baggy T-shirt. "You know I'm grateful for the chance you gave me at the *Intruder*. I appreciate how flexible you've been with my work schedule." No question, she would have been screwed without this job. And she would still need it if things fell apart with Duarte. "I hope you'll remember the information I've shared exclusively with you."

"And I trust you'll remember that I know plenty about you, Ms. Harper." His voice went from lighthearted slimy to laser sharp. "If I don't get the headlines I need, I can send one of my other top-notch reporters to interview your sister. After all, you of all people should know that even royalty can't keep out an *Intruder* reporter."

Seven

Phone in hand, Duarte paced across the sitting area between the two bedrooms. While not as large as his Martha's Vineyard quarters, this suite would still accommodate him and Kate well enough for a few days.

If they even stayed in Washington, D.C., after this conversation with his youngest brother.

Duarte's restless feet took him to the blazing hearth. "How high is his fever?" he asked Antonio—Tony. "Do they know the source of the infection?"

They'd only recently learned that their father had suffered damage to his liver during his escape from San Rinaldo. Enrique had caught hepatitis during his weeks on the run in poor living conditions. His health had deteriorated over the years until their perpetually private father couldn't hide the problem from his children any longer.

"His fever's stabilized at 102, but he's developed pneumonia," Tony answered. "In his weakened condition, they fear he might not be able to fight it off."

"What hospital is he in?" He knelt to stoke the fire in the hearth. Windows on either side of the mantle revealed the night skyline, the nation's capital getting hammered by a blizzard. "Where are you?"

"We're all still at the island, not sure yet when we'll go back to Galveston." His brother's fiancée had a young son from her first marriage. "He's insisting on staying at his clinic, with his own doctors. The old man says they've kept him alive this long, so he trusts them."

Frustrated, Duarte jabbed the poker deeper into the logs, sparks showering. The other suites had gas fireplaces, but he preferred the smell of real wood burning. It reminded him of home—San Rinaldo, not his father's Florida island fortress. "Damn foolhardy, if you ask me. Our father's an agoraphobic, except his 'house' is that godforsaken island."

Tony sighed hard on the other end of the phone. "You may not be far off in your estimation, my brother."

"Okay, then. I'll scrap our next stop, and we'll head straight to the island instead once the snowstorm here clears." He hadn't planned to take Kate there for a few more weeks, but he wasn't ready to leave her behind. "Maybe meeting my charming new fiancé will give him a boost."

"He seemed to take heart from the wedding plans Shannon and I have been making." Tony had proposed only a couple weeks ago, but the pair didn't want to wait to tie the knot.

Duarte had been surprised they chose the island chapel for the ceremony, but Tony had pointed out that place offered the best security from the prying paparazzi. Good thing they'd been amenable to Duarte's suggestion of one reporter for a controlled press release. The *Intruder* wouldn't have been his first choice—or even a fiftieth choice—of outlets for such an important family event, but he'd resigned himself on that point since Kate would serve as the press envoy.

And if he could make a better job open up for her? He cut that thought short.

When Antonio got married at the end of the month, Kate would walk away with her pictures and her guaranteed top-dollar feature. Why should her leaving grate this much? He'd only known her a few days. Tony had dated his fiancée for months and everyone considered their engagement abrupt.

Duarte replaced the iron poker in the holder carefully rather than risk ramming the thing through the fireplace. "Congratulations, my brother," he said, standing, his eyes trained on his fiancée's door, "and I look forward to telling you in person as soon as Kate and I arrive."

"Be happy for yourself, too. Maybe this will help the old man get back on his feet again, then you can ditch the fake engagement."

"What makes you think it's fake?" Now why the hell had he said that?

"Hey now, I know we don't hang out every Friday, but we do communicate and I'm fairly sure you would have told me if you were seriously seeing someone, especially the individual who exposed our cover to the whole world."

"Maybe that's why I didn't tell you. Hooking up with Kate isn't the most logical move I've ever made." That was an understatement, to say the least. But he'd committed to this path, and he didn't intend to back away. "If I'd asked for your opinion you might not have given the answer I wanted to hear."

"Perhaps you have a point there." Tony's laughter faded. "So you really kept this relationship a secret for months? You've actually fallen for someone?"

Bottom line, he should tell Antonio about the setup. He and his brothers didn't live close by. They'd only had each other growing up, which led them to share a lot, trust only each other.

Yet, for some reason he couldn't bring himself to spill his guts about this. "As I said, we're engaged. Wait until you meet her."

"Hanging out with reporters has never been high on my list of fun ways to spend an evening. You sure you're not just looking to poke the old man in the eye?"

Dropping into an armchair and propping a foot on the brocade sofa, he considered Tony's question to see if deep down there was some validity, then quickly dismissed the possibility. It gave his father too much control over his life.

Being with Kate appeared to be more complex than some belated rebellion against his dad. "He will be charmed by her no-B.S. attitude. What's the word from Carlos?"

Their oldest brother kept to himself even more than their father did, immersed in his medical practice rather than on some island. It could well be hours before they heard from Carlos, given the sorts of painstaking reconstructive surgeries he performed on children.

"He's his regular workaholic self. Says he'll get to the island for the wedding, and that he will call Dad at the island clinic. God, I hope the old man can hold on long enough for Carlos to decide he can leave his patients. I'd considered moving up the wedding, but..."

"Enrique insists plans stay in place." His father was stubborn, and he didn't like surprises. For security purposes he preferred life remain as scheduled as possible. Life threw enough curveballs of its own.

Tony rambled on with updates about travel and wedding details. Duarte started to rib his brother over mentioning flower choices for the bride's bouquet—

Across the suite, Kate walked through the door in a knee-length nightshirt. His brain shut down all other thoughts and blood surged south.

"My brother," Duarte interrupted. "I'll get back to you later about my travel plans. I need to hang up."

Kate twisted her hair into a wet rope and hurried barefoot into the sitting area connecting her bedroom to Duarte's.

Almost certainly she should have gone straight to sleep after her conversation with Harold. Except her editor's threat of plastering Jennifer's picture all over a tabloid story sent bile frothing up Kate's throat. She'd played it cool on the phone while reminding Harold of how much she could deliver. Then she'd cut the conversation short rather than risk losing her temper.

Before she could think, she'd rushed to the door, knowing only that she needed the reassurance of Duarte's unflappable calm.

Setting aside his iPhone, he kept his eyes firmly planted on her. "I'm sorry my assistant forgot to order nightwear. The hotel does supply complimentary robes."

"Your assistant didn't forget. This belongs to me. I had it tucked away in my camera case." Kate tugged the hem of her well-worn sleep shirt down to her knees. A picture of a camera marked the middle, words below stating *Don't Be Negative.* "Did everything go all right with your phone call?"

Hopefully his was less upsetting than hers.

"My father has taken a turn for the worse." His body rippled with tension, his hands gripping the carved wood arms of his manor chair. "He has developed pneumonia. And yes, you can leak that to the press if you wish."

Her heart ached that he had to suspect her motives when she only wanted to comfort him. He seemed so distant in his tux against the backdrop of formal damask wallpaper. She searched for the right words to reach him.

"I wasn't thinking about my job. I was asking because you look worried." Seeing the shutters fall, Kate padded past the brocade sofa to the fireplace. She held her chilly hands in front of the blaze. "What do you plan to do?"

"Let's talk about something else."

Like what? She wasn't in the mood for superficial discussions about art. How long could they shoot the breeze about the oil paintings in her room, or the lithographs in his? She'd noticed sailing art in his Martha's Vineyard quarters. Maybe there could be something to those lighter conversations, and certainly she could use the distraction from worries about Jennifer.

"Hey," Duarte said softly from behind her.

She hadn't even heard him move.

The cedar scent of his aftershave sent her mind swirling with memories of how close they'd come to having sex in the elevator. She'd wanted him so much. The fire he'd stirred simmered still, just waiting to be rekindled. She was surprised to find herself with him so soon after. Had she come back in here purposely?

Had she used her frustration over the call from Harold as an excuse to indulge what she wanted?

She looked over her shoulder at him. "Yes?"

Or perhaps she meant *Yes!*

"Is something wrong? You seem upset."

How had this gone from his concerns to hers? Was he avoiding the subject because he didn't trust her? She decided to follow his lead for now and circle back around to discussing Enrique later.

"I'm just worried about Jennifer." She stared back at the fire. "And what will happen if the press decides to write something about her. I have to admit, it's more complicated than I expected, being on the other side of the camera lens."

His angular face hardened with determination. "No one will get past my security people to your sister. I promise."

If only it could be that simple. Nothing was simple about the achy longing inside her. "You and I both know I can't count on your protection long-term."

"After you publish those wedding photos, you'll be able to afford to hire your own security team."

No wonder he didn't trust her. She'd been chasing him down for photos from the start with no thought to the implications for his family. And now her family, as well. She was responsible for putting Jennifer in the crosshairs. Her emotions raw, Kate shivered.

His arms slid around her. "Do you need a robe?"

The cedar scent of his aftershave wrapped around her as temptingly as his hold.

"Is the shirt that ugly?" She looked back at him, attempting to make light, tough to do when she wanted to bury her face in his neck and inhale, taste, *take*.

"You look beautiful in whatever you wear." He eyed

her with the same onyx heat she'd seen during their elevator make-out moment. "I was only worried you might be cold."

"I'm, uh, plenty warm, right now, thank you."

His eyes flamed hotter. The barely banked craving spread throughout her. She couldn't hold back the flood of desire and she swayed toward him. Duarte's arms banded around her in a flash, hauling her toward him.

She met him halfway. Her arms looped around his neck, she opened her mouth and herself to him, to this moment. She couldn't remember when she'd been so attracted to someone so fast, but then nothing about this situation with Duarte qualified as normal.

The warm sweep of his tongue searched her mouth as he engaged her senses. He gathered up her hair in his hands, his fingers combing, massaging, seducing. She pressed closer, his pants against her bare legs a tempting abrasion that left her aching for closer contact. She stroked her bare foot upward, just under the pants hem along his ankle. Hunger gnawed at her insides.

Without breaking contact, he yanked at his loose tux tie and tossed it aside, leaving no doubts where they were headed. Her life was such a mess on so many levels, she couldn't bring herself to say no to this, to taking a few hours of stolen pleasure.

Her fingers crawled down the fastenings, sending studs and cuff links showering onto the floor like her hairpins in the elevator. She tore at his shirt. Finesse gave way to frenzy in her need to verify her memories of him undressing that first night. He took his hands from her long enough to flick aside the starched white cotton in a white flag of mutual surrender.

She peeled off his undershirt, bunching warm cotton in her hands and revealing his hard muscled chest.

The chandelier hanging from a ceiling medallion cast a mellow glow over his chest. He didn't need special photographer's lighting to make his bronzed body look good.

Duarte was a honed, toned *man*.

Kate swayed into him. Her stolen glance when he'd undressed had let loose butterflies in her stomach. Being able to look her fill fast-tracked those butterflies through her veins.

And his body called to her touch as much as it lured her eyes.

Entranced, she tapped down his chest in a rainfall path. Every light contact with the swirls of dark hair electrified the pads of her fingers. Pausing, she traced the small oval birthmark above his navel, an almost imperceptible darkening. Seeing it, learning the nuances of him, deepened the intimacy.

Her fingers fell to his pants.

Duarte covered her hands with his, stopping her for the moment. "We can stop this, if you wish. I don't want any question about why we're together if we take this the rest of the way. This has nothing to do with your job or my family."

Pulling her face back, she stared into his eyes. "No threat of charging me with breaking and entering?"

Even as she jokingly asked him, she knew in her heart he never would have pursued that angle. If he'd wanted to go that route, he would have done so at the start. Somehow, this attraction between them had caught him unaware, too.

He winced. "I want to sleep with you, no mistake about it." The hard length of him pressing against her stomach proved that quite well. "Now that it appears you're in agreement, I need to be sure you're here of your own free will. You have enough information and pictures to set yourself up for life. There's the door."

She could walk now. He was right. Except her life would never return to normal, not after the past few days. Leaving now versus in the morning or three weeks from now wouldn't make any difference for Jennifer.

But having tonight with Duarte felt like everything to Kate. "I'm a little underdressed to leave, don't you think?"

His hot gaze tracked over her, cataloguing every exposed inch and rousing a fiery response in its wake.

Bringing their clasped hands up between them, he kissed her wrists. "I'm serious, in case you hadn't noticed."

"It's tough to miss." She met and held his intense eyes. "Although in case you didn't know it, I'm serious, too."

"When did you figure out I was never going to turn over that tape to anyone?"

"A few minutes ago." Hearing Harold's threat against Jennifer, Kate realized what real evil sounded like. Duarte was tough, but he wasn't malicious. If he'd wanted to prosecute her, he would have done so up-front from the start.

She kissed him once, hard, before pulling back. "No more talking about anything outside the two of us in this suite. I need to be with you tonight, just you and me together in a way that has nothing to do with your last name or any contacts I may have. This is completely private."

"Then there's only one last thing to settle." His hands stroked down her sides until he cupped her hips. "Your bed or mine?"

She considered the question for a second before deciding. "I don't want to engage some power play. Let's meet here, on somewhat neutral ground."

Aside from the fact that they were in his hotel, the symbolism of not choosing one bed over the other still worked for her. She waited for his verdict.

"I'm good with that." He burrowed his hands under her T-shirt, whipping it up and off until she wore nothing but the champagne-colored satin strapless bra and matching panties.

The yellow diamond and filigree gold earrings teased her shoulders.

Like the sweep of Duarte's appreciative gaze. And for some wonderful reason, this hot-as-hell prince was every bit as turned on looking at her as she was looking at him.

She reached, half believing she'd fallen asleep back in her room and was dreaming. Beyond that, what if she'd somehow imagined the magnetic shimmer while kissing him in the elevator?

Her fingers connected with his chest and—*crackle*. A tingle radiated up her arm. This was real. He was real. And tonight was theirs.

This time when she reached for the fastening on his pants, he didn't stop her. His opening zipper echoed in the room along with the *pop, pop* of sparks in the fireplace. He toed off his shoes and socks as she caressed his pants down.

His hands made fast work of her bra and panties. "And now we're both wearing nothing."

He guided her toward him and pressed bare flesh to flesh. They tumbled back onto the sofa in a tangle of arms and legs. She nipped along his strong jaw, the brocade rough against her back, his touch gentle along her sides then away.

Following his hand, she saw him reach into the end table and come back with a condom. Thank goodness at least one of them was thinking clearly enough to take care of birth control. A momentary flash of fear swept through her at how much he affected her.

Then all thoughts scattered.

The thick pressure of him between her legs, poised and ready, almost sent her over the edge then and there. Her breath hitched as she worked to regain control. He thrust deep and full, holding while she adjusted to the newness of him, of them linked. She arched into the sensation, taking him farther inside her. Fingernails sinking deep half moons into his shoulders, she held on to the moment, held back release.

He kept his weight off her with one hand on the back of the couch, the other tucked under her. She rolled her hips under his and he took the cue, resuming the dance they'd started earlier, first in the ballroom, then in the elevator and now taking it to the ultimate level they'd both been craving.

Cedar and musk scented the air, and she buried her face deeper into his shoulder to breathe in the erotic blend. He kissed, nipped and laved his way up to her earlobe, his late-day beard rasping against her jaw. Her every nerve tingled with the memory of that first night in Martha's Vineyard when he'd stroked up her neck. She should have known then she wouldn't hold out long against the temptation to experience all of him.

Control shaky, she wrapped her legs around his waist and writhed harder, faster. Her knee bumped against the back of the sofa, unsettling their balance. She flung out her arms, desperate to hold on to to him, hold on to the moment.

"I've got you," he growled in her ear as they rolled from the brocade couch.

He twisted so his back hit the floor, cushioning her fall. He caught her gasp of surprise and thrust inside her. Her hair streamed over him as she straddled his hips, rug bristly under her knees. He cupped her bottom, guiding her until she recaptured their rhythm.

Were his hands shaking ever so slightly? She looked closer and saw tendons straining in his neck with restraint.

She braced herself, palms against his chest. Delicious tremors rippled up her arms as his muscles twitched and flexed with her caresses. His hands slid around and over her again. He cradled her breasts, teasing and plucking her to tightened peaks that pulled the tension tighter throughout.

Her head lolled and her spine bowed forward. Each thrust of his hips sent her hair teasing along her back. In a distant part of her mind, she heard his husky words detailing all the times he'd watched and wanted her. She tried to answer, truly did, but her answer came out in half-formed phrases until she gave up talking and just moved.

He traced her ribs, working his way down to her waist, over her stomach. Lower. He slid two fingers between them, slickening her taut bundle of aching nerves. She doubted she needed the help to finish, but enjoyed his talented touch all the same.

Carefully, precisely, he circled his thumb with the perfect pressure, taking her so close then easing back, only to nudge her closer.

She gasped out and didn't care how loud. She simply rode the pulsations rocking through her. He gripped her hips again, his hold firmer as he thrust a final time. His completion echoed with hers, sending a second round of lights sparking behind her eyelids and cascading around her until she went limp in the aftermath.

Sagging on top of him, she sealed their sweat-slicked bodies skin to skin. His hands stroked over her hair, his chest pumping beneath hers. She should move and she would, as soon as her arms and legs worked again.

She gazed at him in the half light, her eyes taking in the strong features of his noble lineage. God, even here in his arms she couldn't escape reminders of his heritage, his wealth. She was in so far over her head.

Being with him was different in a way she feared she could never recapture again. Would the rest of her life be spent as a second-best shadow?

And if he made this much of an impact in less than a week, how much more would he change her life if she dared spend the rest of the month with him?

Eight

Yellow moon sinking out of sight, Duarte cradled a sleeping Kate to his chest and carried her to his room. They hadn't spoken after their impulsive tangle. Instead, they'd simply moved closer to the fire for a slower, more thorough exploration. Afterward, she had dozed off in his arms.

Her legs dangled as he carried her. The simple yarn-and-bead-braided string stayed around her ankle. He'd asked her once why she never took it off. She'd told him Jennifer made it as a good luck charm. He didn't consider himself the sentimental type, but he couldn't help but be moved. That she wore the gift even when her sister wouldn't have known otherwise revealed more about her than anything she'd said or done since they'd been together.

Elbowing back the covers, he settled her on the carved four-poster bed and pulled the thick comforter over her.

He eyed the door. He should check his messages and make plans for a morning flight out to see his father, but his feet stayed put.

The allure of watching Kate sleep was too strong. He sat on the edge of the bed, *his* bed. Her hair splayed over the plump pillow, and his hands curved at the memory of silky strands sliding between his fingers.

He'd gotten what he wanted. They'd slept together. He should be celebrating and moving on. Except from the moment he'd been buried inside her, he'd known. Just once with Kate wouldn't be enough.

Already, he throbbed to have her again. The image of her bold and uninhibited over him replayed in his brain. He could watch her all night long.

Why hadn't he told her about going to the island when she'd walked in the room? The truth itched up his spine. After their impulsive kiss in the elevator, he'd sensed they were close to acting on the attraction. But he'd needed her to want him as much as he wanted her. He'd offered her a free pass to walk with all her photos and held back telling her about his imminent trip to see his father.

Now he knew. There was no mistaking her response. And instead of making things easier, his thoughts became more convoluted.

Kate rolled to her back, arm flung out in groggy abandon. Her lashes fluttered and she stared up at him, her eyes still purple-blue with foggy passion. "What time is it?"

"Just after four in the morning."

"Any further word about your father?" She sat up, sheet clutched to her chest her hair tumbling down her shoulders.

"Nothing new." He swallowed hard at the thought of

a world without his father's imposing presence. Time to invite her into a private corner of his life ahead of schedule. "But I'm putting the rest of the trip around the U.S. on hold to see my father first…just in case."

"That's a good idea." She squeezed his knee lightly. "You don't want to have regrets from waiting."

Resisting the urge to touch her proved impossible. He stroked a silken lock from her shoulder and lingered. As much as he wanted her here, he had to know. "My offer for you to take your pictures and walk away free and clear still stands."

Her hand slid from his knee, her eyes wary. "Are you telling me to go?"

Exhaling hard, he gripped her shoulders. "Hell, no. I want you right where you are. But you need to know that when we leave for the island, your life will be changed forever. Becoming a part of the Medina circle alters the way people treat you, even after you walk away, and not always in a good way."

Sheet still clutched to her chest, she studied him before answering. "I have one question."

His gut clenched. Could he really follow through on letting her go while the scent of her still clung to his skin? "Okay, then. That would be?"

"What time do we leave?"

Relief slammed through him so hard he wondered again how this woman could have crawled under his skin so deeply in such a short time. Not that he intended to turn her away. In fact, he even had an idea of how to make her life at the island easier. "We'll go in the morning, once the ice storm has cleared."

Jet engines whispering softly through the sky, Kate snuggled closer to Duarte's chest. Their clothes were scattered about the sleeping cabin in the back of the airplane.

Ten minutes after takeoff, she'd snapped photos of him, thinking the well-equipped aircraft with both a bedroom and an office would provide an interesting window into the Medina world. But she'd found her photographer's eye less engaged with his surroundings. Instead she'd increasingly closed in on his face as if she could capture the essence of him just by looking. Too soon, seeing him through the lens hadn't been enough and they'd reached for each other simultaneously, leaving their seats for the private bedroom. Yes, she was using sex to avoid thinking, and she suspected Duarte was, as well.

Tension rippled through his lean muscled body, and she could certainly empathize. Life had been spiraling out of control for her since they'd met.

And now they were winging to some unknown island. Shades covered all the windows so she didn't know if they were traveling over land or water. Duarte had told her the clothes appropriate for the "warmer climate" would be waiting.

What a mess she'd made of things. How was she supposed to report on a man she'd slept with? Should she have taken his offer to walk away?

Her fingers curled around his bare hip, his body now so intimately familiar to her. How much longer could she avoid weightier issues?

Duarte sketched the furrows in her brow. "What's bothering you?"

"Nothing," she said. She wasn't ready to let him know how being with him rocked her focus. Better to distract him. "I've never made love in a plane before."

"Neither have I." His fingers trailed from her brow to tap her nose. "You look surprised."

"Because I am." She expected this man had done all sorts of things she couldn't imagine. "I would have thought during all those three-month relationships, you would have joined the mile-high club at some point."

"You seem to have quite a few preconceived notions about me. I thought journalists were supposed to be objective."

"I am. Most of the time. You're just… Hell, I don't know."

He was different, but telling him that would give him too much power over her. Was she being unfair to Duarte out of her own fear? Was she making assumptions based on an image of a privileged playboy prince?

Swinging her feet off the bed, she plucked her underwear from floor.

Duarte stroked her spine. "Tell me about the man who broke your trust."

"It's not what you think." She pulled on her panties and bra. Where was her dress? And why was she letting his question rattle her? "I haven't had some wretched breakup or bad boyfriend."

"Your father?" Duarte said perceptively as he pulled on his boxers.

Kate slipped her kimono-sleeve dress over her head and swept it smooth before facing Duarte again. "He isn't an evil man or an abuser. He just…doesn't care." Parental indifference made for a deep kind of loneliness she couldn't put to words. Only through her camera had she been able to capture the hollow echo. "It doesn't matter so much for me, but Jennifer doesn't understand. How could she? He cropped himself right out of the family picture."

"Where is he now?" He stepped into his slacks and reached for his chambray shirt.

"He and his new wife have moved to Hawaii, where he can be sure not to bump into us."

"The kind to send his checks as long as he doesn't have to invest anything of himself?"

She stayed quiet, tugging on her leather knee boots.

His hand fell on her shoulder. "Your father does send help, right?"

Bitter words bubbled up her throat. "When Jennifer turned eighteen, he signed over his rights and all responsibility. They were going to put her in the state hospital since she can't live on her own. I couldn't let that happen, so I stepped in."

Duarte sat beside her, taking her hand lightly, carefully. "Have you considered taking him to court?"

"Leave it alone." She flinched away from him and the memories. "Bringing him back into her life only gives him the option to hurt her more than he already has. Jennifer and I will be fine. We'll manage. We always do."

Duarte cursed low. "Still, he should be helping with her care so you don't have to climb around on ledges snapping photos to pay the bills."

"I would do anything for her."

"Even sleep with me."

His emotionless voice snapped her attention back to his face. The coldness there chilled her skin. Confusion followed by shock rippled through her. Did he really believe she could be that calculating? Apparently what they'd shared wasn't as special to him if he thought so poorly of her.

Hurt to the core, she still met his gaze dead-on. "I'm here now because I want to be."

He didn't back down, his face cool and enigmatic. "But would you have slept with me to take care of her?"

And she'd thought she couldn't ache more. "Turn the plane around. I want to go back."

"Hey, now—" he held up his hands "—I'm not judging you. I don't know you well enough to make that call, which is why I'm asking questions in the first place."

Some of the starch flaked from her spine. Hadn't she thought the same thing herself, wondering ways she may have misjudged him? "Fair enough."

"Has your father called you because of the publicity surrounding your engagement?" he asked, his eyes dark and protective. "People develop all sorts of, uh, creative crises when they think they can gain access to a royal treasure trove."

"I haven't heard a word from him." Although now that Duarte had given her the heads-up, she would be sure to let voice mail pick up if her father did phone. "Other than the obligatory holiday greeting, we haven't heard so much as a 'boo' from him. I guess that's better than having to explain his dropping in and out of our lives."

His hand slid up into her hair, cradling her head. "Your sister is lucky to have you."

"Jennifer and I are lucky to have each other." Kate stood abruptly, refusing to be distracted by his seductive touch.

This conversation reminded her too well that they knew precious little about each other. She'd known her jerk of a father all her life and still she'd been stunned when he dumped his special-needs daughter without a backward glance. What hurtful surprises might lurk under Duarte's handsome surface?

Watching her through narrowed eyes, Duarte pulled on his shoes and gestured her back toward the main cabin. "We'll have to put this conversation on hold. We should be landing soon. Would you like your first glance of the island?"

"The secrecy ends?"

"Revealing the specific location isn't my decision to make." He opened the window shade.

Hungry for a peek at where Duarte had grown up, she buckled into one of the large leather chairs and stared outside. An island stretched in the distance, nestled in miles and miles of sparkling ocean. Palm trees spiked from the landscape, lushly green and so very different from the leafless snowy winter they'd left behind. A dozen or so small outbuildings dotted a semicircle around a larger structure, what appeared to be the main house.

A white mansion faced the ocean in a U shape, constructed around a large courtyard with a pool. Details were spotty but she would get an up-close view soon enough of the place where Enrique Medina had lived in seclusion for over twenty-five years, a gilded cage to say the least. Even from a distance, she couldn't miss the grand scale of the sprawling estate, the unmistakable sort that housed royalty.

Engines whining louder, the plane banked, lining up with a thin islet alongside the larger island. A single strip of concrete marked the private runway, two other planes parked beside a hangar. As they neared, a ferry boat came into focus. To ride from the airport to the main island? They sure were serious about security. Duarte had said it wasn't his secret to reveal. She thought of his father, a man who'd been overthrown in a violent coup. And his brothers, Carlos and Antonio, had a stake in this, as well. None of the Medina heirs had signed on for the royal life.

God, she missed the days when her job had been about providing valuable information to the public. It had been two years since she'd been in the trenches uncovering dirty politics and the nuances of complicated wars as opposed to shining a public flashlight on good people who had every right to their privacy.

The intercom system crackled a second before the pilot announced, "We're about to begin our descent. Please return to your seats and secure your lap belts. Thank you, and we hope you had a pleasant flight."

A glass-smooth landing later, she climbed on board the ferry that would transport them to the main island. Crisp sea air replaced the recycled oxygen in the jet cabin. Her camera bag slung over her shoulder, she recorded the images with her eyes for now. Duarte would call the shots on when she could snap photos. Her stomach knotted even though there wasn't a wave in sight, a perfect day for boating. A dolphin led the way, fin slicing through the water, then submerging again.

An osprey circled over its nest and herons picked their way through sea oats along the shore like a pictorial feature straight out of *National Geographic*. Until you looked closer and saw the guard tower, the security cameras tucked in trees.

A guard waited on the dock, a gun strapped within easy reach to protect the small crowd gathered to greet them. She recognized the man and woman from recent coverage in the media. "That's your youngest brother, Antonio, and his fiancée."

Duarte nodded.

The wedding he had mentioned made perfect sense now. She'd started the ball rolling digging up information about the shipping magnate and his waitress mistress. But then they'd fallen off the map. Apparently Alys Cortez hadn't shared everything she knew about the Medinas.

The brothers shared the same dark hair, although Antonio's was longer with a hint of curl. Duarte had a lean runner's build, whereas she would have pegged his brother as a former high school wrestler.

What sort of school experience would the young princes have had on a secluded island?

As the boat docked, she realized another couple waited with Tony and Shannon. Javier Cortez stood with a woman just behind him. They couldn't possibly have permitted his cousin Alys to stay after she betrayed them. Although they allowed a reporter into their midst...

Duarte touched the small of her back as they walked down the gangplank. "There's someone here to see you."

She looked closer as Javier stepped aside and revealed—

Jennifer?

Disbelief rocked the plank under Kate's feet. What was going on? She looked back at Duarte and he simply smiled as if it was nothing unusual to scoop her sister out of her protective home without consulting Kate. Not that Jennifer seemed to notice anything unusual about this whole bizarre day.

Jumping with excitement, her sister waved from the dock, wearing jeans, layered tank tops and a lightweight jacket. Her ponytail lifted by the wind, she could have been any college coed on vacation. Physically, she showed no signs of the special challenges she faced. But Kate was all too aware of her sister's vulnerability.

A vulnerability that hit home all the harder now that Kate realized how easily someone could steal Jennifer away without her knowing. How could she ever hope to go on a remote shoot without worrying? What if her editor had been the one to pull this stunt?

Kate loved Jennifer more than anyone in the world. But the balance of that love wavered between sibling and motherly affection. The maternal drive to protect Jennifer burned fiercely inside her.

And Duarte had stepped over a line. How dare he use his security people to just scoop up Jennifer? He was supposed to be protecting her.

Her lips pursed tight, Kate held her anger, for now. She didn't want to upset her sister with a scene.

Jennifer hugged her tight before stepping back smiling. "Katie, are you surprised? We get to visit after all. Isn't it beautiful? Can we go swimming even though it's January? It's not snowing, like at home."

Kate forced a smile onto her own face, as well. "It might be a bit cool for that even now. But we could go for walks on the beach. Hope you brought comfy shoes."

"Oh, they have everything for me. He—" she pointed to Javier "—said so when he picked me up at school. I got to fly on an airplane and they had my favorite movie with popcorn. All these nice people were waiting to meet me when I got here a few minutes before you. Have you met them?"

Shaking her head, Kate let Jennifer continue with the introductions, which saved her from having to say anything for a while. More specifically, it offered her the perfect diversion to avoid looking at Duarte until she could get her emotions under control and him alone.

On the surface this seemed like a thoughtful gesture, but he should have consulted her, damn it. Thinking of Jennifer going off with people she didn't know scared the hell out of Kate.

As for the supposedly great assisted-living facility, they never should have let Jennifer leave without calling her first.

So much for giving him the benefit of the doubt, assuming he could be an ordinary, everyday kind of guy. Duarte assumed his way was best.

No worries about joining the ranks of his three-month-rejects club. Because she would be walking out on Duarte Medina on their one-month anniversary.

Nine

Duarte wasn't sure what had upset Kate, but without question, she'd gone into deep-freeze mode after the ferry crossing. He'd known the discussion about her dad made her uncomfortable, but not like this. He'd hoped seeing her sister would trump everything else and make her happy. He'd been wrong, and he intended to find out why—after he'd seen his father.

Two vehicles waited, as he'd requested. A limousine would take the women to the main house and Duarte would use the Porsche Cayenne four-wheel drive to visit the island clinic with Tony.

Watching Jennifer finish her introductions, Duarte was struck by how much she looked like her sister. They shared the same general build and rich brown hair, the strong island sun emphasizing caramel-colored highlights. But most of all, he couldn't miss how much Jennifer adored her older sister. The love and protectiveness Kate displayed was clearly returned.

Bringing them together had been the right thing. And here on his father's island he could offer the sisters some of the pampering they had been denied.

Duarte turned to Kate. "Javier will take you both back to the house. Shannon will help you settle in while I go see my father with Tony. Anything you need, just ask."

He dropped a quick kiss on Kate's cheek, playing the attentive fiancé.

Jennifer quickly hooked arms with her sister. "Let me see the ring…"

Their voices drifted off and Duarte faced his brother alone for the first time since he'd stepped off the ferry. Tony's normally lighthearted ways were nowhere in sight today.

Duarte took the keys from his younger brother's extended hand. "Any change in his condition?"

"His fever is down and the breathing treatments help him rest more comfortably." Tony closed the car door, sitting in the passenger seat. "But the core problem with his liver hasn't been solved."

He turned the key and the Porsche SUV purred to life. "Has he considered a transplant?"

"That's a sticky subject for the old guy." Tony hooked his arm out the open window as they pulled away from the ferry. "For starters, he would have to go to the mainland. His doctors are of mixed opinion as to whether he's a good candidate."

"So we just wait around for him to die?" What had happened to their father, the fighter? "That doesn't seem right."

Enrique may have turned into a recluse, but he'd

rebuilt a minikingdom of his own here off the coast of Florida. Duarte guided the vehicle along the narrow paved road paralleling the shore.

When he'd first arrived here as a kid, the tropical jungle had given him the perfect haven. He would evade the guards and run until his heart felt like it would burst. Over time he'd realized the pain had more to do with losing his mother, with watching her murder. Then he'd begun martial arts training as well so he could go back to San Rinaldo one day. So he could take out the people responsible for his mother's death.

By the time he reached adulthood, he realized he would never have the revenge he'd craved as a child. His only vengeance came in not letting them win. He wouldn't be conquered.

He'd thought his father carried the same resolve. Duarte forced his attention back on the present and his brother's words.

"His health concerns are complicated by more than just the remote locale. There's the whole issue of finding a donor. Chances are greatly increased when the donor is of the same ethnicity."

"Which means we should be tested. Maybe one of us can donate a lobe," Duarte said without hesitation.

"Again, he says no. He insists that route poses too great a risk to us." Tony stared out over the ocean. While Duarte had used running to burn off his frustration, the youngest Medina brother had gravitated to the shore for swimming, surfing and later, sailing.

"He's stubborn as hell."

Tony turned back, his grin wry. "You're one to talk. I'm surprised you actually brought Kate Harper here. And that you gave her our mother's ring. You're not exactly the forgiving sort."

It wasn't Beatriz's wedding ring—Carlos had that—and in fact Duarte hadn't remembered her wearing that one as clearly as he recalled the ruby she'd worn on her other hand. As a child, he'd toyed with it while she told him stories of her own family. She'd been of royal descent, but her parents had been of modest means. She'd wanted her sons to value hard work and empathize with the people of San Rinaldo.

What would life have been like if she'd made it out of the country with them?

But she hadn't, and what-ifs wasted time. Her death must be weighing heavier on his mind because of his father's failing health. And now, he would see his father for what could be the last time.

The clinic—a one-story building, white stucco with a red tile roof—sported two wings, perched like a bird on the manicured lawn. One side held the offices for regular checkups, eye exams and dental visits. The other side was reserved for hospital beds, testing and surgeries.

Duarte parked the car in front and pocketed the keys. Guards nodded a welcome without relaxing their stance. They weren't Buckingham Palace-stiff, but their dedication to their mission couldn't be missed.

Electric doors slid open. A blast of cool, antiseptic air drifted out. The clinic was fully staffed with doctors and nurses on hand to see to the health concerns of the small legion that ran Enrique's island home. Most were from San Rinaldo or relatives of the refugees.

Tony pointed to the correct door, although Duarte would have known from the fresh pair of heavily armed sentinels. Bracing, he stepped inside the hospital room.

The former king hadn't requested any special accommodations beyond privacy. There were no flowers or balloons or even cards to add color to the sterile space. The stark room held a simple chair, a rolling tray, a computer...

And a single bed.

Wearing paisley pajamas, Enrique Medina needed a shave. That alone told Duarte how ill the old man was.

He'd also lost weight since Duarte's last visit in May when he'd brought their half sister Eloisa over for her first trip to the island since she was a child. His father had been making a concerted effort to reconcile with his children.

A sigh rattled Enrique's chest and he adjusted the plastic tubes feeding oxygen into his nose. "Thank you for coming, *mi hijo.*"

My son.

"Of course." He stepped deeper into the room. The old man had never been the hugging type. Duarte clapped him on the shoulder once. Damn, nothing but skin and bones. "Antonio says you're responding well to the treatment. When are you going to get a liver transplant?"

Scowling from one son to the other, Enrique said, "When did you become a nag like your brother?"

Tony spun on his heel. "I think I hear the guards calling me."

When the door closed, Duarte gave no quarter. "Still as stubborn as ever, I see, old man. I just didn't expect you to stop fighting."

"I'm still alive, am I not? My doctors wrote me off months ago." He waved a hand, veins bruised from IVs. "Enough about my health. I have no interest in discussing my every ache and ailment. I want to know more about your fiancée."

Duarte dropped into a chair. "Ah, so you held on long enough to meet her? Perhaps I should delay the introduction."

"If one of you promised a grandchild, you might get nine more months out of me."

"It's unfair to put your mortality on our shoulders."

"You are right," Enrique said, his calculating eyes still as sharp as ever in spite of his failing body. "What do you intend to do about it?"

Duarte weighed his next words. The old monarch passed on his sense of humor to Antonio and his intense drive to Carlos.

Duarte inherited his father's strategic abilities. Which told him exactly what he needed to say to get Enrique out of the hospital bed.

"You can meet Kate...when you get well enough to leave the clinic and come back to the house."

Kate had expected an amazing house. But nothing could have prepared her for the well-guarded opulence of the Medina mansion. Every *ooh* and *aah* from Jennifer as she caught her first glimpse reminded Kate of the awkward position Duarte had placed them in. Although she certainly didn't blame her sister.

Who wouldn't stare at the trees and the wildlife and the palatial residence? She and Jennifer had grown up in a small three-bedroom Cape Cod–style house outside Boston, comfortable in their second-story rooms. Kate had painted Jennifer's a bright yellow to go with photos she'd snapped of sunflowers and birds. She'd put a lot of effort into creating a space for her sister, the way a mother would have done. Jennifer had called the room her garden.

No wonder her sister was entranced by the botanical

explosion surrounding the Medina mansion. The place was the size of some hotels. Except she usually wasn't escorted to her hotel by a scowling head of security. Javier sat beside Shannon, eyeing Kate suspiciously the whole drive over.

The limousine slowed, easing past a towering marble fountain with a "welcome" pineapple on top—and wasn't that ironic in light of all those guards? Once the vehicle stopped, more uniformed security appeared from out of nowhere to open the limo.

Even a butler waited beside looming double doors.

Once inside, Kate couldn't hold back a gasp of her own. The cavernous circular hall sported gilded archways leading to open rooms. Two staircases stretched up either side, meeting in the middle. And she would bet good money that the Picasso on the wall wasn't a reproduction.

Shannon touched her elbow. "Everything will be taken up to the room."

"We don't have much." Kate passed her camera bag and Jennifer's backpack to the butler. "Duarte told me they—"

"—already have everything prepared. That's the Medina way," Shannon said, her words flavored with a light Texas twang. "Let's go straight through to the veranda. I'd like you to meet my son, Kolby."

Her footsteps echoing on the marble floor, Kate thought back to what she knew about Antonio Medina's fiancée and remembered the widowed Shannon had a three-year-old child from her first marriage, the boy she'd called Kolby.

Kate walked past what appeared to be a library. Books filled three walls, interspersed with windows and a sliding brass ladder. The smell of fresh citrus hung in the air, and not just because of the open windows. A tall potted orange tree nestled in one corner beneath a wide skylight. Mosaic tiles swirled outward on the floor, the ceiling filled with frescoes of globes and conquistadors. She pulled her eyes from the elaborate mural as they reached French doors leading out to a pool and seaside veranda.

A million-dollar view spread in front of her, and a towheaded little boy sprinted away from his sitter toward his mom. Shannon scooped up Kolby, the future princess completely natural and informal with her son.

Kate decided then and there that she liked the woman.

Shuffling Kolby to her hip, Shannon turned to Jennifer. "What would you like to do today?"

"What do I get to pick from?" Jennifer spun on her tennis shoes. "Are you sure it's too cold to go swimming in the ocean?"

Kate's heart warmed at Shannon's obvious ease with Jennifer.

"You could take a dip in the pool out here. It's heated." Shannon patted her son's back as he drooped against her, eyes lolling. "There's also a movie theater with anything you want to see. They've added a spa with pedicures and manicures even recently."

Jennifer clapped her hands. "Yes, that's what I want, painted toenails and no snow boots."

Laughing, Shannon set her groggy son on a lounger and walked to the drink bar. "You're a kindred spirit."

"What does that mean?" Jennifer asked.

Shannon poured servings of lemonade—fresh squeezed, no doubt. "We're sister spirits." She passed crystal goblets to each of them. Her eyes were curious behind retro black glasses. "I live to have my feet massaged."

"And when Katie marries Artie—" Jennifer's brown eyes lit with excitement as she clutched her drink "—we'll be sisters for real since you're marrying his brother."

Shannon spewed her sip. "Artie?"

Stifling a smile, Kate set aside her lemonade. "He prefers to be called Duarte."

Seeing how quickly Jennifer accepted these people into her heart sent a trickle of unease down Kate's spine. This was just the kind of thing she'd wanted to avoid. Explaining the breakup would have been difficult enough before. But now? It would be far more upsetting. Her frustration with Duarte grew.

Jennifer hooked arms with her sister. "I know you're the one who is going to marry Artie—uh, Duarte. But I already feel like a princess."

Duarte had done his best to leave his princely roots behind and lead his own life. But there was no escaping the Medina mantle here. Even the "informal" dinner at this place was outside the norm, something he realized more so when seeing the all-glass dining area through other people's eyes. Shannon's young son loved the room best since he said it was like eating in a jungle with trees visible through three walls and the ceiling.

Throughout the meal, Kate had stayed silent for the most part, only answering questions when directly asked. He wanted to tell himself she was simply tired. But now, watching her charge through her bedroom taking inventory of her surroundings and setting up her computer, she brimmed with frustrated energy. Her dress whipped around her leather knee boots.

No more waiting. He had to know what had set her off. "Tell me."

"Tell you what?" She spun away from the canopy bed, anger shooting icicles from her eyes. "It's helpful to a person when you elaborate rather than bark out one- and two-word orders."

He was completely clueless as to what pissed her off and that concerned him more than anything. He should at least have some idea. "Explain to me what has made you angry, and don't bother denying that you're upset."

"Oh, believe me." She sauntered closer, stopping by her camera case resting on a chaise at the end of her bed. "I wasn't planning to deny a thing. I was simply waiting for a private moment alone with you."

"Then let's have it."

She jabbed him in the chest, the kimono sleeves of her dress whispering against him. "You had no right to interfere in my life by bringing Jennifer here."

What the hell? Her accusation blindsided him. "I thought seeing your sister would make you happy."

"Do you have any idea how hard it was to get her into that facility, a place that fits her needs but also makes her happy?" Her words hissed through clenched teeth as she obviously tried to keep her voice down. "What if they give someone else her spot?"

That, he could fix. "I will make sure it doesn't happen."

"Argh!" She growled her frustration. "You can't just take over like that. You're not responsible for her. You have no say in her life. And while we're on that subject, how did you even arrange for her to leave? Good God, maybe I should move her anyway if security is that lax in the center. I'm shelling out a small fortune for Jennifer to live there. What if someone had kidnapped her?"

All right, he could see her point somewhat, even if he didn't agree. "I told you before. I had round-the-clock guards watching her *and* the facility—" he saw her jaw tighten and added "—which is quite nice by the way, like a boarding school. You've done an admirable job for your sister."

And she'd done it all alone without her father's help. That kind of pressure could explain her over-the-top reaction.

"I searched long and hard to find a place where she could live given how much I have to travel." Her chest heaved and her cheeks pinked with her rising emotions. "It wasn't easy and now you've jeopardized that. I simply can't let it pass that they released her to you without even consulting me."

Now he was starting to get pissed off himself. He'd been thinking of her and he wasn't accustomed to explaining himself to people. "I'm not a random stranger claiming a connection. It's well documented and, thanks to your job, highly publicized that I'm your fiancé. My name is known at that facility whether you like it or not and Javier was acting on my authority. We have the space for Jennifer here, as well as the staff on hand for anything she needs. In case you didn't notice, she's very happy with the arrangement."

"Of course she's happy. And that's going to make it all the tougher when we have to go back to our everyday, middle-class life. I can't afford—" she gestured around her wildly, her eyes lingering on a framed Esteban March battle painting "—all of this. I don't want her getting attached to the lifestyle."

Then it became clear. He stroked down her arm,

ready to entice her anger away in the canopy bed. "*You* don't want to get attached."

She dodged his touch. "You'll be out of my life in about three weeks. You've only been *in* my life less than a week. Be honest, you don't want a real relationship with me any more than I want to be a part of your crazy world. This needs to stop before someone gets hurt. We have to go back to our original arrangement."

Like hell. Anger kicked around inside him as hard as her words in his brain, her insistence that she didn't want to be involved with the Medina mess. "Do you think backing off will erase what happened last night and again today? Will you be able to forget? Because I damn well can't."

He could see those same memories scrolling across her mind.

Her gaze locked on him as firmly as his stayed on her. Moonlight played with hints of the caramel-colored highlights in her brown hair, glinted off the deepening blue of her eyes. He wanted her so much he went rock hard in a flash.

His life would be so much simpler without this attraction.

"Duarte, I haven't forgotten a second," she whispered.

Heat flared in her eyes as hot as the fire licking through his veins and he knew he wouldn't trade a second of the connection with Kate. He knew she couldn't ignore this any more than he could. Duarte started across the room just as Kate joined him, mouths meeting, passion exploding.

They fell back onto the canopy bed.

Ten

Duarte tucked Kate under him on the canopy bed, her frenetic kisses tapping into all the frustration burning his insides. Static lifted strands of her hair toward him, crackling off his face in an echo of the charged need snapping through him.

After their fight tonight, he hadn't expected another chance to be with her. Her seductive wriggle he now knew encouraged him to press his thigh closer. She sighed, urging him on with her gasps and fingers digging deeper into his back.

Their legs tangled in the spread. Without moving his mouth from hers, he wadded the coverlet and flung it on the floor. He tunneled his hand under the hem of her dress. The cool sheets slithered underneath them, the high thread count nowhere near as silky as her skin.

"Clothes," she whispered between nips, "we have too many."

He knew an invitation when he heard one.

"Let me help you with that."

Drawing his mouth from hers, he nuzzled down her body until he reached her long legs. She'd driven him crazy all day long with the killer boots. As he eased down one knee-high leather boot, he kissed along her calf, her skin creamy and soft. Her breathy moan, the impatient grapple of her hands on his shoulders encouraged him. He tugged the other boot down and sent it to the floor with a resounding thump.

Kate curled her toes, wriggling the painted white tips in a delicious stretch that called his fingers to her delicate arches. Stretching to the side, she switched on the bedside lamp.

He stroked along her arm and gathered her against him again. "You don't shy away from the light. That's a total turn-on."

She hooked a leg over his hip. "You're such a *guy*."

"Obviously." His erection throbbed between them.

Her eyes narrowed with purpose. "Lie back."

"We'll get there." He slanted his mouth over hers.

She flattened her palm against his chest. "I said for you to lie back." Determination resonated from her words as sure as the unremitting surf rolling outside the open veranda doors. "You give a lot of orders. I think it's time for someone to take charge of you."

"Are you challenging me to a power struggle?"

"I'm daring you to give your body over to me. Or does the prince always have to be in control?"

Her question hinted at their argument earlier, and damned if he would let this moment be derailed. His hand glided up to cradle her breast. "What do you have in mind?"

"No, no." She shook her head slowly, tousled hair

a sexy cloud of disarray around her face. "If I spell everything out, you're not taking much of a risk."

Her meaning crystallized in his mind. "So I trust you a little and you trust me a little?"

"You first," she said, the mix of vixen and vulnerability winning him over.

He whipped his shirt off, reclined back. And waited.

Standing at the foot of the bed, she bunched the hem of her dress in her hands, inch by inch exposing her thighs to his hungry gaze. Then showing her cranberry-red panties and bra he'd peeled from her earlier in the airplane.

Her dress covered her face for an instant before she flung it aside. The salty sea air through the French doors fluttered the canopy overhead and her breasts beaded visibly against the satin bra. His hands fisted in the sheets as he resisted the urge to haul her against him right then and there. She shook her hair from her face, flicking it over her shoulders.

"Your turn," she demanded.

God, she was hot and turned him inside out in a way no other woman had. He tugged his pants and boxers off, ready to cut short this game of dare or strip poker or whatever she wanted to call it.

She quirked a brow then reached for the center clasp—he swallowed hard—to unfasten her bra. Red satin fell away and he couldn't resist. He arched off the bed toward her.

Shaking her head, she covered her breasts and backed up. He reclined again, his arms behind his head. She lowered her hands and hooked her thumbs in her panties. A slow shimmy later, she kicked aside the underwear.

Her eyes blazed bold and determined as she knelt on

the bed. Crawling up the mattress, she climbed toward him. He slid his hands from behind his head, flattened along the sheets, but didn't touch her, not yet. The intensity in her eyes said she wanted to play this out a while longer. He didn't delude himself that this would magically fix their argument, and they might be better served talking.

But damned if he could find the words or will to stop her.

She fanned her fingers over his chest. A primitive growl rumbled free ahead of his thoughts. She dipped her head and flicked her tongue over his flat nipple. Again. She devoted every bit as much attention to him as he'd enjoyed lavishing on her beautiful body earlier in the plane. Drawing circles down his stomach, she scratched lightly down and down. His abs contracted under her touch.

Lower still she traced just beside his arousal until his teeth clenched. Then her cool hand curled around him and stroked, deliberately, continuing until his eyes slammed shut and his senses narrowed to just the glide of her touch. The caress of her thumb. The warmth of her mouth.

Dots specked behind his eyelids, the roar in his ears rivaling the crash of waves. His jaw clamped tight as he held back his release, fought the urge to move.

"Kate…" he hissed between clenched teeth.

Shifting, she stretched upward again, her lips leading the way as she kissed, licked, nipped until she reached his face.

Once he opened his eyes, she stared down at him. "Where do you keep the birth control?"

His desire-steamed brain raced to keep pace. "In my

wallet. I would reach for it, but someone told me not to move. Do you mind?"

With a fluid stretch over the side, she plucked his wallet from his pants and pulled out a condom. Flipping the packet between her fingers, she smiled at him with such a wicked glint in her now-near-purplish-blue eyes that he knew she wasn't through with her control game. Not by a long shot. She smoothed the condom down and took him inside her with such sweet torturous precision he almost came undone.

The restraints snapped and his hands shot up to cup her breasts. She pushed into his palms, tips harder and tighter than ever before. Her instant response to his touch sent a rush of possessiveness through him.

She cradled his face as she rocked her hips. "I would love to capture your expression on film."

"There I have to draw the line." He finger-combed her hair, bringing her mouth to his as he thrust again and again.

"I have to agree," she murmured against his lips, eyes wide, intimate as they watched, touched, even talked, both completely into each other and the moment. "As much as I would love to take your picture right now, the last thing we need is someone hacking into my computer and finding naked photos of you."

She'd surprised him there. But then he should be used to the way she lobbed bombshells his way. "You want to take risqué pictures of me?"

"I beg your pardon? I had something more artistic in mind." She ground her hips against his as she continued to whisper her fantasy. "But yes, you would be totally, gloriously, naked."

He throbbed inside the satiny clasp of her body. While he couldn't imagine himself pulling some pretty-boy naked modeling session even for Kate, he absolutely enjoyed hearing her fantasize. "Artistic how?"

"You're a mesmerizing man. The way light plays across the cut of your muscles in your arms, the six-pack ridges. Everything about you is stark angles. And shadows. The things I see when I look in your eyes…"

"Enough." He kissed her hard to break off her words, uncomfortable with the turn her scenario had taken. To hell with giving over control. He rolled her to her back and she didn't protest.

In a flash, she hooked her legs around his waist and took charge of her pleasure—of theirs—all over again. And it was every bit as combustible as before. The glide of sweat-slicked skin against skin, the scent of her with him lingering in the air. He couldn't get enough of her. Even as they thrust toward completion, he knew the sex between them would always be thus.

And it hadn't brought them any closer to resolving their argument.

A week later, Kate snapped a photo of Jennifer lounging in a hammock strung between two palm trees. Jennifer tucked in one earbud for her new iPod, boy-band music drifting from the other loose earpiece.

Click. Click.

Kate had photos galore, much to Harold Hough's delight, although in his emails he kept pressing for one of the king. She could answer honestly that she hadn't seen him. The monarch was still in the hospital. She hadn't been allowed access.

Focusing on her favorite Canon camera and her job rather than her confusing relationship with Duarte, Kate swung the lens toward her next subject. Antonio straddled a paddleboard in the shallow tides with little

Kolby in front of him, both of them wearing wet suits for the cooler waters. *Click. Click.*

These photos would be her wedding gifts to Shannon and Tony. Some pictures she considered off-limits to Harold Hough, the *Intruder* and the public in general. During the past week, she'd found herself more protective of the images than even Duarte. These people had welcomed her into their lives and they trusted her to represent them fairly in the media. She'd learned there were some moral lines she refused to cross, even for her sister.

Lifting the camera, she went back to work on images for her gift to the bride and groom. Two large dogs loped in the surf, the king's trained Rhodesian Ridgebacks named Benito and Diablo. *Click.* The dogs might look scary but they were pussycats around the little boy.

A strange squeeze wrapped around Kate's heart as she took a close-up of the child and his soon-to-be dad in matching wet suits. The towheaded little boy sported white zinc oxide on his nose and a big grin on his face.

Lowering her camera, she wondered how Duarte would act with his children someday. He wasn't the lighthearted playmate sort like Tony, but she'd seen his gentle patience and understanding with Jennifer over the past week. Her heart went tight again.

Don't think.

Duarte wore jeans and a lightweight pullover, wind threading in off the ocean and playing with his hair the way she longed to. From a distance he may have appeared casual, lounging back against a tree. But through her lens, Kate saw the iPhone in his hand and he sure wasn't playing music. His brow furrowed, he seemed intent on business.

Their week together had been guarded to say the least. While the king stayed isolated in the hospital, they'd settled into an unspoken standoff, participating in five-star family dinners. Smiling at movie nights in the home theater. Sailing. Swimming. Even going to the gym with a stationary bike for her to work off all the meals while Duarte completed a martial arts workout looking like sex personified.

Most would have considered the week a dream vacation.

Except Duarte hadn't apologized for his autocratic move in bringing Jennifer to the island without consulting her. And she simply couldn't tell him never mind, it didn't matter. Because it *was* important.

Although, she didn't understand why she felt so compelled to make her point. They would be out of each other's lives in another two weeks or so when she took the photos of Tony and Shannon's wedding. She should just enjoy the sex and let the deeper issues float away like palmetto fronds on the waves.

And the sex was most definitely enjoyable.

While their days together might be tension packed, the nights were passion filled. In her bed or his, they never planned ahead but somehow found their way into each other's arms by midnight, staying together until sunrise.

Pictures. Right. She'd forgotten.

Click, click, click. She captured Duarte in photos just for her personal collection when she left the island. After all, she would probably need proof for herself that it all happened in the first place. Every moment here felt surreal, a dream life she'd never been meant to live.

She shifted the lens.

Shannon sat cross-legged on a beach blanket with

a basket, arranging a picnic lunch. "Okay, y'all," she drawled, nudging her glasses in place, "we have roasted turkey and cheese with apricot-fig chutney on a baguette, spinach salad with champagne vinaigrette, and fresh fruit tarts for dessert. And for Kolby..." She pulled out what appeared to be lunch meat rolled in tortillas. Her blonde ponytail swished in the wind as she called out to her son and future husband. *Click. Click.* "Caterpillars and snakes."

Jennifer swung a leg over the side of the hammock and toe-tapped it into motion, rocking gently. "Tortillas as snakes? You're a fun mom, Shannon."

The young mother placed the deli rollups on a Thomas the Tank Engine plate. "Anything to make mealtime an adventure rather than a battle."

Swiping moisture off the lens, Kate refocused on her sister. "This reminds me of home in the summer, with picnics by the shore."

Before life had turned vastly complicated.

Jennifer adjusted her pink polka-dot visor. "Except it's January. I could get used to no snow." Her younger sister glanced at Duarte leaning against the tree at her feet. "Why did you wanna live somewhere so different from here? This is perfect."

"Not that different." He looked over patiently, tucking away his iPhone in a waterproof backpack. "Living on Martha's Vineyard reminds me of the parts of home that meant most to me, the rocky shore, the sailboats."

Something in his voice told Kate by "home" he meant San Rinaldo, not this island. For Duarte growing up, the luxury here must have seemed a poor substitute for all he'd lost. The sun dimmed behind a cloud.

Slipping from the hammock to stand beside Duarte, Jennifer pulled out her earbud and wrapped the cord around the iPod. "And when your toes get too cold, you can simply visit one of your other resorts."

"Like your sister travels with her job."

Kate's finger twitched on the next shot.

Her sister scrunched her nose. "Yeah, but the post-cards aren't as fun anymore." Jennifer's face cleared. "I still have the one she sent me from an airport in Paris when she was on her way to somewhere else. I don't remember where, but the postcard has the Eiffel Tower on it. Cool, huh?"

"Very cool, Jennifer."

"Hey." Shannon smiled from the blanket. "Duarte and Kate can fly you to the Eiffel Tower in their family jet."

Kate gasped and bit her tongue hard to keep from snapping back while Jennifer chattered excitedly about the possibility of such a trip. Shannon had no way of knowing she'd raised Jennifer's hopes for nothing. Kate nearly staggered under the weight of her deception. The future Medina bride had no idea this whole engagement was a farce. Kate hadn't foreseen how many people would be affected—would be hurt—by this charade.

Including herself.

What a time to realize she didn't want this to end in two weeks. She wasn't sure what the future held, but how amazing it would have been to date Duarte for real, let a real relationship follow its course. Her thumb went to the engagement ring, turning the stone round and round. Her camera slid from her slack grip to thud against the sand.

Oh, God. She dropped to her knees and dusted the camera frantically. She didn't have the money to replace her equipment. She knew better than to get caught up in some fairy-tale life that included flights to Paris and inherited family jewels, for crying out loud. What was the matter with her?

A shadow stretched beside her a second before Duarte knelt near her, offering her lens cloth. "Need this?"

"Thank you." She felt so confused. He'd given her nothing more than himself this week, making his body delectably available to her increasing demands, but never letting her have a glimpse of the heart within.

How long could they play this sensual teasing game before they hurt too many people to count?

"You miss it," he said. "The travel with your old job, before *Intruder* days of star chasing."

Ah. The least of her troubles right now. But then, Duarte had no idea he'd touched her heart in a way she could never seem to penetrate his.

Wary of being overheard, she checked on the rest of their party and found they'd moved away from the blanket, involved in setting up an elaborate new sunshade tent for Kolby's lunch. She looked back at Duarte quickly.

"My sister needs continuity," she responded and evaded his question. "This is the only way I can earn a living that provides for her."

"Perhaps there are different ways to find continuity than living in one particular place."

Did the man learn nothing? There he went again, presuming to handle Jennifer's life for her. Frustration from the past week boiled to life again. "Spoken like a man who lives in hotels, a man scared of having a real home."

A real connection, damn it.

They stared at each other in a standoff that had become all too common over the past seven days. Except with her heart aching she wondered how she could simply indulge in heated, no-strings sex with him tonight when they had failed to find common ground in every other arena of their lives.

Swallowing back a lump in her throat, she stood. "I should go and upload these photos. My editor's expecting an update and I would hate to miss a deadline."

Duarte clasped her arm, his eyes broadcasting his intent to press her for more…when a Jeep roared in the distance, rumbling across the sandy beach toward them. As the vehicle drove closer, Javier Cortez came into sight behind the wheel. The four-wheel drive skidded to a stop, spewing sand from the tires.

The head of security grabbed the roll bar and swung to the ground. "Duarte, I wanted to tell you in person."

Shannon shot to her feet, gasping. "Is it their father? Is he…?"

Tony rushed up the shore, his board under one arm, his other hand holding tight to little Kolby. "Javier?"

Cortez held a hand up. "Calm down, everyone. It's good news that I thought you should hear face-to-face. The king has recovered enough to be released from the hospital. He will be home by the end of the day."

The weight on Kate's shoulders increased as she thought of fooling yet another person with the fake engagement. This time, they added an old man in frail health to the list of people who would be hurt. And right now, she worried less about how she would be able to forgive Duarte and more about how she would ever forgive herself.

Eleven

His father was home.

Duarte had been as stunned as everyone else by Enrique's surge of energy. But the old man made it clear. He wanted to meet Kate.

Guiding her down the hall toward the wing housing his father's quarters, Duarte kept his hand on her back to steer her through the winding corridors. He barely registered the familiar antique wooden benches tucked here, a strategic table and guard posted there, too preoccupied with the introduction to come.

What the hell was up with the edginess? He'd planned this from the start, to bring her along to appease the old man. They'd made a business proposition. So why did the whole thing suddenly feel off?

Because they'd clearly gone from business to personal in the past week and that rocked him to the core. He wanted more. Over the past weeks, she'd surprised him in ways he never could have foreseen. Like how she'd left her camera behind for this meeting with the king.

She'd told him that she planned to limit her photos of the king to the old man's appearance at Tony's wedding. For that matter, Duarte had been surprised at how few pictures she opted to send to the *Intruder* overall. Since the world was getting a steady flow of photos, news outlets ran those and weren't searching as hard for others. The interest hadn't gone away, but Javier's security team back home wasn't peeling as many reporters off the fences.

Now, entering the monarch's private suites, Duarte tried to focus on the present. While the mansion sported a small fortune in works of art by Spanish masters, Enrique saved his Salvador Dali collection for himself, a trio of the surrealist's "soft watches" melting over landscapes.

The old guy had become more obsessed with history after his had been stolen from him.

Cradling his antique Breguet pocket watch, Enrique waited in his bed, sitting on top of the cover, wearing a heavy blue robe and years of worries. His father's two Rhodesian Ridgebacks lounged on the floor at the foot of the bed. Brown, leggy and large, the dogs provided protection as well as companionship. Kate leaned down to pet Benito, the dogs accepting her because she was with Duarte.

Frail and pasty, Enrique appeared to be sleeping. Then his eyes snapped open with a sharp gleam in his gaze.

"Father." Duarte kept his hand planted on the small of her back. "This is Kate."

Enrique tucked his watch into his robe pocket and stayed silent, his coal-dark eyes assessing Kate. Duarte slid his arm farther around her, bringing her closer to his side. "Father?"

Kate rested a hand on his softly and stepped forward, facing the old man head-on and bold as always. "I'm glad you're well enough to return home, sir."

Still, his father didn't speak and Duarte began to wonder if Enrique had taken a turn for the worse. Was his once-sharp mind now failing, as well?

Kate stepped closer, magnificent in her unfailing confidence. "Do you mind if I sit?"

Still staring intently, Enrique motioned to the leather armchair beside his bed.

Sinking onto the seat, Kate perched a bit more formally than normal, her legs tucked demurely to the side. But other than that, she showed no sign of nerves in meeting the deposed king.

She pointed toward the framed painting closest to his bed. "I've always been a fan of Dali's melting watch works."

"You've studied the Masters?"

"I took art history classes in college along with my journalism degree. I can't paint or draw to save my soul, but I like to think I capture natural art and tell a story with my lens."

"I've seen some of your earlier photographs in our security file on you. You have an artist's eye."

She didn't even wince over the background check, something his father appeared to have noticed, too.

Pushing against the mattress, Enrique sat up straighter. "You're not upset that I had you investigated?"

"I investigated your family. It only seems fair you should have the same freedom."

Enrique laughed, rumbly but genuine. "I like the way you think, Kate Harper." He lifted her hand and eyed the ring, thumbing the top of the ruby once before nodding. "A good fit."

With that succinct endorsement, his father leaned back on the pillow, his eyes sliding closed again.

That was it? Duarte had expected…something more. Digs for specifics on a wedding date. Hints for grandchildren. Even a crack at her profession, and that made him wonder if perhaps there'd been something to Javier's accusation that he'd chosen Kate to jab back at the old man, after all.

If so, the joke was soundly on Duarte, because seeing Kate reach out to his father stirred a deeper sense of family than Duarte had ever felt before. Watching her in this setting finally pounded home what had been going on for weeks without him even noticing. Kate was more a part of his world than he was. She was a seamless fit in a high-stress environment, a strong but calming influence on the people around her, an intelligent and quick-witted woman who knew her mind and took care of her own.

What a kick in the ass to realize Kate was right about his lack of commitment to even a house, much less a relationship. He'd always prided himself on being a man of decisive action, yet when it had come to Kate, he'd been living in limbo—granted, a sex-saturated limbo—but limbo all the same.

Time to take action. He had about two weeks until his brother's wedding and he needed to utilize every second to persuade Kate to stay in his life after the thirty-day deadline.

Whatever the cost.

Gasping, Kate bolted upright in her bed. Alone.

Her heart pounding out of her chest, she searched the

room for him…but no luck. She'd fallen asleep in his arms, slipping into a nightmare where she'd melted away like a Dali watch, sliding from the ledge of Duarte's resort on Martha's Vineyard.

Sliding away from him.

She scraped her hair back from her face, the sheets slithering over her bare skin. The scent of his aftershave clung to the linens as surely as he lingered in her memories. He'd been so intense, so thorough tonight.

Stretching, her arm bumped something on the pillow. She jolted back and switched on the Tiffany lamp. A wrapped present waited in the cradle left by the imprint of his head. She clamped a hand to her mouth at the flat twelve-by-twelve package, a maroon box with a gold bow and no card. Not that she needed a card to know. Receiving a gift was different from the jewels and clothes he'd given her as part of the public charade. This was a private moment.

Why hadn't he stayed to see her reaction? Could he be as unsure as she was about where and how to proceed next?

Her stomach churned with excitement and fear. Maybe she was working herself up for nothing. Wouldn't she feel foolish if the present turned out to be a new gown to wear to the wedding? Or some other accoutrement to play out their fake engagement?

Her heart squeezed tight at the memory of meeting Enrique, a delightful old man who took her at face value and reeled her right in. Guilt had niggled at her ever since deceiving him—a warm and wonderful father figure to a woman so sorely lacking in that department. She hated to think about all the lies yet to come.

But there was only one way to find out what the box held. She swept the gift from the pillow, heavier than she'd expected. Curiosity overcame her fear and she tore off the crisp gold bow, then the thick maroon paper. Lifting the lid from the box, she found…

A small framed black-and-white photo—oh, God, an Ansel Adams of a moonrise over icy mountain peaks. Her hand shook as her fingers hovered over the image. He'd remembered. Just one conversation about her favorite photographer and he'd committed it to memory, choosing this gift with her preferences in mind.

Yes, he'd overstepped in spiriting Jennifer away, but he was obviously trying to woo her. And not with something generic that could have been ordered for any interchangeable woman.

Kate set the gift aside reverently and swept the covers away. She had to find him, to thank him, to see if she was reading too much into one gift. She stepped into the closet—good heavens, Duarte and his family had closet space to spare. She grabbed for the first pair of jeans and a pullover. Dressing on her way out of the room, she scanned the sitting area for Duarte.

The balcony door stood open.

Different from the wrought-iron railing she'd seen on the other side of the house when she'd arrived, this terrace sported a waist-high, white stucco wall with potted cacti and hanging ferns. In her time on the island, she'd realized the house had four large wings of private quarters, one for the king and three for his sons. Here, wide stone steps led down toward the beach, yellow moon and stars reflecting off the dark stretch of ocean.

She scanned and didn't see anything other than rolling waves and a small cluster of palm trees. As she turned away, a squeak stopped her short. She pivoted back and peered closer into the dark.

Moonlight peeked through the clouds long enough to stream over a hammock strung between two towering trees. The ghostly white light reminded her of the gorgeous photograph he'd given her. Duarte lounged with one leg draped off the side, swinging slowly. She couldn't think of when she'd seen him so unguarded.

Hand dragging along the wall, she raced down the steps. A chilly breeze off the water lifted her hair, night temperature dipping. The squeak slowed and she realized he must have heard her.

As she neared, her eyes adjusted to the dark. Duarte wore the same silky ninja workout clothes as the night they'd met. Looking closer, she saw a hint of perspiration still clung to his brow. He must have gone to the home gym after she'd fallen asleep. She was increasingly realizing he channeled martial arts moments to vent pent-up frustration.

Breathless—from the sight of him more than the jog—she leaned against the palm tree. "Thank you for the gift."

"You're welcome," he said softly, extending an arm for her to join him on the hammock.

Almost afraid to hope he might be reaching out to her on an even deeper level, she took his hand.

"It's such a perfect choice," she said as she settled against his warmth, the hammock jolting, rocking, finally steadying. "An Ansel Adams gift? Very nice."

"Any Joe with a big bank balance could have done that."

"But not just any Joe would have remembered what I named my cat." She brushed a kiss along his bristly jaw. "I can't wait to find just the right place to hang it."

Back at her apartment? Every time she looked at it,

she would be reminded of him. The air grew heavier as she breathed in the salt-tinged wind.

His arm under her shoulders, he fit her closer against him. "I'm glad you're happy."

It was one thing to talk in the course of a day or even in the aftermath of sex, but cuddling quietly in the moonlight was somehow more…intimate.

Furthermore, was she happy? At the moment, yes. But so much rode on the outcome of this month. She still feared disappointing so many people with a failed engagement.

"You're not what I expected, you know." She traced the V-neckline of his jacket. "But then that's my fault. It was easier to paint you as the arrogant rich prince. You try so hard, even when you screw up."

"Such as bringing Jennifer here without asking you." His deep voice rumbled over her hair, his chin resting on her head.

"Bonus points for admitting you were wrong." She stroked her toes over his bare feet beside hers.

"I *am* sorry for not consulting you before bringing Jennifer to the island."

She shifted to look up at him. "Did that apology hurt coming up?"

"I beg your pardon?"

Laughing, she swatted his chest. "I bet you've never begged for anything in your life. You're too proud."

"You would be wrong," he said so softly she almost missed the words. Then he squeezed her hand lightly. "I would give you an Ansel Adams gallery if you wish."

"Thank you, truly." She stretched to kiss him, just a closemouthed moment to linger and languish in the rightness of touching him. "But no need to go overboard.

The clothes, private planes, guards—I have to admit to feeling a little overwhelmed."

"You? Overwhelmed?" He sounded genuinely surprised. "I've only known one woman as bold as you."

For the first time that she could recall, he'd offered up a piece of personal information about himself. Another sign that he was trying to make amends? Get closer?

Her heart pounded so hard she wondered if he could feel it against his side. Was there a hidden, lost love in his past? "Who was the other woman?" she asked carefully. "The one as bold as I am?"

His heart beat so hard she *could* feel it under her palm. She waited, wondering if she'd misread his slip. And how would she feel if he suddenly revealed he'd been in love with someone else?

Finally, he answered, "My mother."

Everything inside her went still. Her senses pulled tightly into the world around her. The pulsing of her blood through her veins synched with the tide's gush and retreat. The palms overhead rustled as heavily as Duarte's breaths.

Kate stroked his chest lightly. "I would like to hear more about her."

"I would like to tell you…Carlos and I used to talk about her, verifying that our memories weren't becoming faulty with time. It's so easy for some moments to overtake others."

"The little things can be special."

"Actually, I'm talking about the bigger events." He paused, his neck moving against her in a long swallow. "Like the night she died."

She held her breath, terrified of saying something wrong. She'd covered dangerous and tragic situations in her job, back in the beginning, but she'd been seeing it all through a lens, as an observer. Her heart had ached for those suffering, but it was nothing compared to the wrenching pain of envisioning Duarte as a young boy living out one of those events.

"Kate? The fierce way my mother protected us reminds me of how you take care of Jennifer. I know you would lay down your life for her."

And he was right. But dear God, no woman should ever have to pay the price his mother had to look after her children. She closed her eyes to hold back the burning tears as she listened to Duarte.

"That night when the rebels caught us…" His chest pumped harder. "Carlos whispered for me to cover Antonio and he would look after our mother. When you said you couldn't imagine me ever begging…" He cleared his throat and continued, "I begged for my mother's life. I begged, but they shot her anyway. They shot Carlos because he tried to protect her…"

His voice cracked.

Her throat closed up with emotions, and now it wasn't a matter of searching for the right words because she couldn't speak at all. He'd planted an image so heartbreaking into her mind, it shattered her ability to reason. She just held him tighter.

"Once our mother died," he continued, his slight accent thickening with emotion, "time became a blur. I still can't remember how Antonio and I got away unscathed. Later I was told more of our father's guards arrived. After we left San Rinaldo, we spent a while in Argentina until we were reunited with our father."

Shivering more from the picture he painted than the cool night wind, she pushed words up and out. "Who was there to console you?"

He waved her question aside. "Once my father

arrived, we stayed long enough to establish rumors we'd relocated there. Then we left."

His sparse retelling left holes in the story, but regardless, it sounded as if there hadn't been much time for him to grieve such a huge loss. And to see his oldest brother shot, as well? That hadn't appeared in any news reports about the Medina family. What other horrifying details had they managed to keep secret?

Shadows cast by the trees and clouds grew murkier, dangerous. "It's no wonder that your father became obsessed with security and keeping his sons safe."

"And yet, he risked trips to the mainland those first couple years we were here."

"Your father left the island?" Where was Duarte going with this revelation? She had no idea, but she did know he never did anything without a purpose.

And she'd been so hungry for a peek inside his heart and his past for clues as to what made this man tick. She would be glad for whatever he cared to share tonight.

"My father had developed a relationship with another woman," he said, his voice flat and unemotional, overly so.

What he said merged with what she knew from covering his family. "You're talking about your half sister's mother." Kate knew the details, like the age of Enrique's daughter. Eloisa had been born less than two years after the coup in San Rinaldo. That affair had to have been tough for three boys still grieving the loss of their mother. "How did they meet?"

"Carlos's recovery from his gunshot wounds was lengthy. Between our time in Argentina and relocating here, Carlos had a setback. Our father met a nurse at the hospital." The muscles in Duarte's chest contracted. "He found distraction from his grief."

So much more made sense, like why Duarte and his brothers had little contact with their father. "His relationship with the nurse created a rift between you and your father."

It was easy to empathize with either side—a devastated man seeking comfort for an immeasurable loss. A boy resentful that his father had sought that comfort during such a confusing time of grief.

"You probably wonder why I'm telling you this."

She weighed the risks and figured the time had come to step out on an emotional ledge. "We've been naked together. While being with you is amazing, I would like to think we have more going for us than that."

"You've mentioned my numerous short relationships."

She hated the pinch of jealousy. "Your point?"

"I've had sex, but I don't have much experience with building relationships. Not with my family. Not with women. I've been told I'm an emotionless bastard."

"Emotionless? Good God, Duarte," she exclaimed, shifting over him, hammock lurching much like her feelings, "you're anything but detached. You're one of the most intense people I've ever met. Sure you don't crack a bunch of jokes and get teary eyed at commercials, but I see how deeply you feel things."

He silenced her with a finger to her mouth. "You're misunderstanding. I'm telling you I want more than just your body."

Her stomach bumped against her heart. Could he really mean...

"But, Kate, I can't be sure I have the follow-through. Given my history, I'm a risk to say the least."

Hearing this proud man lay himself bare before her this way tugged at her heart, already tender from images of a hurting young boy. She thought of the considerate gift, left on her pillow rather than presented in person. Could he be every bit as unsettled by their relationship as she was? He acted so confident, so in control.

Unease whispered over her like the night wind blowing in off the ocean. He'd said a relationship with him was a risk and she was just beginning to realize how much she had to lose—a chance with Duarte, a chance at his heart.

So much had changed so fast for both of them. If he was every bit as confused and stunned by the feelings erupting between them, perhaps the best answer would be a careful approach.

"Duarte," she whispered against his mouth, "how about we take it one day at a time until Tony and Shannon's wedding?"

Shadows drifted through his eyes like a stark Ansel Adams landscape playing out across Duarte's face. Then he smiled, cupping her head to draw her mouth to his.

The breeze blew over her again, chilling her through as she thought of how he'd opened up to her, and wondering if in her fear she'd fallen short in giving him her trust.

They'd eaten an honest-to-goodness family dinner.

Working his kinked neck from side to side, Duarte cradled his post-meal brandy in the music room. Well, it was more of a ballroom actually, with wooden floors stretching across and a coffered ceiling that added texture as well as sound control. Crystal chandeliers and sconces glowed.

And the gang was all here, except for Carlos, of course. But their numbers had grown all the same.

Shannon played the piano, her son seated beside her

with his feet swinging. Tony leaned against the Steinway Grand, eyes locked on his fiancée. His brother was one hundred percent a goner.

Sweet Jennifer sat cross-legged on the floor by the mammoth gold harp, petting Benito and Diablo, blessedly oblivious that she played with trained guard dogs while armed security flanked the door. What the hell had he brought Kate and her sister into?

Enrique reclined in a tapestry wingback chair, his feet on an ottoman. The bottle of oxygen tucked by a stained glass window reminded Duarte how very ill their father still was. Kate sat in the chair beside him, her foot tapping in time with the "Ragtime Waltz" that Shannon whipped through on the ivory keyboard.

Kate.

His eyes lingered on her. Her basic little black dress looked anything but basic on her curves he knew so intimately well. His gaze skated down her legs to her sky-high heels. If only they could stay in bed, this attempt at a relationship would be a piece of cake.

It had been tougher than he'd expected spilling his guts for her last night in the hammock, but that's what women wanted. Right? Yet somehow he'd missed the mark because still she held something back.

The last ragtime note faded, and Duarte joined in the applause.

Tony retrieved his drink from beside the music. "Hey, Kate, maybe you can persuade Duarte to play for us."

She turned toward him, surprise stamped on her face. "You play the piano?"

"Not well." Duarte lifted his drink in mocking toast to his brother. "Thanks, Tony. I won't be forgetting that. Keep it up and I'll tell them about your harp lessons."

Laughing lightly, Tony returned the air toast. Carlos

was the only one of them to catch on during music class. Tony had never been able to sit still long enough to practice. The teacher had told Duarte he played like a robot.

Great. Tally another vote for his inability to make an emotional commitment—even to a piece of music.

Enrique angled toward Kate. "Duarte might not have been the best musician, but my goal was simply to give my sons a taste of the arts so they received a well-rounded education. We may have been isolated, but I made sure they had top-notch tutors."

"Hmm." Kate nodded. "I don't see you as the sort of person who sits back and turns over control. So tell me, what did you teach them?"

"You are a good reporter."

"That's gracious of you to say." She winked at Enrique, as at ease with him as if she spoke with the mailman. "Considering who I work for."

"I taught my sons art history." Enrique continued on about his favorite Spanish masters.

Duarte swirled brandy in the snifter. Kate's jab at the *Intruder* surprised him. But then he'd seen her scruples show in the photos she chose. Would she have taken a job she didn't like just for Jennifer?

Of course she would.

His determination to win her over multiplied. He still had ten days left. His mind churned with plans to romance her between now and the wedding. Time to fly her to the Museum of Contemporary Photography in Chicago, to live out the pretend courtship they'd concocted.

She might not have understood that he was reaching out last night. But he could tap every last resource in the coming days up to the wedding to ensure she stayed.

His will strengthened, Duarte looked forward to his first step—a surprise trip this weekend to woo her with art in the museum she'd never visited. He savored the vision of another plane ride with her until—

Tony waved for everyone's attention. He hefted Kolby up and slid his other arm around Shannon's waist. "We have an announcement to make. Since our family is here, why not proceed with the wedding? Or rather we will as soon as Carlos arrives in the morning."

Enrique's pocket watch slipped from his hand. Duarte lunged and scooped it up just shy of the floor.

"We don't want to wait until the end of the month," Tony said, his eyes zipping to their father just long enough for Duarte to catch his fear that any delay could be too late for Enrique. "We want to get married this weekend."

Duarte's brandy turned bitter in his mouth. They'd moved the wedding up, cutting short everything he needed to do to ensure Kate remained his forever. He only had her promise of cooperation until Tony and Shannon tied the knot. And after the wedding, Kate would have no reason to stay.

She'd asked for a day at a time. And his time with Kate had just been cut abruptly short.

Twelve

"You may kiss your bride," declared the priest, vestments draping from his arms as he blessed the newlyweds at the chapel's altar.

Kate blinked back tears, raised her camera and *click, clicked*. She'd photographed weddings to earn extra money in college, but she'd never witnessed a more emotional, heartfelt union. Tony and Shannon had exchanged their vows in a white stone church with a mission bell over the front doors. Duarte had told her the quaint chapel was the only thing on the island built to resemble a part of their old life. It wasn't large, but big enough to accommodate everyone here—Enrique, the rest of the Medina family, the island staff. Kate realized she and Jennifer were the only outsiders. Shannon had no family or friends attending other than her son, and Kate felt a kinship with the woman who'd faced the world alone.

Until now.

Once the embracing couple finished their kiss, they faced the select crowd, their happiness glowing as tangibly as the candlelight from their nighttime service. As Beethoven's "Ode to Joy" swelled from the pipe organ, Tony swept up the little ring bearer. Kolby hooked his arms around his new father's neck with complete trust and the happy family started down the aisle, wedding party trailing them.

The Medina princess Eloisa served as maid of honor in an emerald empire-waist gown. Her bouquet of evergreens and pink tropical flowers from the island was clasped over the barely visible bump of her newly announced pregnancy. As she passed her husband seated by the king on the front pew, she smiled with unabashed love.

Duarte followed, leanly intense and breathtakingly handsome in his tuxedo. She never in a million years would have sought out a mega-rich prince, yet the more she learned about Duarte the man, the more she wanted to be with him. To hell with day-by-day. She wanted to extend this beyond their deadline. She wanted to take that risk.

And then Duarte moved past her, followed by Carlos—the brother she hadn't met yet—ending the bridal party. Kate lowered her Canon. Carlos's steps were painstakingly slow as he limped down the aisle. He clearly could have used a cane. Something about the proud tilt of his chin told her that he'd opted to stand up for his brother on his own steam.

This wounded family was breaking her heart.

She brought her camera back to her face and kept it there all the way outside into the moonlit night. A flamenco guitarist played beneath the palm trees strung with tiny white lights.

Sweeping the crowd with her lens, she snapped photos randomly for the album she planned to give to Tony and Shannon. She would upload the images and burn a disc for the couple, presenting her gift at the reception in case she didn't see the newlyweds again.

Although maybe, just maybe... A wary thread of hope, of excitement whispered through her.

She adjusted her focus on Jennifer, her sister's face animated as she took in the lights twinkling overhead in the trees. Love for her sister filled her. Jennifer wasn't a burden, but protecting her innocence was a responsibility Kate didn't take lightly.

A wide smile creased Jennifer's cheeks and she waved enthusiastically until Duarte stepped into the picture.

"Yes, Jennifer?" His voice carried on the ocean wind. "What can I do for you?"

"I don't need anything," Jennifer answered. "You do lots for everybody. I wanted to do something for you."

Jennifer extended her fist. Duarte's face creased with confusion.

"This is for you," Jennifer continued, dropping into his hand a beaded string of braided gold thread with a metal ring at one end, "since you're going to be my brother soon. I didn't think you would like a bracelet or a necklace like I make for Katie. But you drive a car, so I made you a key chain. Kolby's nanny got me the supplies. Do you like it?"

He held it up, ring dangling from his finger as he made a big show of admiring it. "It's very nice, Jennifer. Thank you. I will think of you whenever I use it."

"You're welcome, Artie—uh, I mean—"

"You can call me Artie," he said solemnly. "But only you. Okay?"

"Okay." Her smile lit her eyes as she rose up on her toes to give him a quick peck on the cheek before she raced across the sand toward the bridal party.

More than a little choked up, Kate swung the lens back to Duarte just as he pulled his keys from his pocket. Her breath hitched in her chest... He couldn't actually be planning to actually use it...

But, oh, my God, he attached the beaded gold braid alongside keys to his high-end cars and an island mansion. Thoughts winged back to that first night in Martha's Vineyard when they'd made up their mythical first date, complete with a vintage Jaguar and *cat*viar.

Her hands fell to her side, camera dangling from her clenched fist. Tears burned her eyes as she fell totally, irrevocably in love with Duarte Medina.

And she couldn't wait to tell him once they were alone together tonight.

The rest of the evening passed in a blur of happiness until before she knew it, Kate was waving to the departing newlyweds. Everything had been magical from the wedding to the reception in the ballroom with a harpist. She had almost hated to miss even a second when she'd slipped away to her computer to burn the disc. But she'd been rewarded for the effort when she pressed the DVD into Shannon's hand. They'd insisted they didn't want gifts, but every bride deserved a wedding album.

Kate arched on her toes to whisper in Duarte's ear. "I'm going upstairs to change. Join me soon? I have a special night planned that involves you, me and a tub full of bubbles."

"I'll be there before the bath fills."

The glint in his eyes spurred her to finish up her last bit of business all the faster.

In her room, she sat in front of the computer to dispense with this last obligation to Harold. Duarte had even given her the thumbs-up to select the wedding photos on her own. He trusted her...

Her computer fired up to the homepage and she logged on to the internet, eager to be done with this as quickly as possible so she could freshen up in a bubble bath and dig through the drawers of lingerie for just the right pieces. The news headlines popped onto the screen with thumbnail images. She frowned, looking closer in disbelief. Déjà vu hit her as she stared at the strangely familiar images.

Pictures of Tony and Shannon's wedding.

The same photos she'd loaded to make the disc, but hadn't yet sent to Harold.

Not just any photos, but *her* work all stored on this computer.

Confusion built as she clicked on article after article from different news outlets, all with photos she'd just taken tonight. How could this be? She flattened her hands to the computer that both Duarte and Javier had assured her only she and Duarte could access.

Had Javier turned on the family like his cousin? She quickly dismissed that possibility. Before she'd made that fateful trip to Martha's Vineyard, the *Intruder* had tried more than once to get the inside scoop from everyone in Duarte's employ. No luck there. Javier had stayed loyal. Which only left Duarte, and he'd made it clear from the start that he sought revenge for what she'd done to his family with her photo exposé.

Her heart shattering, she felt like such a fool. Duarte had wanted retribution and he had succeeded. He'd maintained total control of how his family appeared in the press. And he'd ensured she didn't profit a dime off her efforts.

She'd been so close to admitting she'd fallen in love with him. But she would be damned before she let him know just how deeply he'd wounded her.

Five more minutes and Duarte would finally have Kate alone. He didn't hear the bath running, but then if all went according to schedule, he would have her on an airplane soon.

Tony and Shannon's early wedding hadn't left him much time to expedite his plans to take Kate to the Chicago museum. But he'd pulled it together. A jet was waiting, fueled up and ready to wing them away from here.

All he needed was her okay on plans for Jennifer—he'd learned his lesson well on not usurping Kate when it came to her sister. Hopefully, after tonight he would have a larger role in her life, one where they shared responsibilities. He was determined to make his pitch in Chicago, to persuade her that they should extend their relationship beyond tonight, beyond the island.

Looking through the open doors, he saw her still sitting at the desk in her room in front of her computer, not in the tub but every bit as alluring to him even with her clothes on. So many times they'd gone over her pictures together before she had sent them. She'd been careful about giving him a chance to veto photographs even though more often than not she nixed a picture first. He didn't even feel the need to look over her shoulder now.

He trusted her. What a novel feeling that almost had

him reeling on his feet. He turned away to gather his thoughts, bracing a hand on his four-poster bed.

Fast on the heels of one thought came another. He more than trusted her. He'd been mesmerized by the woman who'd stood toe-to-toe with him from the start. Someone he could envision by his side for life.

He'd known he wanted her with him long-term, but how had he missed the final piece of the puzzle? That he loved her.

The sense of being watched crawled up his spine and he turned around to find Kate standing in his open doorway. And she didn't look happy.

Pale, she stood barefoot, still wearing the midnight-blue dress with Medina sapphires and diamonds.

He straightened, alarms clanging in his brain. "What's wrong?"

Blinking back the shine of tears and disbelief in her eyes, she braced herself against the door frame. "You sold me out. You released my photos of the wedding to the press."

What the hell? He started toward her, then stopped short at the fury in her eyes. "Kate, I have no idea what you're talking about."

"Is that how you want to play this? Fine, then." She dropped her hands from the doorway, her fists shaking at her side. "I started to send the wedding photos, only to find they had already been released to every other media outlet. My big scoop stolen from me." She snapped her fingers. "That fast. You're the one who gave me that computer, totally secure you assured me. You were very specific about the fact that only you and I had access. What else am I supposed to think? If there's another explanation, please tell me."

Every word from her mouth pierced through him

like bullets, riddling him with disillusionment, pain, and hell, yes, anger. He may have decided he trusted her, but clearly that feeling wasn't returned.

"You seem to have everything figured out."

"You're not even going to deny it? You've had this planned from the start, your revenge on me for the story I broke exposing your family." Her composure brittle, she still stood her ground. "I was such a fool to trust you, to let myself care—"

Her throat moved with a long swallow as his plans crumbled around him. She'd clearly made up her mind about him. It was one thing if she had concerns or reservations, but for her to blatantly question his honor. She could ask for explanations all night long. Pride kept his mouth sealed shut.

Face tipped, she met his gaze without flinching. "I knew you were ruthless, but I never even saw this coming."

Was that a hint of hurt, a glint of regret in her watery blue eyes? If so, she had a damned strange way of showing it.

"You climbed onto my balcony to steal a picture." He tapped one of her earrings quickly before she could back away. "Sounds like we're a perfect, ruthless match."

She pulled off both earrings and slapped them into his palm. Her chin quivered for the first time and fool that he was, he couldn't bring himself to wound her further.

He pivoted away, hard and fast, earrings cutting into his fist. "There's a plane fueled up and ready on the runway. I'll send instructions to the pilot to take you and Jennifer back to Boston."

Watching her reflection in the mirror, he caught his last glimpse of Kate as she slipped the ruby engagement ring from her finger, placed it on his dresser and walked out of his life as barefoot as she'd entered.

Strapped into the private plane, Kate stared out the window at the fading view of the island lights. The shades would come down soon and the magical place would vanish like some Spanish Brigadoon.

Within an hour of her fight with Duarte, she and Jennifer were airborne as he'd promised. How could she have been so completely duped by him? From the second she'd found the internet explosion, she'd hoped he would explain how wrong she'd been. Even with the evidence barking that he'd set her up from the start, Kate had hoped he would reassure her of his love and come up with an explanation for the mysteriously leaked photos…

She didn't pretend to understand him. But then, he'd refused to explain himself, refused to give her even the satisfaction of knowing why he would choose this means for his revenge.

Jennifer sniffled beside her, a Kleenex wadded in her hand. "Why can't we stay at the island?"

Most of all, she hated the hurt she'd brought to her sister. How could plans to provide a better life for Jennifer have gone so wrong? "I have to work, honey. How about you just try to get some sleep. It's been an exhausting day."

They'd come a long way from the excitement of preparing for the wedding. She'd had such high hopes a few short hours ago.

"Why did you break up? If you're married to Duarte, you won't have to work anymore." She tore the wadded tissue then clumped it together again.

"It isn't that simple." Nothing about her time with Duarte had been simple.

"Then why did you get engaged?"

As hurt and angry as she felt, she couldn't put the entire blame on Duarte. She'd played her own part, going in with eyes wide-open, deceiving her sister and so many other good people. She deserved all the guilt Jennifer threw her way. "People change their minds, and it's good if that can happen before the couple walks down the aisle."

"But you love him, right?"

Unshed tears burned her eyes, tears that had been building since she'd stared at that computer. She didn't understand why he'd given her the Ansel Adams. Why he'd indulged her sister in a private moment with the key chain, never knowing Kate had been watching the whole time. Kate couldn't explain any of the moments he'd been so thoughtful and warm, appearing to share a piece of himself with her. But she understood the missing photographs hadn't sent themselves.

Her heart hurt so damn much.

Her sister thrust a fresh Kleenex into her hands. "Katie, I'm sorry. I didn't mean it." Jennifer hugged her hard. "You shouldn't marry him for me. You should only marry him if he loves you, like in Cinderella and Beauty and the Beast, except Duarte's not a beast. He just scowls a lot. But I think it's because he's unhappy."

"Jennifer." Kate eased back, clasping her sister's hand and searching for the right words to make her understand without hurting her more. "He doesn't love me. Okay? It's that simple, and I'm really sorry you got so attached to all the pampering and the people."

Most of all, the people.

"You're my family." Jennifer squeezed their clasped

hands. "We stick together. I don't need any spa stuff. I can paint my own fingernails."

The hovering tears welled over and down her cheeks. She didn't deserve such a dear sister. "We'll go shopping together for different colors."

"Blue," Jennifer said, her smile wide, her eyes concerned, "I want blue fingernails."

"It's a deal."

Jennifer hugged her a fast final time and reclined back in her seat, asleep before the steward came through to close the window shades. With a simple request for blue nail polish, Jennifer had given Kate a refresher course on the important things in life. Like her values. If she expected to be a true role model for her sister, she needed to reorganize her priorities. Jennifer deserved a better sister than someone who crept around on ledges to steal a private moment from someone's life.

Even if it meant hanging up her camera for good.

Thirteen

"Didn't you forget something?" Enrique asked from his bed.

His father's question stopped Duarte in his tracks halfway to the door. "And what would that be?" He pivoted toward Enrique, the old king perched on his comforter with his breakfast tray. "You asked me to bring your morning coffee and churros from the kitchen. If something's wrong you'll need to take that up with the chef."

"You forgot to bring your fiancée."

Was Enrique losing his memory? Duarte had already told him about the broken engagement when he'd asked for the tray in the first place. Concern for his dad's health momentarily pushed Duarte's mood aside. "She and I broke things off. I told you already. Don't you remember?"

His father pointed a sterling silver coffee spoon at

him. "I remember perfectly well the load of bull you fed me about going your separate ways. I think you screwed up, and you let her go."

He hadn't *let* her go. Kate had walked out on him, more like *stormed* away, actually. And even though he had a pretty good idea who'd stolen her photos and sold them to other outlets, that didn't change the way she'd believed the worst of him.

Not that he intended to let the individual who'd broken into her computer and taken her work get away with it. Since she had only used the computer for work while on the island, he would bet money her editor had had his IT department hack her account during communications about prior photos. Then Harold Hough had probably sold the pictures to other outlets for personal profit. The Medina computers had top-notch security, but no cyber system was completely immune to attack.

By the end of today, Javier and his team would hopefully have proof. Then Duarte would quietly make sure Harold Hough never took advantage of Kate again. While that wouldn't heal the hole in his heart over losing her, he couldn't ignore the need to protect her. More than his own hurt at losing her, he felt her losses so damn much. He hated the idea that she'd lost her big payday and was right back in a difficult situation with her sister's care.

"Well?" his father pressed.

Duarte dropped into a chair beside his father's bed with four posters as large as tree trunks. "Sorry to disappoint you." Best to come clean with the whole mess so his father wouldn't keep pestering him to chase after Kate. "We were never really engaged in the first place."

"And you think I didn't know that?" His father eyed him over the rim of his bone china coffee cup.

"Then why did you let me bring her here?" Maybe he could have been saved the stabbing pain over losing Kate.

Except that would have meant giving up these past weeks with her, and he couldn't bring himself to wish away their time together.

Enrique replaced his cup on the carved teak tray. "I was curious about the woman who enticed you to play such an elaborate charade."

"Has your curiosity been satisfied?"

"Does it matter?" His father broke a cakey churros stick in half and dipped it in his coffee. "You've disappointed me by letting her leave."

"I'm not five years old. I do not need your approval." And he did not have to sit here and take this off his dad just because Enrique was sick. Duarte gripped the arms of the chair and started to rise.

"Since you are grieving, I will forgive your rudeness. I understand the pain of losing a loved one."

Duarte reeled from his father's direct jab. He'd had enough of the old man's games. If he wanted a reconciliation, this was a weird way to go about it. "Strange thing about *my* grief, I don't feel the least bit compelled to jump in bed with another woman right now."

Flinching, Enrique nodded curtly. "Fair enough. I will give you that shot." Then his eyes narrowed with a sharpness that no illness could dull. "Interesting though that you do not deny loving Kate Harper."

Denying it wouldn't serve any purpose. "She has made her choice. She believes I betrayed her and there's no convincing her otherwise."

"It does not appear to me that you tried very hard to change her mind." Enrique fished in the pocket of his robe and pulled out his watch, chain jingling. "Pride can cost a man too much. I did not believe my advisers who told me my government would be overthrown, that I should take my family and leave. I was too proud. I considered myself, my rule, invincible and I waited too long."

Enrique's thumb swept over the glass faceplate on the antique timepiece, his eyes taking on a faraway look the deeper he waded into the past. "Your mother paid the price for my hubris. I may not have grieved for her in a manner that meets your approval, but never doubt for a minute that I loved her deeply."

His father's gaze cleared and he looked at Duarte, giving his son a rare peek inside the man he'd been, how much he'd lost.

"*Mi hijo,* my son," his father continued, "I have spent a lot of years replaying those days in my mind, thinking how I could have done things differently. It is easy to torment yourself with how life could be by changing just one moment." Gold chain between two fingers, he dangled the pocket watch. "But over time, I've come to realize our lives cannot be condensed into a single second. Rather we are the sum of all the choices we make along the way."

The Dali slippery-watch artwork spoke to him from the walls in a way he'd never imagined. Lost time had haunted his father more than Duarte had ever guessed. During all those art lessons his father had overseen, Enrique had been trying to share things about himself he'd been too wounded to put into words.

"Your Kate made a mistake in believing you would betray her. Are *you* going to let your whole life boil down to this moment where you make the mistake of letting your pride keep you from going after her?"

He'd always considered himself a man of action, yet he'd stumbled here when it counted most with Kate. Whether he'd held back out of pride or some holdover pain from losing his mother, he didn't know. But as he stared at the second hand *tick, tick, ticking* away on his watch, he *did* know he couldn't let Kate slip out of his life without a fight.

And now that he'd jump-started his mind out of limbo, he knew just the way to take care of Harold Hough and let Kate know how much faith he had in her. But first, he had barely enough time to extend his father an olive branch that was long overdue.

"Thank you, *mi padre*." He clenched the old man's hand, grateful for the gift of a second chance.

January winds bitterly cold in Boston, Kate anchored her scarf, picking her way down the snowy sidewalk—toward the redbrick building that housed the *Global Intruder*. Not an overly large place, the *Intruder* headquarters conducted most of its business online. She'd dreamed of a more auspicious retirement when the time came to hang up her media credentials.

But she didn't doubt her decision for a minute.

If she spent the rest of her life taking family portraits for tourists, then so be it. She had found a day facility for Jennifer, but her sister would be living with her. Hesitating at the front steps, Kate rubbed the braided charm that now hung on her camera case, the anklet she'd worn for luck not so long ago.

At least she would have her integrity, if not Duarte. She squeezed her eyes closed against the dull throbbing pain that hadn't eased one bit in spite of two nights spent soaking her pillow with tears.

A well-tuned car hummed in the distance, louder as it neared. She hopped farther onto the sidewalk to avoid a possible wave of sludge. How long had she stood on the curb of the one-way street?

She glanced over her shoulder just as a vintage Jaguar with tinted windows pulled alongside her. Her heart kicked up a notch as she wondered could it possibly be... A *red* vintage Jaguar, like the one Duarte had told her that he owned when they planned out their faux first date.

The driver's side door swept open and Duarte stepped out into the swirl of snowflakes. Long-legged, lean and every bit as darkly handsome as she remembered, he studied her over the roof of the car. She couldn't see his eyes behind the sunglasses, but his shoulders were braced with a determination she recognized well.

While she didn't know how to reconcile her heart to what he'd done with the photos, she couldn't stifle the joy she felt over seeing him here. Without question, he'd come for her. She hoped her weak knees would man-up before she did something crazy like walk right back into his arms.

Securing her camera bag on her shoulder, she walked closer to the car, appreciating the barrier between them. "Why are you here?"

"Because this is where you are. Jennifer told me."

"Not for much longer." She clutched her bag, too weary to give him a hard time for calling her sister. Jennifer missed "Artie" no matter what a brave face she put on. "I'm quitting my job at the *Intruder*."

"Why don't you hold off on that for a few minutes and take a ride with me first?" He peered over his sunglasses.

"You may not have noticed, but we're starting to attract a crowd."

Jolting, she looked around. Cars were slowing with rubberneckers, pedestrians who would normally hurry to get in out of the cold were staring curiously at the man who looked just like…

Heaven help her, they were celebrities.

Kate yanked open the passenger-side door. "Let's go."

Leaping into the low-slung vehicle, she clicked the seat belt into place, securing her into the pristinely restored Jag just as he slid the car into drive.

And didn't Duarte have a way of dragging her into his world when she least expected it? Sweeping snow from her coat, she cursed her weak knees, but she couldn't regret ditching the gathering throng. Funny how a red Jag drew attention. A Medina man beside it didn't hurt, either.

He dropped a large envelope onto her lap.

"What's this?" She thumbed the edge of what appeared to be a stack of papers.

"Documents transferring ownership of the *Global Intruder* to you."

Shock sparked through her, as blinding as the morning sun through the windshield.

"I don't understand." And she couldn't accept it if he offered it out of some sense of guilt over what he'd done to her. She thrust the papers back toward him. "No, thank you. I can't be bought."

Not anymore.

"That's not my intent at all." He guided the sports car effortlessly over the ice along narrow historic roads. "You lost out on the payment for your end of the bargain for the wedding photos. You even left behind the other pictures you took that the public hasn't seen. Why did you do that?"

"Why did you buy the *Intruder* for me?"

"You have a voice and honor I respect," he answered without hesitation. "I know you'll bring humanity to the stories you cover."

"You want me to work for you?"

"You're not listening." Pausing at a stoplight, he turned to face her and pulled off his sunglasses. Dark shadows of sleeplessness marked beneath his eyes much like the weariness on her face. "The *Intruder* is yours regardless. But it is my hope that you'll accept my apology for not clearing the air the minute you came into my room after the wedding."

The magnetism of his deep onyx eyes drew her even when she guarded her heart. Much longer alone with him and she would cave to the wary hope spiraling through her like smoke from the chimneys.

"All right." She hugged the papers to her chest like a protective shield, wondering how Duarte had managed this all so fast. But then he was a man of decisive action when he chose to be. "I accept the apology and the *Intruder*. You're off the hook. You can leave with a clear conscience."

He parked on the roadside within sight of Long Wharf and the Aquarium, the tinted windows shielding them from view.

Turning toward her, he pulled off his gloves and cupped her shoulders in a gentle grip. "I don't want to leave. I want you. And not just today, but forever if you'll have me."

Just like that, he thought he could drive up and buy her off with a big—albeit amazing—gift? She looked away from his magnetic eyes. Think, she needed to think.

She stared at his key chain swaying in the ignition. She struggled to be reasonable, for Jennifer's sake. Her sister had been so crushed over the breakup, Kate needed to be completely certain before she invited Duarte back into her life. Jennifer had braided that key chain for Duarte with such hope and love…

She tapped the swaying braid attached to Duarte's keys. "You kept Jennifer's present."

Frowning, he hooked his arm on the steering wheel. "Of course I did. What of it?"

The way he hadn't even considered hiding or tossing aside Jennifer's gift opened Kate's eyes in a way nothing else had. Like someone had taken off the lens cap, she saw him, really saw him for the first time. And in that flash she saw so many things clearly.

"*You* didn't distribute my photos," she said, her voice soft. "You didn't try to lash out at me for revenge."

He stroked back her hair with lingering, delicious attention to her sensitive earlobe. "I did not betray you, but I understand how it could be difficult for you to trust me."

What she'd realized—after seeing the key chain, hearing him say the words, witnessing the honesty in his eyes—felt so damn good. The love she'd only just found took root and began to flourish again. "Thank you for being the calm, reasonable one here. I don't even know how to begin to apologize for assuming the worst of you."

What it must have taken for a proud man like Duarte to overlook her accusation and come for her anyway. Regret burned right alongside the joy until she promised herself to make it up to him.

"Kate, I realize your father hasn't given you much reason to have faith in men or trust a man will be there for you." His palm sought the small of her back, drawing her closer. "I want the chance, I want the *time* to help you put that behind you. Most of all, I just want *you*."

Gripping the lapels of his wool coat, she brushed her lips over his. "I have one question for you."

The hard muscles along his chest tensed, bracing. "Okay, I'm ready."

"Can we spend a lot of that time making love?"

"Absolutely." He slanted his mouth over hers, familiar, stirring, a man confident in the knowledge of exactly what turned his lover inside out.

Five breathless heartbeats later, Kate rested her forehead against his. "I can't believe you bought the *Intruder*."

"I had to figure out a way to fire Harold Hough."

"You fired Harold?" Thinking of her boss's threat to expose Jennifer to the harsh light of the media, Kate didn't bother holding back the downright glee at hearing he'd gotten his just deserts.

"Inside that envelope you'll also see some of the proof Javier put together showing how Hough is responsible for selling all those photos to other media outlets. He pocketed the money for himself. He accessed your computer through a virus he sent in an email. After a, uh, discussion with me, he decided it was prudent to step aside and avoid a lawsuit."

"Why didn't you tell me this the second we got in the car together?"

"It was nice having you decide to trust me on your own. Although if you hadn't, I would have still pulled the plug on Harold for what he did to you and our family."

Our family.

He'd said it without hesitation, and she couldn't miss the significance.

"I want you to help me house hunt."

Now *that* declaration surprised her. He spoke like a man ready to put down roots, a man coming to peace with his past.

"You're really ready to give up the cushy hotel living?"

"I was thinking of something on the outskirts of Boston, large and on the water. Big enough for you to move in when you're ready, Jennifer, too." His accent thickened as it always did when emotion tugged at him.

"I love you, Kate. While I'm willing to give you all the time you need, I don't need more time to be sure of that."

He reached into his pocket and pulled out her ruby-and-diamond engagement ring. "This is yours now. Even if you walk away, no other woman will wear it. It will always be waiting for you."

The beauty of his words, his whole grand gesture in coming here and presenting her with the *Intruder,* offering to buy a house calmed any reservations. She peeled off her glove and offered her hand without a second thought. He slid the ring back in place and she knew this time, it would stay there.

Duarte closed his hand around hers and rested it over his heart. "Did you notice the car?"

"Your vintage Jaguar…" How far they'd come since that night she'd scaled the outside of his resort.

"I told you I would pick you up in it for our first date. Do you remember where we would go?"

"The Museum of Contemporary Photography in Chicago." How could she forget?

"And before you can protest, remember you own the *Intruder* so you can give yourself at least twenty-four hours off to regroup. If it's okay with you, I would like Jennifer to meet us at the plane. And lastly, you can bring your cat. It's my plane, after all. And—"

"No more details." She covered his mouth with her hand playfully. "Yes, I trust you completely with my life, my sister, my heart."

"Thank you." His eyes closed for a moment, the sigh shuddering through him telling her just how much her rejection had wounded him. She vowed to show him how dear he'd become to her in such a short time, and could only imagine how much more he would mean to her in the coming years.

His eyes opened again and he pressed a tender kiss into her palm. "So what about that trip to Chicago? Are you ready to leave?"

She slipped her arms around his neck and her heart into her eyes. "Yes, I will go to Chicago with you and house hunt after we return. I will wear your ring, be your princess, your wife, your friend for the next thirty days, thirty years and beyond."

Epilogue

Wind whipped in off the harbor, slapping the green bathrobe around Kate's legs. Her cold toes curled inside her slippers as she stood on the balcony of Duarte's Martha's Vineyard resort.

The lighthouse swooped a dim beam through the cottony-thick fog, Klaxon wailing every twenty seconds and temporarily drowning out the sounds from an early Valentine's party on the first floor.

A hand clamped around her wrist. A strong hand. A *masculine* hand.

Grinning, Kate turned slowly. His fingers seared her freezing skin just over her newest braided bracelet made by her sister. A good luck charm to celebrate her engagement. And Kate certainly hoped to get lucky in about five more minutes.

Nestled against the warm wall of her fiancé's chest, she savored the crisp chest hair, defined muscles and musky perspiration. Oh, yeah, she was more than a little turned on. Kate stared her fill at the broad male torso an inch from her nose. A black martial arts jacket hung open, exposing darkly tanned skin and brown hair. Her fingers clenched in the silky fabric of his ninja workout clothes.

Kate looked up the strong column of *her* ninja's neck, the tensed line of his square jaw in need of a shave, peering into the same coal-black eyes she'd photographed many times.

"You're not a ninja," she teased.

"And you are not much of an acrobat." Prince Duarte Medina didn't smile. But he winked.

The restrained strength of his calloused fingers sparked a welcomed shiver of awareness along her chilled skin.

"We should go back inside before you freeze out here."

"The moonlight on the water is just so beautiful." She leaned into the warmth of his chest, now plenty toasty thanks to the heat he generated with just a glance her way. "Let's stay for just another minute."

There hadn't been many seconds spent standing still over the past couple weeks. After returning from Chicago, they'd gone by the island to visit his father. Seated around the dinner table, Enrique had announced he intended to go to a mainland hospital for further assessment. A hospital in *Florida*.

If she'd put her mind to it, she probably could have guessed the Medina island was off the coast of St. Augustine, Florida, given the weather. And while the island sported a mix of English, Spanish and even a little French…her journalistic instincts said the place carried an American influence. But admitting that to herself then would have been more knowledge than she was comfortable having.

Knowledge that had far-reaching safety implications for the Medinas.

And now that she was a de facto Medina by engagement, she had a whole new perspective on the PR angle. No doubt, handling publicity for the Medina family would be a full-time job. She had retooled the *Global Intruder* into *Global Communications*.

Arching up, she kissed her fiancé, who also happened to be the proud new owner of a sprawling Boston mansion on the water, a forever home with room for Jennifer and any future little princes and princesses. "I love you, Duarte Medina."

"And I love you." He swept her up, sporting real strength to go with those ninja workout clothes. Strength and honor to count on for life.

* * * * *

Look for Carlos's story,
coming soon from Desire™.

HIS HEIR, HER HONOUR

BY
CATHERINE MANN

One

"Cover the family jewels, gentlemen," Lilah Anderson called into the men's locker room at St. Mary's Hospital. "Female coming through."

High heels clicking on tile, Lilah charged past a male nurse yanking on scrubs and an anesthesiologist wrestling with a too-small towel, barely registering the flash of male flank here, masculine chest there. Smothered coughs and chuckles echoed around her in the steamy tiled area, but she remained undeterred.

Completely focused on locating *him*.

No one dared stop her on her way past benches and lockers. As chief administrator of Tacoma's leading surgical facility, she could have any of them fired faster than someone could say "Who dropped the soap?"

Her only problem? A particularly stubborn employee who seemed determined to avoid her every attempt to speak with him over the past couple of weeks. Therefore, she'd chosen the one place she could be certain of having Dr. Carlos Medina's complete attention—a public shower.

The stall tactics would end here and now. And speaking of stalls…

Lilah stepped deeper into the swell of steam puffing around a cream-colored plastic curtain. His secretary, Wanda, had warned that he couldn't be reached since he was washing up after a lengthy surgery. He would be exhausted and cranky.

Not deterred in the least, Lilah saw this as the perfect opportunity she'd been seeking to corner him. She'd grown up with two brothers, and she would have been left out of everything if she didn't occasionally invade their male inner sanctums. She eyed the line of showers.

Three of the five were in use. The first sported a shadowy, short and round male figure. Not Carlos.

From the second, a balding head peeked around the industrial curtain with shocked green eyes. Also not her surgeon in question.

She nodded to the head of pediatrics. "Good afternoon, Jim."

Jim ducked back into his stall, which left her to focus on the third tiled cubicle. She marched forward, heels tapping almost as fast as her heart.

Stopping, she planted her feet and checked first. Through the plastic folds, she studied the lean outline standing under the spray, scrubbing his hands over his head. Without even pulling aside the curtain, she knew that body well, intimately so.

She'd found him, Carlos Medina—doctor, lover and,

as if the guy didn't already have enough going for him, also the eldest son of a former European monarch. His princely pedigree, however, didn't impress her. Long before she knew about his royal roots, she'd been drawn to his brilliance, his compassion for his patients....

And a backside that looked damn fine in scrubs. Or wearing nothing at all. Definitely not what she needed to think about right now.

Lilah gathered her nerve as firmly as she clenched the curtain and swept it aside, metal rings *clink, clink, clinking* along the rod.

A wall of steam rolled out, momentarily clouding her vision until the mist dispersed and exposed an eyeful of mouthwateringly magnificent *man*. Water sluiced down Carlos's naked body turned sideways, revealing long lean muscles flexing and bunching. And heaven help her, she had a perfect view of the curve of his taut butt.

Beads of moisture clung to his bronzed skin, arms and legs sprinkled with dark hair. No tan lines marked him since he spent most of his time indoors either in surgery or asleep. But his natural olive coloring gave him an allover tanned look, as if he'd bared himself unabashedly to the sun.

As he turned his head toward her in a slow, deliberate move, not even a whisper of surprise showed on Carlos's face. His eyes shone nearly black...heavy lidded...darkly enigmatic. She couldn't suppress a shiver of desire as his intense gaze held hers. Her stomach knotted with a traitorous ache that could only serve to distract her from her mission today.

He raised one thick eyebrow, slashing upward into his forehead. "Yes?"

His subtle Spanish accent saturated the lone syllable like the steam in the air, so hot she felt the urge to ditch the jacket on her power suit.

In the next stall, water shut off in a hurry as the head of pediatrics made a hasty departure from the locker room. Others lingered, backs studiously turned as they retrieved clothing.

Lilah tugged her jacket more firmly in place. "I need to talk to you."

"A telephone conversation would have saved my coworkers some embarrassment." He spoke softly as always, never raising his voice as if he knew innately that people would hang on his every word.

"What I have to say isn't for an impersonal call." And wasn't that the understatement of the year? What she needed to tell him also wasn't for the curious ears behind her, but she would have Carlos alone soon.

All alone?

Static-like awareness popped along her nerves until the hair on her arms rose. Was that an answering spark lighting his dark eyes? Then he blinked away any hint of emotion.

"It does not get much more personal than this, boss lady." He turned off the shower. "Could you pass me that towel?"

She snagged the white cotton draped on a hook. The hospital name and logo were stamped along the bottom. She pitched the towel to him rather than risk an accidental touch. As he looped it around his waist, she couldn't resist staring for a stolen second.

Water soaked his hair even blacker, shiny and swept back from his face. Every hard and hunky angle of his aristocratic cheekbones and nose was revealed. Dark brows slashed over brown eyes that rarely carried humor, but turned lava lush when he made love to her.

Pivoting, his back to her for the first time, he snagged his shampoo. Her eyes quickly left his slim hips and taut butt, drawn more to the scars along his lower back. In the four years she'd known him, he'd chalked up his permanent limp to a teenage riding accident. The one time she'd pressed him, the first time she'd seen those scars, he'd brushed aside further questions with distracting kisses along her bare skin.

While she was a lawyer and not a doctor, her tenure working at the hospital—and flat-out common sense—clued her in that he'd suffered a major physical trauma.

Toiletries bag tucked under his arm, he leaned toward her. His shoulders, then his eyes, drew her in until the rest of the space faded away. She swallowed hard.

He stared back, unblinking, unflinching. "Let's make this quick."

"Your charm never ceases to impress me."

"If you're looking for charm, you hired the wrong man four years ago." He'd been thirty-six then to her thirty-one, a lifetime ago. "I've spent most of the day repairing the spine of a seven-year-old Afghani girl injured by a roadside bomb. I'm beat."

Unwanted sympathy whispered through her. Of course he was exhausted from the drawn-out, tragic surgery. Even when he caved to his pride and used a chair during extended operations, the toll it took on him was always evident. But she couldn't afford to weaken now.

They'd been friends for years only to have him turn into a cold jackass because of an impulsive one-night stand together after a Christmas fundraiser. It wasn't like she'd dropped a wedding planner in his lap five seconds after the third orgasm waned.

Yep, *three*. Her toes curled inside her pumps at just the memory of each shimmering release.

The sex had been amazing. Beyond amazing actually, and after that impulsive hookup, she'd envisioned them transitioning into a relationship of friends with kick-ass benefits. A nerve-tingling, *safe* option. But he'd pulled away as fast as he'd pulled on his pants the next morning. He was cold, withdrawn and *painfully* polite.

But she wasn't backing down. "I don't have the time for niceties. I'm just here to say my piece. So grab some clothes and let's talk."

He ducked his head until his voice heated her ear. "You're not the type to create a scene. Let's set up a time to talk when you're calmer. This is already awkward enough."

Her nose twitched at his fresh-washed scent. Yes, she'd chosen an unconventional route for her confrontation, but Carlos Medina's tenacious—stubborn—reputation was legendary. She felt confident the hospital board would cut her a little slack for her scene. And if they didn't? Then so be it. Sometimes a woman had to make a stand.

This was her time. She couldn't afford to wait much longer.

"I'm not setting up an appointment. I'm not delaying this conversation." She lowered her voice, although from the sound of retreating footsteps behind her there must not be many people left. "We talk. Today. The only matter up for discussion is whether we chat right here in front of everyone or if we speak in an office. And believe me, if we stay here, it's going to get a lot more awkward very quickly."

Carlos cocked an eyebrow.

From behind her, a cleared throat echoed, or a stifled laugh perhaps. She looked up at Carlos, suddenly painfully aware of just how close they stood to each other with nothing but a towel covering his oh-so-generous family jewels.

Whispering, she struggled not to back away—or move closer still. Carlos had ignored her for nearly three months, hurtful and flat-out insulting given their friendship. Or rather, their *prior* friendship.

One way or another, she would get a reaction from him. "It's not like I haven't seen you before. In fact, I recall in great—"

"Enough," he silenced her with a word.

"The almighty Medina prince has spoken," she mocked, backing a step to snag surgical scrubs from the top of a stack. "Get dressed. I'll wait."

She thrust the folded green set his way and turned away. A trio of half-dressed men faced her, their jaws slack and eyes wide. The magnitude of the scene she'd caused hit her full on for the first time. She resisted the urge to squirm.

This was too important to show any vulnerability. She just hoped she could maintain enough distance to get through the conversation during their first time alone together in so long. She pressed her fingers to her lips, still unable to forget the rush of passion from their first impetuous kiss, a clench that had led to so much more with lasting consequences.

Once Carlos put on his clothes and they moved to another room, he would learn the truth she'd only just begun to accept herself. A truth she could no longer avoid.

Dr. Carlos Medina was a little over six months away from becoming a princely papa.

Carlos Medina was about six seconds away from losing his temper, something he never, never allowed to happen.

Of course, *he* was the person who needed chewing out for foolishly allowing himself to sleep with Lilah nearly three months ago. He'd wrecked a top-notch working relationship.

Sidestepping a janitor slopping an ammonia-saturated mop over the floor, Carlos followed her down the otherwise empty hospital walkway, wearing fresh surgical scrubs, tennis shoes and ten tons of frustration. Fluorescent lights overhead lined the path down the corridor. Windows flanked either side. Murky late day sun fought to pierce the dreary drizzle outdoors. But his focus was locked in on the woman two steps ahead of him on the way to his office.

His office. Not hers. His territory.

She may have tipped the controls in her favor with the shower confrontation, but he wasn't giving ground again. His office would also provide guaranteed privacy. Once his Medina name had been exposed, the hospital had been flooded with paparazzi. He'd feared he might have to resign his position in order to ensure the safety of his patients.

But he'd underestimated Lilah.

She'd slapped restraining orders and injunctions on the press in a flash. She'd increased security at the hospital. And she'd moved his office to the farthest corner of the building. Overzealous paparazzi would have to run a gauntlet of two layers of security and a half-dozen heavily populated nurses' stations before reaching his newly relocated inner sanctum. No one in the press had succeeded to date.

Yes, he'd underestimated her then, something he wouldn't do now. He needed every edge he could muster around this woman when all he could think about was her bold entrance into his shower, her gaze raking over his body as if she wouldn't mind a touch. A taste. Maybe even a bite. Damn, but he hadn't expected to see her again without the defense of even a pair of boxers.

The understated twitch of her hips encased in a black power suit held his gaze far longer than any simple passing interest. His eyes glided up the rigid brace of her spine to the vulnerable curve of her neck, exposed with her auburn hair swept into a tight twist. One stubborn curl escaped to caress her ear the way he burned to do even now when he was angry as hell with her.

He'd wanted her for years, but knew she was the one woman he had to keep his hands well off. She was too insightful, too good of a friend and one who mirrored his workaholic ways. Anything more than a professional friendship would be disastrous. For a man who'd had precious few friends in his life, he'd valued the unexpected camaraderie he'd found with Lilah.

Clearing the hall and entering his reception area, he tore his eyes away from the enticing curve of her butt and nodded to his secretary, an efficient woman with photos of her twelve grandchildren neatly lined up on her desk. "Hold my calls, Wanda, unless it's about the Afghani girl in recovery."

His back twinged with a reminder of just how long

he'd spent cleaning up bone fragments along the child's spine, of working to relieve pressure, doing all he could to ensure she had as much use of her arms as possible even though she would almost certainly never walk again. Entering his office, he braced a hand on the door frame, then the sofa, using walls and furniture to steady himself at the end of a long day. His uneven gait contrasted with the efficient click of Lilah's killer red heels.

Skimming her fingers along a row of leather-bound medical journals, she stopped in front of a framed oil painting by Joaquín Sorolla y Bastida, a gift from his middle brother, Duarte. The canvas came from Bastida's *Sad Inheritance* preparatory pieces, a painting of crippled children bathing in healing waters.

No matter how much distance Carlos put between himself and his homeland, influences from his heritage called to him. He couldn't escape the reality of being the oldest son of deposed King Enrique Medina from San Rinaldo, a small island country off the coast of Spain. He couldn't ignore or forget how his father had fled with his family, relocating to live anonymously off the coast of Florida for decades.

Only recently had the press picked up the Medina trail. Carlos and his two brothers, all now adults, lived in different locations across the United States. Until four months ago, they'd even managed to fly under the radar with assumed names.

For most of his adult life he'd been known as Carlos Santiago. Yet in the stroke of a media pen's exposé, it became impossible for people to think of him as anything other than Carlos Medina, heir to a defunct monarchy.

Lilah was the one person who hadn't treated him differently after the news had broken about his Medina heritage. She hadn't been impressed or even angry over his years of deception. She understood his reasons for keeping his identity hidden.

The only question she'd asked after the story broke? As the hospital's administrator, she'd requested verification that all his medical credentials were valid and in order, given his assumed name.

She was a logical woman to the end.

So what the hell made a sensible person like Lilah decide to waltz into the men's locker room and confront him in the shower? A confrontation that still had him imagining scenarios where he pulled her under the spray with him to peel off every stitch of her clothing until she was as naked and hungry as him.

He closed the door to his office, sealing them inside the sparse space. He kept his world streamlined, only bare essential leather furniture, the painting from his brother and his books.

Leaning back against the wall to take pressure off his aching spine, he faced Lilah for the first time since she'd stared him down through a thin veil of mist. Her back was still straight but her face was pale. Very pale.

Worry whispered over him as his doctor senses blared an alert. She was obviously under great stress. Only extreme measures would have driven her to act so rashly. Normally, she calmly presented her case and made her move, with a legal eagle precision that served to make her a top-notch lawyer with a fast-track start to a brilliant career. He should have realized that. He mentally kicked himself for assuming her confrontation had something to do with their encounter two and a half months ago.

Carlos studied her green eyes, noting the dark circles beneath. "Is it bad news about funding for the new rehab wing?"

"This isn't about work…." She hesitated, chewing the red lipstick from her kissably full mouth.

Concern scratched deeper. He pushed away from the door toward her, drawn by threads of their old friendship and the scent of her perfume. If he whispered in her ear again as he had earlier, he would smell a hint of her body wash along her neck. Not a heavy perfume by any means given the hospital's fairly strict rules about scented lotions, soaps and colognes. Just enough pure Lilah to send his heart pumping faster.

Her eyes tracked him and each uneven step, his limp aggravated by the hours he'd spent operating today. Long ago, he'd gotten over any self-consciousness. Life held much more important issues and concerns than whether people noticed the impairment or pitied him. He knew he was damn lucky to be walking at all.

He closed the space between them. "Then what's so important that you felt the need to cause a scene big enough to feed hospital cafeteria gossip for at least a month?"

"It's about what happened after the Christmas fundraiser."

He stopped short. With a few simple words, she filled the room with memories of the night they'd stumbled back here, into his office, then finished the night at his house because it was closer than her condo. The memories were too vivid, so close on the heels of her bold move striding into the shower. Good thing she'd passed him the towel so fast because he'd been damn close to presenting her with an unmistakable visual on how much she still moved him. Turning his back to her under the pretense of gathering his soap had offered him a few seconds to scavenge control of his careening libido.

He'd been reckless enough to cave into the temptation to sleep with her once before. Every day since then, he'd been tormented by reliving that night and knowing just how easy it would be to succumb to temptation again. Still feeling the near-tangible caress of her eyes on him from earlier, he tried to remember all the reasons he should keep his hands off her.

Somehow his finger landed on the lone curl teasing around the shell-like curve of her ear. The softness of her skin, the silky texture of her hair wrapping around his touch as if drawing him closer, each nuance of Lilah tapped aside the paper-thin remains of his restraint.

Awareness glinted in her jewel tone eyes a second before he cupped the back of her neck and stepped toward her, until God help him, every curve of her body pressed to him in a perfect fit. The give of her breasts, the cradle of her hips, the familiar feel of her broadsided his senses with memories of their night together.

"Carlos," she whispered, her palms flat against his chest, pressing, "you're so damn arrogant."

But she swayed into him anyway. His brain shut down a second before he sealed his mouth to hers.

Need knifed through him with surgical precision, sharp and inescapable. She tensed slightly before gripping the front of his scrubs, her fists tight, insistent and more than a little angry as she hauled him closer. The taste of her, the sweep of her tongue meeting his stroke for stroke reminded him of how quickly they could combust. Keeping his distance the past weeks had been necessary and futile all at once.

This was inevitable. Spearing his fingers into her hair, he loosened the tight roll until silken strands cascaded over his skin. How easy it would be to sweep aside her suit and ditch his surgical scrubs. His leather sofa beckoned from across the room.

His desk was closer.

Sweeping his hand along smooth mahogany, he cleared a penholder, calendar and notepad in one efficient swipe that sent the lot clattering to the floor. He angled her back, cupped her bottom, hitched her up onto the edge. He released the top button on her suit jacket, a satiny camisole of some sort gliding over the backs of his knuckles.

Writhing, she moaned encouragement against his mouth and he made quick work of the fastenings, one after the other until he stroked aside the suit coat to reveal her silver, body-hugging shell. He kissed and nipped along her jaw, down her neck, trekking his way to the generous swell of her breasts. His memory hadn't done her justice. As he nuzzled the scented valley, her head lolled back. He tugged her camisole from her skirt and tucked his hand into the waistband, palming the slight curve of her stomach.

Lilah froze in his arms.

The chill radiating off her brought him back to earth like a shower turned icy cold. Months of restraint had gone down the drain in one impulsive moment. He pulled himself from her and leaned against the desk beside her, dragging in air as she yanked her jacket back on with shaky hands, her hair trapped inside.

He needed to fix this mess of his own making. "Lilah, clearly I have made an error in attempting to ignore what happened between us after the Christmas fundraiser. We need to figure out a way to deal with it so we can regain a level working environment."

"Damn straight, it happened." She thrust the buttons through openings with fierce speed, the fabric flower pin on her shoulder nearly quivering from her barely contained energy. "Believe me, I'm not likely to forget."

He pinched the bridge of his nose in frustration as the only answer pounded through his brain. "My life is complicated in so many ways by virtue of the Medina name. I wish, for your sake, things could be simpler, but they're not." Committed to his new course of action, he skimmed her hair free of her jacket. "I think we should consider an intimate friendship."

Her eyes went wide and unblinking. She sagged back against the desk again, her mouth opening and closing twice before a burst of laughter sliced the air. Wrapping an arm around her stomach, she laughed harder. Her eyes squeezed shut as she shook her head from side to side in obvious disbelief.

"Lilah?" He tucked a knuckle under her chin and turned her face toward him. "This really will be the best option for us to work through this attraction until our lives return to normal."

Her laughter faded, eyes turning somber. "At one time, I may have agreed with you. But it's too late for that now, Carlos."

Disappointment surged through him with more force than he would have expected for his ill-advised plan. He should have approached her sooner. Perhaps she held a grudge that he'd stayed away from her for so long.

Well then, he would dismantle her objections one by one. "I don't agree."

"You don't have all the pertinent information." She straightened to her full height, all of about five feet six inches, bringing her to his shoulder even in her heels. "I'm pregnant. Nearly three months along. And you're the father."

Pregnant?

Shock hit him square in the solar plexus. Followed by disbelief. Then jaded acceptance of her betrayal.

Just when he'd thought he couldn't be any more disillusioned by how easily people could deceive others. A bitter laugh rolled around in his gut and burned a bilious path up his throat.

She crossed her arms under her breasts defensively. "If this is some kind of payback for my laughter earlier, I don't appreciate it. I don't find this in the least amusing."

"Believe me, neither do I." The scars on his back throbbed with a reminder of all he'd lost over twenty-five years ago during his family's escape from San Rinaldo. He told the world the scars had come from a teenage riding accident. That lie was so much more palatable than the truth.

Her mouth went tight, her anger palpable. "This isn't going to make much of a story to tell our child some day."

"Our child? I think not." If anyone had cause to be angry, it was him. "I'm going to give you the benefit of the doubt and assume you're just mistaken about which guy fathered your baby, because I would hate to think you would deliberately try to pass off some other man's kid as mine."

She slapped him, sharp, fast and stingingly hard. "You jackass."

"Excuse me?" he asked, working his jaw from side to side to give himself a chance to weigh his words and tamp down his temper.

"You heard what I said. Believe me, that was the most benign word on my list right now. We may not be…friends…anymore, but I expected better from you than this." She waved her hand through the air as if that could somehow sum up what had transpired between them a minute earlier. "You may be cold, but I thought you were a man of honor."

Scrubbing a hand over his face, he held back the urge to call her on the accusation. She was pregnant—even if it wasn't his. God, the thought rattled him, especially with the leftover surge of hunger for her still cooling in his veins. So much for friends with benefits.

He forced himself to reign in his anger. "Lilah, I'm sorry. But it is *not* my kid."

She tugged her jacket into place again. "I won't force you to love or acknowledge your child. This baby deserves better than that. He or she deserves better than *you*. I've completed my duty in doing the right thing and letting you know. Now you can go straight to hell."

Something in her voice, the intensity of her anger set off warning bells in his brain. She truly thought the child was his when he knew that couldn't be true. If she had the due date wrong by even a couple of weeks, he could see how she might draw that conclusion. Not that he could think of any other man she'd been seeing, but then he'd made a point of avoiding her since their night together.

"Listen closely." He gestured toward her stomach. "That is not my baby, which means you do need to speak to the real father."

A surprise bolt of jealousy shot through him as he fully grasped for the first time the fact she'd slept with someone else close to the time they'd been together. His mind scanned the hospital roster for... Damn it, no. He couldn't go down that path right now.

He forced himself to continue speaking, to make her understand. "You're right that the man deserves to know. And that man can't possibly be me." Not after what had happened to him that night on the run in San Rinaldo. Rebel bullets had killed his mother and nearly killed him while he tried to protect her. Tried. And failed.

He held up a hand to keep her from interrupting—or leaving. "The accident that caused my limp had other physical ramifications as well." Carlos forced himself to say the words he hadn't shared with anyone. "Lilah, I'm sterile."

TWO

Lilah had faced her fair share of shockers in her years as a city prosecutor and then administrator at the Tacoma hospital. Certainly learning Dr. Carlos Medina had been hiding his royal lineage had stunned her silly. But his words now beat all other surprising revelations, hands down.

Gripping the edge of the mahogany desk to steady her shaky world, she searched Carlos's face for some sign of what possessed the innately honorable man to deny his own child.

Her hand still stung from her impulsive slap when he'd called her a liar. She hated the momentary loss of control then…and during his kiss earlier. No man affected her this way. She'd fought too long and hard not to be won over so easily like her mother. Yet a simple brush of Carlos's mouth against hers and she'd almost ditched her panties again with this man.

A very virile man who now seemed intent on denying the consequences of their encounter.

"You're sterile?" she repeated, wondering if perhaps she'd heard wrong. She *must* have heard wrong because she carried the living proof of his virility inside her. So either he was wrong or he was a coldhearted liar.

"That's what I said." He shifted his weight to one foot in a manner that to most would look casual. But after years of knowing him, she recognized the subtle way he favored his aching leg and injured back, something he inevitably did when he was under stress.

Carlos Medina was one of those docs with a godlike status around the E.R., the surgeon most likely to pull off a miracle when a gurney wheeled in the impossible. She'd noticed that most people only saw that glow of success and intelligence around him—when they weren't noticing his obvious good looks. Not many people saw past that to detect the fallout of the intense pressure he put on himself. The shifting feet. The tendency to plant his spine against any vertical surface.

Except she could not think of that now. She had too much at stake to get sucked in by all the things she found compelling about this man, not the least of which were these small signs that he was human underneath all that cool professional brilliance.

"Why didn't you say something when we were together that night?" she asked skeptically.

"I didn't see the information as relevant since procreation wasn't on our agenda." His sardonic tone needled at her already tender nerves.

"But you used condoms…even if one failed in the hot tub."

Just thinking of the combustible connection, their total loss of control threatened her balance even now. They'd started in his office, then raced to his home to spend the rest of the night together, awake and making the most of every moonlit minute.

"Safe sex has to do with more than pregnancy," he pointed out practically.

Of course she knew that. She'd freaked when the condom broke, only partially calming down once he'd reassured her he was disease free. Yet in the back of her mind she'd heard the haunting sound of her mother's sobs behind a closed bedroom door. Lilah had been a preteen at the time, but old enough to understand the gist of her parents' fight.

Her father's latest reckless affair had passed along a disease to his wife.

The STD had been treatable, thank heavens, but Lilah had been stunned by how quickly her mother forgave her husband for his infidelity. Again. And again.

Rather than forcing back the memories of her mom, Lilah embraced them for motivation to stand firm now. To push for answers. And to hold Carlos accountable. "This is your child. I don't want money from you and I certainly have no interest in the whole royalty thing. I only want my baby to know his or her father."

"That isn't my baby." His voice echoed with a surety she couldn't miss.

His denial of his own child infuriated her all over again.

"All because of a riding accident when you were a teenager?" She wasn't a doctor but something sounded off in his explanation, in spite of his utter confidence. Still, she couldn't ignore the gravity in his voice, the set serious lines on his aristocratic face.

"The trauma from the accident, coupled with a postsurgical infection, left me sterile. I'm a doctor, in case you've forgotten." He pulled a leather-bound book from the shelves and dropped it on the desk with a resounding thud. "But if you're still in doubt, there's a full chapter in here that discusses such complications. I'll be more than glad to mark the pages for you. The fact remains, though, that your child must have been fathered by someone else."

A shadow smoked briefly through his eyes, something dark and perhaps angry even, but was gone before she could confirm her impression.

If anyone deserved to be mad here, it was her. She wanted to shout her frustration. She *was* telling the father, whether he believed her or not. "Carlos, you aren't listening to me. There is no one else," she explained slowly, carefully, hoping he would hear the truth in her words even if it revealed her vulnerability in wanting only him. "There hasn't been anyone other than you in eight months."

A frown furrowed his forehead, but his silence encouraged her to continue.

"It is absolutely impossible for me to be pregnant with another man's child. And believe me, I *am* pregnant." Her voice shook for the first time. "I've seen the ultrasound. Our baby is alive and well."

The enormity of how much her life had changed so quickly threatened to overwhelm her. She'd always managed to tackle anything life threw her way, whether it be law school at Yale or standing up to a state supreme court judge.

Never had the stakes felt more important than now as she fought for the tiny defenseless life inside her.

Carlos's eyes relayed sympathy and, even worse, a hint of pity. "You really believe this."

"And you really don't."

Finally, she heard and accepted what he'd been saying since she first told him about the baby. She'd anticipated a number of reactions and prepared her rebuttals as carefully as any legal brief. However, she certainly hadn't foreseen this turn of events. Obviously his doctors had been wrong in their diagnosis of Carlos, and his refusal to even consider the possibility, his insistance on believing she'd lied, cut her to the core.

Disillusionment seeped through her veins like a chilly IV flooding through her system. Even though she'd assured herself she didn't need him, she'd hoped for…something…*anything* more than this.

Their kiss a few minutes earlier meant nothing to him. She meant nothing to him. And she needed to numb herself so *he* meant nothing to her.

Lilah pulled in a steeling breath, a trick she'd learned early on to keep her cool when her insides threatened to bubble over with too much unruly emotion. "I've done my part by informing you. A paternity test after the baby is born will confirm I'm telling you the truth. And you're going to feel like a *royal* jerk when you're faced with the proof."

Determined to leave with her pride, Lilah held her head high as she fought back the urge to cry over how terribly the confrontation had gone. While she hadn't expected exuberant cheers by any stretch, she'd hoped for acceptance, followed by stalwart emotional support as they agreed to spell out the practical details of bringing a child into the world. Carlos was a private, reserved man, but he'd always been quietly honorable. Even after his cold shoulder recently, she'd expected better from him than this.

She closed the door with a quiet but firm click, wishing her aching heart was as easy to seal off.

The click of the closing door echoed in his ears, along with the first hints of doubt.

Carlos leaned back against his desk, staring at the space where Lilah had stood seconds before. She'd seemed so certain. In all the years they'd known each other, she'd been an honest woman—a boardroom shark in fighting for the hospital—but always frank and truthful. He admired that about her. For years, in fact, he'd used that admiration of her character to temper his more…primal response to her.

What if…

The possibility of actually being a father rocked his balance far more than the injuries that still caused him to limp to this day. He flattened his clammy palms against the legs of his green hospital scrubs.

While he'd engaged in a number of careful affairs over the years, never had he let a woman truly break through his laser focus on his work. But Lilah was different. He was damn impressed by the way she fought for the hospital, stood up to million-dollar donors and politicians when it came to patients' rights—hell, the way she faced down even him when he dug in his heels too deeply and lost focus on the bigger picture. She had a sharp mind and she wielded it artfully in her profession.

Would she use those same skills against him even now if she thought it would benefit her child?

His father had taught all three of his sons not to trust anyone, anytime. Everybody had a price, including the cousin who had sold out their escape plan. The queen, his mother, Beatriz Medina had died as a result of the ambush that ensued on their way out of San Rinaldo. Carlos had spent his teenage years undergoing surgeries to recover from the gunshot wounds. That he could walk at all was considered a miracle. Doctors told him to be grateful for that much, even if he would never have biological children.

Could he trust Lilah?

As much as he trusted anyone, which wasn't much. God forbid the press should get a hold of this tidbit before he settled the issue. He needed to provide Lilah with concrete proof while keeping matters quiet.

First step, arrange to have the lab run a sperm count test. As much as he balked at the invasion of his privacy, the current results would end this once and for all.

The pesky "what if" smoked through his mind again, the possibility that through some inexplicable miracle her kid turned out to be his after all. Then, he needed to keep Lilah close at hand until the baby could be tested.

Because if against all odds she carried a Medina, nothing would stop him from claiming his child.

Suddenly weary to her toes, Lilah sagged against the closed door. The reception area outside Carlos's office echoed with emptiness, thank goodness. But there was no telling how much longer before his secretary, Wanda, returned to her desk. Her computer already scrolled a screen saver photo of her dozen grinning grandchildren at the Port Defiance Zoo.

Lilah squeezed her eyes closed. The memory of her argument with Carlos rang in her ears. Her belly churned with nausea, unusual for this late in the day. She still battled morning sickness and, no question, upset emotions made it worse. She curved a hand protectively over her stomach, the baby bump barely discernable so early in the pregnancy. Carlos hadn't even noticed when he'd pulled her camisole from her waistband. But she could feel the changes in her body, the swollen tenderness of her breasts, a heightened sense of smell and an insatiable nightly craving for marinated artichokes, a food she had previously hated. While circumstances were far from perfect, she loved her baby with a fierceness that still overwhelmed her at times.

A lock of hair slithered over her cheek and she realized her French twist must be wrecked from Carlos's hands as they'd kissed in his office. Her nipples tingled in lingering awareness of just how fast and high he could stoke desire inside her. She plucked pins from her hair and let the rest slide free around her shoulders, not as professional as she preferred at work, but no doubt better than the sexed-up mess she'd been seconds ago.

For her child's sake, she needed to think rationally rather than with her emotions—or her welling hormones. Carlos obviously believed he was sterile and had only her word that the baby was his. While she wanted to think four years of friendship would have convinced him of her trustworthiness, that clearly wasn't the case.

He was a reserved and private man by nature. His aloofness—hell, his inaccessibility—the past months let her know their friendship wasn't as deep as she'd believed. That she'd been forced to chase him down in the shower to tell him...

Releasing another trapped breath, she refused to get wound up again. She needed to take a step back from him and wait. Time would prove his paternity.

Content she'd regained even ground, Lilah straightened just as the door to the hall opened. She tucked the handful of bobby pins into her jacket pocket and smoothed a hand over her hair to clear any signs of her clench from Wanda's perceptive eyes. There was a reason they called Lilah "The Iron Lady" around this place, and she intended to keep her reputation intact.

The door opened wider, revealing...not Wanda. Lilah tensed for a second, concerned about the press infiltrating the multiple layers of security she'd put in place. Then she recognized one of their newer radiologists, Nancy Wolcott. Her lab coat sported multiple decorative buttons on the lapel. Nancy had once relayed she wore the nonregulation "flair" to put her younger patients at ease. She must be working on the surgical case Carlos was so concerned about.

"Hello, Nancy." Thank heaven her voice stayed steady. "Dr. Medina and I just finished our meeting. I'm sure he will be anxious to hear an update on his young Afghani patient from this afternoon's surgery."

"Oh, I'm not on that case." Smiling hesitantly, the willowy brunette straightened a light-up shamrock pin. "Actually, I'm here on a personal note."

Unease feathered over her. "A personal note?"

"I'm here to meet him for dinner. It's after hours, so

no worries about an administrative sanction. I'm not on the hospital's clock right now." She shrugged out of her lab coat and draped it over her arm.

Oh, God, Lilah really didn't like where this conversation was headed, and the timing couldn't have been worse. She should have seen this coming. Carlos had never been lacking for dates before his Medina identity became public. He was a hunky, wealthy doctor, after all. Albeit a workaholic, temperamental doc. Women were swarming him now that he'd tacked prince onto his list of attributes.

She scrambled for something to say and a way to get out. Fast. "No one can fault your dedication. I know well how many days you've worked longer shifts when we needed you. Now if you'll excuse me—"

The younger woman stopped her with a light touch to the arm. "I should explain. Carlos—Dr. Medina—and I have been going out for the past few weeks. We've been careful to keep it under wraps." She adjusted one of the dozen frames on Wanda's desk. "He really hates how intrusive the media can be, so we're waiting for the perfect time for a controlled press release."

No worries about steeling a breath. Nancy Wolcott had knocked Lilah into next year without even trying. Carlos, of course, hadn't said a word about it.

And they'd been dating for weeks, not days, not a onetime outing over coffee. But a relationship that needed a freaking press release.

Lilah bit back bile. "I hadn't heard."

"I wanted to keep it quiet, too. I know he has a reputation for keeping relationships light but I think this might be headed somewhere." Nancy laughed nervously, seemingly oblivious to the fact she was gushing. "Perhaps he kept his distance before, back when he had to maintain his royal background. But now that everything's out in the open about his Medina name, he's free to pursue anyone he wants."

Hearing the infatuation in Nancy's voice, Lilah wanted to hate her, to dismiss her like the royalty groupies who'd come out of the woodwork lately. She longed to find fault in someone who'd captured Carlos's interest when a night of sex with her hadn't moved him in even a passing way.

And yet she couldn't be catty. Nancy didn't know about that night with Carlos. No one did.

Furthermore, of every unattached female on staff, this one seemed least likely to be a gold digger or fame seeker. As a part of her job, Lilah knew the history of each employee. Nancy Wolcott was a nice person who very obviously had stars in her eyes over the new man in her life. Who could blame her?

Perhaps a woman who already had Carlos's child swimming around in utero.

A cold ache gelling inside her, Lilah tuned in to the rest of Nancy's lovelorn ramblings.

"I know I'm probably jumping the gun here, but he's such a gorgeous, moody man. A woman can't help but want to touch those inner depths." Nancy pressed a hand to her heart, her eyes fluttering closed as she inhaled.

Lilah wanted to give the woman a good swift kick in her unrealistic expectations about Carlos Medina. Even when he'd dated in the past, she'd seen how emotionally detached the man could be, something that hadn't changed one bit since the whole "son of a deposed monarch" revelation.

Not that she was surprised. There was no such thing

as a fairy-tale ending. Libraries labeled it fiction for a reason. She'd seen firsthand with her parents how quickly love soured, how easy it was for a woman to turn into a pathetic moony-eyed doormat.

Her father had used his job as a Hollywood agent to seduce countless wannabe starlets. To this day his wife—Lilah's mother—did her level best to ignore the indiscretions that messed with her perception of happily ever after with her hunky, rich dream man. On occasion, the bimbo of the month set her eyes on a ring or got angry when the contracts didn't flow in and would confront the Mrs., forcing her to face her husband's infidelities.

A fight would ensue. Tears would flow. He would offer up jewelry or a romantic getaway to "reconnect" and all would be forgiven until the next time when they repeated the same dysfunctional cycle all over again— leaving Lilah with two drawers jam-packed full of tourist T-shirts brought home by her lovey-dovey parents. In fact, her parents were on one of their make-up cruises now, and once they returned she would have to tell them about the baby.

About Carlos?

Listening to Nancy detail her evening with Carlos at the symphony, Lilah had to accept that the woman wasn't blowing anything out of proportion. He really had asked her out on honest-to-God dates. Not that Lilah had entertained dreams of such with him. But damn it, they had slept together. They had been friends before that. And while he wasn't the warm fuzzy kind, she deserved better from him than the way he'd treated her since their one-night stand.

She definitely deserved better than what she'd experienced in his office a few short minutes ago.

Nancy eyed his door warily. "I hope he's not in a bad mood after your confrontation."

Shock jolted her already ragged nerves. Nancy couldn't possibly know about the baby. Had someone been outside the door listening? Wanda, perhaps?

As she calmed down enough to look at Nancy's curious face, she realized the woman was just that—curious. She wasn't shocked or mad, none of the reactions that would be normal if she'd heard rumors that her new "boyfriend" had fathered a child with someone else. "I assume you're referring to the incident in the men's locker room."

"I'm sorry." Nancy pulled up straighter, fidgeting with her logo buttons until they were all cockeyed. "I shouldn't have said anything. I didn't mean to be so chatty."

Lilah eased between her and the exit. "I'm truly curious how you heard this quickly. Please, be frank."

Nancy winced. "I heard in the cafeteria. The buzz is pretty intense as people try to figure out what he did to make you that angry. Bets are being taken for possible reasons."

"And what would those guesses be?"

She nibbled her lip, hesitating for a moment before continuing warily. "Most think you're upset because he blew off that board meeting earlier this week. Others wonder if you're freaking out over him taking on too many pro bono cases. For what it's worth, my money's on the latter. He's such a bighearted man under that gruff exterior."

Lilah gripped the bobby pins in her pocket so tight

they would probably leave holes in her fingers. "Hope you didn't bet the bank on that because you'll lose your life's savings."

If the hospital rumor mill was already churning over one confrontation—granted, a pretty theatrical one—she hated to think how soon her own personal life would be fodder for cafeteria gossip. Good God, she would have to be so much more careful to protect her child's privacy. For the first time it really sunk in that she was carrying a royal child, a person who would be dogged by the press for a lifetime.

Would the news of her child fit on the same press release as Carlos's new girlfriend?

Panic roiled. So much for her decision to opt for an even-keeled "wait and see" attitude. She'd been fooling herself. Her visceral reaction to this woman made it clear too many emotions were involved already.

She needed to keep on fighting rather than letting him roll over her. She would not let her child be hurt by Carlos. She would shield this precious life as best she could from the pain of a father's neglect.

The click of a turning doorknob snapped her attention back to the reception area a second before Carlos's office door opened, the man of the hour filling the frame with his broad shoulders. A flash of surprise raced across his dark eyes.

Anger, frustration and, hell yes, hurt chased through her. Quickly, she stifled the urge to vent the steam building inside her. She'd already made a large enough scene for one day, and she didn't intend to let Carlos know just how deeply he'd wounded her.

That didn't mean she had to balk at making him squirm.

Lilah flicked her loose hair, hair mussed by him during their out-of-control kisses, over her shoulder. "Hello again, Dr. Medina. I was just talking to your new girlfriend."

Three

The shots just kept coming today.

Carlos looked from one woman to the other. How much had Lilah said before he interrupted? Apparently not much since Nancy appeared blessedly oblivious. She was a nice person he'd gone out with a couple of times in hopes of erasing Lilah from his memory.

Nancy was everything he wanted in his personal life. She was intelligent, witty, with common interests and made no demands on his emotions. She should have been perfect for him, except she left him cold. Rather than helping him move on from that colossal mistake, the presence of his "girlfriend" reminded him of just how much every woman paled alongside Lilah.

He'd been planning to break things off with Nancy tonight, even before today's shocking revelation. Continuing to see her when he had unresolved issues with Lilah wasn't fair. Damn shame he hadn't spoken to Nancy a day earlier.

The new radiologist looked from Carlos to Lilah and back again, confusion stamped on her face. "I don't mean to interrupt if you two need to talk business. I can always come back later for our dinner date."

Carlos nodded. "That would be best."

"All righty." She arched up on her toes as if to give him a quick kiss, then paused.

Either she realized such a public display of affection would be inappropriate in the workplace—or she saw Carlos's scowl. Regardless, the woman got the message and pulled away fast.

He caught Lilah's raised eyebrow and added, "Actually, I have an appointment I need to take care of as soon as I check on my patient."

He'd contacted his doctor and the lab about checking his sperm count. He already felt certain of the outcome, but he needed to confirm for Lilah's sake.

And if by some fluke he could father children? Then he would tuck aside his reservations about the way she unsettled his world and launch an immediate campaign to win her over. No half measures, he would be all in, 24/7, until they settled things between them once and for all.

Turning away from Nancy, toward Lilah, he took in her tumbled hair, remembered how it got that way, felt the inevitable kick to his balance. "We will be talking again tomorrow."

Leaving the hospital lab, Carlos walked down the corridor back to his office in a daze. It had been a helluva day. He'd started out operating on a child who reminded him too much of himself, a child caught in the crossfire of war. Before he'd found even five minutes to regain his footing, Lilah had swept aside his shower curtain. Now, his day had ended with the surprise revelation from his own doctor. Not definitive results, by any means, but there was a very slim chance he could father children.

Even the possibility rocked him to the core. He needed time to hole up in his office and plan his next move.

He rounded the corner. Nancy waited beside the door, shuffling from foot to foot while she texted on her cell phone. Apparently she'd been busy while he was gone. She'd changed from her work clothes into a dress—a silky sort of thing for a nice dinner out.

There was no way he could sit through dinner waiting for the right opening to break things off. He needed to make his position clear now. It was the only fair thing to do for Nancy and Lilah.

"Nancy, I'm sorry to have kept you waiting."

"No need to apologize." She tucked her cell phone into her tiny black bag. "I was just telling my best friend about our date tonight."

He winced. "About that." He pushed open his office door. "Let's step into my office so we can talk."

"Oh, um, it's too late in the evening, isn't it?" She scrunched her nose and stayed in the hall. "You need to cancel. I understand. We can go out tomorrow instead. Or how about I cook you dinner—"

"Nancy," he cut her ramble short as gently as possible. "I'm afraid I've given you the wrong impression. This isn't something we should discuss in the hall."

She chewed her lip for a second before smiling, too brightly. She charged into the office ahead of him. He felt bad for misleading her. He'd made a mess of his personal life. He couldn't change the past, but starting now, he could make things right.

As he followed, he decided no more hesitation. No more avoidance. Just as he needed to be clear with Nancy now, he should have settled things with Lilah before.

He wouldn't make the same mistake again. As soon as he finished this confrontation with Nancy, he would go straight to Lilah's—tonight, not tomorrow—and tell her the results of his lab test.

Standing in the open doorway to her penthouse condo, Lilah wished she'd checked the peephole first. But then why hadn't the doorman rang to let her know Carlos was on his way up? Even royalty shouldn't be given a free pass into her building.

Granted, she wouldn't have sent Carlos away, but she would have liked a second to prepare herself before facing him again.

Corridor sconces bathed him in a halogen glow as he waited. Moisture from the light rain clung to his hair and glinted on the hint of silver at his temples. Too easily, she could envision him damp from his shower earlier. Except now he wore clothes. His long trench was open, revealing his gray suit, red tie trekking down his chest the way her fingers itched to mimic.

The hall echoed with intimate silence, everyone else tucked in for the night inside their units in the restored waterfront building. Carlos had been here in the past for informal gatherings, drop-ins and dinner parties, but always with others. Never alone.

Totally alone. Like now.

She gripped the brass doorknob tighter. "I thought you said we would be speaking tomorrow."

The scent of the salty outdoor air clung to him, teasing her nose.

"My appointment took care of itself faster than I expected." Palm flattened to the door frame, he looked past her shoulder into her condo. "We should step inside."

Even fully covered in silky sleep pants and matching green paisley top, she was too aware of the nighttime, her PJs and *him*. "It's polite to ask to be invited in rather than demand."

His jaw flexed with irritation. "Let's stop with the word games. We have important business to discuss."

Of course, he was right. She just resented that he'd caught her unawares, dictating the time and manner of their meeting. "Come inside, then. But don't get too comfortable. It's been a long—" *disappointing* "—day. I'm tired."

Careful to step well clear of him, she pressed her back against the hall rather than risk an accidental brush of her body and his. His uneven gait thudded against the freshly restored hardwood floors as he walked deeper into her condominium. She loved her two-bedroom haven full of character from the whitewashed brick walls to the soaring ceiling with exposed beams and a loft office. A wall of windows revealed the twinkling lights of the Tacoma skyline, historic Foss Waterway and a fog-ringed mountain in the distance.

Shrugging out of his trench coat, Carlos stopped just shy of her burgundy sofa, half in, half out of her place, much like he kept himself from committing to any people, emotions, relationships. "About Nancy—"

She cut him off with the wave of her hand. "I don't care who you date." And maybe if she kept saying it often enough, she would believe it. "That's your business and has nothing to do with us. We were never a couple. You and I have nothing more to say to each other outside of hospital business until after the paternity test."

"Nancy and I are not an item, never were," he ignored her final jab, sticking to the point he seemed determined to press. "We had a couple of casual dates, and I'd already decided to break things off before today."

"How convenient, but still not relevant." She padded closer to him, her bare feet whispering along the cool, bare flooring. "If that's all you came to say, then we're done."

She pointed to the door.

He flung aside his trench to rest on the back of a striped chair and clasped her wrist in a big but gentle grip. Silently, slowly, *deliberately,* he folded her arm back against her chest, which brought him closer to her. His eyes turned smoky with intensity....

And focused on her mouth.

Her heart somersaulted in her chest. "Don't even go there, Carlos," she warned, but didn't pull away. "Any urge to kiss you evaporated once you refused to believe me about the pregnancy."

Teasing his thumb along her speeding pulse, he stilled her again with his eyes. "I came here to tell you that I'm willing to entertain the possibility this could be my baby."

The sensual tug, the raspy allure of his callused fingers on her skin sidetracked her, delaying her brain from absorbing his words for three, needy heartbeats.

Then awareness faded from her body as his words

penetrated, followed by realization of the reason for his surprise visit. She leaned nearer, her breasts so close to his chest a simple deep inhale could skim her tingling nipples against him.

She kept her breathing shallow, even as she lowered her voice into a husky whisper sure to heat his exposed neck. "Got a sperm count check, did you? That was quick."

A fleeting dry smile twitched his mouth. "It helps having connections in the medical world."

Confirmation of her suspicion didn't make her feel one bit better. He wasn't here because he had a change-of-heart decision to trust her word. He'd gotten his proof. While she understood on an intellectual, practical level, she was currently feeling anything but sensible.

Let alone amenable.

"How nice for you." She wrenched her wrist from his grip, wrapping her arms around herself and stalking to the window wall. "What a shock it must have been that you still have swimmers."

"How nice that you find my medical history so amusing."

"I don't find any of this at all funny. Particularly your insinuations about my honesty earlier." She half looked back at him over her shoulder. "Have you let your new girlfriend know?"

Ouch, she hadn't meant to bring up the whole Nancy issue again and sound—God forbid—jealous. She looked away quickly before he could see any betraying emotions on her face.

His footsteps echoed behind her, closer, the sound and feel of him too familiar. "I told you already." He stroked back her hair from her ear. "I broke things off with her."

Goose bumps rose on her skin, twinkling boat lights on the water blurring as everything faded but the sound of his breathing, the light skim of his fingers. Good God, his surgeon hands had such a capacity for minute movements, meticulous attentiveness until he turned even an inch of her shoulder into a volatile erogenous zone.

"Well, she should know you can still—"

Her words hitched up short on her next breath, heat flooding through her body and pooling low. The crisp scent of him—night air and ocean breeze—drew nearer, stronger, until she flattened her hand against the cool windowpane to steady herself.

He cupped her shoulders in broad, careful hands and turned her to face him. "She does not need to be informed."

Did that mean they weren't sleeping together or that he'd been more careful? She tried not to care about the answer, hating that he had such power over her feelings. The way her temperature spiked when she simply looked at him, the sensation of the room shrinking to just the two of them. All too easily she could lose sight of how important it was to keep her head clear.

Shifting her focus from herself to her child, she asked, "What did the doctor have to say?"

His fingers slid down the length of her arms before he tucked his hands into his trouser pockets. "I can give you the lengthy technobabble about motility and counts if you wish. But while chances are very low I can father a child," he swallowed hard, "the chance does exist."

That simple slow swallow spoke emotional volumes

from such an aloof man. Sympathy for him stirred against her will. What a shocker this day must have been for him on a number of levels, which didn't excuse the way he'd betrayed their friendship over the past few weeks with his aloof behavior. But still, the hurt and disappointment eased at having him backtrack. Now, finally, they could make plans for their baby.

She chewed her lip, tasting toothpaste from her earlier attempt to brush away the persistent memory of his kiss. "I realize this must be a big surprise for you—"

"My feelings are irrelevant," he charged over her, his face set again in a mask she'd seen him don during especially taxing surgeries. "I spoke with a GYN colleague and we can have a chorionic villus sampling done in your twelfth to fourteenth week of pregnancy to determine paternity."

An early paternity test? He *still* doubted her? So much for sympathetic leanings on her part.

Anger starched up her spine again vertebrae by vertebrae. "Fine. You've said what you came here for—"

"Actually, I haven't finished."

"Well, good for you. However, I've had more than enough of your company for one day."

"That's my point. Today hasn't gone well for either of us. And regardless of how that test comes out, we're going to be tied to each other, whether through the pregnancy or through work. I'm assuming you have no intention of changing jobs and neither do I."

"That hasn't stopped you from being a jerk since December." She jabbed him in the chest with her pointer. "Other people—" *like Nancy* "—may be willing to put up with your moodiness because you were a hospital legend even before you turned out to be some kind of royalty, but I happen to think that excuses nothing."

"You're absolutely correct on all counts." His angular face creased with the first smile she'd seen from him in so long, longer than she could remember. The power of it was so much stronger than it should be.

Her arm fell to her side. "Pardon me?"

"You heard me." He stroked back a lock of her hair then withdrew his hand before she could object. "You're right. I've been a—what did you say earlier?—a jackass."

She sank onto her sleek red sofa, trying to process this latest surprise turn from him, tough to do when he scattered her thoughts with a simple touch or heated look. "What brought you around to my way of thinking?"

Settling onto the gray-and-white striped chair beside her, he leaned forward, elbows on his knees—closer to her. "Actually, seeing you and Nancy in the office together. I should have given our impetuous night together some closure before moving on."

Stunned anew, she bit her tongue, afraid if she spoke, his surprising chattiness would dry up as quickly as it started.

"I still stand by what I said the morning after we were together." He stared at her intently, his linked hands so close to her legs if she even twitched, they would make contact. "I shouldn't have let things go that far between us, but I also shouldn't have assumed things could return to normal either."

She refrained from mentioning the past months had brought anything but a return to normal. He'd become even more of a workaholic than normal, leaving not even a free half hour for a simple shared coffee as they'd done in the past. Although apparently he'd found time for dates with Nancy Wolcott.

Damn, that green-eyed monster was a tenacious beast. "What is your point?"

"We have about a week's window before the paternity test to find even ground. I propose that we make the most of it."

Suspicion prickled. Could he be making a move on her because of that kiss? While she might have caved to the temptation of that passionate clench a few weeks ago, now that she knew about the baby she needed to be more cautious. "Make the most of it in what way?"

"Let's both take a week of vacation. We leave Washington and work behind to focus 24/7 on clearing the air."

Except he never took time off. Ever.

His offer to step away from the hospital rocked her, and also made her wonder if he could actually be serious. Her own calendar was packed solid. However, he had a point about the future. And she already knew how that paternity test would turn out. This truly could be her only chance to resolve her feelings for Carlos. Her only chance to protect her heart for the many times she would have to face him in the coming years.

"A week off from the hospital," she parroted, needing confirmation even if she didn't know what she would do once she got it. "Just you and me?"

"That's what I said." He nodded curtly, a lock of hair sliding across his forehead. He worked such insane hours he even missed regular haircuts.

"What about your patients? And what about the little girl you operated on this afternoon?"

"My part in her medical plan is complete. As for my

other cases, everything can be handled by doctors on staff."

Heaven knows there were plenty of physicians who owed him for the times he'd stepped in for them and countless holidays spent on call so they could be with their families.

Still, she didn't quite trust he would simply drop everything in Tacoma. There must be a catch. "Where would we go?"

"How about Colorado? My family owns a house there."

Panic tickled. "Who else lives there?"

"No one. It's a resort property. It's empty now and completely at our disposal."

Alone? Just the two of them? While she wasn't ready for a meet-the-parents moment, she also wasn't sure total isolation with her hot onetime lover was such a brilliant idea either.

Although memories of what a jerk he'd been today could provide plenty of protection. Then she thought of the tiny life growing inside her and knew she didn't have any choice. Certainly this was a surprise baby at a time when she'd begun to wonder if perhaps motherhood wasn't in the cards for her. But from the moment she'd seen the heart fluttering on the ultrasound, she'd known she would do anything, absolutely *anything* for her child.

Including spend seven tempting days alone with Carlos Medina.

Outside Lilah's condo building, Carlos closed the door on his Mercedes SUV and hooked his arm over the steering wheel.

Puget Sound stretched out beyond his windshield, hazy through the misty rain. Through the tinted windows, he soaked in the sight, gaining some mystical comfort from the light roll of waves.

Water locales drew him, his brothers as well, likely because it reminded them of their island homeland of San Rinaldo. His middle brother, Duarte, had left their father's fortress to scoop up seaside investment resorts before settling in Martha's Vineyard. Antonio, the youngest Medina son, had been drawn to the warmer climate of Galveston Bay, where he'd become a shipping magnate. Ironically, even their half sister, Eloisa, spent most of her life in Pensacola, Florida, before settling with her new husband in Hilton Head, South Carolina.

He could only conclude that the shores called to something centuries old in their genetics. The scientist inside him didn't make so much as a peep in protest of the illogical thought. He felt the proof surging through his veins. Only once had he felt anything as strong—the night he'd spent with Lilah. The past few months he'd been fighting the temptation to lose himself in her again. He'd tried to move on.

Today had proved his failure on that front all too well. Now, he had a full week with her. Seven days to level things with her, setting the course for the rest of his life. He would either tie her to him so they could parent their child or work her out of his system so he could walk away if she'd lied about the baby's paternity.

To accomplish his goal, he needed to get her away from here, in a setting under his control, no surprises from work or the press.

He fished his phone from the inside of his suit coat

and thumbed speed dial for his brother Duarte, the next in line after him for their father's tarnished crown.

Before the second ring even finished, his brother's voice came across speakerphone, "Speak to me, brother."

Carlos didn't bother apologize for calling late, even more so for Duarte who was three hours ahead on East Coast time. He and his siblings didn't speak every other day by any means, but when one called, they dropped everything else.

"Just calling to check up on our father." Enrique Medina had been near death for over six months from a failing liver. "How's he doing?"

"Still holding on. He's tough. I'm starting to wonder if maybe he will beat this after all."

Carlos knew the poor odds too well from a medical perspective so he opted to switch the subject instead. "I may be coming for a visit in a few days. I'm not going to say anything to him until I'm sure—" *sure if the baby is mine* "—but want to give you the heads-up."

"Just name the time and Kate and I will be there."

The sound of rustling sheets and a sleepy female mumble echoed through the phone line. Duarte was engaged to a reporter, a surprisingly illogical choice, especially given his brother's usual methodical ways. But he'd fallen and fallen hard. There'd been no doubting that when Carlos had seen him with her at Antonio's wedding a couple of months ago.

Normally, he balked at returning to the isolated compound where they'd relocated after escaping San Rinaldo, so many bad memories linked to their new "home." The island complex had been outfitted with a top-notch physical rehab center, where he'd spent most

of his teenage years. His brothers had been his only
friends during those days, and even so with the surgeries
and recoveries, there hadn't been much time to learn
about relationships.

Although he felt anything but "brotherly" around
Lilah.

His gaze shifted from the shoreline to the historic
brick complex housing Lilah's restored condo. "I may
be bringing someone with me."

"Care to share details?"

"Not yet."

Looking up to the tenth floor—the penthouse—he
could swear he saw Lilah outlined in her window for
a second before she clicked off the light. Preparing
for bed? He hardened at the thought of peeling off her
clothes. Lowering her onto the mattress. Imprinting
himself on her. And hoping like hell that baby was his
so he could take Lilah again and again, and damn the
consequences to his carefully constructed world.

He hauled his attention off her condo and back to
the conversation. "She and I are going to spend some
time together over the next few days while I check on a
couple of Father's holdings."

Enrique owned investment properties around the
U.S., and even a few outside the States. Savvy financial
purchases, yes, but they'd also been bought to create
more confusion over where the deposed king had
settled.

Enrique had already begun parceling off parts of his
estates to each of his sons. While Carlos couldn't have
cared less about any inheritance, he saw the wisdom in
protecting the family interests if for no other reason than
he could donate additional monies to the charities of his

choice. He could make it possible for more children to receive the surgeries they needed, to have a chance at enjoying their youth in a way he couldn't.

However, he refused to wallow in self-pity or bemoan all he'd lost. He preferred to charge forward and take control of the future, and normally he succeeded. Except on a day like today, the past, the injury, the acute cut of loss, were thrown in his face in an unavoidable way. Flexing his aching leg, he pushed back the temptation to imagine the face of an infant, his child.

God help Lilah if she'd lied to him.

And God help him if she hadn't. Because then he couldn't seal himself off from the past with a solitary existence any longer.

"Duarte, I'll keep in touch. Sleep well, my brother."

He disconnected the call, his eyes drawn up to the darkened penthouse where Lilah slept. Alone for tonight, but not much longer.

Tomorrow, he would begin his campaign to get back in her good graces with a trip to the family lodge in Vail, Colorado. Hopefully a few intimate nights by the fire would melt her walls and burn away the cold fist that had stayed lodged in his chest since the morning she'd left his bed.

Four

Lilah had been running full-out since the minute she'd rolled out of bed this morning. The day had been jam-packed with continuous phone calls to the hospital in attempts to clear her schedule for a week while she packed, dressed and prepped her condo for her reckless getaway with Carlos.

Now, ensconced in his limousine on the way to the airport, the enormity of what she'd done washed over her until her fingers dug deeply into the supple leather seat.

Late-day rain pattered on the limo's clear sunroof, streaks muting the already cloudy sky. Much like her nerves, it made her apprehension all the worse. She could barely believe she'd agreed to this crazy plan of his, an impulsive idea so unlike the normally methodical man. Perhaps that's why she'd agreed. He must be every bit as thrown by life as she was right now to even suggest such a plan.

Although he looked anything but rattled as he checked updates from the hospital on his phone. While he may have transferred his cases to another physician, he obviously hadn't off-loaded the concerns from his mind. Intense concentration furrowed his brow, his dark, chocolate-brown eyes taking on a distant look as he stared out the window, his mind obviously still on his young patients.

Even in casual jeans and a black cable sweater, he was one hundred percent in charge. His dedication softened her heart, which kept her from tapping on the privacy window and asking the chauffer to take her home.

Today, Carlos was particularly involved in checking up on his very young patient from yesterday's surgery. The deep, low rumble of Carlos's bass filled the roomy limo with his exotic Spanish accent. Even with the blast of the vehicle's heater, the chill of the damp day seeped into her and made her ache to cuddle into the heat of the warm-blooded—undoubtedly hot—man beside her.

Her cashmere blend dress suddenly itchy against her oversensitive skin, she scratched the back of her neck, tucking her hand under the concealed zipper.

Carlos clipped his phone to his jeans and turned his attention toward her. "I assume everything is fine for you to travel. I didn't even think to ask last night and I should have. My apologies."

His concern touched her. "I spoke with my doctor this morning to be sure. And yes, travel is fine or I wouldn't be here. I packed my vitamins and am taking care of myself."

"Would you like something to drink? Some spring

water?" He gestured to the gleaming silver minifridge. "A light snack?"

"No, thank you." Her hands were trembling so much she would likely spill it anyway. "Maybe later."

"Any morning sickness?" he asked in his oh-so-familiar physician tone.

"Some," she responded slowly, curious as to his grilling. "The nausea's not pleasant, to say the least, but tolerable."

Suspicion niggled as she wondered if his questions had more to do with relegating her to a safe, distant role of patient rather than genuine concern for her, for their baby.

Hurt grated against her already ragged nerves. "Why the sudden interest in this pregnancy? Are you searching for clues that I'm not as far along as I say? Is that what this trip is really all about? You must realize a person can travel 'til nearly the eighth month."

He stretched his arm along the back of her seat, inches away from encircling her shoulders. The scent of him mingled with leather and new car smell. "Let's not begin a fight. This time together is about finding common ground."

While he was right on that point, resentment still simmered. "How can you simply shut down unpleasantness in a snap? I'm not accustomed to compartmentalizing my life that way."

"How then do you function during a crisis at the hospital?" he retorted without missing a beat.

"That's different." Wasn't it? "That's a unique moment in time. Life isn't one continual crisis."

He grunted noncommittally. "If you say so."

Was her pregnancy being relegated to crisis level?

So, then, what was this time with her through his eyes? Damage control? "Surely you must have some way to relax, making time to lower those thick walls you put around yourself."

A one-sided grin creased his cheek but never reached his eyes. "Letting down your guard is highly overrated, not to mention dangerous."

Dangerous? A pall settled over their conversation. "Because you're royalty?"

Which meant her child was a royal as well. She resisted the urge to lean back into the safety, the protection, of the hard-muscled beam of his arm.

He teased a lock of her loose hair. "Ah, you remember my Medina roots after all."

"That's a strange thing to say."

His head tipped to the side, his smoky eyes raking her with an appreciative gaze. "I appreciated the way you didn't treat me differently after the news story broke about my family's hidden identity."

The compliment soothed her raw nerves and also made her wonder. "Is that why things changed between us, why you made a move on me at the party?"

Hesitating, he scrubbed a hand over the five o'clock shadow already peppering his strong, square jaw. "In part. You were the one person who didn't want to talk about San Rinaldo."

Because she'd seen how people suddenly treated him differently. She'd noticed how uncomfortable the kowtowing made him. And, quite frankly, she'd found his work at the hospital to be infinitely more admirable than any royal fortune or regal bloodlines.

That he preferred anonymity to media attention impressed her all the more. "Thank you, Carlos."

"For what?"

"For telling me that." For helping reassure her going with him now was the right thing to do. She needed these insights as to what made Carlos tick. She needed this trip.

She needed *him*.

Her eyes fell to his mouth, a strong masculine slash that could turn so tender on her bared body. Memories flooded her mind of the first time he'd kissed her at the hospital fundraiser, standing out on the balcony with a romantic flurry of snow casting a crystal sheen on everything around her. The second Carlos's mouth had covered hers, she'd been warmed to her toes.

Like the heat rekindling in her veins now.

It would be so easy to lean into him, to recapture that magical connection. What a mixed blessing these feelings were. What she felt with him surpassed anything she'd experienced before, but that meant all other men paled in comparison. She ached from wanting something so wrong for her. They still had so much left unsettled. He still didn't trust her.

But an answering blaze flared in his eyes.

The patter of the rain closed out everything but the sound of their breathing, the brush of his thigh along hers as he shifted. Carlos dipped his head silently, close but not near enough to make contact. Clearly he was letting her know he wanted to kiss her every bit as much as she wanted him, but was leaving the next move up to her. Her thudding heartbeat echoed in her ears as the moment ticked out.

Did she dare say to hell with it all? Make the most of this time together before the baby complicated matters further? Indulge herself in the unsurpassed pleasures she'd found with Carlos?

The spacious limousine became full of possibilities. She could straddle his lap and take control with ease, thanks to the dress she wore. Or she could lean back and invite him to stretch his muscular length over her. The tingling need skipping through her veins gathered between her legs until she pressed her knees together against the sweet ache.

The limo slowed, turning off the highway and signaling the nearing end of their drive. A flush burned up her face as she realized how close she'd come to throwing herself at Carlos. She inched toward her door, tugging the hem of her sapphire cashmere dress securely over her knees until it touched the tops of her black leather boots.

Carlos angled away and back to his side, supple leather seat crackling softly under the give and shift of bodies. Just as it would have sounded had she acted on her desire to have him here and now. Every sound, each nuance, felt so intimate in light of the time they would be spending together.

The luxury vehicle rocked gently as the car slid to a stop. They'd arrived at the airport, and while they would leave the confines of the car soon, they were simply exchanging the solitude of the limo for the seclusion of a private jet.

Before she could stem her fluttering nerves, the driver opened the passenger door, holding an umbrella over her head to protect her from the light drizzle. She swung her feet out, her eyes sweeping the small, private airport, a simple one-story red brick building with four hangars and a lone runway. A Learjet swooshed upward into the murky sky.

A pair of businessmen with matching black umbrellas rushed toward the covered walkway. A family of four huddled underneath the shelter as an SUV rumbled toward them. Lilah couldn't tear her eyes from the frazzled family tableau. While the father snagged his son from stomping galoshes through a puddle, the mother scooped up a toddler in a yellow duck raincoat that swallowed the child so fully it was impossible to determine gender.

Her hand gravitated to her stomach and she swallowed back a betraying sigh. But it was difficult to stem the flood of hopeful images, especially when Carlos had already made a first step toward opening up.

Warily hopeful, she shifted her attention to the tiny terminal where they would officially launch their journey. A woman stood by the door with a tomato-red umbrella. Actually an umbrella with a tomato stem on top, with a familiar female waiting and waving underneath the bright shelter.

Lilah stumbled on the curb.

It couldn't be….

But a closer look confirmed her suspicion. None other than Nancy Wolcott, Carlos's supposedly "ex" girlfriend, waited at the airport entrance.

Holy hell.

Wincing, Carlos scrubbed his bristly jaw. What was Nancy Wolcott doing here at the private airport?

And clearly waving at them.

Her presence didn't make sense. He had made himself clear, in a polite fashion. They were both adults. She'd seemed to understand. Yes, she'd seemed disappointed and expressed regret, but not overly so.

He took the offered umbrella from the chauffer and slid under alongside Lilah. Her gasp let him know she'd seen the woman too and was none too happy. The timing couldn't have been worse. All the progress he'd made on the ride over was blasted to bits now. His body was still strung taut with desire and images of how easy it would have been to lean Lilah back on the leather seats....

He cut the thought short and focused on the mess at hand. Planting a hand on the small of Lilah's back, he steered her with him, toward the airport entrance. Toward the waiting train wreck.

"Yoo-hoo," Nancy called, her waving intensifying, raindrops sliding from the umbrella faster in her animation. "Over here!"

He shot a quick assessing glance at Lilah and found her lips thin and tight with irritation, her boots clicking in a snappy fast pace he recognized as angry. He'd heard the same stomping rhythm before as she left a particularly frustrating board meeting. Now was not the time to ponder the reason he knew her well enough to read the mood of her footsteps.

Stopping beside Nancy, Carlos reined in his own frustration over the woman's surprise arrival.

Nancy's smile widened. "What perfect timing. I'm so glad I caught you before you left, Carlos."

Lilah stayed silent, but Carlos had different plans. There were important details to learn before he sent Nancy on her way. "How did you know to come here? And what time?"

"It's not a state secret, is it? I just wanted to tell you goodbye." She stared at Lilah curiously, closing her umbrella slowly and shaking it dry. "I didn't realize the two of you would be traveling together. You didn't tell me that yesterday, Carlos."

Blown away by the way she'd shown up here when he'd made it clear yesterday they both needed to go their separate ways, he wondered how he could have misread Nancy. Not that he'd really known her well when he asked her out.

What had made him gravitate to Nancy so soon after his time with Lilah? On the surface, the women were total opposites in many ways. Which made him wonder if perhaps he'd chosen Nancy for just that reason.

Had that one night he'd shared with Lilah sent him running scared? That possibility rocked his world in a way it would take some serious time to process.

Carlos stepped aside for the pair of businessmen passing. "Nancy, quite frankly, I prefer to keep details of my travels low-key and private."

"Of course." The woman nodded quickly, clutching her shiny red umbrella closer. "I only want to speak to you alone for a few minutes, you know, about what we discussed at the hospital before you left." She glanced at Lilah pointedly.

Before Carlos could insist she stay, Lilah hitched her purse higher on her shoulder and said, "I need to make some work calls. If you'll excuse me."

"No. Don't go." He clasped Lilah's arm while keeping the other, unpredictable woman clearly in his sights. Who knew what she might do next? "Nancy, I'm sorry, but let's not make this awkward for anyone. There's nothing more to say. I believe I covered everything yesterday."

He kept his voice firm and no-nonsense while

working not to be outright cruel. But she needed to understand there could be nothing more.

Nancy's face froze, her grin turning brittle. "You're right. I apologize for wanting to send you off on a nicer note." Her icy smile included Lilah now. "Have a safe business trip."

Tomato umbrella swooping up and sending a fresh shower of water outward, Nancy raced out into the parking lot toward her hatchback. Regret bit at him that he hadn't handled things better with her the day before. He hadn't meant to be a coldhearted bastard, but…damn. Maybe he should have thought of that before they'd dated.

Annoyed with himself and with Nancy, Carlos watched to make sure she got into her car and left. Once her car cleared the parking lot, he turned to Lilah again.

Frowning, she swept water from her wool coat and the hem of her cashmere dress. "Have many more groupies waiting to waylay us before we board?"

Instinctively, he reached for his phone. "I'm more concerned with how she found out we're here and how much more she knows about our travel plans."

A call to his family's security team was in order. As much as he wanted to launch his quest to seduce Lilah, nothing could take precedence over her safety. Once they were secured on the plane, he would turn his attention to discovering how Nancy Wolcott unearthed his travel itinerary and just how much she knew.

Jet engines humming softly, Lilah unbuckled from her seat for a better view out the window at the night sky. Anything to distract her from what she really wanted to study. Carlos, reclined and sleeping an arm stretch away, kept stealing her attention.

Before they'd even left the ground, he'd been working his phone assigning some security team—apparently he kept one on retainer?—to figure out how Nancy had tracked them to the airport. A security team, for crying out loud. Once his "people" had been given their marching orders, Carlos had fallen asleep in a blink, a skill he'd picked up catching catnaps during long shifts at the hospital.

How could he look so familiar but seem so different out of their medical realm? She wasn't a millionaire, but she was financially secure in her own right. She'd also grown up with her fair share of glitz due to her father's connections to the Hollywood scene—although he'd been known to live beyond his means, which led to a feast-and-famine lifestyle for his family.

Still, even her own experience of brushing elbows with the rich and famous hadn't come close to the scope of influence she was only just beginning to see Carlos wielded. While she couldn't deny Carlos attracted her physically, she refused to be swayed by the wealth of his world of secretive itineraries, plush limousines and private jets. And a very determined female radiologist whose behavior bordered on stalking.

Lilah gripped the leather armrests tighter. Seeing Nancy Wolcott waiting and waving had provided a hefty reminder for how little she knew about Carlos. And how important it was to gauge her moves carefully.

She looked away from the starkly handsome man snoozing across from her and turned her attention to the sleeping world of tiny lights below. If only things were as straightforward as they'd once been with Carlos, just a few shorts months ago before that fateful Christmas fundraiser. Back during a time when she'd been able to rein in her wayward attraction to the brooding surgeon who haunted her dreams.

Carlos didn't believe dreams came only in black-and-white. His always felt far more vivid than that as the real world mixed with the slumber sphere. Perhaps because he'd slept lightly for as long as he could remember.

As a child, he'd been taught to stay on guard against threats to him as heir to the throne. Then he'd been denied REM sleep by the claws of pain recovering from the shooting. And, finally, he'd needed to stay on alert for his patients.

Right now, his dream mixed with the recycled plane oxygen blending the scent of Lilah with some kind of pine air freshener...taking him back to that night at the hospital fundraiser nearly three months ago....

Lighted pine trees decorating the sprawling hospital conference room, Carlos stirred his sparkling water, refusing anything stronger until the fundraiser finished. And then, just call him Scrooge, because all bets were off.

Christmas meant celebrations and special family moments to most people. Carlos preferred a bottle of memory-numbing bourbon to get through the holidays.

But first, he had to fulfill work obligations.

He tugged at his tux tie absently. He hated the damn thing, but his presence was required at the formal event. Wealthy contributors liked to rub elbows with the doctors who used their money to save lives.

Apparently he was the celebrity of the hour since news of his Medina heritage had broken. He would give over his entire inheritance if it would get him out of this diamond-studded circus. Even his family's fortune wouldn't be enough for him to bid farewell to fundraiser dog and pony shows.

His back hurt like hell after a relentless day of surgery after surgery. Seeing Lilah offered the first distraction in an otherwise crappy day. Her auburn hair was swept up in a bundle of loose curls rather than her regular tight twist. During office hours she wore button-up power suits, linen and layers that left him imagining peeling each piece off. Now, however, there was much more of her creamy skin on display. Not in an overt way, but enough that his fingers curled in his pockets from restraint.

The gold silk gown wrapped around her curves, giving her a Grecian goddess appeal. Beaded details glinted from the chandelier's light. The luminescent glow of her bared shoulders, however, outshone everything else.

She smiled at him, leaned toward the person she'd been speaking to—excusing herself?—and walked toward him. Silky fabric swirled around her legs with each graceful glide.

For four years he'd resisted the attraction. Persistent. Ever present. Increasingly painful appeal.

Tonight, with memories of that final, ill-fated Christmas in San Rinaldo pounding in his head like the unrelenting bullets that had killed his mother, his ears ringing, ringing, ringing, he didn't have the willpower to resist....

Five

The airplane phone rang and rang and rang, jarring Lilah from her dazed stare out the window at the distant mountain peaks below. She started to walk across to answer the phone before the jangling disturbed Carlos's catnap, but he bolted upright in the reclined lounger and snagged the receiver.

"Speak," he barked into the phone in his normal gruff fashion.

Some parts of his blunt personality were still all too familiar.

He scrubbed a hand over his eyes, his groggy look clearing in a flash as he transformed back to the alert surgeon, the intense man she knew from work. He returned his seat to the upright position. After a few clipped responses of "good," "excellent" and "keep me posted" rumbling from him, he disconnected the call.

Unbuckling, he stood with an almost disguised wince and started toward her. "Apparently Nancy figured out my plans to fly out from a note Wanda had jotted on her desk. If that's the case, then Nancy knows nothing more about our travel plans than the airport location."

Lilah thumbed the brass casing around the window, polishing a nonexistent smudge. "It's a relief to know we don't have to worry about Nancy waiting for us when we land in Vail."

"We can move on to the vacation part of our plans with a clear mind." He glanced at his watch. "Sorry to have napped so long. You must be hungry. Our steward can bring a light snack or supper even. Whatever you wish, I'll make it happen."

"How about a double bacon cheeseburger with a mint chocolate chip milkshake?" she asked, only half joking. She was learning just how tenacious pregnancy cravings can be.

He reached for the call button. "I'll see what he can put together."

Resting her hand on his wrist, she stopped him. "I was kidding. Really, I'm not hungry yet. I just need to stretch my legs. The seats are fabulous—" as was everything on this top-of-the-line private craft "—but my back hurts if I sit too long."

His brow furrowed as he studied her. Muscular shoulders encased in warm black wool called to her fingers until everything else faded. Her mouth went dry. Carlos's gaze fell to her mouth and she couldn't stop her tongue from teasing along her lips. His nostrils flared with awareness.

She and he had a sensual connection, without question. But there was no emotional connection of any substance. Right? As long as she remembered that, she should be able to protect her heart.

His hand settled at the base of her spine, as if already testing her resolve. She started to inch away, but he pressed ever so slightly, ever so perfectly, against the spot that ached. Again, she reminded herself the physical was different from the emotions. Why should she deny herself the comfort—the undiluted pleasure—of his touch?

His fingers circled with deepening pressure and she sighed. A hint of a moan hitched a ride on the gusty breath making its way up her throat.

While massaging in increasingly larger circles, he reached past her to slide open the shade further to improve the view of the clusters of city lights below. "How much does your back hurt?"

"Just a little...right there."

His intuitive touch gave her pause as she realized just how he knew what to do. He lived in constant pain without a complaint.

Straightening, she inched aside. "It's nothing I can't handle."

He followed, his hands never leaving her body. "There's no need for you to handle it all. I'm trying to be nice, so stop arguing. Doctor's orders."

"Okay, then." She began to offer to rub his back in return and then almost gasped.

An urge to laugh followed, chased by a bittersweet sense of how special this would have been had it happened the morning after they'd been together. Or if he'd apologized nicely yesterday for being a jerk these past months, providing a perfectly logical explanation for his behavior.

But she wasn't whimsical. She was practical. Therefore she would enjoy this blasted backrub to the fullest. It was about the physical, nothing to do with her emotions.

Talking, however, would help keep her grounded more in reality and less in the sensual play of his fingers working tension from knotted muscles. "We haven't gotten to talk since boarding. Is the plane yours?"

"My family owns controlling interest in a small charter company," he answered softly from behind her, his subtle accent curling around each word and into her. "It's an investment that also enables us to fly wherever we wish with minimal discussion of our plans."

"No one knows your itinerary."

"That's the idea. I've been able to lead a relatively normal life at the hospital since my identity became public. You run a tight ship and I appreciate that. But out in the real world, I need to be careful."

Which explained why he was especially concerned to find Nancy waiting for them. Her shoulders rose with tension. He skimmed upward to cup them, rubbing until they lowered again. Relaxation radiated through her as he became some kind of medical magician.

"That's better. Just let go," he said, his mouth closer to her ear this time.

Unable to resist, she soaked in the heat of his breath against her neck, inhaled the peppermint scent of his toothpaste. What would it be like if he were telling her to "just let go" while they were doing other, more intimately pleasurable things?

She dragged her attention off his command in her ear and scrambled for something coherent to say.

"You've got a family-owned air taxi service for the rich and famous." She traced the teakwood encircling the portal, brass edging gleaming. She'd ridden with her father in similar crafts as a kid. Of course, thinking about her dad was worse than thinking of Nancy.

"Actually," Carlos's thumbs pressed between her shoulder blades with intuitive precision that sent waves of pleasure radiating outward, "Enrique—my father—diversified the company a few years ago so that when the planes are not in use for the needs of our family and our associates, they are used on call for search-and-rescue emergencies."

"Your father sounds like quite a philanthropist." Different from what she'd expected from a recluse monarch. "He sounds like you."

His hands stilled for the first time. "You're the first to say that."

"How would you describe your father?" She glanced back at him, catching a hint of tensed jaw before his face became a smooth, handsome mask again.

Carlos stared past her, through the portal, his massage resuming. "He's ill."

Not at all what she expected him to say. She tried to turn toward him but his touch became steely for the first time as he held her in place without hurting her, but unmistakably insistent.

Accepting his wishes to keep his face hidden from her, she gripped the window as clouds obscured the specks of light below. "I'm very sorry to hear that. What's wrong with him?"

"His liver is failing," he answered, his voice emotionless other than a thickening of his accent. "During the escape from San Rinaldo, he spent a lot of time on the run in poor living conditions."

She'd read the basics about the coup in San Rinaldo, but there weren't many details available. Hearing the event from Carlos, envisioning the terror the Medinas—Carlos—must have experienced, made her chest go tight with pain for them.

"How awful that must have been for your family. I can't even begin to imagine."

"It was not an easy time in our lives," he understated simply. He stroked her shoulders, down her arms, never missing a beat even when his breathing became heavier against her hair. "We were not with him. My mother, my brothers and I went a different escape route once the rebels attacked. My father didn't want to risk us being captured with him so he attempted to make them follow him instead."

The picture unfolding in her mind was beyond imagining, but he seemed unwilling to take any comfort from her. Hell, he wouldn't even let her look at him.

"How old were you?"

"Thirteen," he answered starkly.

He traced up her arms again and stopped at the back of her dress. He slid a finger inside along her neck, just under the zipper, stroking one vertebra at a time. His sensuous touch was at such odds with their stark discussion, but then Carlos had always been a huge contradiction. The compassionate surgeon, gruff professional.

Tender lover, reserved friend.

And he clearly wanted to keep things on a physical level rather than emotional. How perfect since she'd thought the same thing herself not too long ago. Her head lolled forward and his hand tucked under the cashmere, fanning along either side of her spine, kneading nerve endings.

The zipper parted, only an inch, but still she gasped at the boldness of his move. Cool air brushed the tiny patch of bared flesh a second before his knuckles warmed her skin.

"Shhh," he coaxed. "I'm not doing anything other than rubbing your back to make the trip more comfortable."

She laughed softly. "Do you think I'm foolish?"

"Let me rephrase," he said against her ear. "I will not do anything more unless you ask."

Her heart stuttered at the image that conjured and the sensual power that gave her. What would it be like to claim the toe-curling bliss he could give her so easily? So dispassionately?

She forced her thoughts to disengage from the path, dismayed to think he could pull away from her as smoothly as he could set her whole body to flame. No amount of temptation could lure her into that dangerous terrain. She wouldn't be his next Nancy Wolcott, sprinting to the shelter of her little hatchback car in the rain while Carlos watched with his cool, unmoved gaze.

"Well, take note then, Carlos, because I won't ask for more from you." She was only willing to let the physical side go so far. For now? Until when?

"That sounds like a challenge."

She turned slightly, meeting his eyes, their mouths so close every word was almost a kiss. "Do you really promise not to do anything more?"

With the full power of his intense dark gaze staring

at her with frank honesty and desire, there was no mistaking what he wanted. He wasn't thinking of any woman but her.

"You have my word. Tell me to stop and I will, without hesitation." His low, husky vow vibrated the air between them.

"Then by all means," she said, her voice breathier than she would have liked to admit, "continue what you were doing."

She could handle this.

Carefully, she turned her back to him again, her breasts prickling with awareness as she wondered how far this game between them would go. His hands spread and the zipper parted further link by link. The top of her dress stayed on even as cool recycled air swooshed over her back. He worked his way south to her waist, thumbs circling along small but persistent knots of tension and strain.

Down, down farther still, he went until massaging almost at the base of her spine, his skillful fingers teasing along the top of her bikini panties. His hands spanned all the way across her lower back, then wrapped forward to rub lightly against her hip bones.

Her dress eased precariously forward, until she crossed her arms to hold it in place. Yet she couldn't bring herself to tell him to stop. The pressure of his hands so intimately close to where she really wanted, *needed*, him to touch her only served to stoke the ache hotter.

They played with fire here and she knew it. Yet she trusted him when he said he wouldn't take this further without her permission. So she surrendered to the sensations washing over her.

The man had the art of touch mastered. The glide of his hands on her back soothed and stirred at the same time, the healer and the infuriating prince.

Oh God, it had been so long since she'd had a man's touch on her, his touch. Her body soaked up the gentle rasp of his callused fingers, his every move so precise as he explored her, relaxed her, totally in tune as to exactly where she needed his care.

According to the pregnancy books she'd read, the backaches would only grow worse, as if in some cosmic prelude to labor. Nerves pattered in her chest as her mind fast-forwarded, anxiety intensifying at the notion of facing that day alone.

"Shhh," Carlos whispered in her ear. His hands skimmed around to her rib cage and pulled her back against him. "Whatever you're thinking about. Don't. You're tensing up again. As much as I'm enjoying having my hands on you, I hate to think my efforts here have been for nothing."

His hands rested right below her breasts, so close her nipples peaked against her bra, tight and needy. As he stepped closer, his body against her back, the rigid length of him pressed to her spine with unmistakable arousal. She longed to writhe against him and tempt him higher, harder. How she burned to lift his palms to cover her breasts, to ease the ache with the warm pressure of him.

It was just physical, she reminded herself. Heaven knew she wasn't too happy with the man himself right now. But her willpower was beginning to wane.

She cuffed her fingers around his wrists and shifted his touch an inch lower. "I think it's time to call a halt to this."

Just that fast, his hands slid away. Not a word, not even a hint of a protest from him. However, her body shouted loud and clear over the loss of his touch. Her skin tightened, tingly and hot with awareness. Dragging in breaths that did nothing to steady her racing heart, she held her dress in place and faced him.

His features were taut, his eyes as molten as his dark cable sweater.

"We both—" Her voice shook and she steadied the betraying tremble before continuing, "We both know I'm attracted to you, and it's a safe bet to say you're attracted to me as well. I also know I can want you while not liking you very much. However, I'm not so sure that jumping each other is the wisest move—"

"Whoa, hold on there." He held up his hands while keeping them well off her. "I have no intention of seducing you."

"Oh." The guy sure knew how to take the wind out of a girl's sails. "Then what the hell was that erotic massage all about?"

He lowered his hands, still not so much as brushing her, while outlining her shape, her breasts, waist, hips, around and stopping an inch away from curving her bottom. "To put you at ease and reassure you of my self-control. You can enjoy what I'm about to do because you don't have to keep up your guard."

His confidence was unmistakable, the luxury cabin echoing with the regal sense of surety in his every word. Even in casual jeans and a sweater, this man was royal born, destined to lead, and right now she very much wanted to follow wherever he led.

A simple sway would bring her flush against him.

Breathe, she reminded herself. *Breathe.* "And what exactly are you about to do?"

He grinned ever so slightly at her words, his predatory look lifting the hairs on her arms.

"I'm going to kiss you."

<u>Six</u>

The luscious feel of Lilah still tattooed in his memory, burned in his brain, seared in his soul, Carlos lowered his mouth to hers. No subtle skim of lips over lips. He simply took her.

He'd warned her, giving her a chance to pull away. Still she had not uttered a syllable of protest, no request to stop. Perhaps that pushed the boundary of his promise to her, but he needed her to know how much he wanted her. It would hurt like hell to pull away, but he would honor his word.

He angled his mouth over hers more firmly, exploring, plundering, and wondered how she felt so familiar after only a few kisses. He would have recognized her taste, her scent, her fingers gliding along his jaw. Her touch was so exact, she could have been a surgeon herself, thoroughly dissecting his restraint and leaving him bare to the powerful draw of pure, undiluted Lilah.

She peeled away layers of his reserve as fully as she inched up his sweater and T-shirt to explore his chest with her cool, soft hands.

As smoothly as he'd eased the zipper down her dress earlier.

Sliding inside her open dress, he palmed her bottom. With only her silky panties between his fingers and her flesh, he fit her against him, his arousal. He'd told her they would use this time to find level ground but the floor beneath his feet felt more unsteady than ever.

She gripped fists full of his sweater, anchoring herself to him. So fast, so perfectly, she seduced him right back with a simple stroke of her hands, her tongue, her body brushing against his.

Already rock hard from wanting her, still he throbbed harder. Nobody turned him inside out the way Lilah did, until he forgot about the ever-present pain in his back, the persistent ghosts of his past. In her arms, he could even let go of his driving need to erase loss and agony from the endless stream of children who needed him, children who he too often failed....

And for all those reasons, he needed to keep himself carefully guarded around this woman. The one woman who could make him lose sight of his only path to redemption for his own failure.

Drawing in a shuddering breath that did little to sweep away the sense of Lilah invading every niche inside him, Carlos pulled away. Full of regret, he withdrew his hands and slipped her zipper up inch by inch until he cupped the back of her neck. He took in her passion-dazed emerald eyes, her kissed moist mouth, all signs of his effect on her.

She flattened her hands to his chest, her fingers plucking at his T-shirt peeking from the V-neck of his sweater. "I thought you weren't going to seduce me."

"You were seduced by just a kiss?" He took small comfort in that much.

"Don't be a jerk." Her smile went wobbly. "You know what you did."

"I also know what else I would like to do to you, but I promised not to take things further unless you asked." He tipped his ear toward the whine of jet engines. "Besides, I believe we are beginning our descent."

As if on cue, the intercom crackled a second ahead of the captain's voice. "This is your captain. Please return to your seats and buckle in for landing in Eagle-Vail, Colorado. On behalf of myself and my copilot, I hope you've had a pleasant flight."

They had arrived. And shortly, he would have Lilah all to himself in a house with eight empty bedrooms. He couldn't decide if he was a genius or a moron.

If there was even a remote chance that Lilah proved to be the mother of his child, they needed the chance to get to know each other better outside of the workplace. So this trip made sense. And the heat blasting over him even now from that kiss reminded him how good it could be between them.

But—baby or no baby—he needed to find a way to clear Lilah from his system before the need for her leveled all his defenses.

Permanently.

* * *

A few days alone in Vail, Colorado, with Carlos suddenly felt like an eternity.

As their SUV climbed the icy driveway winding up a hill, Lilah studied the house ahead of them and crossed her fingers for a large staff. Not because she wanted or expected to be waited on, rather she hoped for some human buffers between herself and the increasing need to jump the man beside her. She searched the looming structure for signs of life as Carlos spoke softly beside her, detailing enticing factoids about the area.

Of course he could make a hut in the woods sound amazing with that luscious accent.

The house, she reminded herself. *Check out the house.*

Three stories tall at the center, the cedar home sported varying heights and levels on either side in a sort of art deco Swiss Alps style that instantly charmed her. Built with logs that could only have come from the fattest, most ancient trees, the size of the structure seemed about right for the mammoth mountain it was perched on. Generous windows shone a welcoming yellow glow into the night, a positive sign there might be people inside.

Carlos guided the four-wheel drive past towering pines, branches still wearing heavy snowcaps. She hugged her coat tighter around her, which only served to remind her how much warmer his arms had been earlier in the airplane. Since the pilot had announced their approach, Carlos had shifted from seductive lover to considerate tour guide.

Finishing his spiel about amenities in Vail, he pulled the SUV into the six-car garage that appeared to be nearly two thousand square feet on its own. She'd grown up with affluence around her, but even she was taken aback a bit by the scope of vehicles surrounding her, everything from a Lamborghini to a Mercedes sedan to top-of-the-line snowmobiles.

Carlos might live a Spartan lifestyle in Tacoma, but apparently his family spared no expense when it came to their "toys."

Before she could unbuckle her seat belt, he'd come around to open her door, his shoulders broad in a black sweater and open ski jacket. His limp was more pronounced, reminding her what a long day this had to have been for him as well, yet he didn't complain. She'd noticed a cane in his office once, although she'd never seen him use it. He was a prideful man, no doubt. Offering him her arm would be out of the question.

What would it be like to have the freedom to slide her arm around his waist, intimately touching and helping without bruising his pride? No matter how well this time together went for them, she would never know that kind of closeness with Carlos. That stung her more than she could have foreseen a few short months ago.

Lilah followed him through the garage and into a narrow hall, pausing each time he stopped to disarm yet another security system, like peeling away layers of an onion. A very protected, paranoid onion. Hanging up her coat alongside his on a cast-iron coat tree, she eyed the massive floor-to-ceiling windows with new perception, suddenly certain the glass was bulletproof.

Trees had been thinned away from the house, giving a clear view of the empty snow-covered ground and walkways laid out with the precision of an English garden. Or a well-thought-out security plan…

Now *she* was becoming paranoid.

Focus on the perks of being here. Both indoor and outdoor pools loomed large, each with a breathtaking view of a distant snowcapped mountain range apparent even in the dark thanks to the last bit of twilight flaring along the peaks. She still hadn't seen any staff in the quiet house, only the sound of her footsteps and Carlos's on thick Aubusson rugs cutting the silence.

Walls were dotted with oil paintings of mountains, keeping with the chalet appeal. She had to admit it. He'd picked the perfect retreat.

"The Pyrenees," he filled in simply, referring to the range between Spain and France depicted in the paintings. "My family used to ski there."

Before the coup that destroyed San Rinaldo.

Before his birthright to be king had been stolen.

Before he lost his home, his mother.

She trailed her fingers along a carved mahogany frame. How many other hints of European heritage did he incorporate into his life that she must have missed over the years? How bittersweet those reminders must be of a home that had been ripped from him just as he stood on the brink of manhood.

He swept open the next door to an enormous gourmet kitchen, top-of-the-line appliances with stone and stainless steel decor. Dark green granite glowed under the heavy black iron pendant lamps illuminating the breakfast bar. A temperature-controlled wine refrigerator took up the entire base of a massive island, the exotic labels of the expensive vintages apparent through the lit glass doors.

Carlos leaned against the breakfast bar, feet crossed at the ankles. "The staff has been sent on vacation, but they left everything we should need to eat and a cleaning service will come in when needed."

Well, that answered the question about chaperones and buffers. She needed to put on her big girl hat and decide on her own whether or not she would sleep alone tonight. Or in his bed.

A whisper of longing huffed over her skin, and she loosened her hold on the coat she'd been clutching so tightly. Suddenly, she felt plenty warm. "I can wash my own dishes, thank you."

He pulled open the industrial-size refrigerator, dark blue denim hugging his hips. "Then what do you say to some food before we settle in for the night?"

Fifteen minutes later, she was curled up in the corner of an overstuffed sofa with Carlos sprawled on the couch across from her in the main living room. A roaring blaze crackled in the fireplace, warming her bare toes; her boots were resting beside the sofa. The polished stone hearth stretched up to the vaulted ceiling, the same as the stone fire pit outdoors on the sprawling rustic veranda that overlooked the mountain view. The whole place smelled like pine and cedar, right down to the fragrant wood crackling in the fireplace.

Still edgy from the kiss on the plane and woefully in need of something to ease the tension crackling through her veins, she cupped her mug of warmed cider, a plate of assorted finger foods on the end table beside her. Carlos devoured a larger, more substantial sandwich on pumpernickel. Not that he seemed to even notice how someone had gone to a lot of trouble to make even deli food look like a masterful creation, all the way down to the lettuce curling artfully around the edges.

He ate as he always did, efficiently, regarding the

food as nothing more than fuel for his body. The meal was nothing more than a necessary regimen, much like how he must wash his hands before surgery. She couldn't help but admire him in this moment. He had all of this wealth and privilege at his fingertips, yet he chose to live out his life serving others. There was an unmistakable honor in that.

Although she'd also seen in her job how easy it was for the driven humanitarians to burn themselves out. Perhaps he needed this time away for reasons he hadn't even begun to recognize.

Lilah sipped her cider, the stoneware warming her hands. "This place is...beyond words."

And it was exactly what she needed after the way work had overwhelmed her these last few months. The stress of finding out about the baby and not being able to share it with Carlos had taken its toll in ways she was only starting to appreciate. Right now, she couldn't help but feel grateful for this time out from real life to sort out her future. Somehow the secluded mountain mansion felt warm and welcoming. A safe haven in a crazy time.

At least she hoped it was the house making her feel that way and not the magnetism of the man.

Wiping his mouth with a linen napkin, he finished chewing. "Once my father accepted that his sons were not going to live their adult lives in hiding with him on his island, he tried to make sure our other properties were set up to have everything at our fingertips." Mug in hand, he gestured round the room with a semicircle sweep. "Less reason to step out into everyday society."

She shivered to think of all the worries a parent carried around in a normal world—to shoulder all the fears for his sons' safety that Enrique Medina faced seemed overwhelming.

Her hand slid protectively over her stomach. "He had reason to be fearful for your safety."

"Understood. But a life in hiding is no life at all." He polished off the last corner of his sandwich.

"Even if that life is spent in pampered luxury," she said, trying to inject a tone of levity into a suddenly too dark conversation.

"Especially so." He tossed his napkin on his empty stoneware plate and swung his legs up onto the sofa, almost managing to disguise his wince of discomfort. "All that said, however, this does make for one helluva vacation. It's even equipped with a golf room with a full swing simulator. Although we'll have to bypass the wine cellar this time since you're expecting."

This time? There would be more visits here?

Of course, once he realized this was his child there would be so many reasons for their paths to intersect. Whether or not he appreciated it yet, she knew her life was unequivocally intertwined with his forever. So many new concerns had come her way of late, it seemed impossible to absorb them all before another came rocketing through her brain. She struggled to follow his words.

He scratched the back of his neck, stretching the sweater taut across his broad shoulders. "The personal sauna is probably a no go too. I seem to recall from med school that pregnant women should use caution when it comes to saunas and hot tubs."

Heat flooded her face as she thought of their encounter in the hot tub at his place, the night they'd made the baby. His home had been starkly utilitarian except for the mammoth jetted bath, large enough for two. Intellectually, she knew he likely had the luxury installed for practical purposes because of his back, but they'd most certainly put the spa bathroom to totally impractical, indulgent good use that night.

The air between them snapped with awareness as she saw in his heavy-lidded eyes that he was remembering that night as well. And it affected him. Not surprising given their out-of-control kiss earlier on the plane.

But since that evening at the party when he'd really touched her for the first time, she hadn't been able to think of much else except the feel of his hands on her skin….

From the hospital rooftop garden, Lilah stared out at the Christmas lights twinkling through Tacoma's skyline. So intent on taking a breather from the overloud band and press of patrons at the party inside, she almost missed the sound of footsteps approaching behind her.

She stiffened in alarm, then heard the uneven gait she recognized well after four years of working with Carlos. And quite honestly, she could use the distraction of his company tonight after the disturbing call with her mother, in tears over finding the receipt for a nightie— red and not her size. Lilah gripped the icy rail tighter.

A second later, Carlos's hand skimmed her bare arms as he eased a velvet wrap around her shoulders. "Wouldn't want you to catch a cold out here."

"Thank you." She hugged her wrap closer as snow sprinkled from the sky. "You were especially nice to the board of directors tonight. I'm not going to grouse if you want to cut out early."

He stuffed his hands in his tuxedo pockets, dark eyes reflecting the string of tiny white lights strung around a potted evergreen. "Are you insinuating I've been less than polite in the past?"

"I know these sorts of gatherings aren't your thing." *She scrunched her icy toes inside her pumps.* "You usually have that vaguely tolerant look that lets us all know you've got one eye on your watch so you can get back to work."

"It's impossible to look at any watch when there's someone as beautiful as you to admire instead."

Her jaw dropped then snapped shut quickly. They'd been work friends for a long time, always careful never to cross that line. She'd accepted her attraction to him but never guessed he'd noticed her. "Uh, thank you?"

Her heart fluttered in a way that was totally out of character for her. She was usually so controlled.

"Obviously, I'm much better at hiding my emotions than you give me credit for if you've never noticed how you affect me."

A suspicion tugged at her mind. "Have you been drinking?"

"Not a drop." *He crossed his heart with two fingers like the Boy Scout she couldn't picture him being.*

"Me neither." *Her breathy answer puffed into the cool night air.*

"Actually, I've had a helluva day and something in your face tells me you have, too. The kind of day no alcohol can fix." *He zeroed in with a perception that had her eyes stinging.*

Thank goodness the rest of the partiers were still inside and out of sight. How he'd found her here, she didn't know. Maybe he needed the peace as much as she did.

She blinked hard and tried to tell herself it was just the biting wind making her tear up. Emotions aswirl like the spiraling snow, she boldly tugged both sides of his tuxedo tie. "You look quite stunning yourself, Dr. Medina."

His fingers banded around her wrists, hot and strong and so very enticing. Like him. "Then since we're both clearheaded, lovely Lilah," he whispered, nipping her ear once, lighting a static spark in her veins, "there's no reason not to do this."

Was that moan from her?

Deliberately, slowly, his lips grazed her cheek in a slow trek that had her gripping the rail to keep her legs from folding.

"And do this." His arms swept around her as he captured her next sigh with his mouth....

"Lilah?"

Carlos's voice startled her from her daze, back to the present in his Vail, Colorado, mountain retreat. The memory of his kiss then was as real and stirring as the one he'd given her earlier. She reached for her mug of cider, needing to ground herself in the moment. "I'm sorry. What did you say?"

She eyed him over the top of her mug, inhaling steaming scents of cinnamon as a log shifted in the fireplace, launching a shower of sparks. Those pinpricks of light didn't come close to the kind of sparks Carlos could set off inside her.

He set aside his mug on the coffee table. "Why have you never married?"

His abrupt shift to the personal stunned her into silence for two pops of the logs in the fireplace. How in the world had their conversation shifted to that topic while she'd been daydreaming? Not that she intended to offer up what she'd really been thinking about.

"Why haven't you?" she retorted carefully. "You're older than I am."

"Touché." He saluted her lightly. "I apologize for the sexist sound to my question. To show my contrition, I'll answer first. I decided a long time ago to stay a bachelor."

"Because...?" she asked, suddenly curious to the roots of her hair.

"Standard eternal bachelor reasons," he answered with a wry grin. "I'm a workaholic. I didn't want to subject any woman to the Medina madness."

The last reason was far from standard. "There have been women lining up outside your office ready to volunteer for that mayhem. In fact, Nancy seems ready to hustle to the front of the queue."

His smile flattened to a humorless scowl. "I haven't asked for or encouraged any of them."

"Yet still they flock to your side." The second the words left her mouth, she winced at sounding jealous. But she was carrying the man's child after all. Any of those women would be a part of her child's life through him.

Great. Now she was jealous *and* concerned.

Carlos massaged his knee absently. "They're flocking to the title and the money that comes with it. They wouldn't care if I was a troll with an extra eye in the middle of my forehead."

Laughter burst free and she clapped her hand over her mouth.

He cocked an eyebrow. "I wasn't joking."

"I know, but still, the image you painted…" She couldn't stop laughing. She knew the giggles had more to do with releasing tension than anything else. Her body was wound so tight from the events of the past two days she needed the outlet, a release for her swelling emotions.

And her emotions weren't the only thing that would be swelling soon. Her hand slid to her stomach.

Just the thought of that jolted a fresh burst of laughter until she clapped a hand over her mouth again. Carlos stared at her as if she was half-crazy, and maybe right now… Who knew? She hiccupped and a tear fell free. Then another. More. Until she couldn't stop the flood of an altogether different emotion as a sob tore its way through her heart and up her throat.

Seven

Carlos had seen patients cry more times than he cared to remember. Although he didn't like to think he'd become jaded, he couldn't afford to let tears sway him or he wouldn't be able to treat his patients.

But seeing Lilah so upset sliced through what little restraint he had left.

Unable to keep his distance, he swung his feet from the sofa and knelt beside her before she finished scrubbing her wrist across her cheeks. Only once had he known Lilah to lose it, about three years after he'd begun working for the Tacoma facility. She had gone to the mat with the insurance company for a patient of his, a child whose spine had been fractured in an amusement park ride accident—at the C7 vertebrae. The parents were supposed to be grateful their child could use his thumb to work the electric wheelchair.

Lilah had crushed opponents standing in the way of getting that boy everything he needed.

Late on the night of the boy's surgery, Carlos had been making rounds and found Lilah sitting by the kid's bed, a tear-soaked tissue in her hand. To this day he could envision her face in silhouette, a single tear clinging to her chin, as if that drop of water was every bit as stubborn as the woman, refusing to surrender. He'd never known why that case hit her harder than others, or if he'd just never before caught her during the emotional fallout. But something had shifted inside him then, releasing a gnawing need that dogged him until he gave in to temptation the night of the Christmas party.

A log dropped and popped as he knelt in front of her.

He knuckled a fresh tear from her cheek. "Are you all right?"

"Yes and no and I don't know." Her words jumbled on top of each other. "I almost wish I could blame it on hormones."

"The past couple of days have been overwhelming." For him, too.

"An understatement." She nodded tightly, her last bit of control obviously brittle.

Hooking his arm around her shoulders, he slid up beside her on the couch and drew her to his chest. Her shoulders trembled as she choked back sobs, then finally let go, crying into his sweater. He rested his cheek against the top of her head and inhaled the scent of her shampoo, lightly floral and so different from the antiseptic world they usually inhabited together. His hands skimmed up and down her spine, the soft cashmere reminding him of the massage he'd given her on the plane. Right now, though, her zipper would stay firmly in place. She needed something different from him and, by God, he would deliver.

He stroked her back, made what he hoped were soothing noises and held her until her tears slowed. Each gentle breath pressed her breasts to him. He gritted his teeth against the temptation to pull her closer and savor the lush curves of her. Nearly three months of no sex—of no Lilah—sent desire grating through him.

He felt like a bastard for being turned on while she was so blatantly upset. Protectiveness and passion got tangled up inside him. All the barriers he'd worked to resurrect around her crumbled.

Sniffling, she finally eased away, swiping her hair from her face and straightening her dress. She braced her shoulders and faced him, chin jutting with determination.

"Okay," she said simply.

Huh? "Okay what?"

"Let's make the most of this time away and have sex 24/7." She reached behind her neck to tug down the zipper on her cashmere dress. "Starting now."

Shock stunned him still until the rasp of her zipper brought him out of his stupor. Yes, he'd wanted her naked, but not this way, not when she wasn't thinking clearly.

Not when his own mind was such a mess.

"Whoa." He gripped her shoulders to keep the top in place, confused as to what brought her abrupt about-face and concerned about what had upset her. "Hold on there a second, Gypsy Rose Lee."

Her forehead pleated in frustration. "You're telling *me* to stop?"

"As much as it pains me to say this…" He took in the generous swell of her breasts so close, only an inch away from where he clasped her wrists. But he had to hold strong. "We need to talk this through."

Confusion faded from her face, replaced by increasing anger snapping from her as tangibly as the crackles in the stone hearth. "I'm not sure what kind of head game you're playing here, but I do not appreciate it. I could have sworn back in the plane today that you were totally turned on."

"Believe me, I was." He winced. "I am."

A slow, sexy smile creasing her face, she swayed closer, her green eyes glinting jewel tones. "Then what's stopping you?"

As much as it pained him, he forced out the words that would push her away for the night. "It would be wrong to take advantage of a woman when she's drunk or crying."

When they went to bed together again—and he was damn determined that they would—he wanted her every bit as certain as he was. Although the anger tightening her face made it clear his road back into her arms might not be smooth. He'd wounded her pride.

"Fine, then." She yanked up her zipper and swiped her fingers under her eyes a final time, clearing away all signs of tears.

Except for a tiny smudge of mascara streaking into her hairline. He thumbed the splotch and she jerked away.

He wished life's messes were as easily cleared. "Sleep on it. If in the morning when you're dry-eyed and rested you're still interested, then believe me, I'll have you on the nearest flat surface before the crepes cool."

The anger in her face eased a hint to reservation. "You can cook crepes?"

"Is that such a surprise?" He wanted to coax a smile to her face, end this day on a lighter note, anything to keep tears from her eyes. "I would have made them for you that morning if you'd stayed around."

She studied him with a narrowed, discerning gaze. "Is that what the cold shoulder has been about these past months? Because I left before breakfast? I remember things differently."

"Tell me what you recall." He could only think of how much he'd gone through the motions that morning, his insides shredded by the memories of his mother's assassination. He'd been intent on not letting Lilah get too close, maintaining the distance that protected him from a past he didn't stand a chance of reconciling.

"I remember the scent of bacon in the air along with the gruff tone in your voice and the way you hauled on your clothes for work." Hurt leaked into her voice, filling him with regret. "Can you deny that breakfast together would have been decidedly awkward?"

The last thing he wanted was to revisit the past in any form, especially given how poorly he'd handled it all in the ensuing months. He mentally kicked himself for bringing up that night in the first place. "Why don't we focus on now, rather than then? Meet me for crepes in about—" he glanced at his watch "—nine hours."

Steeling himself from taking things further tonight, he pressed a kiss to her cheek and tasted the salty remnants of her tears. He stood quickly before she could pull away or get angry again, and gestured the way toward her room. As she walked ahead silently, he realized that while her crying had stopped, he could still see the tension rippling through her spine. He'd accomplished nothing to help her.

God, he hated being mystified when it came to this woman. He always, always could reason his way through anything. But the way he felt about Lilah had wreaked havoc on his self-control.

With the scent of her still on his skin bringing back memories of their night together, it was all he could do to keep from charging after her and taking her up on her enticing offer....

He watched Lilah across the ballroom. Their kiss on the rooftop garden had spiraled out of control until they were seconds from having sex right there. Only the prospect of frostbite had convinced them to relocate. To his office. ASAP.

Anticipation ramped his heart rate as he tracked her making her way through the throng toward the exit, doing her best to disengage herself from the other partiers attempting to snag her attention. Jim—the head of pediatrics—was especially persistent, but then the guy wanted a substantial chunk of some grant money that had just come through.

Vaguely, Carlos registered his own name being called. He half glanced to find the new radiologist— Nancy Something—waving to snag his attention. He nodded politely then surged ahead before he could become entangled in a conversation. His full focus was on Lilah and their assignation.

His office was distant and private since Lilah had relocated his space after the Medina exposé hit the news and brought reporters rushing into his life. And speaking of the press, he checked his back to make sure no one followed him down the back hall.

He slid his key into the office lock just as a hand fell to rest on his shoulder. Lilah. Turning, he looped an arm around her and sealed his mouth to hers again, reaching behind to open the door.

Her fists tightened in his tux, her kiss increasingly frantic. Their legs tangling, he backed into his workspace, kicked the door closed and flattened her to the door.

He didn't know how this had flamed so high so fast, but he'd never wanted a woman as much as he had to have Lilah. Here. This minute.

Her hands fell to his pants and made fast work of his belt. Even now, the woman was bold and efficient. Strong. He admired that about her. He wanted to wrinkle her perfect dress, to ruck it up to her waist and bury himself inside her until she was lost in the moment. Out of control. Calling out his name. Especially with her fingers nudging down his zipper.

Good thing he was always prepared. He pulled the condom from his wallet and plucked out the packet of protection.

Reflexively, he pushed back thoughts of the children he would never have. Of how he didn't even dare risk adoption, risk exposing any child, any woman, to the dangers his family had faced. He would not, could not live through the nightmare of watching another woman suffer because of her connection to the Medina name.

Restraint shaky, he gathered Lilah's dress, bunching the silky fabric upward. He revealed his Grecian goddess inch by inch of creamy leg, nudged aside her panties and sunk inside. The warm clamp of her body

*took him to a level beyond anything he'd experienced...
beyond anything he would feel again since this was the
only night he could have with her....*

Embers blurring as he stared, Carlos rubbed his
fingers together, the moisture from Lilah's tears soaking
into his skin. Had he done the right thing in turning
away from her, sending her to her room? Hell, half the
time he didn't know what he was doing when it came
to her. He reacted with his gut instead of his brain.

The tears she'd cried were so different from the ones
shed by his patients and their worried parents. In those
cases, he knew how to respond, his eyes firmly fixed on
healing. Here, he didn't know how to ease her pain.

Then it hit him like the logs blazing back to life.

He was the cause of her tears and her tension. He'd
sensed her anger the day she'd told him about the baby—
tough to miss when she'd slapped him. But so intent on
protecting her with distance, he'd missed the obvious.

Intellectually, he'd understood she believed him to be
the father. He'd assumed she must have mixed up dates.
Yet as he thought back to what she'd said in his office,
he recalled her emphatic insistence that there hadn't
been anyone other than him for months.

She had no reason to lie. Lilah had never been
impressed by his money or his pedigree.

Bracing a steadying hand on the mantel, he let the
implications line up in his brain. That left him with two
possibilities. Either the baby really was his or someone
had taken advantage of Lilah without her knowledge,
not as far-fetched as it sounded. Some bastard could
have slipped any number of date rape drugs into her

drink. His hands fisted at even the possibility of her being taken advantage of so callously. So criminally.

A fresh wave of protectiveness—*possessiveness*— flooded him until he accepted the inevitable. She was his. Which made her baby his regardless.

The reality of that settled inside him. There was no cutting her out of his life. No turning his back. She and her child were his to keep safe. He hadn't planned on linking his life to anyone else's. Being a Medina had never brought peace to anyone, most certainly not to his mother.

But walking away from Lilah was no longer an option.

The next morning, Lilah combed her fingers through her damp hair, wide awake thanks to her shower. Sleep had been hard to come by.

Sure, she'd been reckless throwing herself at Carlos last night. Still, his rejection had hurt.

She hadn't cried again though. She'd refused to waste another tear on him. Instead, she'd stared dry-eyed at the soaring ceiling, warm honey-colored cedar planks overhead bathed in moonlight, then with the first morning rays.

Now the window let blazing sunshine through, but shed little illumination on her confused emotions. Hitching her jeans over her hips, she raised the zipper, then realized she couldn't button them any longer. Her waist was expanding. Time was ticking away to settle her life.

Could she trust he'd only pulled away out of honor? If so, could there be some hint to an answer about why he'd kept his distance in recent months?

Or was this just more of the same evasiveness from Carlos? There was only one way to find out.

Refusing to hide in her room all day, she yanked a pale pink angora sweater over her head—and down to cover her thickening waist. She would face whatever the day held with her eyes dry and her chin up. For her child. For her own pride. Lilah yanked open her bedroom door and padded down the hall, her socked feet sinking in the handwoven wool rugs. The second her foot hit the top step on the lengthy staircase, she smelled…

Breakfast. Sweet and fruity. Crepes, perhaps?

She'd almost forgotten about that part of their discussion, so focused on how he'd pushed her away. At the base of those stairs, a decision waited. Gripping the banister, she stared down and weighed her options, her heart racing. Her gaze settled on another of those framed oil paintings of the Pyrenees. She gripped the railing tighter, the reminder of Carlos's tumultuous childhood softening her heart just when she most wanted an excuse to be with him.

The sweet and bready scent of breakfast drifted up the stairs and this time she inhaled deeply, unreservedly soaking in this simple moment of domesticity from her royal lover. Each breath brought a surge of desire and anticipation as she thought of him preparing the meal for her, of him following through on his promise. He was showing her he hadn't been rejecting her last night—he'd truly been thinking of her.

Right now, she wanted him every bit as much as she had last night when she'd been so overwhelmed with fears about her future. Her hand settled on her stomach. The open button poked against her sweater, reminding her that all too soon she would need to put the concerns of her child first.

This could be her last chance to be with Carlos again.

Committed, she walked down the stairs and to the kitchen, the delicious aroma growing stronger. Her feet carried her closer, closer still, until she stopped in the cedar archway leading into the gourmet kitchen.

Carlos stood with his back to her, shuffling crepes from the stove to a serving platter. Plump raspberries and apricots filled a bowl. Her mouth watered, but more because of the broad shoulders of her personal chef than from the food itself. Her eyes lingered on his hands, as careful with the cuts on the apricots as he would be in the O.R. Strong, capable hands.

A copper tea kettle whistled and she nearly jumped out of her skin.

Pouring the water over a tea leaf infuser, he glanced back at her.

Lilah spread her hands wide. "No tears."

If he showed the least hesitation, she was out of here. She wanted him, but she'd made as much of a first step as her pride would allow.

He set aside a crystal flagon of syrup on the cutting board. His eyes flared with unmistakable heat. Her breath hitched at the power of his smile. Still, she didn't move, needing him to come to her.

One step at a time, he advanced, his limp reminding her of all the baggage they both brought to this encounter. Two wary people past the days of first-blush love.

Two people who couldn't deny the flame between them.

Carlos stopped in front of her in jeans and a plain

white T-shirt, his bare feet brushing her toes. "Are you hungry?"

"Starving," she answered, knowing full well neither of them referred to food. "No more talking."

No more chances for doubts and reservations to steal this moment.

He nodded. She exhaled a breath she hadn't even realized she'd been holding.

His hands slid up to span her waist with a bold large grip. She cupped his shoulder, ready, eager to step into his embrace.

In one smooth move, he lifted her onto the granite counter. She gasped in surprise. The stone chilled through the denim of her jeans. "Wow, somebody's in a hurry. Didn't anyone ever tell you not to bolt your food?"

"Apparently nobody's ever had anything as delectable as you on the menu."

He tore off a corner of the crepe and stirred it through the fruit. He brought the bite to her mouth. She tasted from his fingers. Her eyes slid closed at the burst of sensation on her tongue. The sweet fruit mixed with the lightly salty taste of his skin as he withdrew his fingers slowly. She couldn't resist sucking gently. His pupils widened in response. A low growl rumbled up his throat.

Pushing away the plate of crepes, she cupped the back of his neck, urging him closer. *Closer.* Until he stepped between her knees and kissed her. She tasted raspberries and syrup on his tongue. Apparently he'd sampled his own cooking along the way.

Her senses sharpened, the taste of him on her tongue, the scrape of his unshaven face under her fingers. The scent of fresh-washed man and the food he'd prepared for her filled her as tangibly as he would soon fill her body.

Clamping her legs around his waist, she locked him nearer, gripped by the connection she'd been aching to recapture. She banned all other thoughts from her mind but the here and now.

His hand slid under the hem of her sweater, his touch fiery against her bare flesh. He tunneled further until sweeping the angora up and over her head. He growled low in appreciation as he cupped her breasts. The creamy lace provided a flimsy barrier between her and his circling thumbs. Her nipples went hard, the lace suddenly itchy, her skin everywhere tightening with a need for more of his touch, more of him.

Arching toward him, she pressed for a fuller connection and he took her cue well. His hands slid behind her and freed her bra in a deft sweep.

She bunched his T-shirt, gathering, raising until she flung the body-warmed cotton across the room to rest on top of her sweater. She made fast work of the top button and zipper on his jeans while he tugged hers down her hips, lifting her briefly, then pulled them down her legs. He backed away, removing her pants inch by torturous inch.

His washboard stomach gleamed in the morning sun as she looked her fill at the strong expanse of his chest. She reached to trace down, down, down further still, following the crisp sprinkling of hair in a narrowing trail to his open button, down the links of his open zipper.

No underwear.

Carlos flung her pants to the floor and stepped closer.

The granite felt cool and slick against the backs of her bare legs. Only her silky panties separated her from total exposure. Her eager hand freed his arousal and his eyes slid closed. He flattened a palm on the counter for a second as if to steady himself.

A surge of feminine power curled through her as she stroked him, her thumb rolling over the glistening first pearly dampening. His throat worked in a long swallow before he opened his eyes. The intensity, the raw passion in his gaze left her breathless.

With slow deliberation, he swiped two fingers through the raspberries, squeezed the juice along her collarbone and cleaned it away with his mouth. The warmth of his tasting tongue and the cool air provided the most delicious contrast on her oversensitized skin. He nipped the last taste up at the base of her neck, then scooped up more of the fruit, eyeing her chest with only a hint of warning that he intended to…

Yes.

The drizzle of warmed juice flowed over her like the desire spreading throughout her body. Her head fell back as he laved his undivided attention on one breast and then the other. The gentle sucking along her skin and the light rasp of his tongue sent shivers of pure pleasure down her spine. She gripped his shoulders, her fingernails sinking in deep. He braced a hand against the counter and leaned into her.

A fleeting thought chased through her mind, concern for his back, for the strain he thoughtlessly put on his body. "Carlos, let's take this to the sofa."

Her fingers trailed down the flex of muscles on his back until she reached the puckered ridges of his healed flesh.

He popped a raspberry into her mouth. "I dreamed all night long about having you here." Pulling her hands away and replacing them on his shoulders, he nipped up her shoulder to draw on her bottom lip. "Nothing's going to steal that fantasy from me."

His words sent a thrill up her spine, almost chasing away her concern for him. She sought a way to express her worry without stinging his pride. "But what if..."

"What if my legs give way?" He raised an eyebrow and hooked a finger on either side of her skimpy panties. "Then you can join me on the floor and we'll finish there, because don't doubt for a minute we're taking this to the conclusion we both want."

He twisted his fingers in the fragile fabric until her panties gave way. "I will see this through any and every way I can have you."

Air brushed along her damp and needy core, stirring her higher. Just air, for heaven's sake. Her heart tripped over itself in anticipation of his touch.

He inched her hips nearer to the edge. "Condoms or no condoms? I'm clean. There's been nobody but you in a year."

A year? His words along with the thick pressure of him, right there so close, teased her perilously near completion too fast.

"Go ahead," he urged, "let go. I'll take you there again as many times as you want."

His bold confidence sent a charge through her, reminding her of how he'd coaxed her to let go before. And she realized—he wasn't going to fall. He was in complete control of this moment between them.

"There is no need for a condom, Carlos. None. It's only you and me."

Her fingers dug deeper into his flanks as he thrust inside, his low growl of possession echoing through the spacious kitchen. Clamping her legs around his waist again, she urged him deeper, faster. Still she wanted more of him, no restraint. She whispered her wishes, her wants, her secret fantasies in his ear, delighting in the feel of his throbbing response to her words.

Just like after that party, she lost herself in the frenzy of the moment. Even wondering all night long if this would happen, still the powerful need caught her unaware. She'd known their sex was one of a kind before, but her memories…well… Nothing could compare to the pulsing draw she felt now in his arms.

Carlos brought her just shy of release again and again until their bodies were slicked with sweat. The scent of them together blended with the sweet stickiness of the raspberries and sugary fruit juice.

Flattening her hands behind her on the counter, inching closer, closer again, hungry to be nearer still, she rolled her hips against his. Her eyes fluttered open and shut, giving her glimpses of the mountain range stretching across the horizon. They were completely isolated up here, alone to explore each other, to explore the complex, confused feelings that had erupted between them over the past few months.

His pulse throbbed in his temple. He dipped his head to her breasts, increasing her pleasure with a flick of his tongue. The tingling in her veins gathered low and pulsing, tighter still until she gasped.

Once.

Twice.

The third carried her moan of release to echo into the cedar rafters. Sweet sensations exploded inside her, filling every corner until she could have sworn even the roots of her hair shimmered.

She bowed upward and into his arms as he thrust again, again, again, until finishing with a hoarse shout muffled against her neck. The throb of his completion triggered an aftershock through her. Caught unaware, she shuddered, her bare chest against his. Her arms went limp with exhaustion around his neck. She tried to hold on but her body had gone boneless with bliss.

Carlos's hold on her tightened just in time to keep her from slipping off the counter. "Lilah?"

"What?" she answered simply, unable to scrounge more than the single syllable.

His fingers dug deeper into her hips, giving only a second's forewarning of his increased intensity before he demanded, "Marry me."

Eight

The force of his release still pounding through his veins, Carlos wondered how he'd let amazing sex steal his ability to think rationally. He hadn't meant to blurt out his proposal quite that way. As he'd prepared breakfast, he'd planned for something more…eloquent maybe, after they shared crepes in front of the soaring mountain view.

Feeling Lilah frozen in his arms relayed her shock, but not much else. He searched her face for some hint as to how she felt, but she quickly averted her eyes.

Silently, Lilah inched to the side and back to the floor. She snatched his T-shirt from the butcher block and yanked the white cotton over her head in a swift move. With defiant eyes, she all but dared him to comment on the fact she wore his shirt.

Her bravado waning fast, her hands shook as she

pulled free her sex-tousled hair. "Um, we've already had sex, more than once I might add. So a proposal for 'compromising' me isn't in order."

"You didn't answer." He zipped and buttoned his jeans, wincing.

Fisting her hands by her side, she finally faced him full-on. "My answer is no."

Her refusal stung him more than he would have expected. He didn't want to get married, damn it. "I thought you would be happy. You didn't even think about my proposal."

"And you did?" she retorted.

He might be confused about a number of things when it came to this woman, but he could answer this question honestly. "It's all I thought about."

"Why did you ask me? And why now of all times?" She padded closer across the tile until she stood toe-to-toe with him. "Is it because I shed a few tears last night? Am I suddenly one of your needy cases to save?"

"I want the child to be mine." He gripped her shoulders, working to keep the fierceness inside him from escaping. "I want to protect you both. Is that so wrong?"

She shook her head fiercely. "That's not the same as believing me."

Why did she have to keep pushing this? He was doing what she must have wanted from the start. What he had to do now. "I'll take care of you and the baby, claim it as mine, regardless of what the test shows. You and I are alike. We make a logical match."

"A logical match," she repeated cynically. "Your single life suited you fine up to now. You've said so yourself on more occasions than I can count. In the four years we've known each other, you haven't even hinted—"

Frustration tore at his gut as he tried to find the right words to offer her. "What the hell do you think that night we spent together was about?"

"I don't know, Carlos." Her jaw went tight, but she didn't shed even one of the tears sheening in her eyes. "I do know that the months that followed were about you moving on as if I didn't exist. Maybe I'm not as logical or practical as you believe, because I couldn't just rationalize away the time we spent together."

He should have waited and proposed as he'd planned, in more of a romantic setting. He scrambled for something to say to give her more of the flowers and stars kind of affirmation he should have offered in the first place. "What we experienced rocked me."

"That's it? I rocked your world?" Shaking her head, she backed up. "Well, hello, you rocked my world, too. It's called great sex. Not something particularly logical to build a marriage on."

Spinning away, she made fast tracks toward the stairs, proving loud and clear how badly he'd messed up.

"Lilah! Lilah, damn it. Let's talk this out." He started after her.

His cell phone rang from beside the bowl full of raspberries and memories of tasting Lilah. He reached to thumb the ignore button, only to hesitate when he saw his youngest brother's number on the caller ID. He had to take the call. Maybe giving Lilah a few minutes to cool down would be a wise idea anyway.

"Antonio?" he said into his phone. "Speak to me and it better be important."

"It is." His brother's voice filled the airwaves. "It's

our father. He's taken a turn for the worse. The doctors don't expect him to live through the week if he doesn't get a liver transplant."

Leaving Vail far behind, Lilah peered through the airplane window at the dark sky and clouds. From her work at the hospital, she'd seen often enough how a family health crisis derailed any other concerns.

Just when she'd thought her life couldn't be flipped upside down any further.

Once she'd returned to the kitchen in her clothes, she'd been ready to roll out a speech she prepared, asking him to stop any further marriage proposals or she would leave. The news about his father had changed everything. Carlos had asked her to come with him. How could she say no?

This could be her only chance to meet her child's grandfather. She could learn important information about Carlos that might help her deal with him in the future.

And there was one completely illogical, emotional reason to stay right by his side. She couldn't let him face his father's death alone, especially not when he'd asked for her. Carlos never asked for anything for himself. Ever.

So here she sat, on the plane with him again. This time they were flying through the night sky to some super-secure island off the coast of Florida, which was more information than she'd ever read in the media about the location of his well-protected father. That Carlos would tell her such a closely guarded secret stirred a scary kind of hope inside her. In spite of his unromantic proposal chock-full of "practical" and "logical" reasons to get married, they obviously still shared a respect and trust that they'd possessed once upon a time as friends.

Well, at least as far as either of them seemed capable of trusting, which wasn't saying much.

Sitting across from her as before, Carlos checked his messages, his face inscrutable. The window beside him displayed the receding U.S. shore as they traveled over a murky view of ocean waters.

Their packing and leaving had been so rushed she'd barely had a chance to process their explosive encounter in the kitchen. The scent of raspberries still clung to her skin even after her hurried shower.

The casual lover was long gone now, replaced by the preoccupied doctor she knew so much better. His gray suit was tailor-made, fine quality, yet it hung a bit loose on his lean muscled body, as if he worked so hard he forgot to eat—or get a haircut. She clenched the armrests to resist the temptation to stroke back the salt-and-pepper hair brushing his brow.

With a muttered curse, he jammed his phone inside his jacket again.

She toyed with a loose string along the hem of her dress, her clothing options becoming limited until she went shopping for maternity jeans. "Anything new about your father's condition?"

Shifting uncomfortably in his leather seat, he shook his head. "Only a message from my youngest brother confirming our arrival time."

"I'm sorry. You must be frantic."

He stared at his hands clasped loosely between his knees. "It's not like I haven't known this day was coming soon."

"We've both seen enough cases at the hospital to realize that preparation doesn't erase the pain."

"Talking about it won't change anything." He waved away her sympathy and straightened abruptly. "I apologize for springing the whole family on you so abruptly. I had planned to hold off on that until the end of our time alone."

Surprise cut through her. He'd never mentioned planning this trip to meet his relatives. More of those confused and warily hopeful feelings stirred in her gut. "Both of your brothers are already there?"

"My brother Antonio, his wife and stepson. Duarte and his fiancée. And my half sister is there with her husband. I'm surprised she traveled so late in her pregnancy, but Antonio said she's emphatic about being there." He pinched the bridge of his nose as if battling a headache. "Sorry to introduce so many people at once. The estate is large enough for you to have your own space if you need to escape. My brothers and I each have our own wing. There's also a guesthouse if you prefer that to staying with me. "

"I'm sure your wing will be fine."

"The island is secure, without question, but there's everything you could need there. Our father built it all—from a clinic to a chapel to an ice cream parlor café. He said he wanted us to have 'normal' childhood memories, whatever those are."

"It sounds like your father tried to do his best in an unimaginable situation."

"The violence directed at our family was very real and damn dangerous." He extended his legs in front of him, drawing her attention to the way his muscular thighs stretched the fine gabardine, the sinews defined so well that the veneer of luxury didn't begin to mask the raw power of the man underneath the clothes. "Actually, I appreciated the privacy when I lived there. My brothers hated it on the island, but I didn't want any part of the real world again."

Why had he left if he felt that way? Then she realized. "Now I understand how you work those insane hours at the hospital. You actually don't mind being cut off from day-to-day life."

Carlos arched an eyebrow, half smiling. "Is that a loaded question to figure out if I can change enough where you could envision living with me?"

Admiration and attraction weren't going to be enough to make a relationship work. "You're assuming I'm willing to live with you."

All humor faded from his face. "I want us to do more than live together. I meant what I said back in the kitchen. I want us to be married."

Married?

The word still packed a powerful jolt. She knew part of her knee-jerk reaction to the idea had to do with the train wreck that was her parents' screwed up union. But she knew this would be rushing it.

As much as she didn't want to upset him when he had such heavy worries about his father, she couldn't let this marriage nonsense continue. What if he said something in front of his family? "If you keep proposing, I'll have to sleep in that guesthouse. This was about no pressure, remember?"

"Then let's back up to the living together." His eyes narrowed with that sleepy-sexy look she was beginning to recognize so well. "More importantly, let's get back to *not sleeping* together."

His words stirred memories of frantic lovemaking on the counter, bringing the sweet taste of raspberries exploding through her senses like the aftershocks of a world-rocking orgasm. She suspected he wasn't really serious, but rather found such outrageous talk a distraction from concerns about his father.

All the same, she squirmed uncomfortably in her seat, leather creaking as the tension and the need inside her increased. "Now that you've mentioned sleeping, I think I'll catch a catnap for the rest of the flight."

"Fine," he said, a wicked gleam mingling with the steam in his eyes. "But remember that bacon cheeseburger and mint milkshake you said you'd been craving? The steward has both ready for you. Of course, I can cancel the order."

Her mouth watered. And quite frankly, she welcomed the lighter air he seemed determined to inject. Weightier concerns would come soon enough once they landed. "You're using food to blackmail an expectant mother into conversation? That's not playing fair."

"I'm only trying to help," he said practically. "I want to take care of you. Not just what you eat or helping you with an aching back. Getting married makes sense."

Deftly, he'd shifted the conversation right back to that confusing proposal of his. What was his real motive for this about face?

Yet what did *she* want? Her heart clenched as she realized she was more like her mother than she cared to admit, because she did want the fairy-tale romanticism after all. "Thank you, but in case you haven't noticed, I'm capable of taking care of myself."

Silence stretched between them until she looked away, focusing instead on the view below where Carlos's family waited. And what about *her* family? She couldn't delay calling them for much longer. She just wanted to have her life more settled first.

She wanted to have her feelings for Carlos resolved.

In the distance, an island rested in the middle of the murky ocean. Palm trees spiked from the landscape, lushly thick and so very different from the leafless snowy winter they'd left behind.

Curiosity about Carlos's home drew her until she nearly had her nose pressed to the glass as she catalogued details. It was a small city unto itself, a surprise splash of lights in the sea so vast that, like a Lite-Brite design on the water, the island began to take shape. A dozen or so small outbuildings dotted a semicircle around a larger structure, what appeared to be the main house, bathed in floodlights.

The white mansion faced the ocean in a U shape, constructed around a large courtyard with a pool. Details were spotty in the dark. Soon enough she would get an up close view of the place where Enrique Medina had lived in seclusion for over twenty-five years, a gilded cage for his sons to say the least. Even from a distance she couldn't miss the grand scale of the sprawling estate.

The intercom system crackled a second before the pilot announced, "We're about to begin descending to our destination. Please return to your seats and secure your lap belts. Thank you, and we hope you had a pleasant flight."

Her stomach knotted with nerves over meeting his family.

Engines whining louder, the plane banked, lining up

with a thin islet alongside the larger island. A single strip of concrete marked the private runway, blinking with landing lights in the night. As they neared, a ferryboat came into focus. To ride from the airport to the main island? They sure were serious about security.

She thought of his father, a man who'd been overthrown in a violent coup. The detailed planning of the island made her wonder if every step this family made had ulterior motives. Nothing seemed left to chance.

If that was the case, why then had he brought her here?

Carlos steered the SUV through the scroll-work gates separating his father's mansion from the island. The machine gun-toting guards didn't so much as flinch as he drove by. He and his siblings had agreed to gather at the house to reconnoiter, then go to the island clinic to see their father.

He thought he'd prepared himself for this visit, prepared himself for his father's death. But as he stared at the white adobe mansion where he'd spent his teenage years recovering, the past came roaring up like a rogue tidal wave.

Slowing the vehicle, he eased past a towering marble fountain with a "welcome" pineapple on top. Ironic.

When he'd been here for his brother's wedding, he'd been able to numb himself. However, for some reason, he felt raw this time in a way that he hadn't experienced since a surgeon had retooled most of his insides. His fingers clenched around the steering wheel reflexively before he forced himself to relax and turn the vehicle over to the uniformed staff member opening the passenger door.

His shirt stuck to his back, and Carlos tried to chalk up the perspiration to the warmer Florida climate. But he couldn't lie to himself. The doctor inside him couldn't deny the physiological reaction to the stress of being here.

Carlos circled the front of the car and before he consciously registered the motion, he reached for Lilah. Strange how her presence here kept him going. One foot in front of the other, in spite of the stabbing pain increasing at the base of his spine. His body shouted subliminal alarms left and right. He tucked his hand against her waist under the guise of being gentlemanly since she would probably think he was nuts if he clasped her hand.

This arrival together was important to him, a commitment from him to her, even if she didn't realize it. Bringing any outsider to the island was a huge step. Especially for him. His family would recognize that right away.

Lilah was his now.

The butler motioned them toward the library. Lilah stayed silent, eyeing her surroundings as they walked through the cavernous circular hall, two staircases stretching up either side, meeting in the middle. He guided her through the gold gilded archway, past his father's favorite Picasso.

Finally, he reached the library, his father's domain. Books filled three walls, interspersed with windows and a sliding brass ladder. Mosaic tiles swirled outward on the floor; the ceiling was filled with frescos of globes and conquistadors. Scents from the orange trees drifted in through the open windows along with the feel of the ever-present warm ocean breeze.

Beneath a wide skylight, the family had all gathered while his father's wingback chair loomed empty. Enrique's two Rhodesian ridgebacks stood guard on either side of the empty "throne."

"Lilah, these are my brothers, Duarte and Antonio."

Duarte stepped forward first, his hand extended precisely. His middle brother would have made the perfect military officer if they'd stayed in San Rinaldo. Their assumed identities as adults had made it impossible for Duarte to sign on as a U.S. serviceman. Instead, he'd become a ruthless businessman.

Lilah wore her overly calm expression, the one Carlos had seen her wear during stressful board meetings at the hospital. She shook Antonio's hand next.

The family maverick sported longer hair. He'd left the island at eighteen and signed on to a shrimp boat crew in Galveston Bay, working his way up to shipping magnate. His weathered face showed lines of worry today. His new wife tucked her arms around his waist in quiet comfort.

Once intros were complete, the women circled Lilah in an impenetrable wall—of protection or curiosity? He wasn't sure. But their half sister, Eloisa, Antonio's wife, Shannon, and Duarte's fiancée, Kate, were filling her ears with everything she could possibly need to know about the island.

Carlos turned to his brothers. "Our father?"

Duarte clasped his hands behind his back. "Still holding his own at the clinic."

"I want to know why he left the hospital in Jacksonville." There had been a glimmer of hope when they finally persuaded their father to look beyond the island clinic for medical help on the mainland. Getting their father to agree had been a major coup given what a recluse Enrique had become. "I thought he was on board with seeing specialists."

Antonio shrugged impatiently. "He said he's come home to die with his family."

Duarte's jaw went tight for a second before he continued, "The doctors in Jacksonville support the clinic staff here. Transplant is the only way to go if he wants a chance at beating this."

"Then what's with his whole death march?" Their father had options. A chance. A liver transplant could even be done with a live donor giving a lobe of his or her liver, and Enrique had a room full of possibilities in his children. "We need to get him back to Jacksonville immediately."

Duarte laughed darkly. "Good luck convincing him to agree."

Antonio braced a hand against the dormant fireplace. "Tests show I'm a match as a donor, but the old man shut me down. He's fixated on the notion that he doesn't want me to undergo the risk, even though it will save his life."

Carlos resisted the urge to bark out his frustration at the outright hypocrisy. His father had demanded his son fight to live after the bullets had torn into his back, to endure endless torturous procedures and rehabilitation in order to beat the odds and walk again. No way was Carlos letting the old man simply check out on the family when there was still a chance. "I will just have to persuade him otherwise."

"We would have called you about this sooner, but

you're ineligible to be a donor because of the damage to your liver from the gunshot wounds."

A gasp drew his attention. He turned to see Lilah staring back at him with wide—surprised—eyes, the color draining from her creamy skin. Hell. He'd never told her the real cause of his injuries and he hadn't thought to warn his brothers to stay silent on the subject.

It hadn't seemed necessary to inform her. There hadn't been the right moment. And he knew those were just excuses because he didn't want to revisit that time in his life with anyone.

Seeing the confusion in her eyes, he realized he'd screwed up with her yet again, and that unsettled him as he accepted just how important it had become to have her with him.

Talking with Lilah would have to wait, however. He needed to prepare himself to see his father for what could be the last time.

Nine

Every minute spent on this island only imprinted in her brain how very little she knew about the man who'd fathered her child.

High heels echoing down the marble corridor, Lilah trailed the other women as they gave her a crash course on the Medina mansion, a palatial retreat that felt nearly as large as the Tacoma hospital. They'd already seen the library, music room, movie screening room, pools, more than one dining area and her own suite. Now she was learning where to find the others in their quarters.

Too bad she couldn't just MapQuest the place.

Maybe as she wandered she could collect clues about Carlos from the priceless art collection on walls and pedestals.

Her heart clenched as she remembered the only painting on the wall in his hospital office—a canvas by Joaquín Sorolla y Bastida, one of the *Sad Inheritance* preparatory pieces. She'd always thought the image of crippled children bathing in healing waters to be tied into his own work.

Now she realized how he was connected to that image in a far more tragic way than she could have ever known. Shot in the back? Tears stung her eyes as she envisioned his scars with a deeper understanding.

So far the house wasn't revealing much more about him other than relaying an utter isolation and wealth beyond anything she could have imagined. Her only other option? Ask.

Passing yet another heavily armed and stoic guard, she eyed the women in front of her. Carlos's dark-haired sister Eloisa. Then the girl-next-door blonde sister-in-law, Shannon. And the savvy-eyed brunette fiancée, Kate.

The time with them would be better spent picking their minds about the family than memorizing the floor plan of this mansion maze. She just hoped they weren't as closemouthed as Carlos. Angling to the side, she passed a man vacuuming the molding over a high archway. Given the late hour, she wondered if the staff around here ever slept.

As they walked through a small courtyard, she ran her hand along a sleek jade cat keeping watch over a fountain nestled between the property's vast wings.

Shannon opened yet another door in their marathon tour. "This hall leads to my quarters." Her Texas twang coated each word as silk Italian drapes rippled with their passing. "I hope you won't mind if I check on my son real quick and relieve the nanny. Then we can have that late-night snack I promised."

"Please, take your time," Lilah said, waving the younger mother into the room, balcony doors already parted to admit a gusty ocean breeze. "I'm wide awake on West Coast time."

Soon she would have those same responsibilities, the privilege of a child in her life. Making sure her child had the most stable life possible increased the urgency in settling her confused feelings about the baby's father.

Her shoes sunk into the Persian rug until the toes blended into the apricot and gray pattern as she followed the other women into the rooms Shannon shared with Antonio. The suite sported two bedrooms off a sitting area with an eating space stocked more fully than most kitchens. Seeming to know her way around, Kate brought a tray with a bone china teapot alongside a plate of tiny sandwiches and fat strawberries.

Lilah lingered by a Waterford vase to sniff the lisianthus with blooms resembling blue roses that softened the gray tones in the decor. Trailing her fingers along the camelback sofa, she hesitated, surprised to find a homey knitted afghan.

Softly, Shannon closed her son's door and crossed to the sofa, caressing the worn-soft pewter yarn with reverence. "Their mother made this for Antonio shortly before she died." She looked up, her blue-gray eyes sad. "Antonio was only five when they left San Rinaldo. He told me he thought of the blanket as a shield."

Five years old.

As the other women settled into fat, comfy chairs, Lilah wrapped her arms around herself, chilled to the core by the image of three young boys fleeing the only home they'd ever known. Dodging bullets. Losing their mother. She squeezed her eyes shut briefly. In the four years she'd known Carlos, she hadn't a clue just how deep and dark those shadows in his eyes went.

Sweeping her sleek, black ponytail over her shoulder, Eloisa propped her feet on an ottoman, balancing a plate of shrimp and cucumber sandwiches on top of her pregnant belly with a wry grin. "It's more than a little overwhelming, isn't it? I'm still growing accustomed to all of it."

Resisting the urge to touch her own expanding waistline, Lilah focused on the woman's words instead, eager to learn more about these people who would be family to her baby. "Didn't Enrique have visitation rights when you were a child?"

"My parents never had an official custody agreement drawn up. I only met him once." Eloisa leaned forward for her tea, her silver shell charm necklace chiming against her china plate. "I was about seven at the time of my visit."

Taking a cup of tea from Shannon, Lilah reviewed what little she knew about the Medina history. "That's years after the last sighting of him."

Eloisa smiled nostalgically. "I didn't know where we went when my mother and I flew here. It felt like we took a long time in the air. But of course all travel seems to take forever at that age. I never told anyone about the visit after I left here. I may not have had much of a relationship with my father while I was growing up, but I understood that his safety and the safety of my brothers depended on my silence."

Shivering, Lilah eyed the blanket made by a mother who would never see her children grow up. "Did you meet them as well?"

She sipped her tea to warm herself in spite of the sultry

island air. A burst of chocolate mint flavor surprised her. Had Carlos informed the staff of her recent craving for chocolate mint? The possibility seeped through her more tangibly than the drink.

"Duarte and Antonio were here," Eloisa answered. "Carlos was having treatments at the time."

Her teacup rattled on the saucer. Lilah set it down carefully and busied her shaking hands by picking from the assortment of tiny round sandwiches—goat cheese and watercress. "The whole trip must have seemed strange to you, a child so young."

"More than you know." Eloisa smiled as Shannon held out a tray of fruit—she selected a chocolate strawberry with obvious anticipation. "My mother had remarried by then and had another baby."

Her words sunk in. "How did your stepfather feel about the trip?"

"He never knew about the visit, or about any of the Medinas...until recently when the whole world learned too."

Shannon settled back into her chair, tucking her bare feet under her, expensive shoes forgotten in the timeless ritual of girl talk. "The day that revelation exploded on the internet is definitely one of the most memorable moments of my life."

The everyday sort of gab session wrapped around Lilah with a strange—alien?—feeling. She had so few people in her life to share moments like this. As the only daughter with two much older brothers, as a woman with a high-powered position, she didn't have many female friends with whom she could kick off her shoes.

Lilah accepted a refill from Kate. "When our hospital staff first heard the news, the whole place went wild over the fact that one of our own surgeons had been leading a double life."

She couldn't imagine such an existence of secrecy and fear. She'd been so focused on Carlos's injuries that she hadn't considered how other aspects of his childhood had shaped him as well.

Eloisa waved a hand dismissively. "But my childhood, the whole exposé—" she winked at Kate, whose photos had first started that buzz "—it's all water under the bridge now. I want to tell you about that visit when I was seven. It was amazing, or rather it seemed that way to me through my childish, idealistic eyes. We all walked along the beach and collected shells. He—" she paused, clearing her throat "—um, Enrique, told me this story about a little squirrel that could travel wherever she wanted by scampering along the telephone lines."

Lilah reached to clasp the other woman's hand. "What a beautiful memory."

Would these two Medina grandchildren—Eloisa's baby and Lilah's child—have the privilege of hearing their grandfather Enrique tell them the same story?

Reconciling the image of a man who would tell such lovely tales with the notion of a father ignoring his child unsettled Lilah. Greatly. A man who could detach himself came into focus, bringing fears because Carlos had sliced her from his life just as easily.

Had he learned that skill at his father's knee? Could she be in for another repeat in the future, regardless of how open he'd seemed in the Colorado kitchen?

The attorney inside her blared warnings to protect herself, protect her baby against a family with unlimited resources at their fingertips. People with this kind of power rarely surrendered anything. Once Carlos had the proof in hand about the baby, she didn't doubt for a second that he would claim his child with a fierce determination.

Would he go so far as to try to gain custody of the baby if she didn't marry him? And could she put aside a lifetime of reservations about relationships to agree to a marriage of convenience?

No matter the warm draw of the women around her, the hope of a secure life for her, for her baby—for Carlos—provided a frighteningly heavy allure.

Carlos guided the four-wheel drive over the two-lane paved road, Duarte beside him and Antonio in the back. Only a couple more minutes until they reached the island clinic—and their dying father. He thought he'd prepared himself for this day.

But he was wrong.

Of course he'd been mistaken about a lot of things lately, like assuming Lilah would jump at the chance to marry him. The way she'd thrown his proposal back in his face still grated. As much as he tried to play things calm and laid-back with offers of cheeseburgers and milk shakes, he couldn't escape the sense that time was slipping away. That if he didn't settle his life soon, there wouldn't be another chance for him with her.

In the backseat, Antonio leaned forward, arms resting on the backs of his brothers' seats. "Care to share, Carlos?"

His hands tightened around the steering wheel as he steered deeper into the jungle. "About what?"

"Really, brother." Antonio flicked him on the temple. "You're supposed to be the genius in our family. Who's the lady friend?"

"Lilah and I work at the same hospital. She's the administrator."

"A lawyer?" Duarte loaded the final word with cynicism, his arm hooked out the open window.

Antonio snorted. "You're the one engaged to a *reporter*."

"Photojournalist," Duarte corrected softly, possessively.

Protectively.

His fiancée had been the one to first break the Medina story to the press with a picture she'd accidentally nabbed. Ironically, that snapshot had brought her and Duarte together and now she handled all carefully controlled press releases about the family.

Their youngest brother chuckled. "Journalist or photojournalist. Tomato, tom-ah-to."

Carlos whipped the car around a corner, toward a one-storey building, white stucco with a red tile roof. The clinic sported two wings, perched like a bird on the manicured lawn. One side held the offices for regular checkups, eye exams and dental visits. The other side was reserved for hospital beds, testing and surgeries. The clinic treated not only the Medinas, but also the staff needed to run a small island kingdom.

Everything was top-of-the-line, easy enough to finance with an unlimited bank balance. Enrique had insisted on the best for the facility where his son would spend most of his teenage years. Carlos knew every nook and cranny of the place.

"Ignore Antonio," Duarte said, bracing a hand on the dash. "I'm happy for you, my brother."

Downshifting as he cruised to a stop in front of the double sliding doors, Carlos glanced at his brothers quickly. "Hold off on the congratulations." Better to be honest than risk them congratulating Lilah. "I still have to convince her."

Carlos pocketed the keys and left the vehicle. Guards nodded a welcome without relaxing their stance. Electric doors slid open. A blast of cool, antiseptic air drifted out. The clinic was fully staffed with doctors and nurses, on hand to see to the health concerns of the small legion that ran Enrique's island home. Most were also from San Rinaldo or relatives of the refugees.

Antonio pointed to the correct room number, although Carlos would have known from the fresh pair of heavily armed sentinels. Enrique never relaxed security. Ever. Even when at death's door.

Duarte stopped Carlos with a hand to the arm. "We'll wait out here so you can have time to visit him on your own first. Call when you're ready for us to join you."

Carlos nodded his gratitude, words stuck in his throat underneath the wad of emotion. Bracing himself, he stepped inside the hospital room.

The former king hadn't requested any special accommodations beyond privacy. There were no flowers or balloons or even cards to add color to the sterile space. Just an assortment of machines and IVs and other medical equipment all too familiar to Carlos, but somehow alien in the context of keeping Enrique Medina alive.

His powerful father was confined to a single bed.

Wearing paisley pajamas, Enrique needed a shave. That alone relayed how ill the old man was even more than his pallor. Even on a secluded island with no kingdom to rule, the deposed monarch had always been meticulous about his appearance.

His father had also lost weight since Carlos's brief visit a couple of months ago for Antonio's wedding. Still stinging from his screwup with Lilah, Carlos hadn't been much in the mood for making merry at a wedding. He'd done his family duty then promptly left with the excuse of a patient in need.

"Mi hijo." A sigh rattled Enrique's chest, and he adjusted the plastic tubes feeding oxygen into his nose. His voice was frail, with only a hint of the authority he'd once carried in booming tones.

"Padre." He swapped to Spanish effortlessly. His father had always spoken their native language with Carlos most often of his sons.

Carlos unhooked the chart from the foot of his father's bed and thumbed through it. "What is this nonsense I hear about you rejecting surgery?"

"I will not survive the operation." Enrique waved dismissively, IV clanking against the metal pole. "I will not put anyone's, most especially my child's, life at risk on such a remote chance."

Looking up from the dire vital stats in front of him in black-and-white, he met his father's eyes unflinchingly. "You're quitting?"

"You are a doctor," he said with a pride Carlos couldn't remember hearing before. Their father had railed at each of his sons for leaving the safety of the island for a wide-open world where any nutcase could assassinate them too. "You have read my chart. You can see how weakened I am. I do not have the will to fight any longer."

Carlos hung the chart carefully on the bed, suppressing the urge to fling the lot across the room in rage. "Listen to me, old man," he bit out carefully. "When I begged you to let me end the pain, you refused. You added more nurses and guards to watch me, to push more treatments and physical therapy and any extreme measures you could find to keep me alive, then get me on my feet again."

Memories of this place, of the torturous rehab sessions he'd endured bombarded him. Of the months in body casts and traction. Of surgery after surgery, pins and steel rods implanted inside him only to be replaced again the next time he grew. And always, the pain, which he could have handled had it not been for the pity stamped on the faces of his caregivers.

He'd finally insisted on solitude whenever possible, gritting through one minute at a time.

"So I will say to you now what you said to me then in the room just next door." He leaned in until they were nearly nose to nose. "You will not give up. A Medina does not surrender."

His father didn't even blink. "It is out of my hands."

"*Idiota,*" Carlos exploded, spinning away and damn near falling on his ass in the process. He grabbed a utility sink for balance, dragging in heaving breaths.

"Carlos," his father's voice ordered with threads of the younger ruler resonating. "I did not bring you up to be disrespectful."

"According to your timetable, I am only days away from becoming the head of this family." The king of nowhere. "So who is going to stop me from saying what I think? Certainly not you."

His father nodded with approval. "You have become tougher over the years."

"I am like you, then."

"Actually, your mother was the truly strong one. But even she could not push me to change my mind."

Mentions of his dead mother stabbed through the last of Carlos's shaky control. "Your plan now isn't any better than your plan then."

"My intent now is as it was then." Enrique's voice faltered. "To protect my children."

Carlos clutched the bed rail in a death grip. "Then don't make us bury another parent prematurely."

The hospital room went silent as his father's pale face turned downright chalky. But damn it all, Carlos would do whatever it took to make his father agree to that transplant.

This life had already stolen too much from their family too early. Unless he persuaded his father to fight, no surgery would stand even a chance of saving him.

A way to tether their father's will more firmly into this world whispered through his brain, a way to have it all. And, yes, he would be manipulating his father in order to keep Lilah, but if that protected both of them? Safeguarded both his father and Lilah? The choice was obvious.

"Stick around and you'll get to meet your grandchild. Your heir."

Regret creased Enrique's weary, weathered face. "Eloisa—"

"I am not talking about her child." He cut his father short. "You'll have to hang on longer than a few weeks for the baby I'm referring to." He took a deep breath in preparation for making that final step and found it easier than he expected. "I've brought someone to the island to meet you—Lilah. She and I are expecting a baby."

Shock, then a deep sadness creased his father's face.

"Son, I am not so ill that I have forgotten your medical history."

"Doctors can be wrong in their dire predictions and hopeless odds." The possibility did exist. Regardless, he would raise her child as his. "And I am living proof. My child is living proof."

He only had to convince Lilah to marry him.

His father's eyes went wide—then watery with emotion. Carlos gathered up his tattered self-control, angry with himself for losing it earlier. Everything was too close to the surface in this place—the island, the clinic.

As much as he ached to be with Lilah tonight, to bury himself in the warm softness of her body, he couldn't risk it. The next time he faced her, he had to have his game plan prepared. If she caught him unaware now, he would combust.

Ten

Lilah bolted upright in her bed.

She searched the dark room lit only by moonbeams piercing the curtains, momentarily disoriented at being in a strange space and unsure what had woken her. The room felt empty, no sounds other than the rolling gush of waves outdoors. She rubbed the slight curve of her stomach as if she could somehow apologize to her baby for disturbing her—his?—slumber as well.

Swinging her feet to the floor, she toe-searched along the dense nap of the antique rug until she found her fuzzy slippers. Eyes adjusting to the darkness, she slid from the high bed, curious and now completely awake. Her sleep had been restless anyway, her imagination painting too vivid a picture of a younger Carlos and his brothers escaping San Rinaldo.

But she refused to get sucked into this extravagant

lifestyle simply because her heart hurt for this family. As much as she truly enjoyed beautiful things, she felt stronger in her own world, where hard work had bought every object in her possession.

She flicked on the bedside lamp, the flood of light confirming she was alone. Where was Carlos now? Asleep in his room on the other side of the sitting area? She hadn't even been able to ask him about what Eloisa had shared. Carlos and his brothers had stayed late at the hospital, visiting with their father. Duarte had called Shannon, who'd passed along the message to the rest of them. Lilah had tried to hide the sting of hurt over Carlos not phoning her directly...then mentally kicked herself for being selfish. He had overwhelming family concerns. This wasn't a pleasure trip.

Still, he could have at least said good-night when he returned.

Snagging her white cotton robe from the bench at the end of her bed, she slipped her arms into the sleeves, covering her matching eyelet nightgown. Carlos's suite was decorated far more starkly than the other quarters she'd seen, much as his Tacoma home provided a bare essentials place to crash. All burgundy leather, deep mahogany wood and brown tones, the space shouted masculinity without even hints of softness to welcome a woman.

As she padded away from her four-poster bed toward the sitting area, she felt the floor vibrate under her bare feet. Again. Again. From music?

She tipped her head to the side, listening more closely to nuances underneath the crash of waves. She swung open the hall door. Melodic runs of a piano swelled from the east wing.

She considered stepping back into her room—or waking up Carlos. But her pride kept her from entering his room when he hadn't bothered to speak to her when he came in.

She stepped farther into the hall. Curious. And determined to tap into her practical lawyer side to find out who was playing, and playing quite masterfully. Nodding to a guard, she continued her search. Hadn't Shannon said she once taught music? If the woman couldn't sleep either, perhaps they could talk more, or she could simply listen until she grew groggy again.

Softly, she followed the hall around corners and down stairs until she stopped outside the almost closed door leading to… She peered inside the circular ballroom she'd only viewed briefly during her tour earlier. Wooden floors stretched across with a coffered ceiling that added texture as well as sound control. Crystal chandeliers and sconces cast shimmering patterns. She looked past the gilded harp to a Steinway grand…

And Carlos?

Not Shannon.

Curiosity melded into something deeper, something more emotional. He sat on the simple black piano bench, his suit jacket and tie discarded over the harp. His gabardine pants were still creased perfectly, a sure sign he hadn't been anywhere near a bed since returning from the hospital.

His face intent, distant, he leaned over the keyboard, his fingers flying across the ivories, playing something classical. Flowing from Carlos's fingertips, the music sounded intense, haunting, so much so she felt the first sting of tears at the tortured passion he milked from every note.

Her feet drew her deeper into the room to a tapestry wingback tucked in a shadowy corner by a stained glass window. She felt closer to him, to the man inside, in this moment than ever before. There were no walls between them now, only raw emotion from someone who'd faced the worst life could dish out and was clawing his way back to the light note by note.

Carlos's hands stilled as the final chord faded. Her breath hitched somewhere between her lungs and throat. She wasn't sure how long she'd been holding it, but hesitated to even exhale for fear of disrupting the mood.

Turning his head slowly, he looked at her over his shoulder. "Sorry to have disturbed you. You were sleeping so soundly when I looked in on you."

He'd come to her room? How long had he watched her? The thought stirred her, knowing he hadn't simply turned in. He'd been concerned, checking, letting her rest. She closed the distance between them with a half-dozen hesitant steps, her slippers whispering across the hardwood floors.

"You didn't bother me. I couldn't sleep," she lied, tracing the curved edge of the Steinway. "How did I never know you played?"

He turned on the wooden bench, his eyes tracking her every movement. "It never came up in conversation. I'm not what you would call chatty."

"That's an understatement." She stared back from the far end of the piano.

Awareness vibrated from him to her like another chord from his fingers.

"What do you want to know, Lilah?"

"Who's your favorite composer?"

"That's it? Your big question?" His bark of laughter cut through the otherwise silent room.

"That's a start."

"Rachmaninoff."

"And you picked him because…?" She walked slowly around the piano toward him again. "Come on, help me out here. Conversation involves more than clipped answers."

"My mother played the piano. He was her favorite to play when she was upset or angry." His fingers hammered out a series of angry chords, then segued into something softer. "When I'm at the piano I can still hear the sound of her voice."

His answer stole the air from her lungs. For a stark man, sometimes he said the most profoundly moving things.

She sat beside him on the bench. "That's beautiful, Carlos. And more than a little heartbreaking."

"Keep up comments like that and I'll stop the sharing game." He picked up the pace until his fingers flew across the keyboard again. "Maybe we can play a game I like to call 'Strip for Secrets'."

She covered his hands with hers, stilling him, the sound fading. "Or you could stop with the games all together and simply talk to me about what's upsetting you. How was your visit with your father?"

"His condition remains unchanged."

Upsetting to be sure, but somehow she hadn't reached the core of what was bothering him, of why he chose to play…. "You're thinking of your mother, maybe?"

As tempted as she was to say to hell with it all and lose herself in his arms, she needed something more first. She needed answers to understanding the man she was considering linking her life with.

The thought stopped her short. She was actually considering his marriage proposal, waiting for a sign that she could trust the feelings building inside her. She waited, letting him find his way as she'd learned long ago there was no pushing this stubborn man into saying or doing anything until he was good and ready.

His hand gravitated back to the keys, rippling a five-finger scale back and forth. "Mother was an artist in a thousand ways and in no way formal. She played the piano by ear. She was an amazing cook but said she learned from watching her mother. And needlework…in spite of having unlimited funds, she knitted blankets."

The low rumble of his voice carried shades of grief, loss and nostalgia in the treasured memories of a lost loved one.

Her heart squeezed with sympathy. "She sounds like a very talented and busy woman."

"Busy?" His eyebrows pinched together. "I never thought of it that way since she was always laid-back, never seemed rushed. But what you say fits with what I remember."

She linked her fingers with his. "How old were you when she died?"

"Thirteen." His squeezed her hand, tightly, the line of his jaw taut. "I prefer to celebrate the way she lived, not dwell on how she died."

Cradling his face, she stroked until the tensed tendons under her fingers eased. "I'm sure she would prefer you treasure those happier memories."

The silence between them stretched with only the

sound of their breathing to fill the vastness of the room and the depth of his loss.

His throat moved in a long swallow before he continued, "I play to remember her because there aren't any home videos or even that many photos of our life as a family. Our father kept us out of the public eye even then as much as he could. He destroyed most of our personal items before we left."

And his life had continued in that stripped-down fashion from his bare-bones office to his stark home... even his place here, understated in comparison to the rest of the opulent mansion. The escape from San Rinaldo had marked this family in so many ways, but Carlos bore physical scars as well.

"Your brothers mentioned gunshot wounds this afternoon. So there wasn't a riding accident."

He shook his head, his answer slower this time. "I was wondering what you would think when that was mentioned earlier."

"Do you want to tell me what happened?"

"You could just access my medical records," he joked lightly.

"Leaving aside the ethics for a moment," she answered seriously, "I wouldn't break your trust that way."

"Ah, Lilah..." He tucked a knuckle under her chin, calluses warm and masculine against her tender skin. "That's why I like you. And believe me, I don't say that lightheartedly."

"Then thank you." She leaned into his hand, deepening the touch, the connection. "I like you, too, most of the time, anyway. Help me understand you so I can like you even more of the time."

He looked away, staring into the open top of the grand

piano at the lines of strings. "I was shot in the back by rebels during our escape from San Rinaldo."

She'd guessed as much from what his brother said earlier, but hearing Carlos confirm it brought the reality of that attack so horribly alive in her mind. "I'm so sorry. I can't even begin to imagine how terrifying and painful that must have been for you."

Still he stared into the piano, his fingers stroking over the ivories without pressing. "Not any more frightening than the kids I treat who've been gunned down in their own neighborhood for no reason other than where they live or what color shirt they wore that day."

He had a point, not that it lessened the horror of what he'd endured. "I guess not."

"I tried to save my mother and I failed. If I'd stepped more to the left... I've replayed that day in my mind so many times and there seem to be a million options I could have taken."

Heartbroken for the young boy he'd been, for the man now, she touched his arm lightly, squeezing the tensed muscle gently. "You were only thirteen."

"At the time I thought I was a man." He glanced at her, his bicep flexing under her touch.

"You must have grown up far too fast that day." Her heart hurt at the image stamped in her mind.

"Stop. I don't want your pity, and I don't want to talk about this anymore."

She flattened her hands to the hard wall of his chest, his heart hammering through his shirt. "How can I know this about you and not be moved? How can I just let it go on command?"

Her defenses were impossible to find, much less resurrect around him. She had to face the fact that it was impossible to stay logical and impartial around Carlos. He pulled her closer until the heat blasting from his body seared through her nightgown, through her skin, deep inside and pooling low.

His head lowered until his breath fanned over her face. "I'll just have to distract you, then."

Smoothly, his mouth covered hers with the familiarity of lovers who knew each other well, who knew just how to touch, stroke, taste and nip to drive the other to the edge. Even just when to hold back and draw that pleasure tighter.

How could a man know her body so well, yet still be such a mystery? She reassured herself that she'd learned more tonight. They were making headway. He'd opened up more tonight than ever before.

And those marriage proposals?

She still didn't know what prompted him to make those offers for a lifetime commitment, but right now, she wanted to focus on the feelings, the connection. Her heart ached for him and all he'd been through. While she refused to let that blind her, she also couldn't look away.

He skimmed aside the shoulder on her robe and gown, exposing her collarbone to his kisses, his hand curving around her breast.

She wasn't as adept as him at shuttling aside tumultuous emotions. So many roiled inside her, she needed an outlet. And regardless of what tomorrow held, she couldn't leave him here alone with his painful memories. "I think it's time to lock that door."

Need for Lilah searing through him, Carlos opened the security panel in the wall beside the door. Every room in the house was equipped with one, a way to lock the doors and seal the windows from any outside intrusion. While his father had installed such extreme safety measures for their protection against everything from hurricanes to an attack, Carlos had an entirely different purpose in mind.

Tapping in codes with as much speed as he'd played the piano, he secured the door with a click and hiss. The windows then darkened until the ballroom became a luxurious—impenetrable—cocoon.

Lilah, seated on the edge of the piano bench, gasped in surprise. "I had no idea. And no one can see inside?"

"This is my home, my dominion," he declared, sauntering toward her. "No one will disturb us. No one can see us. I would never put you at risk. I will keep you safe, always."

The evening spent talking with his father and his brothers was such a mixed bag of familiar and torturous. There was a hole in their family that had never been filled.

A void because he'd failed to keep his mother safe.

And while he knew in his head that he'd been one thirteen-year-old against a small band of rebels, that didn't stop him from feeling, knowing, he should have been able to do more. He'd lived with the knowledge for years, but tonight the memories flayed him raw. More than ever he needed the forgetfulness he knew he could find in Lilah's arms.

Rising, she faced him without hesitation. Her hands fell on his shoulders and he gathered the soft cotton of her nightgown set in his fists. When he saw her pupils widen with desire, he swept the fabric up and over her head. He sent the gown sailing across the room in a white flag of truce, not surrender.

She stood before him, unflinching, proudly naked. His hands trembled ever so slightly as he reached to touch her. Trembled, for God's sake. He was known for his ever-steady control under even the most stressful and lengthy surgeries. But nothing had tapped his composure as deeply as Lilah, her beautiful body and creamy skin on display for him.

Only him.

Possessiveness spread further through him, growing roots until he knew he could never escape the feeling. And right now it became vitally important to make sure she was every bit as consumed by desire as he was.

Cupping her shoulders, he eased her back to the bench, guiding her further still until she reclined with her legs draped over the end. Her eyes flared with understanding a second before he lowered her head. Nudging her knees apart with his shoulders, he stroked up the insides of her thighs, following with slow, deliberate kisses. Her sighs encouraged him.

Aroused him.

Softly, *deliberately,* he nuzzled her through the thin satin barrier of her panties. The scent of her filled him every time he inhaled, which he wanted to do over and over again because nothing, absolutely nothing rivaled her.

He skimmed aside her panties and…yes…tasted her essence, teased her sweet folds. Her back bowed upward as she mumbled sweetly incoherent requests for more. He hooked his arms under her knees and brought her closer, urging her pleasure higher. She gripped his shoulders, her nails cutting half-moons into his flesh. Each husky gasp came faster until she grasped his hair.

"Now," she demanded, "I need you inside me."

No need to tell him twice. "Lucky for us both that's exactly where I want to be."

Kissing her slickened, swollen sex gently once, he eased her feet to the ground again. He stole a lingering look at her, reveling in her dazed eyes, flushed cheeks and tousled hair streaming an auburn flame over the edge of the bench. She'd never looked more beautiful.

She arched upward and he caught her around the waist, shifting her onto the keyboard in a jangled chord. She yanked at his pants with frantic hands, tearing at his zipper until she freed his throbbing length. Bracing his hand behind her on the piano, he thrust inside. Her moist heat clamped around him in sync with her legs locked around his waist. Her heels dug into his buttocks as he thrust again and again.

Their speeding hearts, breaths and sighs mixed with the Steinway's own tune. He let her transport him from this room, from the island and the memories slamming into him from all directions. With each incredible grip of her silken body, stroke of her hands, he realized he'd approached things all wrong with Lilah. He'd thought by shutting her out he could avoid the past. Instead, with Lilah like this, the hell of it faded to the back of his mind. If he could stay with her, inside her, he could shut the rest out.

She clenched around him as her release built, increased until she flung her head back. Her cry of pleasure echoed into the domed ceiling. Hearing her, watching her—feeling her—unravel in his arms snapped the last thread of restraint in him. He pulsed inside her, deeply, fully, and somehow nowhere near enough because already he wanted her again.

Holding her as aftershocks snapped through him, he gathered her close and sank to the piano bench with her in his lap. He smoothed her hair and whispered along her brow how much she moved him, other words he couldn't form or remember, except that some poet inside him had come to life with her.

The feel of her against him, perspiration slicking her skin and sealing her to him, felt so damn right. He skimmed his hands down her back and soaked in the leisurely pleasure of her pressed to him, her breasts, her hips... Her stomach curved ever so slightly and he realized... Her pregnancy was beginning to show. Medically, he knew all the stages and changes she would undergo. But for the first time, he allowed himself to think of experiencing that miracle in an up close and personal way.

As a father.

Something shifted inside him and he slid a hand between them, splaying across her stomach, her child. He felt the weight of her gaze on him and looked up. She stared back with an open vulnerability that sucker punched him. In that moment, she was his old friend, his lover now, the soon-to-be mother of his child, and he had to have her.

The warmth in her eyes all but unraveled him. But he couldn't lose focus, not when he needed her in his life for so many reasons.

He would do anything, say anything, pretend to be the man she seemed to want if that's what it took to persuade her to stay.

Eleven

Lounging in the overlarge tub in her suite, Lilah leaned back against Carlos's chest. His long legs stretched on either side of hers with rose petals floating in the water, scenting the air. She'd never seen a place with so many fresh flowers around every corner, even vases alongside the LCD screen and sound system currently piping Beethoven into their tiled retreat.

Two brandy snifters filled with milk sat on a silver platter beside the marble tub. He'd insisted that if she couldn't drink alcohol, then he would abstain as well. The silly gesture touched her as fully as his hands.

He'd made such intense love to her in the music room, and again in her bed before they'd migrated to the spacious bath. Her wary heart wondered if maybe, just maybe, she could trust what they shared. Hopefully he'd resolved whatever freaked him out that first night they'd been together. Without question, Carlos carried heavy baggage from his past. That had to have left some emotional marks.

But as long as they kept open lines of communication, maybe they really had a shot at working this out. Counting on that honesty between them calmed her own fears of ending up like her parents. It had to. Because heaven help her, if Carlos asked her to marry her again, she wouldn't be able to say no.

He swept his foot under the brass faucet, activating the electronic fixture. Warm water flowed into their cooling bath.

What would she have done if he'd proposed right after she told him about the baby? Her hand tightened on his knee. She liked to think she would have told him to take his dutiful proposal and shove it after the way he'd acted. She needed—and deserved—confirmation that he held deep feelings for her, not just because she carried his baby.

Nestled against his chest, she wanted to roll out her thoughts, test their newfound truce, but concerns for his father had to take precedence. No wonder he'd been pouring his heart out through his music.

She stroked up his leg and reached through the rose-covered surface of the water, folding her hand over his cupping the snifter. "The way you played—" her fingers caressed the rougher texture of his "—your hands on the keyboard, it was magical. You're quite accomplished."

"There wasn't much else for me to do during my teenage years. Between surgeries..." His voice rumbled his chest against her back, his low words mingling with the sound of water shooshing from the faucet. "My father had the music room built to be airy, open and bright, like being outside."

"Apparently you spent a lot of time practicing." Pouring out his pain, his loss, his frustration onto the keyboard? What a heart-wrenching image.

"More than average." He brought the goblet of milk to her mouth for a sip. "One especially hot July day, my brothers surprised me by showing up with wheelchairs they'd lifted from the island clinic. They nailed a basketball goal right in the middle of one of our father's murals and gave 'ballroom' a whole new meaning."

She tried to laugh with him, but her mind hitched on one telling word. "Wheelchairs? You were in a wheelchair?"

With careful deliberation, he swept his foot under the electronic sensor again and shut off the water. "For a while, the doctors weren't sure whether or not I would walk again."

"How long is awhile?" she pressed gently.

"Three years before I was on my feet again. Seven more years of surgeries after that." He reached for his milk abruptly and drained the glass.

"Carlos..." she gasped, at a loss, overwhelmed by what he must have gone through. "I had no idea." She tried to turn, to face him, to comfort him, but he locked her in place with one arm around her.

He set aside his snifter and slid his hand over her stomach. "Let's talk about something else instead. You're learning a lot of my crummy past. How about you share up some things about yourself?"

"Strip for Secrets doesn't work when we're already naked."

"I have plenty of other enticements to offer." His

hand dipped below the water, between her legs for a languorous caress.

His obvious attempt to change the subject didn't escape her notice—even though it was growing difficult to think of anything but the talented tease of his fingers.

She angled back to kiss his jaw. "What do you want to know?"

Laughing softly, he moved his hand to her stomach again. "Are you hoping for a boy or girl?"

And, wow, he'd chosen his distracting topic well, because finally they were talking about their child in a way she'd barely dared dream.

"I haven't thought about that one way or the other." She held his hand over her stomach just as she'd done earlier around the goblet of milk. "The baby already is what he or she is."

His fingers circled lightly along her skin. "Are you planning to find out during the ultrasound?"

"It doesn't matter to me either way." She forced herself to relax, to grow comfortable with his hand curving over her stomach as if it belonged there. "Are you hoping for a boy?"

Just yesterday he'd said he wanted the baby to be his. Was he finally settling into the reality of being a father after all? She could see how he would have grown leery of hope after such traumatic teenage years. At the hospital, she'd witnessed more than one patient become cynical to the point of losing reasonable perspective.

If only she'd known more about Carlos's past from the start.

His deep inhale pressed against her back before he

finally answered, "I don't have any preferences other than that the child be healthy."

"We're in agreement on that." She swirled her fingers through the water, swirling red petals before her hand fell to rest on top of his again. "Well then, do you have name preferences?"

"The Medinas typically pull from the family tree."

Everything she'd learned since coming to the island had shed such light, helping her understand this enigmatic man. Did she dare push further? Yet, how could she not when this could be her only window of time? "Your mother's name was Beatriz, right?"

"She didn't care much for her name. She said it sounded too old-fashioned."

"And what about boy names?"

"My family tree is filled with relatives. We have plenty to choose from."

We? Her heart raced against her ribs. "We'll have to make a list."

"What about your family?" He skimmed a kiss across her temple, brushing aside a stray curl that had fallen from the loose bundle on her head. "Any names you wish to use?"

The water went chilly again. "Not really." She toed the drain to release some water and activated the brass faucet again, grateful for what had to be the world's largest hot water tank. "We aren't estranged or anything. My brothers and I keep in touch, but we're not what I would call close. We exchange emails, speak a couple of times a year. I try to make it for special occasions in my nieces' and nephews' lives. But we're not all taking family vacations together by any stretch."

"You've done an admirable job in setting up what

works best for everyone," he said, his tone non-judgmental, another characteristic she liked about him. "Have you told your family about the baby yet?"

"My parents are away on their fifteenth honeymoon."

"Fifteenth anniversary? I didn't realize you had a stepparent."

"No, you heard correctly." She really didn't want to think about this now, but she'd demanded so much from him tonight. She owed him the same consideration. "They're both my biological parents, and it's their fifteenth honeymoon, not fifteenth anniversary. You've heard of couples rekindling the romance with a second honeymoon? Well, my parents are on their fifteenth reconciliation."

"Sounds like they've had a rocky go of it," he offered up another diplomatic answer.

"That's putting things mildly." She sat upright, hugging her knees, all of a sudden weary of dancing around the truth. "My father cheats. My mother forgives him. They go on an elaborately romantic getaway that puts stars back in my mother's eyes until the next time he strays and the cycle starts all over again."

His strong arms went around her, muscles twitching with restraint as he held her gently. "They've hurt you."

"In the past? Yes. Now I'm mostly...numb, I guess you could say." She rested her cheek against his forearm. "When it comes to the two of them, nothing surprises me anymore."

"That's why you were so upset when you bumped into Nancy outside my office."

"And don't forget the airport."

He turned off the water and pulled her to her feet in a fluid movement. Facing her dripping wet and naked, water pooling around their toes on the warmed tiles, he stared directly into her eyes. "I may have gone out with her but I never slept with her. You kept getting in the way."

"What do you mean?" She needed to hear him say it, to spell out every single thought as salve for her wounded ego and hope for her wary heart.

Carlos gripped her shoulders in his broad palms. "She's a perfectly nice and attractive woman, but she bored the hell out of me because she wasn't you."

"You're just saying that to get into my good graces." Although right now she wasn't sure why he would work so hard for that. They were already sleeping together again. And, sure, she hadn't agreed to his proposals, but they had time now.

"I'm sorry your father has made it difficult for you to trust what I say." He'd touched too close to the truth, like poking his surgeon finger right into an open wound.

She snatched up a towel from the warming drawer and tucked it tight under her arms. "Don't put this off on him, and don't blame it on some hang-up I may have." She thrust another towel at him, reminded too vividly of when she'd confronted him in the hospital shower. "You are the one who refused to speak to me after the Christmas party."

"I did what I thought was best for you." He knotted the towel over one hip.

"Easier for you, you mean." How had this conversation gone so wrong so fast? Was she sabotaging herself? Scared to take the happiness just an arm's reach away?

"Then let's make this right." He clasped her shoulders

again to keep her from racing away from him. "Forget taking any paternity tests. I accept the baby is mine and I want us to be married. Tomorrow. No more waiting. We can have the ceremony performed in my father's hospital room."

No paternity test?

He believed her.

Finally, she heard the words she'd been hoping for from the beginning. Almost everything. He hadn't said he loved her. But then her father threw the word *love* around like pennies in a fountain. Cheap and easy to come by. Carlos was offering her something far more precious and tangible. He was offering her the truth.

Drawing in a bracing breath, she took the biggest gamble of her life and placed her hand in his. "Call the preacher." As the words fells from her lips, she tried like hell not to think of the morning after they'd made love for the first time nearly three months ago.

Lilah reached for Carlos, called his name softly as she woke…but her hand found nothing but cool cotton sheets and emptiness on his side of the bed. She might have thought the whole crazy night with him after the fundraiser had been a dream. But her body carried reminders of their impetuous lovemaking, from the tender muscles of her legs after their near acrobatics on his office desk to the scent of chlorine in her hair from his hot tub on the deck of his mountainside home.

How appropriate he should live on a cliff, how in keeping with the edginess of the man himself.

She stretched her arms overhead, her eyes adjusting to the dim room lit only with a few pale streaks of morning sun. Not that she could afford to lounge around. In a Tacoma winter it could be nearly eight in the morning already.

Her toes protesting the chilly hardwood floors, she searched for something more appropriate to wear than a sheet or her evening gown currently crumpled in a corner. She'd kicked the designer dress off and away in her frenzy to be with Carlos again, in his bed, then in the hot tub, before returning to his room, certain she was too exhausted for more. Only to have him prove her wrong.

A smile on her lips, she plucked his tuxedo shirt off the bedside lamp. Apparently she'd thrown his clothes around too. The crisp fabric still carried his scent, stirring her all over again with languid memories of making love until the blend of them together made a sensual perfume.

She found him in his kitchen, another simple room with the bare essentials—stainless steel appliances with black-and-white tiles.

And one hot chef wearing only a low-slung pair of scrubs that showcased his taut butt as perfectly as any tailored tux.

The scent of frying bacon hung in the air as he tended the stove, a second pan in place with batter in a measuring cup.

He pivoted toward her. And with one look at his emotionless eyes, the stark set of his jaw, all the warmth seeped from her. He took in her standing there in his shirt and…nothing. He didn't smile. He didn't reach for her.

Carlos simply turned away. "Do you want breakfast?"

She wanted to tell him to go to hell. Instead she said, "I think it's best if I just go."

Still, like a fool, she hesitated, giving him a chance to say something softer, nicer. Instead, he just opened the refrigerator and pulled out a carton of milk.

Apparently last night had been a dream after all, and it was time for her to wake up....

Unable to sleep, Lilah inched from Carlos's bed, the one in his father's mansion. Although the past and present felt strangely merged at the moment with memories of that wretched morning after hammering in her head.

Careful not to disturb Carlos, she reached into her purse on the bedside table and fished free her cell phone. The scent of roses from their bath filled the room, a much sweeter scent than those chlorine-tinted recollections.

Things were different now, damn it. All the same, she resisted the temptation to crawl under the covers and spoon against his back. She needed to take care of a niggling detail.

Before she surrendered her guard fully to her future husband, she needed to call her parents.

Tiptoeing, she left the room, closing the door softly, before curling up in the window seat to place her call, nerves pattering. She knew they would be happy, but she'd put off the conversation because she had a tough time reconciling herself to a lifetime with a man who had held back from her in so many ways, a man who would never have chosen this life for himself if she hadn't gotten pregnant. She thumbed "seven" on her speed dial and waited through so many rings she almost gave up. Then—

"Hello?" Her mother's voice cut through the static of the distant connection of her parents' "anniversary" cruise. She hadn't been exactly truthful when she'd told Carlos she couldn't call them. It had been one thing to hold the baby news close for a while, another matter to keep an established pregnancy and an impending wedding from her mother.

"Mom, it's me." She hugged her knees, her nightgown draping her legs.

"Lilah, honey, it's so great to hear your voice," her mother said enthusiastically, not even mentioning the hour or how the call must have woken her. "Let me get your father on the phone too."

"Mom, no, really." Her head fell to rest against the warm windowpane. "You don't need to disturb him."

"Don't be silly." Her voice faded as she must have pulled the receiver from her face. "Darren? Darren, wake up. It's Lilah."

Her father's voice rumbled along with the rustle of sheets in their cruise ship cabin. How her parents managed to stay together she couldn't imagine and didn't want to dwell on overlong with her own hastily conceived wedding on the horizon.

"Okay," her mother said, back on the line. "I'm switching you to speakerphone."

"Mornin', pumpkin," her father said groggily.

There wasn't a breath deep enough to prepare her to say the words she never thought she would say to her parents. "Mom, Dad, I'm getting married...."

* * *

His wedding day was overcast, but he was a man of science, not superstition.

Carlos stood by his father's hospital bed in the island clinic, Lilah beside him. His brothers, his sister and their significant others gathered in a corner. Limited visitation rules were out the window for the duration of what promised to be the shortest service on record. A priest waited at the foot of the bed, looking a bit confused as to whether he'd been called for last rites rather than a marriage.

Enrique struggled to sit up straighter. "Are you sure you want to do this?"

Startled, Carlos looked at his father, then realized the old man was speaking to Antonio. The youngest Medina son was the donor match—he would give a lobe of his liver—he would save their father's life. Something Carlos couldn't do in spite of all his medical degrees.

"Absolutely certain," Antonio answered from beside his wife.

Enrique slid the pocket watch from his bedside table. "You used to play with this when you were a boy. I want you to have it. It is a small thing to give you in exchange for a piece of your liver—"

"Thank you. I'll keep it until you're well enough to need it again." Antonio took the watch, swallowing hard before giving his father a brisk but heartfelt hug. "Besides, you pretty much gave me my liver in the first place."

"You are a strange boy." Enrique shook his head, then wheezed for air. His face pale, he continued haltingly, "And Carlos, I have something of yours, *mi hijo*."

Enrique extended a gnarled hand, a black velvet

box in his grip. Carlos didn't even have to open it to know what rested inside…his mother's wedding rings, a platinum diamond set, meant to be worn by a queen. Meant to be worn by Lilah. He was still stunned she'd actually agreed.

The wary hope in her eyes when she'd said yes made him feel like a first-class ass. He wasn't the romantic hero she dreamed of. He wasn't wired that way, a flaw in himself he'd known from the start. But it was too late to protect her from that any longer. They were tied to each other through the fragile life inside her, and he would do his best to make sure she never realized the bad deal she'd made. Taking the box from his father, Carlos turned to Lilah with a king's ransom worth of gems in his hand.

Twelve

Lilah twisted the platinum diamond ring set around and around on her finger, hardly able to process all that had happened in the past thirty-six hours since she and Carlos had exchanged "I Dos" at the island clinic. Now, she and most of the Medinas paced in a private waiting area at the Jacksonville hospital where Enrique had been transferred for his transplant.

While she wasn't a big fan of preferential treatment, she understood how much mayhem their presence would have caused had they been placed in the public waiting area. The Medina fame should not intrude on someone else's crisis.

And she had to admit the quiet for their own emergency was helpful. Her nerves were fried. In her job as a hospital administrator, she'd witnessed so many families facing similar ordeals, but she'd never been on this side of the surgery.

Tests, doctors, plans had filled the past day and a half to the point of exhaustion. For the two nights prior, she and Carlos had made intense love before falling asleep. Any honeymoon plans, even any talking would have to wait. Right now their world was tightly focused into these four walls, with antiseptic air and bad coffee.

The door opened and Antonio's wife, Shannon, walked into the waiting room. She'd been sitting with her husband as he awaited surgery. "Enrique would like to see you."

Carlos, Duarte and Eloisa stood in sync from the steel and pleather sofa.

"No..." Shannon shook her head. "He wants to see Lilah."

Surprise held her still as a Red Cross volunteer pushed a cart full of books and magazines past the open door.

"Me?" Lilah asked. "Are you sure?"

"Absolutely," Shannon said, tucking a limp strand of blond hair back into her hair clamp.

Carlos, her *husband*—how strange that word still felt—shot her a quizzical look before squeezing her hand with encouragement. Standing, she smoothed her dress. While she'd met Enrique just before the surreal wedding ceremony in his room at the island clinic, there hadn't been much time for "get to know you" chats.

A lump lodged in her chest as she realized this could be her only opportunity to speak to him.

She scrounged for composure as she walked closer to the ICU room in front of the nurse's station. Tapping on the door, she waited, the low murmur of staff mingling with the *beep, beep, beep* of medical equipment.

Through the glass window, she saw the critically ill king with a nurse sitting vigil. Enrique raised a hand, IV taped in place, and waved her into the room weakly.

The nurse excused herself quietly and shifted her post to the hall side of the window. Lilah stepped deeper inside the ICU unit.

"Shannon said you wanted to see me." She wasn't sure what to call him. "Your Majesty" seemed awkward given they were relatives.

"You may call me *Padre,* like my boys do," he said in a raspy voice as if reading her mind. Or perhaps he was just an intuitive man. "Sit."

Sit? She stifled a smile at his brusque order, so like his son. Lilah settled into the chair beside his bed. "What did you wish to speak to me about?"

"You are a lawyer. Look at this." He pointed to a folder on the bedside table.

Curious, confused, she opened the manila folder and found… "Your will?"

"I want you to read over it," he insisted.

Clasping the papers to her chest, she studied his eyes for some clue as to why he'd made such a surprise request. "You must have the best of attorneys. Why are asking me to review it?"

"Do not worry. I am not suffering from diminished capacity," he said with a wry grin, his eyes sharp in spite of his critically ill state.

"Your sense of humor is certainly still intact, even if it is a bit twisted." She tapped the folder. "I will read your will if that's what you wish."

"I do." He nodded once. "And before I go into surgery I want to dictate an amendment. I need you to witness it."

The legalese of a king's last will and testament had to be intense. There hadn't been a class on this in law school, and it wasn't something she'd come across in Tacoma, Washington. "Again, I will advise you that you have attorneys in place who are far better versed in your holdings and unique situation."

"Are you going to ask me about the amendment?"

"You will tell me when you're ready." She pulled the pen clipped to the top of the folder and found a legal pad underneath the typed pages.

"You are a patient woman, a necessary quality when dealing with Carlos."

She met and held his eyes. "I hope your decision to have the surgery gives you both a second chance."

"He did not leave me much choice when he told me about the baby you are carrying. I never thought I would live to see Carlos's child." The old man's dark eyes blurred with unshed tears. "While nothing can erase what happened to my Beatriz and to Carlos, there is healing in knowing my decision to send my family away did not cost Carlos everything."

Lilah struggled to process that, but her brain was still stuck on the first part. He knew about the baby? She and Carlos had agreed to wait until after the surgery to tell his family. Hadn't that meant waiting to tell his father too? Perhaps she'd misunderstood Carlos.

And she really hoped she'd misunderstood Enrique.

Ungluing her tongue from the roof of her mouth, she sought clarification. "He told you about the baby to persuade you to have the transplant surgery?"

A smile kicked into one cheek, a laugh rumbling the old monarch's chest until he began coughing. A tear trickled free and he brushed it aside with an impatient swipe. "He certainly did, the very second he set foot on the island. I have to admit I did not think anything could convince me, but Carlos, he is every bit as Machiavellian as his father. Now let us go about writing that child into my will, even though it is my heartfelt hope that I will survive this procedure."

And Carlos hadn't once mentioned to her that he'd twisted the king's arm. If he'd even hinted as much to her—if Carlos had shared anything of his heart and his feelings about his father's grave condition—she might have been able to overlook the fact that he was walling her out emotionally. But she hadn't been given access to Carlos's heart any more than ever. It was like he was still staring at her across that kitchen with the scent of frying bacon in the air and his cold, cold eyes warning her what they shared hadn't meant all that much to him.

As they'd flown to the island, she'd wondered what he wanted from her. Now she knew.

Bottom line, he'd used her.

The wary optimism she'd been feeling since exchanging vows faltered at Enrique's words. Had every one of those proposals been about fulfilling a dying father's wish to see his son settled? About giving Enrique a reason to hang on?

She'd thought the lack of love talk from Carlos meant nothing. That his actions spoke louder. And, sadly, that was true. With Enrique's revelation still fresh on her ears, she knew. Carlos had only married her to ensure his father would have the surgery, that he would fight to live.

How ironic. She wasn't so different from her mother, after all. In spite of all her best intentions she'd allowed herself to be blinded by her feelings for Carlos. And

God, yes, even with hurt and anger coursing through her, she couldn't deny how deeply she loved Carlos Medina. Her husband. The father of her child.

She also couldn't deny the truth staring her in the face. Her marriage was a sham.

Nine hours later, Carlos sagged back in his seat in relief as his father's surgeons left the waiting area. The procedure was a success. Both his father and Antonio were in stable condition. Enrique wasn't out of the woods, but he'd made it over a substantial hurdle.

Eloisa cried tears of relief on her husband's shoulder. Even reserved Duarte was smiling, hugging his fiancée hard. Shannon was already sitting with Antonio in recovery.

Carlos turned to his new bride. Finally, finally, they could celebrate. Her brittle smile gave him pause. Something had been off with Lilah since she'd returned from his father's room. But she'd denied as much, telling him she was simply concerned about Enrique. That they should all focus on the surgery and nothing else. And he had. For nine long, gut-wrenching hours, that had been all he'd thought about.

But with the good news from the king's doctor easing his fears for his father, Carlos now had the clarity to see something was definitely wrong.

She touched his knee lightly. "I'm glad your father and brother both came through so well. If you don't need me anymore, I would like to go back to the hotel."

"You must be tired." He hadn't considered what a physical toll this would take on a pregnant woman. As a doctor, he should have known better. He should have been looking out for her. "Of course. I'll drive you over."

"It's okay." She flinched away from his touch. "I can get there on my own. You stay here where you're needed."

Before he could sort through her words, she started down the tiled corridor, weaving around an aide rolling a laundry cart. What the hell was going on?

She hadn't said anything specific that he could fault. She had every reason in the world to be exhausted. But in the short span of their marriage, not once had she left his side without a kiss. A squeeze of his hand. Some gesture of warmth he'd already grown accustomed to. Now, something in her eyes shouted anger.

Hurt.

And he'd seen that look in her eyes before, a little less than three months ago. She'd stepped into his kitchen—wearing his shirt and looking so damn right in his clothes, in his house, in his life that he'd lost it. He'd shut her out.

Hell. He'd done exactly what he was doing now. He was letting her walk away.

Carlos charged after her, cursing under his breath at his bum leg that made catching her painful and slow.

Finally, he called out, bracing a hand against the hall wall. "Lilah? Lilah, stop."

She slowed and turned silently beside the gleaming stained glass of the hospital chapel door.

Limping, he closed the distance between them in the deserted late-night corridor. "What's really going on here?"

"Just what I said." She folded her arms over her chest,

pulling her cotton dress tighter over her full breasts. "I'm returning to the hotel."

"Wait and I'll come with you," he repeated his offer from earlier.

"There's no need to pretend anymore, Carlos." Her voice was low and tight, her emerald eyes so sad they sliced right through him. "I'm not going to spill the beans to a critically ill man."

Unease scratched at his gut. "I'm not sure I understand what you mean."

Blinking fast, she looked around impatiently, then tugged him into the chapel. Her eyes glinted with a deep hurt. "Your father told me how you persuaded him to get the surgery. How you gave him hope with this baby."

He couldn't deny what she'd said, but he needed to figure out something to diffuse the sadness radiating off her. "Is it so wrong to want to do whatever it takes to give my father a reason to live?"

"Whatever it takes?" She laughed once but her face was devoid of any humor. "We shouldn't have this discussion now. We're both wiped out, and you should be with your family."

"I'm here with you."

"For how long?" She stopped short and held up her hands, a row of candles behind her casting a glow around her. "Forget I said that."

"No," he said tightly. Yes, he'd maneuvered the situation, but in a way that was best for everyone. "We got married, and pardon me if I don't see where that makes me a bad guy."

She backed away from him, deeper into the dimly lit chapel. "I blame myself, too, you know. I was so gullible in believing your quick turnaround in accepting the baby. I mean really, it's only been what? Less than a week since I confronted you in your office and you denied your own child."

Her tearful words pierced through bit by bit until he realized... "You actually believe I had some ulterior motive for marrying you?"

"Your father refuses to have surgery, then you magically give him a reason to live, thanks to this life inside me that you've never felt any connection to at all." She clutched the end of a wooden pew.

He couldn't even refute her. She was a woman of honor and he'd treated her so dishonorably he was ashamed. He'd thrown away this chance to have a life with the child he'd never thought he would have and the loss gutted him. This offspring would be an even greater miracle than his recovering the use of his legs, and instead of doing everything in his power to ensure that child's future, he'd spent the last week driving away the woman who carried his legacy.

"Lilah, I'm sorry," he said simply, sincerely.

"Well, Carlos." She backed away. "You're a little too late, because I'm not so sure I can believe you anymore."

Stunned by the way the day had gone sour so quickly, he watched her turn away, clearly dismissing him. Leaving him with no room for doubt.

His new bride had dumped him.

As Carlos's uneven footsteps faded, Lilah sank onto a wooden pew, her legs giving out. She raked her wrist under her nose, sniffling up the tears and getting a noseful of scented smoke from the half-dozen candles burning by the door. Had she really just tossed away her husband of two days?

She'd kept her silence during the surgery and had planned to wait before packing her bags. Except Carlos had pressed her until the words fell out, until finally she was honest with him the way she should have been right from the start. She never should have stayed silent for months.

What a mess she'd made of her life. She thumbed the wedding set around and around on her finger, the beautiful rings that had come with such hope. A family heirloom that also cost a fortune and didn't belong to her. She needed to return it before she left the hospital.

Stretching her legs out on the pew, she studied the diamonds sparkling as they caught and reflected the stained glass windows. She stared until her eyes grew heavy and closed as sleep drew her in. This time, she knew there wouldn't be any dreams of Carlos waiting to greet her.

The argument with Lilah still reverberating in his head, Carlos watched his baby brother sleep, sitting vigil to give his sister-in-law a break. Sure, Antonio was only eight years younger, but Carlos still saw the kid he'd been when they left San Rinaldo. Carlos held the gold pocket watch in his hand, turning it over and over, remembering another night when their father had given Antonio the antique. They'd been preparing to leave San Rinaldo, and Enrique had told his youngest son to safeguard the timepiece until they met up again.

That long ago day, Antonio had clutched it while wrapping himself in that pewter-colored afghan, telling his brothers the blanket was his shield. The watch was his treasure. He'd been a child trying to find a frame of reference for the unimaginable.

Then the attack had come just two blocks before they reached the ship that was supposed to carry them away from San Rinaldo. They'd been in a park, such a benign place. Duarte and Antonio had thought they were deep in a forest, but their childish minds had misperceived. They'd been so small, everything must have appeared larger than from Carlos's teenage perspective.

Still, when the attack had started, he'd told Duarte to watch over Antonio. And he, as the oldest, would protect their mother. Duarte had succeeded. Carlos had failed. Now, Antonio had saved their father. The baby boy of the Medina family wasn't so little anymore. Antonio filled the bed with his bulk, an avid outdoorsman even now that he could kick back in an office if he so chose.

They'd all come a long way since that nightmare escape from San Rinaldo. Yet, at the moment, he could have sworn he was still stuck there, in that day, with a home and family he could never have back.

Was it any wonder he'd screwed up so badly with Lilah?

His brother's eyes opened heavily, cutting short maudlin thoughts.

Carlos forced a smile and placed the watch on the end table by a cup of ice chips. "Welcome back."

"Our father?" he croaked out, rustling the sheets with slow shifting, followed by a wince.

"Is fine. Resting comfortably. As you should be doing." Carlos passed the cup of ice shavings to dampen Antonio's mouth until his doctor gave the okay for drinking again. "You, my brother, look like hell."

"Is that any way to talk to the guy who saved the day?" Antonio joked in a raspy voice.

"Ah, now I know you're all right."

"Damn straight." He laughed, then coughed with another wince. "Thanks for sitting with me, but don't you have a new bride to spend time with?"

"She's, uh, resting at the hotel."

Antonio's eyebrow shot up, his gaze unexpectedly clear. Canny. Too damn shrewd. "You're a really crummy liar."

"And you're a crummy patient." He passed his brother a small pillow. "Hold this against your incision when you cough. Coughing is good, expands your lungs and keeps you from getting pneumonia. Practice while I find Shannon." He started to stand.

Antonio clamped a hand on his wrist, his grip surprisingly strong for a guy who'd just been through major surgery. "What's wrong? And don't dodge. We know each other too well. You go into doctor mode whenever you're uncomfortable."

His baby brother most definitely wasn't a kid anymore. Still, Carlos didn't want to unload his problems on someone in his brother's condition. Although it was unlikely Antonio would even remember given residual anesthesia still seeped through his system.

And hell, he didn't know what to say to Lilah back at the hotel anyhow.

Carlos sank back into his seat. "Lilah thinks I married her just to make our father have the surgery."

"Did you?" Antonio asked. "I'm not judging. Just wondering."

"Partly. But not fully." Carlos looked at his clasped

hands. "She's pregnant. Apparently I'm not shooting blanks anymore."

"Congratulations, my brother." He raised a fist, woozily, but steady enough to be bumped by Carlos's fist in salute. "So I'm guessing you forgot to tell her you love her. It might not be obvious to the world at large, but to your family it's apparent how far gone you are for her."

His eyes slammed shut. Of course he was. Of course he had been since that morning after the fundraiser when he'd run scared from how Lilah tore down walls inside him, how she forced him to step out of the shadows of the past and face the future. Face the risk of loving, of possibly losing that person.

Because, hell yes, he loved her, with a fierceness that rocked him.

"Far gone? That I am." He couldn't avoid the truth in his brother's words. "What makes you think I botched the proposal?"

"You're a brilliant surgeon and a gifted musician, but when it comes to words?" Antonio shook his head on the pillow. "The years you spent in the hospital cost you communication skills."

Carlos resisted the urge to snap a sarcastic comment. He'd had enough of people raking him over the coals for one day. Standing, he glanced at his brother's vitals, happy to distance himself with the role of doctor. "You should rest."

"And you should listen to me." His gravelly voice carried an undeniable authority. "Women like to hear the words. Unless you are afraid to say it."

Carlos raised an eyebrow. "Calling me a chicken isn't going to work. We're not kids on a playground."

"Granted…" Antonio paused for another cough. "But I can't forget the way it motivated me."

"Pardon?" Was the anesthesia making his brother incoherent? If so, did that mean he could disregard the love advice too?

Antonio set aside the pillow. "That day we were leaving San Rinaldo."

"I still don't know what you mean." His memories of that day were full of blood and pain. "I just remember… Mother."

His brother nodded shortly, his face creased with an agony that clearly had nothing to do with incisions or surgery. "But after she died, you got us out of there. You kept us going, even told me to stop being a chicken and move my ass. Duarte and I would have died without you that day." The steady beep of his heartbeat on the monitor filled the silence as he swallowed another ice chip. "I understand it chaps your hide that you weren't the one to give an organ to save our dad. But, hell, Carlos, you can't be the hero all the time. It doesn't hurt to be a regular guy every now and again."

He hadn't thought of it in quite those terms, but his brother's words resonated. Since their escape, he'd been trapped in the past. Trying to save others, save his father, somehow erase the time he'd failed to save his mother. He'd allowed that day to put a wall between him and moving forward with a normal life.

And he'd allowed that wall to block him from seeing what was right in front of his face—an amazing woman to love. He loved Lilah Anderson Medina, and the time had come to not only show her, but to tell her.

And he wouldn't stop until she believed him.

* * *

Lilah was certain she must be dreaming. Otherwise, how could she be looking into a face full of love?

But the hard church pew hurting her hip felt uncomfortably real enough. She blinked fast to clear her eyes and still Carlos sat beside her, his arms crossed as if he'd been waiting for her to wake. The scent of knotty pine pervaded the chapel. The warm wood walls and rafters remained unvarnished, reminding her of the cabin in Vail where she and Carlos had started this journey.

Sitting up, she scraped her hair back from her face. "Carlos? How long have you been here? Is everything all right with your father and Antonio?"

It must be okay or he wouldn't look so…at peace. "Everyone is fine, all asleep in fact. It's been a long few days. But that's no excuse for the way I handled things with you."

Her heart tripped over itself, but she couldn't allow herself to turn to mush. She needed something more from him this time. She couldn't settle for half measures and avoidance of what really mattered. Her baby deserved better.

She deserved better. "What exactly do you mean?"

"Going to make me work for this, are you? Good for you." He lifted her left hand, thumbing her wedding rings. "I've messed this up from the start, from the way I ran scared from how I felt about you to the way I asked you to marry me. I'm sorry for that. More sorry than can be put into words, but I'm going to try my best."

"Words are good." They both were such workaholic, type A people, neither of them had slowed down long enough to say some important things along the way.

Hope built inside her. She'd slept away some of the anger, enough to listen with a more open heart.

He skimmed a kiss over her knuckles. "I want to be your husband now and always. Not because of my father, but because my life is so empty without you. I will be here for you and our baby every day of my life. I can't promise not to brood, but I vow to share all those brooding thoughts."

The deep tone of commitment in his voice, in his words, bowled her over. This was so much more than she'd ever expected, more than she'd dreamed she might find with such a reserved man.

"Brooding is okay every now and again." She squeezed his hand, encouraging him to continue. After waiting so long for a sign from him, she intended to soak up every second of this.

"I appreciate the way you keep me from sinking too far into that abyss. From losing myself in my work until I'm no good to anyone." His deep voice rumbled low, echoing gently around the empty chapel. "More than my lover, my wife, the mother of my child, you are my friend. You're the one person standing between me and a life of supreme loneliness."

Happy tears clogged her throat for a moment before she could push words free. "Wow, for a man of few words, you're quite poetic when you choose to be. Perhaps some of that artist in you is showing as it does when you play the piano."

"After being scared to death over the thought of losing you, I'm finding it much easier than I expected to be poetic for the woman I love."

Love.

Of all the words he could have chosen, that was the

one she needed to hear most. The one she wasn't sure he would ever voice. But as she looked at the emotion burning strong in his eyes, she didn't doubt him for a second.

"Carlos, I wish I could offer words as beautiful as yours, but right now all I can think about is how relieved I am that we figured this out, that we got it right, because I love you too."

She cradled his face, savoring the bristle of his unshaven cheek, the curve of his smile against her touch. And as she tipped her forehead to his, forging a connection she knew would last a lifetime, she found the right words coming to her. "I adore everything about you, from your brilliant mind to the feel of your hands when we're together. From the way you remember chocolate mint milkshakes to how you devote your life to your patients when you could have so easily taken an easier path." She skimmed her mouth over his, whispering softly against his lips. "You are an amazing man, Carlos Medina, and I look forward to loving you for the rest of my life."

"Exactly what I wanted—but didn't dare hope—to hear." He kissed her deeply, reverently, and the honesty in his touch spoke so clearly she wondered why she hadn't heard it before.

His talented hands stroked down her arms and linked fingers with her. "Will you marry me again?" He gestured to the small, simple altar draped in purple embroidered linens. "Here, now?"

"Of course, my love," she said to her royal lover, her blessedly human husband. "I will. Or rather I should say I do."

Epilogue

Eight months later

Carlos walked the floors of his suite in the island mansion, patting his son's back and singing him to sleep. He wasn't the lullaby sort, but an old Frank Sinatra tune seemed to work just as well. A couple of verses of "Fly Me to the Moon" and the kid was out like a light.

Cradling his seven-week-old sleeping newborn in his hands, Carlos lowered him carefully into the blue eyelet bassinet but didn't—couldn't—step away. Staring at his child had become a favorite pastime of late. Studying the miracle of those perfect hands and feet could keep him mesmerized for a good twenty minutes by this blessing he'd once given up hope of having.

Tiny but long fragile fingers wrapped around Carlos's thumb. "Maybe we've got a future musician in the family with those hands of yours. What do you think, little Enrique?"

Lilah had insisted on naming their child for his grandpa.

The old king had recovered from his transplant surgery with a surprising strength and speed. His will to fight was back in full form so he could walk the beaches with his namesake—and his other new grandchild, Eloisa's daughter, Ginger.

Both infants were so clearly Medinas they looked like brother and sister with their dark hair and stubborn jawlines. Plans were already in place for all the Medina offspring to know each other well with frequent visits to the island, a pattern already started over the past months as everyone rotated helping the senior Enrique recover.

Little Enrique's arms relaxed as he settled into deeper slumber. Carlos grinned over how well he could already read his son's cues. Lilah had opted to take a year's leave from her hospital duties, but Carlos made a point of coming home for longer lunches to give his wife a chance to nap. He cherished the time with his son. And he looked forward to time with his wife.

Without a doubt, today's afternoon wedding and reception had exhausted the baby for what should be a nice long stretch.

Duarte and Kate had insisted their ceremony include everyone from the most senior member—the king—to the babies. Medina gatherings were a frequent event now, with so much to celebrate in their expanding family. They'd packed even the spacious mansion during the past week before the wedding. Little Enrique's baptism had brought out relatives from Lilah's side as well. And while she still harbored reservations about her father, she was able to enjoy her parents' delight in their new grandchild.

Now the time had come for Carlos to round out the day with a final—private—celebration with his wife. He dropped a careful kiss on his son's forehead then backed away quietly.

Tugging his tuxedo tie with one hand and nabbing the baby monitor with the other, Carlos strode toward the sound of spraying water emanating from the bathroom. He flung his tie aside and plucked a rose from the sterling silver vase beside the bathroom door. He ran the rose under his nose before stepping into the steam-filled room.

He set the nursery monitor on the marble countertop and opened the fogged glass door. "I need to talk to you," he repeated her wording from eight months ago when she'd stunned him, dazzled him with her bravado at confronting him in the men's locker room. "And this is the only place I can be certain of catching you alone on an island full of family and our son asleep in the next room."

Water slicked down his wife's body, caressing every luscious inch as he would soon have the privilege of doing in deliberate, leisurely detail. Motherhood suited her well in every way.

"Well, you most certainly have my attention," she said, gathering her water-darkened hair and stretching her arms overhead with a come-here smile.

He stripped off his tux in record time and stepped under the heated spray, rose in hand, eager to explore the new curves childbirth had brought. "And I'll be doing my level best to keep your attention through the night."

"Am I about to be the lucky recipient of another of your amazing medicinal massages?" She looped her arms around his neck, her slick body against his. Warm pellets of water engulfed them from the multiple showerheads.

"My most thorough massage to date." He plucked the petals free and tossed the stem back onto the bathroom floor. Grabbing a bar of French soap, he lathered his hands into a mixture of suds and petals, then rubbed the fragrant mixture over Lilah's creamy skin. The flowery scent saturated the steam along with the perfume of her shampoo.

"Mmm…" She arched into his touch with a throaty sigh. "We should insure those hands. I am such a very lucky woman to have found you."

"I'm the lucky one, and you can be sure I won't forget that for even a second." He stroked upward until he cupped her face. "I love you, Mrs. Medina."

"And I love you, Dr. Medina."

* * * * *

MILLS & BOON®

Christmas Collection!

Unwind with a festive romance this Christmas with our breathtakingly passionate heroes. Order all books today and receive a free gift!

FREE GIFT!

Order yours at
**www.millsandboon.co.uk
/christmas2015**

1015_MB515

MILLS & BOON®

Buy A Regency Collection today and receive FOUR BOOKS FREE!

4 BOOKS FREE!

Transport yourself to the seductive world of Regency with this magnificent twelve-book collection. Indulge in scandal and gossip with these 2-in-1 romances from top Historical authors

Order your complete collection today at
www.millsandboon.co.uk/regencycollection

0915_ST19

MILLS & BOON®
The Italians Collection!

Irresistibly Hot Italians

You'll soon be dreaming of Italy with this scorching six-book collection. Each book is filled with three seductive stories full of sexy Italian men! Plus, if you order the collection today, you'll receive two books free!

This offer is just too good to miss!

Order your complete collection today at
www.millsandboon.co.uk/italians

0815_ST17

MILLS & BOON®

Why shop at millsandboon.co.uk?

Each year, thousands of romance readers find their perfect read at millsandboon.co.uk. That's because we're passionate about bringing you the very best romantic fiction. Here are some of the advantages of shopping at www.millsandboon.co.uk:

* **Get new books first**—you'll be able to buy your favourite books one month before they hit the shops

* **Get exclusive discounts**—you'll also be able to buy our specially created monthly collections, with up to 50% off the RRP

* **Find your favourite authors**—latest news, interviews and new releases for all your favourite authors and series on our website, plus ideas for what to try next

* **Join in**—once you've bought your favourite books, don't forget to register with us to rate, review and join in the discussions

Visit **www.millsandboon.co.uk**
for all this and more today!

MILLS & BOON®
By Request

RELIVE THE ROMANCE WITH THE BEST OF THE BEST

A sneak peek at next month's titles...

In stores from 16th October 2015:

- **Ruthless Milllionaire, Indecent Proposal**
  – Emma Darcy, Christina Hollis & Lindsay Armstrong

- **All He Wants for Christmas...** – Kelly Hunter,
  Natalie Anderson & Tori Carrington

In stores from 6th November 2015:

- **In the Tycoon's Bed** – Maureen Child,
  Katherine Garbera & Barbara Dunlop

- **The McKennas: Finn, Riley & Brody** – Shirley Jump

Available at WHSmith, Tesco, Asda, Eason, Amazon and Apple

Just can't wait?
Buy our books online a month before they hit the shops!
visit www.millsandboon.co.uk

These books are also available in eBook format!

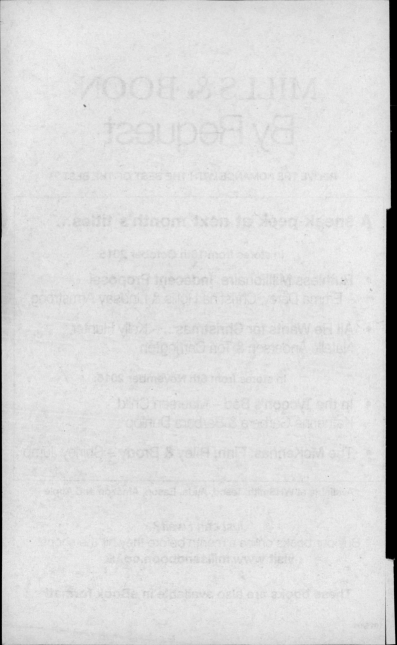